How far
will she
go . . .

SEARCHING FOR A KILLER

"What are you really doing here?" Lucy asked September.

"I thought I'd explained: I want to know what happened."

"I know, I know. But really . . . why this? Why me?"

"I don't like people getting away with things," September answered slowly, as if testing every word for its veracity.

Lucy forced herself to focus. She had a point to make, and she was going to make it. "Okay . . . so why are you here? It's not your job. You said so." She was having a little trouble tracking. "You know, I probably shouldn't talk to you," she decided, then couldn't help asking, "Are you telling me the truth?"

"Yes. Of course," September said, then added, "Listen, I admit I don't know exactly why I'm here, but it feels like there's been some kind of a setup. . . ."

Books by Nancy Bush

CANDY APPLE RED
ELECTRIC BLUE
ULTRAVIOLET
WICKED GAME
WICKED LIES
SOMETHING WICKED
WICKED WAYS
UNSEEN
BLIND SPOT
HUSH
NOWHERE TO RUN
NOWHERE TO HIDE
NOWHERE SAFE
SINISTER
I'LL FIND YOU
YOU CAN'T ESCAPE
YOU DON'T KNOW ME
THE KILLING GAME
DANGEROUS BEHAVIOR
OMINOUS
NO TURNING BACK
JEALOUSY

Published by Kensington Publishing Corporation

Jealousy

NANCY
BUSH

ZEBRA BOOKS
KENSINGTON PUBLISHING CORP.
http://www.kensingtonbooks.com

ZEBRA BOOKS are published by

Kensington Publishing Corp.
119 West 40th Street
New York, NY 10018

All Kensington titles, imprints, and distributed lines are available at special quantity discounts for bulk purchases for sales promotion, premiums, fund-raising, educational, or institutional use.

Special book excerpts or customized printings can also be created to fit specific needs. For details, write or phone the office of the Kensington Sales Manager: Attn.: Sales Department. Kensington Publishing Corp., 119 West 40th Street, New York, NY 10018. Phone: 1-800-221-2647.

Zebra and the Z logo Reg. U.S. Pat. & TM Off.

First Printing: September 2018
ISBN-13: 978-1-4201-4291-4
ISBN-10: 1-4201-4291-7

eISBN-13: 978-1-4201-4292-1
eISBN-10: 1-4201-4292-5

10 9 8 7 6 5 4 3 2 1

Printed in the United States of America

Prologue

Jean-Luc gazed around the kitchen, his heart pounding crazily, as it had ever since he'd taken this job. The place was impossible! The oven was *ancient*. The grill erratic. The counters so badly scarred that Jean-Luc had sprayed them down with disinfectant *himself*. The Crissmans might think their Denim and Diamonds affair was the height of societal fun, but Jean-Luc was the one who had to pull his staff together and create hors d'oeuvres that were *spectacular*.

He'd taken the job because the Crissman family was well-known, well-respected, and well-heeled, or so he'd thought. He'd been stunned at the dismal state of the lodge, downright appalled at the kitchen, and when it was explained that the lodge's "rustic" appearance was in keeping with its 1930s architecture, he'd pasted on a smile and tried to hide his full-body shiver. It was after he'd agreed to take the job that he learned that there were parameters. He was supposed to make something outstanding on a *limited budget*.

Still, he'd done the impossible. He'd put his own twist on some regulars: dates and bacon, tuna tartare, a rustic cheese plate, platters of crudités with his own Roquefort dressing, and those lovely trays of melons, grapes, pineapple, and papaya. There were breads and desserts, a particularly lovely

pear tarte, and oh, his *amuse bouche*! The bite-size morsel
was packed with flavor; his rendition of capers and goat
cheese and salmon that Donovan, his sous chef, had mostly
mastered to correctly put together.

But these people . . . All dressed in their finery, the women
in smooth heels, shimmering gowns, and diamonds—or
maybe zircons, one never really knew—*or*, and this was the
"fun" party, in jeans and casual shirts. One woman had even
worn cowboy boots. Jean-Luc had peeked out at them as
they'd arrived, wondering dourly why he even tried. It was all
a joke to them.

Well, wait till they tasted his food. They would swoon, no
matter how gauche they were.

The event was all for charity. Everybody said so. In fact,
they said it over and over again, as if they couldn't believe it
themselves. He snorted. Maybe they couldn't.

He glanced down at the rows of champagne glasses on
serving trays and sparkling in the drab green kitchen.
Soong-Li was watching over them, making sure everyone
just got *one*. They could buy drinks from the open bar, but
they were allowed only one glass of free champagne . . . or
rather, *sparkling wine*, as there was nothing remotely French
about the California varietal they were serving. Jean-Luc
sniffed, then glared at the kitchen worker, not one of his
regulars, who was trying not to dry out the prawns.

"Watch those!" Jean-Luc told the man, who didn't even
bother acknowledging him.

Imbeciles! Jean-Luc flared his nostrils as he drew in air,
shaking his head. He glanced at the "champagne." Where
was Soong-Li? As he watched, several guests *snatched*
glasses from the serving station, and he could see that a full
tray was missing. No, no! They weren't serving it yet. They
hadn't made the final count. Hurriedly, he placed himself in
front of the glasses and had to block a rather tense-looking
woman in a beaded blue gown with grasping hands.

"Not quite ready," he said with a forced smile.

"Well, I saw a tray go out," she declared aggressively.

"Yes, soon, madam. I will look you up personally and bring you a glass."

She shot him a baleful glare and left. As soon as she was gone, Jean-Luc hissed, "Soong-Li! *Soong-Li!*"

She rushed back in from the serving room. "Mr. Crissman took the tray. I couldn't stop him. I'm so sorry."

Mr. Crissman. "The raspberries?" Jean-Luc snapped.

"All of the glasses had raspberries in the bottom. They're okay. It's okay."

"Ah."

"Should I take out another tray of champagne?"

His ears almost hurt at her words. "No. Serve the cheese tray. It's been forgotten and looks forlorn. I'll watch the *wine*."

She hurried off, and Jean-Luc fumed at being required to attend to such a menial task. There was so much to do. Why was he relegated to this?

He suddenly smelled the scent of burning seafood. "The prawns!" he shrieked, but his words were drowned out by a shout from the main room, a rising chorus of wailing, screaming voices.

Jean-Luc put a hand to his heart. What?

Soong-Li returned, wild-eyed. "A guest has collapsed. Stomach pains. He's . . . *vomiting!*"

Food poisoning. Jean-Luc's face went slack. He saw his own ruin in a series of newspaper headlines . . . *Famed chef poisons guest . . . Health Department called to famed chef's restaurant to check for violations . . . Famed chef blamed for employee's negligence . . .*

"I . . . I . . . think he might be dead," Soong-Li declared, tears of horror standing in her eyes.

With a soft cry of submission, the "famed chef" fell to the ground, hand still on his heart.

PART ONE

Chapter One

One month earlier . . .

Lucy Linfield pressed herself into the back of the padded, oxblood-red booth and sipped her vodka martini, her gaze on the good-looking bartender with the strong jaw and the five o'clock shadow as he moved from one end of the bar to the other, pouring drinks and offering up little ecru napkins. His shirt's white sleeves were pushed up his forearms, and she liked the look of his skin on his arms and the underlying muscles. She also liked the look of his face and his neck above the unbuttoned vee of smooth, hard flesh. She imagined his eyes were blue. She was a sucker for blue eyes.

Narrowing her eyes for a better look—she really should get those long-distance glasses she'd been putting off—she watched him pour a cosmopolitan into a triangular glass and push it toward the server whose breasts were trying to escape the white, ruffled bodice of her wench outfit. This was part of the Pembroke Inn's theme decor, which, if asked, Lucy would label medieval men's club. It was one of the few Portland restaurants that had been open over a hundred years and had been a favorite of her grandfather, Lyle Abbott

Crissman Jr., called simply Junior, and her father, Lyle Abbott Crissman III, called simply Abbott. She'd never asked if her great-grandfather, the original Lyle Abbott Crissman, called simply Criss—the construct of Criss, Junior, and Abbott made to keep their names straight over the years, apparently—had been a patron.

In any case, she was glad to be here today, idly imagining what it would be like to kiss the bartender's firm lips. Mark. His name was Mark, she thought. She'd never seen him before—unlike the male counterparts in her family, she wasn't a Pembroke Inn regular—but she thought she'd heard someone call him by name.

I'll have to ask Kate when she gets here.

Her sister-in-law, married to her brother, Lyle Abbott Crissman IV, simply called Lyle, which was the sanest answer to the family name thing, Lucy firmly believed, had been the one to set up this afternoon meeting. Kate had said she had something she wanted to discuss with Lucy and her sister, Layla, and she'd invited them both to a four o'clock soirée on Tuesday afternoon; well, more like a command performance, knowing Kate, which was why Lucy was here drinking martinis in the first place.

And, well, Mark.

"Mark," she uttered softly, trying it out.

She was in dangerous territory even thinking about him. She'd had crushes before, if you could call them that. Little naught-mentioned obsessions about one man or another: the buff, dark-haired son of the head gardener at Stonehenge, the family's pet name for their estate above the Columbia River; the actor on the drama about that wealthy Southern family whose name she could never remember—she'd watched his episodes over and over again until John had teased her about him and she'd abruptly stopped, embarrassed; the UPS worker with the really muscular arms, the one before the older guy who delivered to them now; and then, of course, lastly, the true lover whom she would not name, sort of like Voldemort, who'd given her Evie and who sometimes, even now, occasionally entered her darkest dreams, and she would remember that night and the pain and the choking shame that came after.

She tossed back the rest of her martini in one swallow, coughing a little. Nope. Not going there again. She knew better. She'd made up way too many scenarios and excuses and reasons, and all of them were lies to explain the unexplainable.

Pushing those thoughts firmly aside, she turned her attention to the massive oak and stone fireplace at the far end of the room, the firebox huge enough that you could practically stand in it, the andirons impossible to move without a forklift. A number of white-haired gentlemen Lucy recognized as friends of her grandfather were congregated by the mullioned windows that opened onto a grassy forecourt. During the day, the restaurant looked like an English country home, but this afternoon, with rain puddling on the walkways and the box hedges glimmering wetly in the fading light, it seemed more like a lodge in the far backwoods of Sherwood Forest, not a bustling restaurant on the east side of the Willamette River, a stone's throw from Portland's city center.

The Pembroke's one bar waitress was leaning across the bar, giving Mark a good, long look at those bursting breasts. He was saying something to her and she nodded, and in that moment one of the male patrons reached over and slapped her lightly on the butt, just above her short little ruffled hem.

Lucy sucked in a breath in surprise as the waitress reared back and gave Mr. Grab-ass a glare that could cut through steel. Lucy glanced at Mark, who seemed to be assessing the situation, wondering, maybe, whether to jump into the fray. But the waitress was clearly holding her own. Lucy read her lips: *Touch me again and die.* The guy was much younger than the group by the fireplace; thirties, she guessed. Drunk, he grinned up sloppily at the waitress, lifted his hands in surrender, and tried to maintain his seat on the barstool with limited success. His friend collared him and sat him back down, then leaned past him to apologize. In the process, he copped a very long, lascivious look at the waitress's burgeoning boobs himself.

Drama. Well, huh. Lucy had new respect for the waitress, whose name was Kitty, she believed. She was pretty sure that was what Mark had called her, though from across the room she wasn't entirely sure she'd heard correctly, and her lip-reading skills weren't that refined. Kitty had a great body, but her face was as stern and humorless as a prison matron's, and the continued stare she gave Mr. Grab-ass was enough to give a sober person fair warning.

When Kitty finally broke focus to glance around the room at the other patrons, Lucy signaled her, pointing to her own drink, then lifting a finger to indicate she needed another. Kitty raised her chin in an I-got-you motion, and said something to Mark, who looked Lucy's way.

Lucy felt a frisson of awareness shoot through her and did a moment of serious soul-searching. Would she go there? Would she? If he was interested? Would she?

Yes. Maybe. . .

Her heart pounded at the thought.

It was utterly depressing to realize how little spark there was left in her own marriage.

A few minutes later, Kitty plopped an icy-cold martini with two olives skewered on a red toothpick in front of Lucy. "On the tab?" she asked, already gazing back at another group of men at the far end of the bar from Mr. Grab-ass and his friend, who seemed to be collecting themselves and getting ready to leave.

"Yes, thanks."

One of the men in the new group was signaling her, and Kitty drew a breath and dutifully walked toward him, standing back on one hip to take his order. He seemed to be having a hell of a time deciding as he smiled up at Kitty in that too-friendly way, like he'd gotten by on charm for way too much of his life. He, too, was all hands, touching Kitty's arm, sliding fingers around her elbow, leaning in just as she turned in the hopes of brushing her magnificent rack.

They were all assholes.

Except Mark.

Well, maybe him, too, but fine. She'd do him anyway. It wasn't like she planned on marrying him. She'd made that mistake already, and though she'd been faithful to John and tried her best over the last four years—well, at least mostly her best—she was suffering beneath the law of diminishing returns. Even when she tried harder, John almost never responded or noticed.

Were they really edging toward divorce?

Yes.

Lucy closed her eyes, sighed, then opened them again. She picked up her drink, took a sip. She had a nice little buzz going and she didn't want it to stop. Besides, if she had to put up with Kate, better to be somewhat trashed. Whatever her sister-in-law wanted, alcohol would make it more bearable.

It occurred to her that she hadn't told John she was meeting Layla and Kate, so he would run right into the babysitter: her neighbor's daughter, who was sliding from fresh-faced cheerleader into gothic pseudo-intellectual, much to John's horror and Lucy's private amusement.

Plucking her cell phone from a side pocket of her purse, she texted her husband: **With Layla and Kate. Bella is babysitting Evie.**

There. She dropped the phone back in the pocket and turned to her drink once more. She knew this wouldn't go over, but she'd deal with the fallout later. She'd left the office early with no explanation. Lately, she hadn't been a model employee at Crissman & Wolfe, her family's department store, but she didn't much care. Though she hadn't wanted to meet Kate, she was happy to walk out and let the other employees figure out their jobs, for once. She wasn't going to earn any points with her brother, her father, or her husband, all connected to the business in one way or another, but sometimes being the mother and decision maker to everyone else just plain sucked.

She heard a text come in just as Layla blew through the heavy oak door, followed by a swirling, cold January wind that made everyone in the bar sit up a little straighter and glare at her as if the weather was her fault. Her sister was a couple of inches taller than Lucy and her curves were more pronounced. She wore a long, dark blue skirt and black boots beneath a thigh-length black coat, a matching blue scarf with dark symbols that looked like runes from where Lucy sat. Layla saw Lucy and nodded to her, her blondish hair touched with rain, the ends sparkling like diamonds.

"You're drinking a martini," she said as she approached, sliding the scarf from around her neck and beginning to unbutton the coat.

"Yes, I am. Grey Goose straight up." She lofted the glass and nearly spilled some.

"Your first?"

"My fourth," Lucy lied. "But who's counting?"

Layla gave her a sharp look, then realized Lucy was putting her on. She shrugged out of her coat to reveal a brick-red peasant-style blouse and hammered, dull gray metal earrings with a matching, looping necklace in a vaguely Native American design. Layla was nothing if not colorful, though she'd never learned the art of makeup, for some reason.

"Since when are you the booze police?" Lucy asked her. Layla was a teetotaler after a traffic accident that, though it hadn't involved drinking at all, had resulted in a young woman's death and robbed her child of a mother. Still, she rarely made judgment calls.

"I don't care if it's your tenth, except I don't want you to die of alcohol poisoning. I need to talk to you before Kate gets here, and I want you to remember it."

"I'll remember." Lucy thought this might be close to an untruth, so she forced herself to focus hard.

"I'm . . ." Layla inhaled, held it a moment, then exhaled. "I'm in flux."

This wasn't exactly breaking news. Layla was always in some kind of a situation, it seemed. "What kind of flux?"

"Maybe I should wait till Kate gets here, so I don't have to go through this twice," she said, changing her mind. Again, true Layla. She could switch gears so fast, you'd suffer vertigo.

"Sounds dire."

"Not dire . . . but life changing."

"Okay. Now you've got my attention."

Layla shook her head, apparently having made up her mind to wait for Kate. "Tell me about Evie. How's it going?"

Lucy's daughter was nine and the apple of her Aunt Layla's eye. "She's being watched by Bella Stromvig, who lives down the street. You remember her?"

"The cheerleader?"

"Yeah, well . . . yes, though she seems to be entering a new phase. Evie thinks she's the greatest, no matter what, so that's good. Sitters are just a challenge; you have no idea. Or maybe it's just me. Other people seem to manage them without a problem, but I find them *needy*. Luckily, we're nearly out of the babysitting phase and it's just a couple of hours after school these days. And I've been shortening my hours." *By simply leaving work.*

A frown line was forming between Layla's brows. Afraid she might actually have heard of Lucy's new work plan, she added before Layla could speak, "Evie's piano lessons are coming along. Luckily, we have that old monster upright from John's mother, and we barely use the living room for anything else, so now it's a music room."

"I hated piano," Layla said on a sigh.

"I remember. Dad made Mom stop giving you lessons because you cried like you were being beaten."

"I've never been good about hiding my feelings."

"Amen." Lucy nearly slopped her drink. "At least they didn't make me take lessons."

"That's because you were so bullheaded, no one wanted to fight with you."

That struck Lucy surprisingly hard. She *had* been bull-headed. "But I'm not that way any longer," she said before she could stop herself.

"You try harder now," Layla agreed, though that wasn't quite the same thing, in Lucy's opinion. Layla, the oldest of the three Crissman siblings, had always been more laid-back than Lucy, who was only a year behind her. In that way, they'd seemed to skip the traditional roles. It was Lucy who was the more responsible . . . or at least she had been. Layla was artier and generally considered the nicer of the two sisters, though they'd certainly had their fights growing up. Lyle, the youngest, had been a pleaser when he was a kid, and the way he kowtowed to his wife these days, that personality trait still seemed to be going strong.

"You changed when you had Evie," Layla added to Lucy's silence.

I changed when Evie was conceived, Lucy thought. She had a moment of remembrance before she pulled herself back from that precipice. "Why don't you tell me your big secret before Kate arrives and sucks all the air out of the room?"

"Well . . ." Layla said, hesitating.

Before she could go further, the inn's front door opened again, and Kate appeared in a hooded white rain jacket. She glanced toward the bar, then looked around with a lifted chin in that way Lucy found distracting and annoying, as if she were royalty surveying her kingdom.

"As soon as she sits down, you're spilling," Lucy warned her sister, her gaze fixed on Kate.

She really couldn't stand her sister-in-law for a whole host of reasons. Kate was single-minded, humorless, and mean-spirited. She didn't like women at all, in Lucy's experience. Men, well, men with money, now they interested her, and whenever they were in a social situation that involved males, Kate zeroed in on the wealthiest, usually older guy in the room and beelined toward him. Said older gentlemen always ate up the attention. It was a marvel that men never seemed to see through her, or maybe they just didn't care. Maybe it was just nice to have someone hang on your every word, no matter that you were boring as dirt. And Kate was certainly pleasant enough to look at. Lucy would never have been able to suffer through it, whereas Kate, always on a mission, appeared attentive and interested.

But, man, was she a sour pill to her sisters-in-law. Maybe to all women, come to that.

Not for the first time, Lucy almost wished Kate would cheat on her brother. Maybe then Lyle would see she was only in it for the family money, of which he, being the only male heir, would get the lion's share, an antiquated part of the will they'd all been made aware of, though no one had seen fit to change it. It was great-grandfather Lyle Abbott Crissman, Criss's wish, and it had remained in place throughout the years. Ironically, dear old dad, Abbott, and her grandfather, Junior, had helped themselves to Great-grandfather's wealth without adding anything to the pot. After a long stretch of profligate spending and bad investments, the once-vaunted Crissman wealth had sorely diminished, and by the time Junior died, after a long stay in a private-care nursing home—a drawn-out misery that had ended the year before—the Crissman fortune was mostly a thing of the past. All, again, according to what she'd heard. Neither Lucy nor Layla had asked for a running account and, as their father was still alive and the sole heir, it also wasn't their right.

Kate spied them, lifted a palm in recognition, then pulled back her hood and headed their way. She wore her blond-streaked hair in a sleek bob and her cherubic face was split by an insincere smile. Kate swung into the chair opposite Lucy and next to Layla. She had icy-blue eyes that never showed the least bit of warmth or humor. Her coldness put Lucy's teeth on edge. Lucy tried very hard to keep a smile on her face whenever they were together, but it was difficult.

Lucy slid a look to Layla, wondering how her sister felt about Kate. Lucy was close to her sister in some ways, oddly separated in others. Layla was . . . different. On the bohemian side and into performance art, which Lucy didn't even pretend to understand. Layla currently had an artist boyfriend who didn't believe in marriage, or working a job, or making money, or pretty much anything bourgeois. As far as Lucy could tell, Layla was barely one step ahead of total ruin, and said boyfriend, Ian, wasn't doing anything to contribute. Of course, Ian hadn't been spoken of for many months, so maybe he was out of the picture. Maybe that was what Layla wanted to talk about? There was another guy she'd mentioned a few times, so maybe not. Lucy couldn't tell if this new guy was a romantic prospect or something else. If it was the former, she hoped to hell he was better, financially speaking, but then, anyone would be a step up from shiftless, layabout Ian. The last time Lucy had been to Layla's apartment, he'd been lying on the floor against Layla's batik-covered cushions smelling of marijuana and incense. His one positive quality was his good looks, and he did the least humanly possible with it. Lucy doubted his man bun had been taken down in over a year.

Her eyes strayed to the bar. She focused again on Mark's tanned, muscled forearms.

"Whew. It's really trying to rain out there," Kate said as she eased out of her raincoat. She wore a soft pink sweater graced by a strand of pearls. Lucy wondered if the gems were real and, if so, where Lyle was getting his money. Kate did work for a charter school, April Academy, founded by April McAdams, a bitch on wheels who seemed to bully people into getting what she wanted, but Lucy didn't think Kate's job earned her the big bucks. Lucy had gotten her info about April McAdams from Kate herself, in a rare moment of female bonding several years earlier, though Kate would never admit it aloud now. Kate conveniently remembered what she wanted to and forgot the rest. No bringing up the truth would dissuade her either. She fit the facts to her own narrative and that was that.

"It sure is," Layla agreed.

Kate noticed Lucy eyeing the pearls and said, "They were a Christmas gift. I couldn't believe it when I opened the box. Lyle is so careful, you know. He's a really good money manager."

Lucy battened down a dozen snippy comments that wanted to burst from her mouth and said simply, "They're beautiful."

Layla asked dubiously, "Lyle really got those for you?" She was apparently less interested in keeping the peace.

Kate regarded Layla coolly. She didn't do well with questions that shone too bright a light on her personal fairy tale. "Yes, he did. I know he's your brother and you have your own opinions about him. I have a brother, too. But Lyle's really tender under that hard crust he shows the world. He saved and saved for the pearls."

Lucy wondered how her brother saved anything; he was currently jobless. Well, sort of. Like herself, Lyle worked for their dad, but whereas Lucy worked in the department store's business office, Lyle worked "from home." He'd had a job at the store itself a few years earlier, but he hadn't liked their father telling him what to do, nor had he liked Miranda Wallace, the store's longest-working employee, being put in charge of teaching him the ropes. Resenting Miranda's authoritative nature, Lyle had complained to Abbott to get Miranda fired, but their father hadn't listened, declaring he would be lost without her. Well, somebody had to do the real work, and that was Miranda, who approved of Lucy because of her work ethic. Well, at least she had. Maybe she would feel differently after Lucy's early disappearance today. In any case, Miranda was still at the store, but Lyle now had the amorphous job of overseeing investments with Abbott. Apart from Crissman & Wolfe and the family property in the Columbia River Gorge, Lucy couldn't guess what those investments might be.

"I'm glad you both could make it. I tried to pick a centrally located venue." Kate flashed a smile, but it seemed forced.

"Figured it was a place you frequent," Lucy said.

Kate acknowledged that with a nod, and one of the white-haired gents mistook the gesture for him. He smiled and winked at her, and she smiled back. "Kenton DiPalma," she said.

"Friend of Junior's?" Lucy guessed.

"And your father's."

"I'm on the east side of the Willamette. This place isn't close for me," Layla reminded.

"Well, there are a lot of bridges," said Kate shortly.

Lucy shrugged. "It's not called Bridge City for nothing." She hefted the remains of her martini. Two down. The buzz was there, but way too slight to dull the anxiety and annoyance she was beginning to feel. She was already tired of waiting for Kate to get to the point, so she took matters into her own hands. "Why did you want to meet?"

"Well, as you know, the days of the brick-and-mortar store—certainly *our* brick-and-mortar store—are almost over. Like everyone else, we're relying more and more on internet sales."

This was hardly a news flash. Lucy knew the store's sales trajectory over the past few years, and it had been on a slow decline. You couldn't turn on the news without hearing something similar.

Kate looked at Layla. "Maybe this doesn't affect you as directly, because you aren't employed by Crissman and Wolfe, but Lucy . . ." She glanced back at her and gave her a commiserating look. "Both you and John are employed by the company."

"What are you saying? Where are you going with this?" Lucy demanded. She didn't need a lecture, and she didn't like the way this was going. Kate was already seriously getting on her nerves.

"John's been Abbott's right-hand man, but now I'm sure I'm not telling you anything you don't already know, with shrinking market share, changes are going to have to take place."

"Are you letting John go?" Lucy demanded, her voice rising.

"You know I don't have that power," Kate said. "But . . . your father's been grooming Lyle for that position for a long time."

"Wait a minute. Wait a minute." Layla held up her hands. "Dad's giving Lyle John's job?"

"No," Lucy said firmly.

Kate's lips tightened. "I'm just saying, things are changing. They have to change."

"How come you're telling us this and not Lyle?" Layla asked.

"Because it isn't true," Lucy snapped.

"I don't even work there, like you said," Layla pointed out. "It seems to me—"

"If Dad were going to fire John, he'd tell him himself," Lucy interrupted. She spoke positively, looking at Kate for corroboration. Her sister-in-law's hesitation spoke volumes. "You're kidding. What? Am I supposed to tell my husband he's been *fired*?"

"Abbott will talk to everyone when the time's right. I was just trying to broach the subject to both of you as family," Kate said.

"As family," Lucy repeated.

"You're not the family member who should be telling us this," Layla pointed out, eyeing Lucy with concern.

"I'm okay," said Lucy tightly.

"Look, I know how you're both feeling. I was a little stunned myself when Abbott first talked it over with Lyle. Change is always hard," Kate murmured.

You don't know the first thing about how I feel.

Lucy thought of a thousand things she wanted to say back. Actually opened her mouth to say at least some of them but was usurped by Layla, who said, "I have something I want to talk about."

Chapter Two

"Go ahead," Lucy said magnanimously. Anything was better than listening to Kate, and she really did want to know what Layla's big secret was.

"Wait, I'm not finished," Kate said. "I just want to be straightforward and aboveboard."

Since when? Lucy thought, downing the last of her martini, wondering if she dared order another. She could take Uber home. Maybe she and Layla could Uber together; that was Layla's main form of transportation these days.

As if blessed with some kind of server's ESP, Kitty showed up at just that moment. "Another?" she asked Lucy as she laid down cocktail napkins for Kate and Layla.

"Umm . . ."

"I'll have a Moscow mule," Kate ordered.

The waitress looked at Lucy expectantly, then shifted her gaze to Layla.

"Could I have an Arnold Palmer?" Layla asked. "With decaf tea?"

Layla rarely drank anything with alcohol. She was into herbal teas and everything natural and organic, but Lucy thought she was making a mistake today. A meeting with Kate was surely an occasion to imbibe.

"You?" Kitty asked Lucy.

"Oh, one more," Lucy said. At this rate, she'd be a screaming alcoholic before sundown, but c'est la vie. Once Kitty departed, she said to Kate, "I think we've got the gist of where you're coming from. I want to hear what Layla has to say."

Kate turned impatiently to Layla.

And then Layla, being Layla, started talking in circles, slowly winding inward to the crux of the matter. First, she invited them both to a production of poetry, music, and a woman who apparently plucked a lute while twisting her body into all kinds of contortions, to which Kate said basically thanks, but no thanks, while Lucy tried to come up with a convincing excuse to skip it as well. Layla didn't wait for their response as she went on to talk about the fact that she'd been helping out a local real estate agent with art and decor for staging properties for sale. This was mildly interesting but hardly the earth-shattering news Layla had hinted at.

"Well," Layla finally said, coming to the point just as Kitty hurried over with their drinks, nearly tipping the tray but catching it at the last moment. "Sorry," she muttered, carefully depositing the drinks on the table. Only a little of Lucy's martini had sloshed over.

"She'd better not expect a tip," Kate observed as Kitty hustled away. She picked up her Moscow mule and took an experimental sip. She liked to drink whatever was the height of fashion at the moment. "Layla, I'm sure you have a lot to say, but I'm really pressed for time."

"Hold on," Lucy said.

"Just give me a second," said Layla at the same moment.

"Fine," Kate said sourly.

Lucy looked toward her sister expectantly, and Layla drew a breath, then . . . stopped. A full thirty seconds went by before Kate rolled her eyes and looked around, as if hoping someone would come to her aid. For some reason, Lucy had a sudden premonition. Oh, God. Her sister was pregnant. She just knew it. As the French rabbits—or dogs; Lucy was never quite sure what they were—in that cartoon Evie had loved so much, *Gaspard and Lisa*, often said, *"Catastrophe!"*

Except Layla couldn't get pregnant. The accident had taken that away from her.

So, no. It was something else.

Kate's indulgence with Layla ended right there. She said, "Your father has decided to shutter Crissman and Wolfe and just go with internet sales. That's why there'll be a reshuffling of jobs. That's what I came to tell you."

"What?" Layla asked.

"The Crissman and Wolfe brand is well respected and we'll still sell online. Fewer costs, once the brick-and-mortar store closes down."

She said it all in a rush, as if it tasted sour, and it sure did to Lucy. Like she'd maintained, it was really no surprise, yet the finality of Kate's words hit home. "Again, why isn't Dad telling us this?" Lucy asked, in a voice she barely recognized as her own.

"I'm just . . . breaking the ice."

"Whose choice was that?" Lucy asked.

"Does it matter?"

"Yeah, I think it does." Layla lifted her chin a bit belligerently. "If Dad can't face us, Lyle should."

"He knew you wouldn't want to hear it, so I offered."

"So nice of you," said Lucy.

"You had to have known this was coming," she insisted.

"We should have been at that meeting, when you all decided. For sure, Lucy should've," Layla stated.

"Yep," Lucy agreed.

"Your father knew it would be difficult for you to look at the situation objectively and—"

"I can be as objective as the next person. And don't tell me about my father," Lucy said tightly. "He's a goddamn chicken. So's Lyle, mostly."

Kate's mouth pinched into a thin line.

"You'd think I'd at least get a company memo," Lucy said.

"In the meeting, Abbott brought up how good you are at your job," Kate said stiffly.

Lucy laughed.

"It sure seems like you just fired Lucy and John," Layla said.

"Oh my God. This is exactly what Abbott knew would happen." Kate looked away for a moment, then added tensely, "I came here today because I didn't want either of you to be blindsided. Sorry for trying to ease into it."

There was a stretch of silence as they all thought about what had been said. Finally, Lucy said, "Well, okay. We're moving to internet sales only. Maybe I have a job, maybe I don't. Guess I'll have to ask Dad."

"That's all he's selling, right?" Layla piped up, looking at Kate. "I mean, just the store. He's not touching Stonehenge."

Stonehenge was their nickname for the rambling, rustic lodge their great-grandfather had built in the thirties in the Columbia Gorge above the Columbia River. The main building and the wings and outbuildings ran along the cliff's edge, looking over the river. The rooms were austere, your basic wooden floors and walls, with bunk beds and thin mattresses. It had been designed as a summer home, but Criss just kept building. Now it was so large, it was rented out by church groups, and schools, and addiction recovery groups, as a place to get away and find inner peace, maybe. It had never been lavishly put together, and it had fallen into disrepair with the dwindling of the Crissman fortunes, but it was a remarkable piece of Oregon architecture and history.

Lucy looked to Kate for confirmation about the property,

but Kate didn't immediately respond. Heart clutching, Lucy declared, "Dad is leaving Stonehenge alone."

"The property in the Gorge isn't really the issue. That's not why I came here." She bent down to dig through her purse, which she'd dropped on the floor, pulled out her cell phone, and touched the screen. "I gotta go."

"You haven't even finished your drink," Lucy pointed out.

"We're not selling Stonehenge," Layla stated flatly.

"No one's talking about the house in the Gorge!" Kate declared. She refused to call the property Stonehenge like Layla, Lucy, and presumably Lyle, though their brother had seemed to diminish and disappear by degrees after his marriage, so it was hard to say. "That place would cost a fortune to renovate to some kind of decent sale price. Anyway, it's the land's that's the value. The house is a white elephant. But we're not selling."

"But, you did talk about Stonehenge with Dad and Lyle," Lucy said, watching Kate's face.

Her sister-in-law set down her phone and reached up to deliberately tuck her hair behind both ears, an unconscious gesture she employed whenever she was annoyed. "I don't want to sell. Like I said, it's a white elephant and—"

"But somebody wants to sell," Lucy cut in.

"You can't sell it. It's a historical property!" Layla declared.

"It's not on the historical registry," Kate came back quickly.

"Who wants to sell?" Lucy demanded, her voice rising.

"Lyle."

Their brother. Lucy felt like she'd been kicked in the gut, and Layla looked much the same way.

"Lyle said you'd go all apocalyptic."

Lucy glared at Kate. "Lyle shubbee talking to us." She cleared her throat after the slurred words.

"How many times do I have to say it? He knew you'd both

be this way and he didn't want to deal with it. He just wants what your father wants."

"So, Dad wants to sell Stonehenge?" Layla demanded.

"Not really. It's not like the store."

"Lyle can't sell Stonehenge without Dad's consent, right?" Layla turned to Lucy.

"That's how I remember it," Lucy answered slowly, carefully. She wasn't drunk-drunk. Just a little tipsy. She didn't want to appear drunk-drunk, but words could get tricky.

"We gotta make sure Dad doesn't buckle," Layla said to Lucy, jaw tight. For someone normally easygoing, Layla could really dig in her heels sometimes, always kind of a surprise.

Kate said, "I don't know why you keep circling around to the property. I told you—"

"'Cause yer not tellin' us the truth!" Lucy blasted back.

"You just said Lyle wants to sell Stonehenge," Layla pointed out.

"Actually, he just wants to tear it down. Not the same thing."

"Worse," Layla said.

Kate shook her head, picked up her copper cup, and downed the rest of her drink. "There. I'm finished." She got to her feet.

Lucy said, "Stonehenge has been in our family for generations."

"Well, it's Abbott's right now. He can do with it as he chooses. I don't know what else to say." Kate had her purse in hand.

"Did you and Lyle get Dad to change his mind?" Lucy asked. "Change" came out a little bit like "chain," but luckily, no one seemed to be acting like the word police.

"Shame on both you and Lyle," said Layla in a quiet voice.

"I had nothing to do with it. How could I? This is your family, not mine!"

You'd be good to remember that, Lucy thought, but wisely didn't try to articulate it. She drank down her water, needing to be completely sober.

Layla accused, "I can't believe you. And my brother. And my father."

"So, when is this teardown happening?" Lucy set down her water glass.

"I'm . . . I don't know. It might not be torn down. It was just an idea. Maybe it'll be an outright sale."

Something in her tone caught at Lucy's brain. Layla heard it, too, because she asked coldly, "Who's buying Stonehenge?"

Kate rolled her eyes toward the ceiling. "I didn't say there was a buyer."

"But you've had an offer," Lucy pressed.

"It's not even listed."

Yet. Lucy could hear the word even though Kate hadn't said it. "Sounds like there's been a lot of discussion about it."

Kate drew a breath, looked impatient. Lucy thought she might storm out, but instead she said tightly, "Jerome Wolfe has made an offer on the property."

"Holy mother," Lucy said, her mouth dropping open.

"You lied to us," Layla accused.

"The offer hasn't been accepted."

Yet. Again, that unspoken word.

Jerome Wolfe was the great-grandson of Criss's business partner, Herbert Wolfe. Unlike the Crissmans, the Wolfes had held on to their fortune through the years, each successive Wolfe seeming to add to the pot rather than take away from it. Jerome Wolfe was no exception, but he was a son of a bitch, or so Lucy had heard.

"Will Dad accept it?" Lucy demanded.

"I don't know. I can't read his mind." Kate was stiff with repressed anger.

"You can certainly speak for him, though," Layla pointed out.

"I'm sorry I even tried." She started to turn away.

"Jerome Wolfe will tear it down for sure and build a modern hotel," Lucy said.

"Over my dead body," said Layla.

The Wolfes had moved from retail department stores to boutique hotels scattered around Portland and down the Willamette Valley to Salem, Eugene, and as far south as Ashland. The hotels were expensive and snooty and everything the lodge was never intended to be.

Kate paused, turning back to add, "This year's charity event at the lodge is scheduled for March for the Friends of the Columbia River Gorge. Still so much to be done after the Eagle Creek fire."

"You're not cancelling it, are you?" Layla was horrified.

"Of course not. Your father wants us all to be there this year. To host. As usual, it's an all-day affair that ends with a silent auction, hors d'oeuvres, and drinks in the evening at the lodge. It's slated for the last Saturday of the month. We're working on the details now, and your dad'll be talking to both of you."

"And then he's selling to Jerome Wolfe." Layla regarded Kate coldly. "You weren't planning to tell us Stonehenge was for sale, were you?"

"I came here to talk about closing the store. Stonehenge is your father and Lyle's decision."

"How come you drew the short straw?" Lucy asked.

"I'm talking to the historical society," Layla warned.

"Do what you have to." Kate's tone was brisk. She was apparently finished with trying to be conciliatory. "Lyle said you would."

"We'll fight you," Lucy declared, at the same moment Layla announced, "I'm going to be a mom. That's my news."

Lucy and Kate both focused on her. "How?" Lucy asked.

"You're pregnant?" Kate asked, slack-jawed.

"You know I can't get pregnant. There are other ways to have a baby," Layla said.

Lucy's senses swam. Too much alcohol. Kate looked about ready to cry, but it had nothing to do with Stonehenge. Kate wanted to have a child. For years, she'd been adamant that she didn't want children, but that was then and this was now. Though Lucy had only heard bits and pieces, smatterings of what was going on with Kate and her brother, she knew they were desperately trying to have a baby and nothing was happening.

Layla added, "A guy I'm seeing wants a son, so we're having one with a surrogate."

Chapter Three

Silence held for a heartbeat or two, then Lucy said, *"What?"* There was so much packed into Layla's last sentence, she hardly knew where to start. And now, suddenly, she couldn't for the life of her remember Layla's slacker boyfriend's name.

"What guy?" Kate asked.

"His name's Neil," Layla revealed.

Ian. That's his name. But she isn't talking about slacker Ian. Lucy shook her head. "Neil? Wait. The older guy you met at the home and garden fair?"

"I didn't meet him there. He's Brooke's client. He admired my painting that was on display at the Bingham house. I told you about it."

"You said you met a guy who took you out for dinner at Cover . . . Covington's, and I said I hoped he had money, so that you didn't have to fit all the bills. Foot all the bills," Lucy corrected. She was too inebriated to be having this conversation, though she was sobering up fast. "You said it was just one dinner."

"Well, it was. Then."

"You're having a baby," Kate questioned. Her skin was chalky.

"I didn't know him that well at first," Layla told Lucy. "But it's over a year since we became friends."

"And you never mentioned him again?" Lucy was hurt.

"Who's the surrogate?" Kate asked.

"I . . . I wasn't sure I wanted to talk about him." Layla turned to Kate. "She's someone Neil knows."

"And she's pregnant? With your egg and this Neil's sperm?" Lucy was trying to keep up.

"*This Neil* wanted a son, and we talked about it, and he didn't know about the accident, so when I told him—"

"Jesus," Kate whispered, staring down at her copper mug.

"—he suggested a surrogate."

"When is the baby due?" Kate's voice sounded an octave higher than normal.

"Well, soon," Layla admitted.

"Layla . . ." Lucy felt utterly betrayed that her sister had kept this from her. "What happened to Ian?"

"Since when do you care about Ian? You always wanted me to break up with him."

"Yeah, but . . . I expected you to tell me."

"What do you mean by 'soon'?" Kate wasn't about to be distracted from Layla's bombshell.

Layla took a sip of her tea. Lucy half-expected another round of prevarication and hesitation, but her sister just swallowed and said, "April."

"April!" Lucy and Kate both chorused, and Lucy sputtered, "You must have made this decision the minute you met him!"

"A month or two in," Layla admitted.

"Why didn't you say anything?" Lucy clasped her water glass and guzzled some more.

"You'll have a baby right after the charity event," Kate said, her face white.

"You're not selling Stonehenge," Layla shot back. "My son is going to be able to play there, just like we did when we were growing up."

"You did this on purpose," Kate accused Layla, her voice uneven.

"Kate, I didn't do it to you," Layla said. "I'm lucky I still have functioning ovaries."

Lucy suddenly felt icily sober. The automobile accident Layla had obliquely referred to had nearly killed her. She was lucky to have just lost her uterus, spleen, and a section of intestine. She was lucky to be alive.

"The surrogate's name is Naomi," Layla told Kate. "If you want, I can get you her phone—"

"No." Kate grabbed her purse and walked out, struggling several times to open the door before yanking it back, letting in another swirl of wind and rain as she practically ran outside.

Lucy said to Layla, "Why didn't you tell me?"

"I don't know. I guess I was worried that things could go bad." She sent Lucy a crooked smile. A bit of tension there, Lucy thought.

"What happened to Ian? All this time, you never even mentioned he was gone."

"He just moved on."

"Before or after you met Neil?"

"After. But Neil was just the straw that broke the camel's back."

"So, who's paying for all this? Neil?" Lucy asked.

"Yes."

"He has some money, then."

"Yes."

Layla's monosyllabic replies weren't exactly elucidating. "Well, that's better than poor any day, right?"

"Yeah . . ." She plucked the tiny paper napkin from beneath

her cup of tea and folded and refolded it. "What are we going to do about Stonehenge?"

"I'll talk to Dad. And Lyle."

"Kate's in on this, too, no matter what she says."

"I don't like her. Have I told you that?"

Layla smiled faintly. "She's not my favorite person either, but she's part of our family."

"A big part, apparently. Dad's faith in her kills me."

"I know."

Lucy slid her empty martini and water glasses aside. "A baby . . . wow."

"I know." Layla smiled, looking hopeful.

"You know Kate'll never get over this. I don't care what she says, she thinks you did it on purpose, and that you did it to her."

"It had nothing to do with her."

"Tell her that. Oh, that's right, you did." Lucy swallowed a laugh. "Tell her again."

"Next time I see her, which I'm not looking forward to."

"So, what's your plan?"

"Plan?" Layla looked at her, a line between her brows.

"Well, are you going to live together? Share custody? Get married? What?"

Layla reached for her purse, so Lucy did the same, signaling Kitty to bring them the tab. Lucy grabbed her credit card, the one with the lowest balance. If she quit work, it would put them in a bit of a financial bind. *You're not quitting. You're just making a point by leaving early. Unless you have no job to go back to . . .*

Layla protested that Lucy was paying, but Lucy ignored her as she signed the bill. Of the three of them, Kate, Layla, or herself, Layla was the most pressed for money.

She and Layla walked to the door together. "You wanna drive my car?" Lucy asked Layla, who didn't have one of her own.

"It's too windy and dark." Layla peered up to the heavens

and shivered. It was a day like today that had caused the accident that had nearly cost Layla her life, Lucy remembered, and it had cost the life of the unfortunate woman in the other car. Both parties at fault, but that didn't mean Layla felt any less guilty, nor that the dead woman's family had ceased suing her.

"We'll take Uber," Lucy said.

As they waited beneath the Pembroke's overhang to be picked up, Lucy asked, "How do you know it's a boy?"

"The viable embryos we chose were male. Only one of them survived."

"You can do that? Choose the sex?"

She nodded. "Neil did PGA testing."

"What's that mean?"

"Preimplantation genetic diagnosis. Embryonic cells are examined for genetic disorders, and it's also a way you can learn the sex."

"Ah." Lucy tried to keep her tone neutral, though it sounded like some kind of sci-fi plot. The kind where a faction, or a fiend, or a government chose to determine the next generation's makeup. It gave her a small case of the willies.

They fell into awkward silence, and Lucy finally broke it with, "So, I'm going to have a nephew? Evie'll be thrilled. She's always wanted John and me to have a baby."

Layla squinted against a swoosh of rain-filled wind but didn't respond.

Lucy said, "You know, Kate would do almost anything for a baby."

"I'll get her Naomi's number. She might not want it yet, but maybe later. I don't know what the problem is exactly, but they seem able to conceive. She just hasn't been able to carry till term."

"Maybe that'll work," Lucy said, unconvinced. She sympathized with Kate's plight, but Kate was the kind of person who could resent Layla for trying to help.

"When my baby comes . . ." Layla trailed off, seemed to want to start again, but in the end just shook her head.

"You're happy about this?" Lucy questioned.

"Oh, for sure. I want him. The baby," she said. "I've already got a name. But I'm pretty sure Neil will want something else. Maybe a family name."

"What's Neil's last name? I don't think you ever said."

Layla looked at Lucy and seemed about to answer, but at that moment a Prius with an Uber sign pulled up to the front of the restaurant and she changed the subject back to Stonehenge. "You've got to keep Dad from selling, Luce. Jerome Wolfe will tear it down given the chance, so we can't give him the chance."

"Okay."

"Promise?"

"Hey, I'll do the best I can."

Lucy climbed into the backseat beside her sister, who seemed to collapse into a blue funk for the rest of the ride.

The Uber driver pulled away, water running off the back tires as it finished the half circle drive after dropping Lucy off. Pulling out her keys, Lucy ran to the front door, head down against the rain. Normally, she entered through the door from the garage, but as she'd left her car at the restaurant, she pressed a key into the front lock and pushed open the iron-banded wooden door that led into the two-story Tudor she'd called home since her marriage to John Linfield.

"I'm home!" she called, walking down the hall to the kitchen and family room.

"Hi, Mom," Evie said. She was on the couch, nose deep into her iPad, her white rabbit—which she'd named after Lisa of *Gaspard and Lisa*, though the jury was out on whether the character was really a rabbit or a dog—sat on the couch beside her today, a sign that Evie was feeling a bit of anxiety. The television was set to HGTV, and Bella looked over at Lucy with a smile on her face. Her hand was just setting down the TV remote, and Lucy suspected the sitter had changed the channel as soon as she'd heard Lucy's return.

"Hello, Mrs. Linfield," Bella said. Her lashes were thick with mascara and her eye shadow was mauve and gray.

"Hey, Bella," she said easily. She wondered what she'd been watching before the channel was changed.

"Evie and I made cupcakes," she said. "We've been talking about surrealism. You know Dalí's *The Persistence of Memory*?"

Lucy had an immediate vision of Salvador Dalí's 1930s painting of melting clocks. Ah, yes. Bella and her newfound intellectualism . . . Lucy found herself yearning for a good old cry of "Defense! Defense!"

"When you say 'we,' you mean you and Evie?" Lucy asked.

"I showed Evie some of the surrealists we're studying in my art appreciation class. There are several theories about what the clocks represent. Time, for certain. Its impermanence. Using 'persistence' in the title with clocks that are melting appears to be a sarcastic statement, which surrealists of the time often used in their work."

"That's really interesting." She looked at her daughter's back. "Did you have dinner, Evie?"

"Leftover pizza," Evie said over her shoulder.

"You okay?"

Evie half-turned so Lucy could see her profile. "Just a lot of homework."

"Okay."

Lucy paid Bella, who was eager to move onto other theories and surrealists as she headed out the door. Bella was still educating Lucy as she walked down the block to her own home, which was just around the corner.

Sheesh.

"How's homework?" Lucy asked Evie, closing the door after Bella and walking back to the family room.

"All done." Evie finally looked up and gave her a bright smile. "You don't have to worry about me."

"Yes, well, good." Lucy smiled back. She picked up the remote and pushed the "Last" button. The program defaulted to network news.

Huh.

She texted John to let him know she was home as Evie asked, "Did you want to know what Bella was watching?"

Lucy looked up and at the TV again. "It wasn't this?"

"No, she was watching On Demand. Something with a lot of f-words. She told me to close my ears."

"Wonderful," Lucy said.

"It's not like I haven't heard it before."

"Okay. Let's not tell your father." She was already wondering if he knew her father's plans to shutter the store and whether either of them still possessed a job.

"I won't tell John if you don't," Evie said.

Evie had never been able to call her stepfather "Dad," even though John had encouraged her to in the beginning. Lucy had hoped for the same thing, a bit selfishly perhaps, because she was tired of explaining the circumstances of Evie's birth, a one-night stand with a guy she'd met in college. That guy had never called her again, and though, when she'd learned of her pregnancy, she'd initially tried to make contact, he'd been long gone.

She'd determined at that moment to raise the child alone, much to the disgust of her father, who'd held it against her ever since, even though he'd grudgingly allowed Evie to worm her way into his heart. Abbott had also let Kate's daughter from her first marriage, Daphne, do the same, so it was no great accomplishment. Not that Daphne wasn't a nice kid. She was. It was just that Abbott seemed extraordinarily interested in anything to do with his son, far less so with either of his two daughters.

"Can I go home with Daphne tomorrow after school?" Evie asked. "She invited me."

"Does Kate know?" Lucy didn't see how that was still on the table.

"Yeah."

Her daughter's voice held enough of a note of uncertainty to make Lucy give her the evil eye. "You sure?"

"Daphne said it was."

"If it's okay with Kate, I guess it's okay."

"Can you text her?"

Lucy wanted to demur, but her daughter's face was so full of hope that she sent a quick text to Kate, saying Daphne had asked Evie to come over after school the next day, but if it wasn't on Kate's radar, no big deal.

"Has Dad called?" Lucy asked as she sent the text. Maybe Evie wouldn't call John Dad, but it was second nature to Lucy.

"Uh-uh. But Grandma did."

Lucy looked over in surprise. Layla's and her mother, Sandra, had divorced Abbott when he'd taken up with Lyle's, whom he'd married and then subsequently divorced as well. Both ex-wives had forged new lives for themselves, marrying new husbands and moving out of state. Lucy and Layla's mom now lived in California, Lyle's in Ohio. Neither of them had enjoyed their marriage to Lyle Abbott Crissman III, and their maternal instincts apparently had been smothered by his overbearing attitude as they weren't close to their children either.

"Did you talk to her?"

"She said she was thinking of coming to visit."

"Wow." Lucy scrolled through her call list and punched in her mother's number. When she reached her, Sandra said,

"Oh, darling, we were trying to come through your way on our trip to Europe, but now I don't think it's going to work out. If I could've reached you and gotten assurances you would be there, I would have made plans. But you're never home."

"Mom, I'm going to get rid of the landline. Then you'll have to call me on my cell." This was a battle Lucy waged every time she spoke with her mother, who simply refused to call any other number for reasons that escaped Lucy.

"But I usually get you at home," her mother protested.

"No. You don't. You call, and I call you back on my cell."

"Let's not fight."

"I'm not fighting, I'm just . . . trying to change your behavior."

"You make me sound like I'm a problem." Her voice moved away from the phone, as if she were pulling away.

"You're not a problem, Mom. You're just . . . our communication could be better."

"Well, I'm sorry I can't come. It was nice talking to Evie. I can hardly believe she's nine. Before you know it, she'll be a teenager. I remember when you were that age, and you and Layla came to visit and you wanted a Shetland pony more than anything and Layla drew you a blue one on a piece of construction paper and you had a fit. . . ." Her mother waxed rhapsodic on the one memory she seemed to have of her girls; she couldn't recall their high school years very well, or anything before. A few moments later, she found a reason to get off the phone, and Lucy was left with the same feeling she always had after speaking with her mother: *I will never be that way with my daughter.*

"You want some popcorn?" Lucy asked determinedly. She had a bit of a headache now that her martinis had worn off.

"Did Aunt Kate get back to you?" Evie dropped the iPad and came into the kitchen, where Lucy was pulling out the popper.

She checked her phone and read from Kate: It's fine.

Hardly a ringing endorsement, but Lucy hadn't really expected anything else.

"Looks like you can go."

"Yay!" Evie said, delighted.

They made the popcorn together, and Lucy realized her jaw was set and she forcibly relaxed it so she could enjoy the snack. She sat beside her daughter on the couch and blindly watched the rest of the news as Evie chatted about the events of the day—she'd made a new friend who wanted Evie to come to her birthday party that weekend—and wondered vaguely why John hadn't answered her text.

She was just about to text again when her phone trilled. She glanced at the screen.

I'll be late.

No explanation why, and she realized she was almost relieved. She didn't want to talk to him about her family and the business and Kate or any of it. If he hadn't heard from Kate yet, well, then, it would be up to her to give him the news about Crissman & Wolfe, which she didn't want to do.

She felt depressed and poked around her feelings to figure out exactly what was bothering her. Well, the store, for sure. Crissman & Wolfe was once a big deal in Portland, and her father was still living off the afterglow. And Stonehenge. Like Layla, she didn't want her father and brother to sell it for any price.

How would her great-grandfather, Criss, feel about that if he were still alive? Not good, she suspected, although by all accounts the man had been a true son of a bitch. A financier who had entered the retail business with Herbert Wolfe, a man with an eye toward development, Lyle Abbott Crissman had founded one of the premier Portland mercantiles of the time. He and Herbert had run in elite circles and married accordingly, both to well-respected women from good families. Criss had showered Lucy's great-grandmother, Edwina, with gems and furs, and had taken her to all the important social events in the first years of their marriage. He gilded the appointments of the interior of their house in the west hills until it looked like a harem, according to family lore and the records of the time. But he was a man who grew bored easily, and he apparently grew very bored of his wife, whom he began denigrating in front of society friends at every opportunity, once even striking her. There was a story of him backhanding her, causing her to trip over an ivory elephant-shaped footstool in the front parlor and crack her head on the marble floor. Apparently, she never was quite the same after that. She kept taking off the now-valued multi-million-dollar diamond ring he'd given her, leaving it lying around the house where anyone could steal it. One of the servants tried once, but the ring was recovered. Sometime later, that maid's body was found floating in the Columbia River. Everyone swore she'd slipped from the footbridge that ran along the edge of Stonehenge's property, where the Crissmans summered, tumbled down the cliff, and into the river to her death. Criss told the authorities the poor woman had been beating the dust from one of the tiger skin rugs that adorned his den, the skins being gifts from admirers, big game hunters who apparently wanted to curry favor with the financier, and the maid had simply lost her footing and fallen to her death. A sad tale, but bad things happen . . . or so the story went.

Sometime after that incident, Edwina disappeared, along with a lot of her jewelry. Criss was beside himself, bellowing and raging, firing all the staff members, who pretty much ran for their lives, as far away from Portland as they could get, terrified of Criss's possible retribution.

Criss's son, Junior, was about ten at the time of his mother's disappearance. Of all the Crissmans, he'd been the quiet one, made more so without motherly protection. Criss hadn't been much of a parent and was a skinflint with his money. He died of a heart attack when Junior was about forty, and that was when the spending began between Junior and Abbott, who was about twenty at the time. Lucy's grandfather and father dismantled all Criss's copious wealth, selling, spending, and losing . . . in an apparently stunningly short amount of time.

Was it any wonder she had reservations about Abbott's decision to shutter the store?

Chapter Four

Lucy popped open a can of club soda, pouring it over ice. It was depressing losing the department store. She supposed she should also be depressed about her grandfather and father's profligate spending, but she'd never really considered her great-grandfather's money as hers . . . although it would have been nice to have the family still possess the fabulous jewels, supposedly worth a fortune in the 1920s and undoubtedly stratospherically valuable in today's market, that Criss had bought for his bride and Edwina took with her when she left.

She was telling herself it didn't matter—families' wealth and prestige rose and fell through generations—when she heard John's car enter the garage. She was standing by the sink, holding her glass of club soda, when he entered the kitchen.

His expression was stiff as he asked, "More drinking?"

His tone got under Lucy's skin. When had it started that everything he said and did annoyed her? "I just can't seem to stop," she told him. "Maybe you should check me in to a rehab facility."

He eyed her carefully. "What's wrong?"

So, Kate hadn't given him the word about the store. Neither had Abbott. Of course.

She looked her husband over. He was lean and tall and wore his brown hair, now slightly silvered, short and clipped close around his ears. He wore a dress shirt and slacks but no coat and tie, the semicasual look that had slowly developed over the past few years at Crissman & Wolfe. He possessed a strong jaw and deep-set hazel eyes and would be considered handsome by most people's standards. If he was unbending and slightly humorless, she'd accepted that when she married him. He was a good man, and she'd been looking for a good man, someone who would take on responsibility, not shirk it.

So why are you so dissatisfied?

She said, "I think we're both out of a job. Dad is shuttering Crissman and Wolfe except for online sales. That's why Kate asked Layla and me to the Pembroke Inn. To let us know."

"I haven't heard anything about it." His tone suggested therefore it wasn't true.

"That's what Kate told us. And they're selling Stonehenge, too."

He smiled faintly. "I can't believe that."

"She said Jerome Wolfe's made an offer."

That connected. John's head snapped back as if she'd slapped him. "You're kidding. What for? A boutique hotel? Not on those grounds."

"Some modern development probably." A wave of sadness swept over her. This was the root of her depression. Not the loss of the business and even their jobs. Stonehenge.

"I think Kate's getting ahead of herself," John said dismissively.

"Man, I wish you were right."

"Abbott would have said something about it," he said stubbornly. John was a great one for sticking to his own narrative, digging in his heels when someone told him something he didn't want to hear.

"Kate didn't want to tell us about Stonehenge. That just came out."

"Maybe Wolfe's made an offer, but it hasn't been accepted yet."

"Yeah, well . . ." She waved a hand at him. She didn't really want to talk about it anymore.

He whipped out his cell phone. "I'm calling Abbott."

"Good. I was planning to do that myself, but I wanted to talk to you first."

"We're not out of our jobs."

"Maybe not today, or tomorrow, but . . ." *The writing's on the wall.*

She fell into silence, waiting for John to connect, but she could tell his call went to her father's voice mail. Her husband's lips tightened, and the line deepened between his brows. She watched his thumbs press the tiny keys as he texted a message and said, "If he doesn't call me back within the hour, we're going to his house."

"I'll tell Evie."

He lifted his head. "Oh, wait. Maybe I should go by myself. I don't want Evie to overhear anything until we know what's going on. You should probably stay with her."

"He's my father, and I work for him, too."

"This whole thing isn't going to be a problem. You just heard Kate's wish list. It's not the truth. Kate's wanted to run Abbott's businesses for a long time, and this is her bid to do it. Luckily, Abbott's got her number."

Lucy didn't respond. She didn't believe it, and she doubted John did either.

"What?" he demanded, seething.

He was getting mad at her. Transference. It kind of pissed her off. She didn't want to lose her job either, and even more than that, she was hurt that she'd had to find out from Kate. Her father was autocratic and sometimes downright mean, and he was no businessman himself. If he had been, he wouldn't be in this situation. He'd always taken too much money out of the store. She knew it, and John knew it, too, though their pleas and the company's down-sliding profit margin hadn't convinced him.

This day was bound to happen.

"You almost seem happy," he accused.

"Happy? Are you serious?"

"Like you don't care, then."

"I care. I care a lot. If you think this hasn't affected me, you aren't looking. This is *my* family. And they haven't treated either me, or Layla, with any respect."

"Layla," he said derisively.

"She's the only one not dipping into the profits," Lucy defended, growing angry herself.

John made a dismissive gesture with his hands and walked away. This was another of his tactics that infuriated Lucy: leave the argument if you feel you aren't winning.

She followed him. "Layla's going to the historical society to put Stonehenge on the list. That ought to slow things down."

"Great idea. Then none of us will be able to sell it."

"I never want to sell it!" Lucy declared. "If we inherited it, I would never sell it!"

"It's a white elephant. Would suck up too much money."

"That's what Kate said! You tell me my father isn't selling, then say why *you* should sell it. Which is it?"

"I don't know, Lucy. What do you want me to say?"

"I don't know! Something else!"

They'd headed up the stairs to their master bedroom, but now he snorted and strode into the bathroom, slamming the door on her. She almost went in after him because she knew this was one of his favorite ways to shut her out. But she didn't want to. To hell with him. This wasn't his battle, it was hers. She shouldn't have waited for him to come home.

She didn't need him confronting her father before she did. She should have called her father immediately.

She headed back downstairs, grabbed her cell phone from her purse, and scrolled to her favorites, looking for her father's landline. Like her mother, Lucy's father chose his landline over his cell. He carried his cell during the day, but in the evenings, it might not be near him. She let the line ring until voice mail picked up, then tried his cell. Nothing.

To hell with it.

Checking on Evie, who'd moved from the family room couch to her bedroom, she ducked her head inside her daughter's room. Evie was on her bed, engrossed in her iPad. Lisa, the white rabbit/dog, was seated in the little chair Evie used for the stuffed animal.

"I'm going to Grandpa's. Grab a jacket and join me," Lucy said.

"Do I have to?"

"You can stay with your father."

"With John," she corrected.

"Okay, with John. Fair warning: he's not in the best mood."

"Okay, I'll come." She tossed down her tablet and got to her feet.

Of course her car wasn't there when Lucy automatically headed to the garage. Muttering a curse, she headed back inside and plucked the keys to John's Acura MDX off the key rack by the back door where he'd placed them when he'd come home.

"Where's your car?" Evie asked, following Lucy into the garage.

"I'm picking it up tomorrow."

"Are we still going to Stonehenge for Easter?" she asked.

Lucy didn't quite know how to answer that one. "Oh, I don't know. I hope so."

Did she? Yes, she wanted to keep Stonehenge in the family,

but a holiday trip to the huge house with her father, brother, Kate . . . It sounded more like torture than anything else.

She drove them to her father's house in the west hills with its view of the city. Parking was terrible on the narrow, winding street, but the curving drive in front of the house was empty, so she pulled up to the front door. She rang the bell and waited under the portico, watching desultory raindrops drip from its eaves, while Evie stayed in the car. No answer. She didn't have a key to her father's home, but she knew where one was hidden on the north side of the house, wedged up tight under a shingle.

But there was no reason to go in if Dad wasn't home.

What if he just isn't answering?

Would he be that much of a chicken?

Sadly, the answer was yes. Lucy stood on the stoop for another five minutes, pressing and repressing the button. She could hear the chimes ring inside, over and over again. A part of her wondered if something was wrong, but then she walked to the garage and looked through the decorative windows on the garage doors that made it look like a carriage house. His Mercedes was gone.

Probably with Lyle and Kate, plotting the dismantling of the company.

"Is something wrong with Grandpa?" Evie asked in concern as they were driving away.

"Nothing more than usual," Lucy muttered.

"That's kind of a mean thing to say."

"Yes, it is. An inherited characteristic."

She was too angry to protect her daughter from the truth of the family, and that truth was, her father was a son of a bitch, just like his grandfather and probably her brother, too.

Layla swept her fob across the black receiver pad and the door to Riverview Place clicked open. She hurried up the steps to the second-floor lobby and the bank of elevators that led to her fourth-floor apartment, conscious of the scents of cinnamon and dark roast coffee from the Starbucks on the first level. She loved living in this part of the city, Portland's funky east side with its vintage clothing stores, food carts, artists' lofts, and biking culture. Her building had been renovated and she'd been part of the decorating team. Some of her own original artwork had been used in staging the model, though mostly her use of bright colors scared designers, who lived in tones of beige, gray, and white.

Inside her unit, Layla tossed her keys onto the black lacquer half-circle table that served as a catchall for her mail, keys, purse, and other miscellany, then walked past the overstuffed tan couch with its maize afghan toward the kitchen. She'd painted the cabinets herself in a dark cherry color, and they gleamed when she switched on the overhead can lights. Layla was happy with her efforts, though the cabinets did tend to stick a bit. She hadn't had the money to have them professionally done, and she hadn't wanted someone else to paint them anyway.

Her bouquet of yellow daisies still looked pretty good, and she transferred them from the clear Mason jar to a deep, royal-blue vase. She set the vase on the wooden table, an antique she'd plucked from a dusty second-hand store in Sellwood, fussed with the flowers a bit, then checked for the time on her phone. She'd pushed it at the Pembroke Inn. Neil was coming over and she always felt slightly breathless when he chose to come to her place. He professed to love it, but she knew he was lying. He was too buttoned-down to truly appreciate her eclectic style and he lied a lot. At least to her.

You should have walked away from him.

She'd wanted to tell Lucy about him for months, about their plan, but hadn't known how to. Lucy would have talked her out of her decisions. Lucy was practical and certain of her choices, whereas Layla mentally wrung her hands over monumental decisions, mainly because she seemed to always choose wrong. Lucy was the responsible one and had said the same for years, her personal badge of honor. "I'm the responsible one, and Layla's the artist." When the sisters were together, that was how Lucy introduced them. It always bothered Layla a little, even though there was no denying its truth. But it implied that Layla wasn't responsible at all, and that just wasn't true. She knew how to behave, what was right and what was wrong, and she felt like Lucy's offhand comments diminished her somehow.

She just seemed to come down on the wrong side of difficult decisions.

She may have made a doozy with Neil.

But it can still be okay.

Layla quickly headed into the bathroom and checked her makeup. She wore a modicum of eye and face makeup at all times, though she knew Neil really preferred more. For all the color she liked in her surroundings, she wanted precious little on her face. She squinted her eyes and grimaced at herself, examining her skin. Wan. Washed out. She needed to look her best tonight, so she added a touch of cream under her eyes to cover purplish shadows and a bit of blush to her cheekbones. Then she stood stock still, staring at herself, before carefully smoothing on soft pink lip gloss.

She fingered her earrings, feeling the hammered raised design. Her heart was racing already.

What are you trying to do? Make him want you again?

Yes, of course she was. She wanted him to want her, like he had in the beginning.

Or at least the way he pretended to.

She left the bathroom for her bedroom, which still smelled slightly musky and maybe just a bit like the weed Ian had smoked like a religion. She'd demanded that he not smoke inside, which he'd adhered to when she was around, less so when she was away.

Annoyed, she opened the sliding glass door that led to the balcony that ran along the whole east side of her apartment. There was another slider that entered the living room, rarely used because she had a chest of drawers pushed up against it with Ian's television sitting on top, one of the many items he hadn't bothered to take when she'd asked him to move out.

She then moved to her desk, a wooden door with ornate filigree around the perimeter set atop feet that were crossed metal bars. There were no drawers, but she had a stack of green plastic boxes from The Container Store, which held all her important papers. She opened the top box/drawer and pulled out the manila folder within, laying it flat on the desktop. Opening it, she drew out the legal-sized document from the law firm Neil used, then flipped to the back page to stare at her own distinctive scrawl and the notary stamp and signature beneath it.

Why had she signed it? Money, yes. He'd paid her well and she'd had debts that needed to be serviced. But she knew she'd buckled under Neil's coercion. He'd been taken aback upon learning she could never bear a child herself, but then he'd come up with "the plan," and Layla had gone along, bobbing on the tide of his decisions. It had been so nice to be the one taken care of, and Neil had a way of taking care of everything, damn near effortlessly.

That's what money could do, she thought. It opened all kinds of doors, even ones that maybe should have remained closed.

She heard the knock on her door and quickly put the legal documents back inside the folder and into the box before hurrying to answer the door.

Neil stood in the outside hallway, water from the persistent rain coalescing in his hair. He was smiling, which froze her insides a bit because he hadn't been happy in months.

"I brought some champagne," he said, holding up a bottle of California sparkling wine.

She was immediately wary. He knew she rarely drank alcohol. But she smiled and accepted the bottle gracefully. She had a lot of territory to cover and didn't need to destroy his mood before they even got started. She figured she could nurse one glass. She just needed him to go along with her.

Neil took off his raincoat and Layla added it to the wooden coatrack by her front door. She had an entry closet but used the space as a pantry in her small abode.

Neil drew a deep breath, smoothing back his dark hair with one hand as he looked around. Layla thought he may have put on a bit of weight. He was looking softer around the jawline in a way she hadn't noticed before. He was fifteen years older than she was, his age being one of the reasons he hadn't wanted to wait in his quest to have a son.

"What?" Layla said to the small chuckle he emitted. She was working the foil off the bottle, and, upon seeing her struggle, Neil gave her an indulgent look and took the bottle away from her, popping the cork over the sink.

"You do have champagne glasses," he said, raising a brow.

"Yes." Layla fetched them from the cupboard next to the sink. Two glasses. All she had room for, but all she needed. "Are we celebrating?" she queried. She'd asked him over tonight to have a serious talk, and she'd thought he'd understood that.

"Well, Naomi's seven months pregnant. Everything's going according to plan." He regarded her expectantly as she handed him a glass. "Isn't that a reason to celebrate?"

Layla held her glass in a tight fist. Her heart was beating hard. In the beginning, she'd thought she and Neil were a couple. They *were* a couple. She'd dreamed of marriage, even though she'd been the one who had scoffed at all the institutions and rules and folderol that went with the usual societal traditions. That, she recognized now, had been her own construct. Something made up basically because she'd never found someone she wanted to "yoke herself to"—her own words—and the Ians of the world had proved her right.

But she hadn't really felt that way, and when Neil crossed her path, admired her cityscape painted in primary colors, paid her way more than she would ever have dreamed of asking, and then turned his attention on her . . . well . . . she hadn't realized how primed she was to get out of the rut she was in. He'd been carrying a list of the artists at the gallery and asked for her specifically, she learned later. One of his first questions was if she was related to the Crissmans of Crissman & Wolfe. She'd said yes, she was Lyle Abbott Crissman III's daughter, and he'd smiled and said he was an acquaintance of her father. This, too, should have been a red alert, but Layla had basked under the attention, not realizing how much she'd yearned for someone to look out for her until it happened. Neil asked her about her family in a general way. In that first meeting, he was charming and interested in her art, her story, her life, and Layla was immediately smitten.

Going back to her apartment and Ian had been a depressing cap to an otherwise wonderful evening. She'd determined right then that, no matter what happened with Neil, she was done with trying to work things out with Ian. He was a weight dragging her down. The only income he provided came from playing guitar in a band that played rock and roll oldies—Ian being the youngest member by twenty years—and he was pretty stingy with adding his share to their combined finances. She'd been blind to his array of faults, making excuses in her own mind for behavior she abhorred. When she asked him to leave, he hadn't believed her. He tried to jolly her out of it, promising all manner of behavioral changes, but Layla was adamant. If nothing else, Neil had opened her eyes to Ian, who had reluctantly and extremely slowly, finally moved most of his things out.

It wasn't long before Layla was spending all her free time with Neil. She'd initially protested having him buy her every meal, but he wouldn't listen to her. She had a job at a local bistro to supplement the money she made from helping a friend who owned a model-home staging company and any of the proceeds from her artwork, which was scattered through a number of Portland galleries. Some months she did okay, some she barely scraped by. Her father had once reluctantly offered her a job at the store as a saleswoman, but Layla had politely declined, relieving them both.

Two weeks into her relationship with Neil, she'd stayed over at his place and they'd tried making love, but he had trouble maintaining an erection.

He was frank about the problem, which apparently had plagued him for a while. He suggested Viagra, which he'd brought with him. Layla was fine with that but very quickly understood he really didn't have much of a sex drive. What he wanted was an heir, a son, and he was looking at her to be the mother of his child.

"You're a Crissman. I'm a Grassley. We have the right bloodlines."

Neil's family had been one of the pioneers who'd helped bring steel to the Northwest. Unlike the Crissmans, his had hung on to their wealth, and he painted a beautiful picture of a life together. It was a cruel joke. With his low sex drive and her missing parts, they were a poor bet to become parents in the usual way.

She'd sadly told him she couldn't carry a child, and he'd countered with, "How would you feel about using a surrogate?"

The question took her by surprise. She'd really expected

him to pack it in and look for someone else. She hadn't really been looking to become a parent. She initially wasn't even sure she wanted children. And on those rare occasions she thought, *Yes, I want kids*, she always thought of it in terms of courtship and marriage.

But his eagerness infected her. "How?" she asked him. "Who?"

He had it all mapped out. There were several women he knew who were possibilities. Naomi Beecham was at the top of the list. She lived in the area, had a child of her own already, and was happily married. She was a perfect candidate.

Layla initially demurred. Things were moving a little too fast for her. Having a child was life transforming. She needed time to think. Neil told her to take all the time she needed, which she learned later wasn't in his game plan at all. He kept subtly pressuring her, all the while taking her to the symphony, the Keller Auditorium for an otherwise sold out touring Broadway play, a trip to Banff for skiing, where she sat in the lodge sipping hot cocoa and he hit the slopes, joining her afterward in front of a fire pit, a Hawaiian cruise where she swam with the dolphins, a weekend spa trip through Oregon wine country . . .

She fell in love with a different life.

Neil learned of the automobile accident that had killed the other woman driver when she explained that she couldn't carry a child. Though the no-fault accident had been blamed on bad road conditions on a dark night, the woman's husband sued Layla anyway, blaming her entirely. Layla's insurance company paid a settlement rather than face a costly court battle, which pissed Layla off, but she was lucky not to have to pay the legal fees herself.

Neil figured out quite quickly that Layla really wasn't making it financially and that she was getting no support from her wealthy family. He offered her a deal: They would make a baby together, her eggs and his sperm. He would pay her for her eggs. They would sign a contract.

No.

The coldness of the proposal brought her up short. She couldn't do it. But Neil assured her that he would pay for everything, and they would share custody. Maybe they would even have a life together . . . ? They were certainly making a good start.

Layla could admit now that she'd let herself be persuaded by the life he dangled in front of her, one she could snatch if she just said yes. So, she agreed to the deal, tentatively, and suddenly there was the document to sign, which gave up her rights to the eggs she donated. She remembered how tightly she'd gripped the pen, how the angel and devil on her shoulders screamed in both her ears. In the end, she listened to the devil and quickly scribbled her name to the pact.

Neil paid for the extraction of her eggs and gave her an additional twenty thousand dollars.

She had yet to touch a dime of it.

"Well, here I am," he said a bit impatiently. "What did you want to talk about?"

"It's no secret. You know I want to share custody of our son." She said it in a rush. "That's always been understood. I just haven't felt lately . . . that we've been communicating enough about Naomi and the baby."

He set down his champagne glass very deliberately on her counter and smiled at her. "I've been busy."

"I know. But the baby's going to be here soon, and I don't know any of your plans. I almost bought a crib the other day. I saw one in a thrift shop off Seventeenth."

"Don't do that."

"Neil, that's what's wrong. You say things like that, but you have no plans for me and the baby."

"Well, technically, legally, he's mine. You signed away your rights."

"I know. But he's yours . . . and mine." She swallowed some of the fizzing liquid in a big gulp. "I want to share him. I don't think that's unreasonable."

"It's not unreasonable, it's just that I paid you for your eggs. It was a business transaction."

"And I can give you the money back. I have it all."

"You signed a legal document."

"Yes. I know I did. I have the copy you gave me." She glanced toward her bedroom. "I'm not trying to interfere with your plans for fatherhood. I just realized I can't completely give up my child. I never really meant to."

"Then you shouldn't have signed."

"I know . . . I know. Believe me, I know. I think we'd be good parents together. There's just no legal provision for me to be any part of his life as it stands now, and I'd really like to fix that."

"I know you've never been in business, Layla, but when a transaction takes place, a legal transaction, that's a binding document."

She could feel the heat rise inside her. "That's why I want to amend it. We started out as friends, and then things progressed to whatever we are now. I'd like to start over."

She drew a breath and waited, her pulse pounding in her ears. She was lying. She didn't want to start over. She was sorry she'd ever connected with Neil. She'd learned very quickly that it was his way or the highway. The wonderful life he'd dangled in front of her was as real as smoke.

But she wanted her child.

When the moment stretched out as long as she could stand it, she said, "I can write you a check right now."

"Keep the money, Layla. I want you to have it."

"I'd rather have some rights to our son."

"You knew what I wanted from the beginning. I didn't hide anything from you. You can have more children. You can use a surrogate, the same way we have. You're young and healthy. From a good family." He carefully rubbed his jaw, thinking over his words. "I'm just not sure you're mother material for my son."

"*Our* son," she corrected.

"Not legally," he reminded her.

With that, he headed for the door, plucking his coat from the wooden rack, nearly toppling it over. He steadied the rack as Layla followed him.

"I'm not giving up," she said. She'd known this was going to happen. In the back of her mind, she'd known it.

"Oh, Layla. Don't turn this into a battle you can't win. I have the means to go a long, long time in court. If you play nice, I'll play nice and let you see him occasionally. But if you fight me, you get nothing. You understand?"

He spoke gently, as if to a child, but she heard the implied threat.

Layla's insides were in turmoil. "I understand more than you know," she bit out.

He smiled and let himself out.

Every once in a while, Layla had a psychic moment where everything aligned. Her own personal syzygy. With crystal clarity, she knew she was going to have her son back. How, when, and where was still a mystery, but it would happen. No matter what she had to do.

Pulling out her cell phone, she hit the button for a number she'd added to her call list earlier, the lawyer she'd gone to see two weeks earlier, when she decided she was going to have her child no matter what it took.

"Eddie," she said, naming him after her great-grandmother Edwina. Neil could call him anything he wanted, but he was going to be Eddie to her.

Chapter Five

Kate leaned into her husband, spooning up against him as she listened to the rain pepper their bedroom windows. She wrapped her arm around his waist and pressed her cheek to his back, listening to his steady breathing stutter a little at the contact. "I love you," she whispered.

"Mmm," was his sleepy response.

She squeezed her eyes closed and tried to lower her anxiety, which had hit a full-blown rollick after meeting with his terrible sisters. Layla! Having a baby with a surrogate! It made her want to weep. Quickly, as she had from the moment she'd heard, she mentally wrapped that information in a box and tied it tightly and set it on a shelf. She might be able to look at it later, open the box and examine the terrible shock of it, dissipating its power. Maybe . . .

She inadvertently tightened her hold, and Lyle shifted rather sharply, she thought. She eased up, fighting back her hurt. When she'd gotten home to him and Daphne, things had really deteriorated, not least of which was that Lyle was mad at her. Mad at *her*. Because she'd done as he and his father had requested and alerted Lucy and Layla to their plans? Kate had been speechless in the face of Lyle's fury.

"What did you do?" he demanded, fingers digging into

her arm as he led her out of the family room and away from Daphne, into their master bedroom.

"You knew . . . you knew . . ." she babbled, too stunned to fight for herself.

"We talked about it with Abbott, but nothing was decided!"

This was patently untrue, but Kate didn't argue with him directly. That never did any good, and she was upset anyway. Lyle lived in awe of his father. Couldn't even call him anything but Abbott. Kate understood this and prided herself on being the liaison between the two men. "Abbott said he wanted to get started, step one being alerting your sisters," she reminded him.

"We were in discussions. That's all!" He dropped her arm and stalked across the room to the window.

Kate had revealed to Lyle that she'd told Lucy and Layla about the plans to close the store. She hadn't mentioned anything about their discussion about Stonehenge. The sale of the lodge was for phase two, and Lyle would be even more livid when he learned she'd unfortunately let that cat out of the bag early. Well, Layla had pressed her on it and she'd tried to fob her off, but the conversation had rapidly grown out of her control and so the deed was done. But what of it? This way they were just one step closer to selling and dividing the Crissman assets. No harm done. It was what her husband wanted, so she wanted it, too. She'd painted herself as a neutral party to Layla and Lucy, but really, everyone would be better off if the family just sold everything. Lyle knew that, but then, he was smarter than his sisters, more business-minded than even Lucy, whose smarts were a little bit overrated.

She'd almost cried out about Layla's news but had stopped herself at the last moment. When Lyle was in one of his moods, there was no room for Kate to appease him. She just had to wait it out, let him do his worst and stay silent while he heaped on the abuse. It was just his anxiety problem. No big deal. The one time she'd recommended meds to lessen the effects, he acted as if she were crazy. He didn't think he had a serious problem, and maybe he didn't. She just knew that when something happened to ratchet up his stress, he looked for her to bring it under control. And that was fine. She could do that. She could be everything to him because he was everything to her.

Briefly, she thought of Daphne's father, who'd bounced from one career idea to another, sucking up her hard-earned money along the way, never sticking to anything. When Lyle crossed her path—Lyle Abbott Crissman IV of Crissman & Wolfe, a store where she'd often shopped—she'd divorced Adam Lawrence and married the man of her dreams. That was seven years ago, and though Lyle's sisters were both straight-up bitches, she'd learned the ways of dealing with Lyle's father, who appreciated her business savvy and bemoaned the wasted lives of his two daughters, well, except for Lucy's overly vaunted business skills, nothing like Kate's own experience in the corporate world. It had been a shock when Abbott had hired Lucy for a job Kate was more qualified for. She'd ended up taking a job at April Academy because April had absolutely begged her to manage the school. She'd accepted the job, figuring it would only be for a short time, just until she and Lyle had their own child, and Kate would quit working and become a full-time mom. Things hadn't worked out on her original timetable, and she'd had to adjust her thinking. It just sucked that Daphne had insisted that Evie come to April Academy and the two girls had worked on both sets of parents to that goal, and, of course, Lucy and John had caved. Lyle hadn't seen how terrible it was, had suggested Kate "get over it." She'd had to swallow back how upset she was and act like she was completely on board with Daphne and Evie's plan, that she'd been about to propose the same plan, but the girls beat her to it. Very difficult. Sometimes she wanted to pull the covers up to her mouth and bite into them while she silently screamed.

But . . . she loved Lyle, and she was blessed by the fact that Abbott trusted her in a way he would never trust Lucy or Layla. Maybe he even thought she was a teensy bit better than Lyle, who'd graduated in business and was proving himself at Crissman & Wolfe until that hard-ass Miranda Wallace had made life so difficult for him. Miranda had thought it was her job, apparently, to school the Crissman children in the ways of Crissman & Wolfe. Fat lot of good it did her, considering the brick-and-mortar store was on its last breath. Kate had initially warned Lyle that he should make nice with Miranda, but Lyle had refused, and Kate saw now that it was best to let Lucy work things out with the controlling bitch. Too bad Abbott listened to Miranda so much. She knew nothing and less about the company business, no matter what she said. Kate could have run the place better if Abbott had let her. He knew Kate's worth, so maybe in time he would turn over the reins of the internet business to her and kick Miranda and Lucy to the curb. Lyle didn't seem to want to make that move, so it would be up to her . . . maybe. She needed to think about that.

Lyle had finally walked back out of the bedroom, but he hadn't said a word. Kate had asked about dinner, but he hadn't been interested in anything she came up with. She'd heard him on the phone later, talking to his father, and she'd made certain Daphne ate the organic salad she'd created with wheat berries, avocado, cherry tomatoes, and kale. Her daughter had made gagging noises and protested that her friends got to eat pizza, her friends like Evie, and that had really burned Kate.

"You can go live with your father anytime," she said, a favorite of hers, which normally brought Daphne in line, although today the girl had looked rebellious for a moment

before she'd gone back to her homework. It was an empty
threat, though Daphne didn't know that; her ex seemed to
have less and less interest in his daughter as the years rolled
by. He'd been dating the same woman for almost five
years and she apparently had the funds to put up with his
schemes and promises, although Kate had heard he'd taken
a job with an investment firm and had been there going
on almost three years. Hard to believe. Lyle's job consisted
of meetings and phone calls with Abbott, which meant
he could pick up Daphne and run her around when Kate
couldn't, which was very nice . . . a godsend, really.

She just wished he received a regular paycheck; Abbott
paid him sporadically because his pay wasn't put through the
regular store payroll. Sometimes it felt like begging for
the very real salary Lyle worked for, but then the store was
about over. Most of the employees would be let go. Such
was the way of progress.

With Lyle disinterested in dinner, Kate had made herself
a peanut butter and honey sandwich, of which she ate half.
She could have used another drink, but she decided on a
glass of white wine instead, sipping away in silence. Peanut
butter sandwich and wine. She would be embarrassed if
anyone knew.

By the time they'd gone to bed, Lyle had been speaking
to her again. Well, Kate was speaking and Lyle was listening. He complained of being tired, so she'd told him to take
a shower and then crawl between the sheets. He took her
advice, and she asked if he wanted anything more to eat, to
which he said he'd stopped by Morton's Steakhouse and
had a little something on the way home. She'd laughed
and asked what "little something" he'd found there, at which
he'd become stubborn all over again.

Now, hours later, she'd slipped in beside him. She'd
wanted him to make love to her, wanted to feel him inside
her. It was about all she could think about. She tried not to

obsess too much about conception, having their baby. That had gotten her nowhere so far, and she knew the more desperate she became, the less the chances. She needed to ratchet down the anxiety and live in the moment. She could feel the box unwrapping in her mind, ready to spring Layla's news all over her again, like raining confetti. Gritting her teeth, she mentally strapped it down hard, yanking on the bow till it was extra tight. No lovemaking tonight. Lyle wasn't in the mood. She'd told herself to be content to just cuddle with her husband, feel his arms around her, burrow into the comfort of his embrace, but with that in mind, all she'd gotten was his back.

Well, fine. She could cradle him. They were a team. Nothing without each other. Abbott understood that, and Lyle did, too.

"Goodnight, lover," she said, waiting, hoping he would turn toward her.

Instead, he just nestled his head farther into the pillow, easing a bit farther from her embrace so that Kate loosened her grip. She pulled back to lie on her back and stare at the ceiling of their bedroom.

Abbott called Lucy on her cell phone while she was at her desk the following morning. She pushed back from her desk and her Excel program to take the call. "Hi, Dad," she said coolly, getting up from her chair and leaving the room. She didn't need Miranda's ears listening in, or anyone else's for that matter.

"I understand you've been trying to get hold of me," he said shortly.

"I came by your house last night when you didn't answer your phone."

"I was having dinner with a friend."

"Ah. After sending Kate to tell us you're shuttering the business and selling Stonehenge?"

He ignored the Stonehenge issue, saying, "You know as well as anyone that sales have been dismal."

"Why couldn't you talk to me about it? Or John?"

"I talked to John this morning. We're not closing the store immediately. We're staying open through the summer. Our lease is up in September. John understands."

"Does he?" Lucy felt the burn of angry tears and forced her voice to stay steady.

"He'll be running the online sales division."

Lucy absorbed that. "Oh."

"With Lyle," he added. "You'll be working with them both, unless you don't want to."

She squeezed her hand around the receiver. That would never work, but it wasn't for her to say. Lyle didn't work well with people, and neither did John.

Her father grumbled, "Kate was supposed to set up a time for us all to meet. We've settled on Friday at my office. I want Layla to be there as well."

"So, this isn't just about the company?"

"I want all of you there. No misinterpretation. Crissman and Wolfe is still my company. You all seem to forget that," her father said.

No, we don't. You never let us. She asked carefully, "Are we going to talk about Stonehenge, too?"

"There's nothing to discuss."

"Kate said there was an offer on the table."

"We can talk about everything on Friday. I'll call Layla next and tell her to join us." He trailed off, and she suspected he wanted her to step in and say she would do it. Lucy might have trouble connecting with her father, but Layla was a complete mystery to him and he was always uncomfortable with her.

Lucy wasn't going to let him off the hook this time. "Call

her. Good idea," she said. "Oh, and I should let you know congratulations are in order. You're going to be a grandfather again."

She clicked off before he could answer. Let him stew on that one. Layla might not have wanted her to spill the beans, but she was feeling ornery . . . and a little hurt. Everyone seemed to be keeping secrets from her. It was a small victory to have the last word with her father, but it felt inordinately good.

"I'm going to have to find a new job," she said aloud. This was not a healthy situation, no matter what the future brought.

She sat in her chair, reviewing every syllable in the call with her father. She had to practically shake herself back to the present. There was still over half a day of work ahead of her, but Lucy was feeling angry and reckless. She grabbed her purse and coat and headed toward the door. What were they going to do to her anyway? Fire her?

She got in her silver Ford Escape and drove toward the Pembroke Inn and Mark the bartender.

Layla pulled away from the gallery with a check in hand. One of her paintings had sold and she'd received the proceeds after the gallery took its cut. She felt almost gleeful, except for the weight on her chest. She needed to make things right for her and Eddie, but it was going to be a tough road.

She went to the bank and deposited the check, feeling slightly better. She wasn't due back to the local bistro where she waited tables until Friday. Luckily, she wasn't working until after the meeting her father had invited her to. Invited, hah! He'd called her up and practically ordered her to attend. Not that she didn't want to go; she did. But it killed her, the way Abbott treated her. Like she was the unwanted child who had to be dealt with. The one he wished would just disappear.

She drove past the Easy Street Bistro on her way home. The place always seemed to be on the verge of bankruptcy, and she sometimes worried she wouldn't be paid for the weekend hours she put in. She wouldn't be surprised to find a sign on the door when she showed up for work sometime. It was a popular spot but horribly mismanaged, and the owner didn't take kindly to suggestions on improving customer service. Layla had quit for a while when she and Neil were first together. She'd wanted her weekend time to spend with him and thought she could make it on the money she received from her home-staging job and the occasional piece of art that sold. But it had been too tight to pay the rent, so she'd gone back to the bistro.

And she would rather die than touch Neil's twenty thousand.

Her appointment with her lawyer to discuss a lawsuit to fight him over custody was slated for tomorrow afternoon. Initially, she would have been satisfied with visitation rights, but since Neil had shown his true colors, she wasn't interested in anything less than joint custody.

She pushed the button on the fob to open the gate to her apartment complex. The building's apartments had been renovated and turned into condominiums during the height of the last recession. None of them had sold right away, but a real estate mogul who'd seen their potential had bought up as many as he could. He'd ended up renting them out as he waited for the prices to rise, which they had. Layla was lucky he'd left her apartment alone so far. She didn't want to move and she could still afford the rent, at least at this point. Having Ian move in with her had made things dicey for a while. His dope smoking was noticed by the next-door neighbors, who didn't want the smell around, even if it was legal now, at least in the State of Oregon, and Layla had been on pins and needles, worrying she might be kicked out at any time.

It hadn't happened yet. The real estate mogul still held a number of units as rentals, Layla's apartment being one of them.

She parked in her designated spot and used her key fob again to open the door to the stairs that led to the interior lobby. Once inside her unit, she dropped her keys and headed toward the kitchen. Her cell phone rang as she was hanging on to the refrigerator door, wishing there was something inside.

She reached over and picked up her cell from the counter, where she'd left it. The name that popped up on her screen was Naomi Beecham, their surrogate.

Layla straightened abruptly. The surrogate didn't call her, as a rule; Layla called her. "Hi, Naomi," she answered. She softly closed the refrigerator door and paced across the room.

"Hi, Layla. I just wanted to call to see how you were, considering everything."

She sounded a bit anxious, and "considering everything" made Layla anxious, too.

"I'm fine," Layla said.

"Okay. Good."

"How are you?"

"Fine. Ooh . . . he just kicked under my ribs! He's head down and bicycling right there. Jeremy was just like him."

Jeremy was her own seven-year-old son. She had a daughter, too, who was six going on thirty, and a husband, who accepted that she was making a baby for Layla and Neil. Layla had marveled that she wanted to do it, but Naomi said she loved being pregnant, and Neil's substantial payment and all medical costs hadn't hurt. "Many of the best surrogates are happily married and have their own families," Neil had informed her when Layla had first marveled about Naomi's choice to be a surrogate. Neil had then explained that she'd already been a surrogate once before.

"Great," Layla had said, slightly envious because her own body would never be able to perform this basic biological function.

Neil had learned of Naomi from satisfied customers: a wealthy, middle-aged couple who ran in his circles. They'd been delighted to learn that Layla was a Crissman and had raved about Naomi. Layla had felt a little uncomfortable with their assumption, and Neil's, that her family name was what really mattered, but they were right about one thing: Naomi was wonderful.

"How's Junior doing?" the woman, Cathie Hyatt, had asked.

"You mean Abbott, my father?" Layla had answered politely. Her grandfather, Junior, had recently died in a private care facility.

"Oh, yes . . . I meant Abbott. I'm so sorry. I knew Junior had passed. My mistake." She sighed. "He was a wonderful man."

Layla smiled. She'd known very little about her father's father, who'd spent his last few years on a long, slow decline. The only time she'd seen her father show any emotion was after Junior's death. He'd pressed his lips together, as if holding something in that was about to break, then said abruptly, "He's gone," the whole extent of the information she and Lucy were given. Lyle had been with Abbott at the time, but he was quiet and sad, grieving in his own way, and didn't want to talk about it any more than Abbott had.

It was later that she'd learned how much money was gone, having slipped through Junior and Abbott's collective fingers over the years. A small shock. Layla had never counted on the money, but it had always been there as a kind of security blanket, something that just *was*.

What she had counted on was Stonehenge. Not as a

source of income, but as a part of their family heritage. The summers she and Lucy and Lyle had spent at Stonehenge, roaming around its grounds and the forests beyond, were her best memories. She wanted that for her child. She wanted it fiercely.

"Well . . . I just called to touch base," Naomi said. "Feel free to call me, if you want. Any time."

This was a bit odd as it had already been established that Layla could contact Naomi whenever she wanted. Pulse accelerating, Layla asked, "Has Neil said something to you about me?"

She hesitated. "He said you weren't . . . going to be as involved."

Oh, did he? Layla almost blurted out how Neil was planning to force her completely away from Eddie, but she knew confiding in Naomi could be a bad, bad mistake.

"Well, that's incorrect. I'm going to be involved," Layla told her, forcing a smile on her face as she spoke the words. Saying something through a smile was supposed to make it brighter and more positive, though she sure as hell felt like snarling. "We're still working out the details."

"Oh, good." She was clearly relieved.

"I was thinking of stopping by tomorrow, just checking in. I have an appointment in the afternoon, but maybe earlier?"

"Would you like to have lunch? Say eleven-thirty?" Naomi invited. "I've just been craving pastrami, for some reason, and I've been making Reubens like it's a job. Come by the house and I'll make you one?"

Layla wasn't much of a meat eater, but she would tackle a beef hindquarter for a chance to be one-on-one with Naomi. She'd never been invited to her house without Neil before. "Sounds wonderful," she said. "See you tomorrow."

Chapter Six

Lucy looked at her empty glass on the Pembroke Inn's shiny, lacquered bar and traced a droplet of condensation from her copper mug along a line in the wood. She was drunk . . . no, pleasantly high . . . no, maybe drunk. She giggled. Uber once again.

She'd asked today's bartender about Mark, earning her a slow look from the man, a heavier, muscle-bound guy in his forties or fifties with a trimmed red beard and a supercilious attitude. She was pretty sure it was supercilious. He just had that *look*.

"Mark comes on at five," he said.

She sensed he was smiling knowingly at her, but he turned away before she could totally discern if that were true or only her own paranoia. She'd been too obvious by seating herself at the bar and asking about him.

Well, fine. She could wait. Evie was going home with Daphne today, so Lucy was free for hours. She knew she should care more that Evie was under Kate's influence, even a little, but truthfully, sometimes Evie popped out with these pithy observations about people and situations. If she had anything to say about Kate after this playdate, all the better.

Lucy could console herself for today's lapse in parenting by telling herself it was probably a good thing. She might actually learn something to use in her fight against Kate, and learning something was always good.

"Pithy," she said aloud, squinting at the face of her phone for the time: 4:30. Half an hour until Mark time.

Mark time. She liked that.

You should text John.

She felt a little thrill of anxiety. John would want to talk to her after he got home from work. Maybe he'd already tried to find her. She'd left too early for him to catch her, though he hadn't tried to text her yet . . . had he?

She'd already tucked her phone back in her purse, which she'd set on the floor in front of her barstool. Now she leaned over to try to snatch the handle—she'd done a great job of snagging it a few seconds ago—but it was just out of reach. She bent over farther, could feel herself slipping off the stool, and grabbed for the edge of the bar at the last second.

"Watch out there, now," the white-haired guy two seats over said to her. One of the old guys who haunted this bar. He looked slightly familiar, so she smiled vaguely and turned away. Was he one of her father's acquaintances? Or maybe her grandfather's? Junior might be gone, but he'd been a regular at the Pembroke from what Lucy had heard.

She managed to grab her purse's handle on her next try and pulled it onto her lap before plopping it on the bar, on the side away from the old guy, who she could still feel staring at her. Was he trying to place her? Lord, she hoped not.

You shouldn't have come back here. You want to fantasize about some hot guy, do it somewhere else.

But no . . . she wanted to fantasize about Mark.

She concentrated on her phone. No text from John. Something from Layla, though. Ah, yes. In a fit of pique, she'd texted her sister about the meeting on Friday after that phone call with dear old Dad.

"Fit of pique," murmured Lucy, eyeing Layla's response.

Dad called. I'm going. We need to stop them.

That's right. She'd made her father call Layla. No need to text her. Layla was right. They needed to stop them.

White hair said, "Weren't you here yesterday?"

Lucy pretended not to hear him. *Go away*, she silently urged. She was here on assignment. A secret agent. A tryst between secret agents.

She drew a breath and reached for the glass of water the red-bearded bartender had thoughtfully placed down along with her second Moscow mule. Yes, she'd ordered Kate's drink, and had belted them both back as if she were getting ready to have surgery performed without anesthesia. My, my, but those drinks had been strong.

Are you starting to have a problem? Two days of drinking in the afternoon?

She thought that over carefully. She almost wanted that to be her problem. Drinking. Something to open up to a therapist about, confess seriously to her closest friends and family. But instead, she wanted to cheat on her husband. And that was all on her. The blame would be intense.

"How are you doing?" red beard asked.

It took her a moment to realize he was referring to whether she wanted another drink or not. Did she? The alcohol was making her melancholy, which was just a stop on the road to maudlin. "Could I order that artichoke jalapeño dip and chips?"

"Sure thing."

"Oh, and a glass of Pinot Gris."

Red beard reappeared with her wineglass a few moments

later, and about ten minutes after that with the appetizer she'd remembered from yesterday's menu. White hair had subsided, but she kept herself half-turned away from him, only to realize as the shift changed that he was no longer there. She forgot him anyway as Mark came on duty, looking wonderfully rakish with that longer, dark chocolate-colored hair and those blue eyes. John's eyes were blue, too, like Layla's. She had a thing about them apparently. She always noticed. Her own were a greenish-hazel that Layla had wistfully said she wished she had; but then, Layla was always looking for the offbeat, the different, the winding road.

Time passed . . . One moment Lucy was nibbling on the artichoke jalapeño dip—she'd forgotten they served it on toasted slices of baguette and she had to keep wiping the little crumbs from her lips—the next she was looking at Mark's strong hands as he slipped her empty glass away and slid the second glass of Pinot toward her.

She heard the ding that denoted a text on her phone. Her move to collect her purse was as ungainly as before, but she managed it without falling off her stool, which was room for congratulations. Her cell phone felt a bit slippery in her hands. Everything was slightly slippery. Her mind couldn't catch on anything.

More dip and baguette, she warned herself, setting her phone down on the bar and then carefully applying the smooth spread on the little piece of bread and taking a bite.

"So, where did your grandmother take off to?" Mark asked.

Lucy had already forgotten they'd been having quite the conversation about her family. She wiped more crumbs from her lips. "No one knows. She was my great-grandmother. Did I not say that? She was a *great*-grandmother and she left my great-grandfather back at a time when it just wuvn't done." She cleared her throat, aware she'd slurred a bit there. "Criss, my great-grandfather, was a real sonuvabitch apparently. I asked my grandfather about him a few times, but he never said much. Grandpa's gone now. I haven't even tried to talk to my dad about any family history. He would just shut me down before we got started. I got my information from my mom, but she only knows bits and pieces about my dad's family. Her family isn't much better. She's an only, and her parents are also gone. I never saw them much anyway. Ah, well." Lucy prepared another slice of baguette and squinted at Mark. "What started this conversation?" She took a sip of wine.

"You said marriages don't last and that your grandmother ran away."

"My *great*-grandmother."

"Okay."

"I meant, it's hard to make a marriage last, no matter how hard you try."

Was he looking amused at her, or was he just thinking she was another drunk groupie, something red beard had implied with that *look* he'd given her.

Another ding. Oh, right. John.

She checked the screen of her phone and read his text: **Where are you? Where's Evie?**

She was feeling more clearheaded. The food. The water . . . but her heart was pounding as if she'd run a marathon.

"Could I have another glass of water?" she asked Mark.

"Sure thing."

Mark went to fill up her glass and several other drink orders as well. Lucy chewed on her lower lip, then texted back that she was at the Pembroke and Evie was with Daphne at Kate's. She was feeling guilty, but she reminded herself she'd done nothing wrong . . . yet.

John texted back: **We need to talk.**

Yeah, well . . . yeah . . . they did need to talk. About a whole lot of things she didn't want to talk about but knew were coming. Things that had gotten away from them over the course of their marriage. Her family . . . his remoteness . . . their lack of sex . . .

When I get home, she texted back.

Mark was back with her glass of water. He was looking at her in a way that made her glad she'd taken a trip to the ladies' room to refresh her makeup before she'd found her seat at the bar.

"Ever found talking to somebody you talk to every day just so *damn hard*?" she said on a sigh.

"You mean your friends yesterday?"

Lucy blinked. "You saw me and them?"

He nodded.

It made her feel kind of squirrelly, thinking about him noticing her, well, and Layla and Kate.

"It looked intense," he said.

"It was," she admitted. "But no, I was thinking of something else."

Was he holding her gaze a little too long, a little too intimately? She'd never been good at reading the signals. She'd made one ghastly error in her youth and had never trusted herself since.

"I'm going out for a cigarette." This was from one of the waitresses, not Kitty, who seemed to be MIA this evening.

"When you get back, take over for me for a minute or two while I take a break," Mark said easily.

"You barely got here," she complained.

"Call the EEO," he drawled, and she simply waved him off and headed through a door behind the bar.

He said to Lucy, "There's a covered walkway around the back."

She eyed him cautiously. "Okay."

"Great place to meet. Private. You can walk out the doors, follow the sidewalk around . . ." He gestured the way to go and to turn around two corners. He lifted his eyebrows at her, his gaze intense.

"Interesting," she said, her mouth dry.

He smiled lazily and brought her the check. He then went back to work, filling orders.

Lucy paid the bill by rote, her gaze flicking toward Mark, away, and then back again. She was still thinking over his words when the waitress returned and took her place at the bar. The crowd was smaller than the night before, maybe a typical Wednesday. Hard to say. Mark gave the waitress a few instructions and then headed through the back door, shooting Lucy a last look before disappearing. Lucy slid off her stool, picked up her coat, which she'd thrown over the stool next to her, casually shouldered her bag, and headed for the door. As she turned to start her trek around the outside of the building, she heard the front door open behind her and glanced back to see white hair heading outside. So, he hadn't left earlier. He lifted his chin at her in recognition and pulled a cigar from an inner pocket, walking the requisite ten feet from the door to light up. Lucy almost chickened out, but he seemed so involved in the ritual of preparing his cigar that she slipped around the first corner when he wasn't looking. She walked rapidly along the side of the building. There were no windows; it was the kitchen end of the restaurant.

At the second corner, she hesitated.

What are you doing?

Her hand was gripped around the collar of her coat, holding it close to her neck as if she were a shy virgin. Snorting, she loosened her grip.

Be careful. Be smart. You need to work things out with John one way or another before anything else. She thought about the night before, the tension between them and John's cold attitude. Remembering made her feel belligerent. To hell with that. She'd spent the last year, the last *two* years, trying to work things out, and she hadn't gotten anywhere.

With bolstered resolve, she rounded the last corner and there was Mark, standing beneath an overhanging eave that was lackadaisically dripping water from the earlier spate of rain. The air was cold and damp, but he was in his white shirt. The black vest the waitstaff wore was unbuttoned.

He said, "I've got about five minutes."

"Okay, well, I don't know what I'm doing here. I think maybe I should—"

She was stunned when he suddenly moved forward and pulled her toward him, backing them both into an alcove. She felt his hands slip under her coat and pull the small of her back toward him. He kissed her hard, then, crotch to crotch, which left no doubt what he was feeling.

When he released her, her head was spinning. "Bold move," she said a bit breathlessly.

"Time constraints," he said, grinning.

He suddenly unzipped his pants, letting his cock spring free. Lucy drew a breath in surprise. Clearly, he went commando and wasn't afraid to let her know. "I—" she started to say on a laugh when he pressed her fingers around his shaft, sliding her hand up and down its length and moaning. His other hand slid farther down the small of her back to squeeze her buttocks.

She had a bright flare of memory. Long ago. Nothing like this, but the end feeling was the same. Being used. Not as a person. As someone's vessel for sex.

She yanked her hand away, stumbled backward, turned to run, not before seeing that his own hand had taken up where hers left off.

She ran around the building and would have darted toward her car, but she slowed to an abrupt stop when she saw her husband's back as he stopped and talked to the white-haired gentleman, who was just finishing his cigar. John was just saying good-bye to the man and reaching for the door. The gent was waving him a good-bye of his own, then he turned toward the parking lot. Lucy stood frozen, praying the man didn't look back at her. If he'd recognized her, he hadn't put it together that she was John's wife, or John surely would have come looking for her instead of heading into the inn.

She watched John pull open one of the inn's double doors and head inside, then waited until the man reached his car, his steps agonizingly slow.

She wanted to run to her own vehicle, peel out of the lot, roar away.

Don't drive.

Frozen, she debated for about ten seconds. Call Uber or face John?

You didn't do anything wrong. You didn't.

Who are you kidding? Of course you did!

Ding.

She pulled out her phone, suddenly wanting to wash her hands like she might die if she didn't get the deed done ASAP. Oh, God. Oh my God.

John wrote: I'm at Pembroke. Where are you?

With shaking fingers, she texted that she was outside, about to call Uber. Then she headed for the double doors, catching sight of her husband heading her way through the glass panels.

He looked coldly furious.

Her face was hot. She felt guilty and used.

Just like before.

Not just like before.

"Were you ever going to come home?" John demanded as soon as he stepped outside.

"Yes." Through the glass she saw Mark reenter through the door behind the bar and head to the bar sink to wash his hands.

She was revolted and suddenly mad. At Mark and at herself. And at John, who was following up his question with a series of complaints about her and her father and was still complaining, ". . . can't depend on either of you. I've been waiting to talk to you, but I come home and you're not there. You're drinking alone at a bar. And you left Evie with Kate. *Kate.*"

"Evie was invited and wanted to go. I didn't—"

"You left work early," he cut her off. "Yesterday and today. And both days you're *here.*"

"I know. John, I know. I shouldn't have. I'm just trying to—"

"Are you drunk?"

"—process the fact that my dad talked to . . ." She trailed off as another older gentleman, this one with silvery-gray hair, came through the door and nodded at them. "Well, I'm feeling pretty sober now," she gritted through her teeth as soon as the man passed out of earshot.

"Why didn't you come home? We've got a lot of shit coming down on us."

"I know."

"I can't rely on you." He tucked his hand under her elbow and moved her away from the door.

When he stopped several feet away from the protective eaves, she said, "It's raining!"

"I don't want to be right next to the entrance."

"I'm not going to stand out here with you." She fumbled for her phone.

"What are you doing?"

"Calling Uber. I'm not completely sober yet, but I'm on a fast track."

"Because of me," he challenged.

She wanted to scream that everything wasn't about him, but, actually, in this case, it was. Instead, she pulled up the Uber app as John swept the phone from her hands.

"I'll drive you," he snapped.

A young couple crossed the parking lot toward the front door as Lucy said, "I don't want to be yelled at all the way home."

His grip on her arm tightened. "Why are you suddenly so irresponsible?"

"Suddenly? I've always been irresponsible. You just haven't noticed."

"Yes, I have. That's how you got Evie."

Lucy jerked her arm from his grip and walked blindly away from him. She stepped into the parking lot. John apparently thought she didn't see the car circling the end of the row and turning toward the inn's entryway because he grabbed her, pulling her arm so hard she stumbled and lost her balance, falling onto her knees, her arm wrenching from her weight.

"Ow!" she cried out in surprise.

"You're making a scene," he said through his teeth, hauling her to her feet with one hard yank. She tried to pull her arm back, but he held her tight. Tears formed behind her lids because it really hurt.

"Let go of me," she hissed, "or I don't know what I'll do. Something irresponsible like screaming or hitting you!"

He dropped her as if she'd burned him and stalked away.

"You okay?" the young man asked. He and his date had stopped at the door and were regarding her worriedly.

"Yes, fine." She straightened and ignored the pain in her arm and her scraped knees.

"Do you know him?" the woman asked cautiously.

She almost laughed. "It's debatable."

"You want me to call someone?" the man asked.

She shook her head. "No."

They looked at each other, then went into the bar. She saw John's taillights light up and the engine turn. He backed out with a little *blurp* from his tires and then sprayed water as he drove away.

With a sigh, she walked to her own car, the rain dampening her cheeks. When she tried to thread the key in the ignition, her hands were cold and wet, and it took her a couple of tries. Maybe she wasn't ready to drive anyway. Maybe she didn't want to go home.

She felt tears dampen her lashes and her nose got hot. Moments later, once she was in her car, she broke down and cried. She covered her face with her hands and sobbed. The windows fogged up. It was almost nice to be cocooned inside. She just needed to pull herself together and . . . what? Go back to the house she shared with John?

After a few moments, she let out her breath in a long sigh. She realized she was pretty darn sober now but decided to wait awhile longer anyway. She texted Kate and communicated with Evie, who was still in no hurry to be picked up. Lucy wrote back that she would be there soon anyway. Evie said okay, and then, a few minutes later, Lucy heard the ding of a new text from her daughter: John's here!!!! Can't I stay???

Groaning, Lucy texted back, I'm sorry. Didn't know he was picking you up. I'll meet you at home.

Lucy pushed the button for the garage door and pulled her car in next to her husband's, grimacing at the headache that had emerged. She'd had some time to think and was regretting her recklessness. Her unhappiness in her marriage was fueling some bad behavior. Maybe she was lucky Mark had turned out to be such an ass. Common sense had reasserted itself. She needed to face her problems with John—and her longtime hurt and anger with her father—and make better choices.

She entered the back door and found John in the kitchen, furiously washing the dishes. This was a task he only did when he was proving a point. Evie was in the family room, standing behind the couch, her body stiff. She rolled her eyes accusingly at Lucy, who realized something had gone down that had gotten her daughter in trouble with John.

"I'm sorry," Lucy said to her husband, who barely glanced her way. "I'm not dealing with things well."

He snorted.

Evie said, "Is it all right if I go to my room?"

"Sure, honey." Lucy frowned.

"She can stay right there and finish her homework. She and Daphne were watching videos they shouldn't have been. Kate was furious."

Lucy looked at Evie. "What videos?"

"They were just people doing stupid things. They were funny!" Evie burst out.

"Talk to Kate," John snapped. "If you're sober enough."

"I will," Lucy said slowly, her temper simmering. "Sorry for putting you out." She should have known John wasn't willing to let this pass, even for a cooling-off period. Lucy got over issues pretty fast. She could usually see the root cause and take steps to right the ship. But John seethed. It was a characteristic he'd managed to hide during their short courtship.

Evie said in a teary voice, "I did my homework already."

"You can go to your room if you want," Lucy decreed.

Evie raced away as if the hounds of hell were on her heels. John clattered the dishes, then slowly turned and regarded Lucy coldly. She could practically see the boiling fury behind his eyes.

"You always undermine me," he said.

"This isn't about Evie." She stood her ground. "This is about you and me and our jobs."

"Oh, is it?"

"I've said I'm sorry. I don't know what else I can say. I'm upset with my father, and I'm glad we have that family meeting on Friday. I'm going to write down all the things I want to say to him, so I don't forget them."

"Don't walk away from me," he warned as she headed toward the stairs.

Lucy turned around and spread her hands in a what-gives? posture. It did no good to argue with him when he was in a black funk. He was itching for a fight, pushing for one. The best thing she could do was nothing.

"I don't want my wife hanging around at bars," he stated flatly.

"Fine. Your wife doesn't plan to hang around bars any-more."

"Why? What happened?"

"I'm going upstairs now, if you have no further objections."

There was a slight smirk on his face as he said, "You look a little pale. Not feeling so well?"

"John . . ." She sighed.

"What?"

She fought back the urge to fight back. Though it never did any good, she was sick of being treated like a schoolgirl. "Thanks for doing the dishes." She turned away from him.

"That's all you have to say?" he called after her.

She didn't answer, and she heard him stride quickly toward her. She was two steps above him when she whipped back to face him. If he touched her, she'd scream bloody murder, but no, she knew he wouldn't. He just liked to intimidate, but she sensed, like all bullies, he was deeply afraid inside.

She wished she'd known all this when she married him, but she'd only seen his good side. A sad song she'd heard over and over again. She'd thought she was too smart to fall for someone like him, but she'd learned the hard way that she was as susceptible as the next person.

He broke the stalemate by brushing past her, heading up the stairs ahead of her.

She knew it would be an icy night in the bedroom, with neither of them getting much sleep.

Sighing, she decided to head back downstairs to the family room. She sank onto the couch. *You need to do something before this marriage devolves into something dangerous.*

Chapter Seven

"Kate, could I have a moment?"

Kate looked up from the pro forma she was working on, the school's profit and loss, to find April McAdams, April Academy's director, standing in the doorway, regarding her soberly and fingering the silver chain around her neck, not a good sign. It meant she was holding back her temper, and her other clenched fist proved the assumption right.

"What's wrong?" Kate asked, glancing at the time. Ten a.m. She wished it was much later. She was anxious to grab Daphne and head home. She had much to do to prep for tomorrow's meeting at Crissman & Wolfe. Having Evie over through dinner the night before had really messed with her schedule, and she was annoyed with herself that she'd ever agreed to it. What had she been thinking? A midweek, after-school playdate? But Daphne had begged and begged and begged, and so she'd buckled. Finding the girls laughing at those videos of people doing inane, dangerous tricks had made Kate want to scream at Lucy, and Lyle had been no help at all.

"Let it go," he'd told her. She'd had to pretend she had, even though she hadn't. His disinterest in anything to do with child-rearing sometimes got to her, especially when it was his sister's daughter who'd started everything. Still, it was lucky he'd been in the kitchen when John came to collect Evie, so she'd managed to have a private moment to let him know what his stepdaughter had gotten Daphne in to. Later, when Lucy texted an apology, Kate showed Lyle the proof of Lucy's rudeness. No phone call, just a few words on a screen, and Lucy hadn't even known what she was apologizing for. Lyle had only cut a look at the words on her cell's screen and shaken his head. Kate had yet to call Lucy to lay the full extent of the transgression out to her. She'd tried to engage Lyle in the issue, but he'd been distracted. He was damn near always distracted lately. She was going to have to find out what was going on with him.

"You're not coming in tomorrow?" April demanded tightly.

"No. I've got a meeting with Lyle's family about their business." *Which I told you about.*

"Well, I need you to come in tomorrow."

"April, I have every other Friday off," Kate reminded her carefully. This wasn't a news flash. April knew as well as Kate did what her schedule was.

April drew a long breath and released it slowly. Kate could see her ropy biceps jutting out from her dark green sleeveless dress as she wrapped her arms around her waist. She was obsessive about working out, using every free moment to head to the gym. Kate could have told her, no amount of exercise would bring back her youth, and with her blond hair and pale skin, April looked another thirty years older than her true age.

April . . . like the month Layla would have her baby.

Kate shut that thought off before it could turn her deaf to her boss, who looked cocked and loaded for a real fight.

"I'm sorry, Kate. I need you here. The representative from KeyBank is going to be here tomorrow, and you know the numbers almost better than I do."

That was patently untrue. April was a stickler for every cent spent and could be a skinflint over the smallest item. Kate had taken to bringing her own staples and pens because April never requisitioned enough office supplies, and Kate was sick of giving hers up whenever April needed something. "I thought the bank was coming next week."

"I had to move them up. I'm leaving on Monday for that conference in San Jose. You know that."

Kate's anger fizzed. When April made plans, she ignored anyone else's. She had an inflated belief in her own importance and expected her employees to just roll over and do as she asked, time and time again. "I'm sorry. I just can't be here tomorrow. This is something I can't miss."

April's thin face suffused with color. "I hired you to be my voice in financial matters. You know that."

"I'll be here next week. We're right on budget. I think the bank will be impressed with how well you manage everything and—"

"They're coming tomorrow," she bit out. "I don't need to remind you that you were the one who wanted to place your child at my academy. And Daphne loves it here." April was obliquely referring to the discount Kate received on her daughter's tuition by being a staff member. A discount that wasn't nearly as substantial as April acted like it was. But still, without this job . . . Kate would likely not be able to afford April Academy.

An icicle of fear stabbed her heart. She needed this job, which was why she'd put up with April's black moods all this time.

Unless the lodge sells . . .

Stonehenge. It wasn't anything like the ruin in England, and she hated their nickname for it. She'd told Lucy and Layla that it was Lyle's idea to sell Stonehenge, not hers, but honestly, she'd be happy to unload the place. It was a huge, rambling building with two wings, all of it old and rustic to the extreme. Yes, the kitchen had been remodeled at one point, and she believed the plumbing had been upgraded, but there was no escaping the fact that it was a money drain. The last time it had been rented out was to a church group Kate suspected was little more than a cult, and she knew for a fact they'd cut a very sweet deal with Abbott, who had no head for numbers. It was a crime how little both Abbott and Lyle knew or cared about making a profit.

And she didn't care how many times Lucy, Layla, and yes, sometimes even Lyle, waxed rhapsodic over remembrances of past times at the lodge. From the way they talked, they'd led this bucolic childhood there, traipsing through the surrounding woods discovering trillium and birds' nests and deer and babbling brooks. . . . Layla was the worst, recounting special moments, like when they'd all sat on the low stone fence that flanked a path along the cliff's edge and stared out toward a cloudy sky above the river, hundreds of feet below. Layla had a penchant for spinning out her memories in a way that sounded like they'd led idyllic lives from a century before. Layla really was an airhead. They could call her arty all they liked, Kate knew the truth.

So, yes, Kate wanted to sell the lodge, and she hoped Abbott was ready to have his children share in the profits from the sale. God knew they needed the money. If Stonehenge sold, Kate could not only quit her job, she and Lyle could maybe, possibly, look in to using Layla's surrogate themselves. Right now, the cost of IVF was outside their budget. But time was tick-tick-ticking away, and so far, they were no closer to Lyle's inheritance. Selling the lodge could be the difference.

Layla was damn lucky to have someone who had the means to pay for the procedures.

It wasn't fair.

"Kate?" April demanded, waiting for Kate to roll over, as she always did.

But not this time. She needed to be at Abbott's and Lyle's sides tomorrow, reminding them to stay on task, no matter what April wanted. She needed to run with Lyle's idea to sell the lodge to Jerome Wolfe.

"April, if I'd known you needed me, I would have asked to reschedule the meeting with my father-in-law. It's just at this late date, I have to be there. This is one of those must-dos."

April blinked at Kate's refusal. Kate held her breath, waiting for her reaction.

After a beat, April said, exasperated, "I'll have to cancel with the bank if you're not there."

"I could come back . . . maybe later in the afternoon?"

"Thank you so very much, Kate. We'll just have to reschedule when I get back."

Before Kate could respond, she twisted on her heel, then tip-tapped angrily back down the hall to her office. Kate jumped when she heard April's office door slam with more force than necessary.

I should quit. See how she likes that. Let her boss some-body else around. I should be at Crissman & Wolfe. I could do all their jobs.

She gripped her pen with all her strength, then hauled back and hurled it across the room. It bounced off the wall next to the door with a small smack. Immediately, she was afraid someone might have heard it. Listening hard, she then got up and hurried to pick up the pen. Back at her desk, she breathed a sigh of relief that no one seemed to have noticed.

A text dinged on her phone. She picked up the cell, which was lying atop her desk. Lyle, she saw:

Won't be home for dinner.

Well, that was just great.
Where will you be? she texted back.

After a long pause, he wrote: **Meeting business associates for a drink.**

Where? she wanted to scream. Who? About what? But she sensed he was playing this very close to the vest, so she kept quiet herself. His actions alarmed her, but she couldn't keep demanding answers. It was the quickest way to shut her husband down completely.

She looked at the clock. Too early to leave for lunch.

With an effort, she settled back into her job, but a little black cloud hovered over her head, darkening her thoughts.

Layla rang the bell at Naomi's house and waited beneath a narrow overhang, trying hard to keep the rain from dripping onto her hair. She'd pulled her blondish tresses into a ponytail at her nape and had picked out her most conservative dress, dark blue with a thin silver belt. She'd wanted to appear competent and in control, so she'd channeled her inner Lucy. She had to assume Naomi would be talking to Neil—he might already know about this lunch—so she was bound and determined to present herself in the best possible light.

Naomi came to the door, her midsection ballooning out beneath a maroon sweater. "I'm a beach ball," Naomi said. "I always am at this point."

Layla couldn't take her eyes off the evidence of the baby. He was going to be here in just a few months. She felt a wave of yearning so deep it made her eyes burn. This was her child . . . *hers* . . . and Neil was trying to take him away from her.

"You look great," Layla greeted her.

"Come on in. I tried to pick up the house, but bending over is a trick these days."

"I don't see anything out of place."

They were walking along the edge of the living room

down a short hallway lined with pictures of her two children at various stages of their life. The last photo was of Naomi, her husband, and Jeremy and their little girl at the beach. They were all in jeans and white shirts, looking at the camera with the sun setting in the background. The little girl was in front of her mother, smiling for the camera, and her brother was standing in front of his dad holding a fistful of wet sand.

Naomi said fondly, "As soon as that picture was snapped, Jeremy threw that sand at Keelie and laughed like a banshee. Got it all over her blouse. It's funny now, but Keelie cried like it was the end of the world. Luckily, it was after the picture."

Layla found she couldn't speak. She wanted this. Wanted it so badly. She didn't know if she could pull off acting like everything was okay between Neil and her.

She managed to make it through the small talk while Naomi put their Reubens together. Somehow, the surrogate didn't notice her distraction, or maybe she just ignored it. In any case, Layla choked down as much of the sandwich as she could manage through a dry mouth and tight throat, while Naomi sighed with pleasure after finishing hers.

"My God, I can eat when I'm pregnant!" she laughed.

Layla smiled and swallowed a last bite.

Naomi picked up their plates, waving off Layla's attempts to help. Layla sat at the table and tried hard to keep her gaze from clinging to Naomi's belly. Finally, she said, "I don't know what Neil said about . . . our relationship, but I do want you to know I would never give up my child. He's mistaken about that."

Naomi came back to the table and sat across from Layla, desultorily picking up a crumb with her thumb. "He said you had a legal agreement that the baby would be his."

"Well . . . yes. That was how it was in the beginning. We were dating, and he wanted a son. . . . You know our history."

"I thought you were going to be parents together."

"Well, yes. We were. We *are*."

"Layla, he said you sold him your eggs."

"I did. I didn't know what I was doing. I thought we were a couple and I wanted to give him what he wanted . . . and I signed something, which I think he's misunderstood. . . ."

"So, you want your child, but you and Neil aren't . . . on the same page."

"That's right. That's what's happened. But I'm giving Neil his money back. It's all been a big misunderstanding. I've always planned to be a part of my son's life. And Neil's," Layla added for good measure. She wasn't in love with him, but if they could make it work together, that would be ideal.

Naomi's brow furrowed. Her dark hair was cut short and feathered around her face. Despite her shape, she had an elfin look about her. "Layla . . . you know Neil's been paying for my services throughout this process, and he's made all the financial arrangements for the hospital."

"Yes."

"I have a contract with him as well."

"We'll work this all out. I'll pay you, or I'll pay Neil," Layla assured her.

"I just don't want there to be some major fallout between you two just as this little guy greets the world."

"No, no. No fallout. Neil and I are talking about everything. We met two days ago and talked about you and the baby."

"Okay. Good. Good to know . . ." She heaved a sigh of relief, then shot Layla a quick look. "So, you know about his girlfriend?"

Her heart contracted hard, then her pulse began to pound. "Oh . . . no . . . I guess not."

Naomi's look of concern returned. "I've met Courtney a couple of times. She seems nice and very interested in the baby."

Layla couldn't speak. Her insides were ice.

Naomi's voice came from faraway. "I hope I didn't say anything I shouldn't have."

"Oh, no. No . . . It's all fine," she said woodenly. "I will . . . talk to Neil about everything; his girlfriend, too. Thank you so much for lunch. It was really good. I shouldn't have put you out."

Layla was babbling, but Naomi seemed to understand. "You didn't put me out. It was good to see you."

She sounded sincere. As Layla left Naomi's house, she felt dizzy. She stood at the end of the drive in the relentless rain, waiting for Uber to collect her. By the time she was picked up she was soaked to the skin and she doubted even a bath could warm up the ice in her core.

Neil has a girlfriend . . . who's very interested in the baby. That traitorous thought rumbled through her mind as she returned to her apartment and stripped off her wet clothes, hanging them over a heat register to dry, then soaked in a hot tub. But the chilling thought that Neil had betrayed her never left.

After the water had turned tepid, she climbed out of the tub and stepped into the same blue dress. She blow-dried her hair and stared at her own haunted eyes in the bathroom mirror.

At three o'clock she left for her afternoon appointment with Dallas Denton, attorney-at-law.

Lucy gazed blankly at her computer screen, determined to stay at work till the end of the day. Evie normally walked from her school to after-school care, which was just a block away, but Lucy was having a heck of a time not racing to pick her up. She wanted to be with her daughter. She wanted to be with her *now*. The two of them against the world. But she couldn't leave work early three days in a row and expect to have any credibility when she met with her father and the rest of the family.

The rest of last night had been a silent war with John. She'd stayed up late, crawling into bed well after midnight, turning her back to him. The space between them felt like a wall of ice. Her making or his? She couldn't tell. Probably both of theirs.

There was a knock at Lucy's office door.

"Come in," Lucy called, turning in her seat to meet the newcomer.

Miranda ducked her short bob of gray hair inside. She smiled at Lucy. "Wanted to see how you're doing."

"Fine. Not bad." This was the first time Miranda had shown that she was even aware of the difficulties facing Lucy and Crissman & Wolfe. "How about you?"

Miranda's smile dropped as she moved into the room, smoothing her gray pullover sweater, its shade nearly the same color as her hair. "Your father is making some hard decisions."

"Yes, he is."

"I hope he makes the right ones."

"You and me both."

Miranda didn't approve of Lyle as her father's right-hand man, and Lucy suspected she was thinking of how both her brother and father listened to each other's counsel above all others'. Lucy had been tempted to confide her own feelings along the same lines but knew that would be a mistake. She couldn't afford to get in an us-against-them mentality, even though her father listened to Miranda. No, she needed to bring her issues directly to her father and hope for the best.

"Let me know if I can be of any help."

"Thank you. I will."

Miranda left a few moments later, and Lucy turned back

to her computer. She went back to puzzling out a series of transactions that had been made in the general account about a month earlier, while she was on vacation with John and Evie—not that it had been much of a vacation, when John had been on the phone to her father and others at Crissman & Wolfe the whole time—that appeared to show a sixty-thousand-dollar deficit. Mistakes were made whenever she was gone, and when they came to light she always ended up spending an inordinate amount of time fixing them. It was just a fact, a part of her job, one she was pretty good at. Lucy didn't think she was irreplaceable, but she knew she was a hard line between keeping the accounts correct and letting them start to slip into fuzziness. When she'd started at the company, she'd spent a long time straightening out a kind of slush account where financial inequities that couldn't be traced were dumped. Before her, these problems were attended to by the company's outside accountants, who charged an arm and a leg for their forensic accounting, but from what Lucy could tell, they never really seemed to get to the bottom of the pile. The truth was, Abbott was sloppy. So was Lyle, and, well, so was John. They moved fast and didn't do all the paperwork they should. Both Lucy and Miranda were their cleanup girls. Lucy wondered, not for the first time, what would happen if she were to lose her job. Nothing good.

She was following up on several transactions that had led to the deficit when her cell phone buzzed. It lay on her desk beside her keyboard, and she looked down at the screen to see Kate was calling. Lucy made a face. She'd texted her sister-in-law the night before to ask about the inappropriate video they were watching, but Kate hadn't responded until now.

She pressed the button to connect and answered, "Hi, Kate."

"Hi, Lucy. I got your text. I thought you and I should talk personally, though."

"Sure."

"Did John tell you what the girls were watching?"

"He just said it was an inappropriate video. What was it?"

"I think it's called *Jackass*."

"That show where they do stupid stunts?"

Lucy started to smile, and Kate must have heard it in her voice because her answer was a curt, "Yes."

"Oh, okay. I'm . . . sorry?" She was so relieved it wasn't something worse that she couldn't work up any real concern. "I'll talk to Evie about it. Where'd they find that?"

"You don't really seem to be taking this seriously," Kate said stiffly.

"I know. I'm trying. I thought . . . I don't know what I thought." Actually, that was a lie. What she'd thought was that the girls had watched something violent or full of graphic sexual content or both.

"I don't know if I can trust the two of them together unless I'm directly in the room with them," said Kate.

"Okay. You're right. And thank you for having Evie over. It meant a lot to her."

"Oh." She sounded somewhat nonplused by Lucy's about-face. "You're welcome."

Lucy said good-bye a few moments later, still smiling. She'd dreaded talking to Kate and then it had turned out to be mostly a big fat nothing. Her mood remained lifted until it was time to head home, but as she grabbed her coat and turned off the office lights, her expression grew grim. John had gotten up early and left while she was getting ready, but she was going to have to face him soon.

Their marriage was broken, and she didn't know if she could fix it, or if she even wanted to.

Chapter Eight

The small meeting room at Crissman & Wolfe was on the third floor, mixed in with the business offices behind customer service. Kate stepped into the room early, nearly a half hour before anyone was due to arrive. Abbott had initially said the family would meet at his office, but there wasn't enough seating there for all six of them, so Kate had opted for the small conference room and Abbott had agreed. Miranda had asked her what she was doing in that snotty way of hers, and Kate had informed the woman that the Crissman family was having a private meeting, and would she be so kind as to make sure they were undisturbed?

Miranda had gazed at her with those dead eyes, which were a complete lie because the woman cataloged everything, then whispered in Abbott's ear, the biggest tattletale in the store, especially about the transgressions of his family and their spouses. In a way, it had been easier when Junior was alive. He hadn't had the reverence for Miranda that Abbott did, and he tended to curb the woman's overreaching. But after his wife Judith's death, Junior had started fading away, which was irony itself because the man was a profligate spender and womanizer. No wonder Abbott couldn't sustain a marriage. His father had been a terrible role model.

Sure, Judith had stuck with him over the years, but they'd really led separate lives. Funny how much her death had affected Junior . . . and how much his death had affected both Abbott and Lyle. Too close a brush with the grim reaper, maybe. The only positive out of all of it was, Junior wasn't around to spend more Crissman money.

Kate placed her notebook in her spot, and then another for Lyle, whom she seated next to Abbott. That left a spot for Lucy or John on his other side, and she had a moment of indecision. Really, that's where she should sit. She was more his right-hand man than even Lyle was, though she would never say as much. But she could see that the other Crissmans would use that as one more sign she was trying to seize control. It was galling how they all watched for her to make a mistake.

Layla would undoubtedly sit next to Lucy, unless John edged her out. If that happened she would sit several seats away from all of them. Layla was the outsider, in many ways, and if she couldn't have Lucy's support, she made a point of it, for some reason. Kate just couldn't fathom the woman. It was shocking what a good job she did in staging homes. Kate had been through several model homes recently, just to see what Layla was doing, and had been impressed despite herself. She had double-checked to be sure there wasn't a mistake, but the information clearly listed Layla Crissman as the stager, and some of the artwork on display—and for sale; shameless self-promotion—was hers as well.

Still, Layla was easier to take than Lucy, who always acted superior, like she always knew best.

Kate walked down the hall to the employee break room, rummaged in the cabinets, and found a glass pitcher. She filled it with filtered water, put it on a tray with six glasses, and walked it back to the meeting room, throwing a dark glance in the direction of Miranda's office as she passed by. If you wanted anything done, you had to do it yourself.

Minutes later, she heard quick footsteps heading her way down the hall. Lucy, she thought. Kate stood behind her chair and pasted a smile on her face, waiting for her sister-in-law. She was surprised when Layla strode in, pale and grim, the peacock-blue scarf draped around the back of her neck beginning to flutter as if it were about to take flight.

"What's wrong?" Kate asked.

Layla stopped short to stare at her. "Seriously? Stone-henge? You're still trying to sell it, right?"

"*I'm* not trying to sell it. I told you that. I was just asking why you look so . . ."

"Where are you putting Lucy?"

Normally, Layla was quiet, keeping most of her thoughts to herself, mostly disinterested in family business, Kate always thought. Today was different in a way Kate couldn't put her finger on. "Lucy will probably sit by her father or John, maybe." She swept a hand to indicate the seats on Abbot's left side.

Layla thought about it a moment, then walked over to the seat next to Abbott's.

"Oh, no. That's not what I meant. I—"

"I know what you meant," Layla interrupted, planting herself down in the chair anyway. She gave Kate a *look*.

Well, honestly. Kate wanted to defend herself, but she hardly knew where to start. That was the trouble with Lyle's sisters. They were so incredibly unfair. They wanted to blame her for everything.

More footsteps in the hallway heralded the arrival of Lucy and John, then Abbott and Lyle. Kate had asked Lyle to come with her, but he'd demurred. She hadn't known why, but now it seemed he'd wanted to see his father before the meeting took place. It pricked her anger a little. It felt like her husband was moving away from her.

Spying Layla, Lucy quickened her steps and took the seat next to her. Lyle sat in the seat Kate had readied for him, leaving John the seat next to Lucy, the farthest away from Abbott. Except that he looked around and focused on the one next to Kate, rounding the table to come to her side. Abbott and Kate were the last to seat themselves, and everyone looked expectantly to the Crissman patriarch, though Kate was acutely aware of Lucy's husband so close to her. She slid a glance across the table at Lucy, who had turned toward the head of the table, her shoulder tucked forward like a wall. Kate could swear she was deliberately snubbing her husband, but then, John didn't appear to want to sit by her either. Trouble in paradise? The idea warmed the cockles of her heart a bit.

"Pass me the water," Abbott said, pointing to the tray in the middle of the table with the pitcher and glasses.

Kate swept up the pitcher and poured a glass before anyone else could, although seriously, none of them seemed to be eager to perform the small task.

"I'd like one, too," John said in her left ear.

Get it yourself. But she was holding the pitcher in her hand, so she grudgingly poured him a glass as well.

Lucy wore a dark green dress and earrings with stones of the same shade. She was a little pale as well, Kate thought, sliding a glance from her to Layla and back again. Lucy's attention was directed totally toward her father. She hadn't turned once to look at her husband.

Kate peered sideways at John. He was dressed in a white shirt, jacket, and no tie. If he sensed her looking at him, he didn't show it. He, too, was facing forward, waiting for Abbott to speak. It felt like there was a force field between Lucy and John. What had happened?

Abbott said, "I'm not going to spend a lot of time holding your hands. Crissman & Wolfe's been busy losing money. It costs too much to keep the lights on in that building and the rent keeps skyrocketing. I told our landlord we wouldn't renew the lease. We're in till August; then we're out."

Kate switched her attention to Lyle. He appeared to be looking at his father, but she could see the distance in his eyes and knew what it meant. He was somewhere else. Maybe worrying ahead of the conversation? She wouldn't be able to stand it if his attention was somewhere else. She put in quickly, "But online sales are doing very well. And we have a distribution center that's hiring right now."

Lyle roused himself to say, "That's true. We've leased more warehouse space. A lot cheaper than office rent."

"Where is the business office going to be?" Lucy asked.

"At the warehouse." That was from John. "On the east side, out near Gresham."

"That's a helluva drive from Laurelton," Lucy pointed out.

Abbott ignored her and, as if everything was said and done and she had no input in those kinds of important decisions, said, "We'll be starting to move there soon. Miranda and John should be in place by the end of March."

Lucy turned her eyes on her husband, silently accusing him of holding out on her.

Abbot brought her attention back to him. "Lucy, you'll be staying at the store for now. You'll be taking over Miranda's duties until we shut down completely. Lyle and I will handle the accounting."

"What?" Lucy asked in surprise.

"You're good at managing," Abbott told her.

Kate drew a sharp breath. That was a lie. Lucy might have a head for figures, but she was terrible in dealing with people. Just terrible!

"So, you and Lyle will be at the warehouse?" Lucy asked carefully.

"Isn't that what I just said?" Abbott challenged. "We'll be setting up all our offices there. It's going to take a while, so we've already started. We should be pretty well set up by the charity auction for the Friends of the Columbia River Gorge. That's taking up a lot of time right now."

Layla asked, "Who's in charge of setting it up?"

"I am," said Lyle.

Well, I am, Kate thought, but she didn't say it.

"What's the theme again?" Layla questioned.

Kate was sure she was trying to be a pain in the ass. Lucy had subsided into silence after learning she'd been promoted. That was the thing. She was looking at her change of status as a demotion, when she should have been thanking Abbott, gushing to him. Not that she'd be any good in the job. Maybe Abbott knew that and was just trying to find a way to edge her out. "Denim and Diamonds," Kate said.

Beside her, John asked, "Your idea?"

"Well, I came up with it, but we're all on board." She looked from Abbott to Lyle and back again. Neither of them said anything, which kind of pissed her off.

"Ah," said John, which definitely pissed her off.

And what about John? Lyle was taking over his duties one by one. Sure, there was a learning curve, and Lyle hadn't really been as on the ball as he could. She'd had to push him along pretty hard, but he was getting there. So, did that leave John out in the cold? She was really starting to hope so.

Layla asked, "So, Lyle's moved up quite a few rungs?"

The hairs on the back of Kate's neck rose. Since when did she get to talk about the company? She wasn't any part of it!

Abbott's eyes glared at his eldest daughter beneath fierce, bushy brows, and Layla added insult to injury by asking, "What about Stonehenge?"

Kate held her breath. Had Layla taken a self-destruction pill? She was purposely questioning her father, and that never worked.

"We're not talking about Stonehenge," Abbott ground out. He flicked a look at Kate, and she felt her face heat. He knew she'd spilled the beans too soon. His own face took on a ruddy hue as well, and he added angrily, "Whatever I decide about it, I'll let you know."

"It should be on the historical registry," Layla said.

"Business-wise, that would be a very bad idea," her father said through a thin smile. "I think I'm lucky you're an artist."

Ouch, Kate thought with a certain amount of pleasure.

"Is Jerome Wolfe buying Stonehenge?" asked Lucy.

"You have any questions about *the business*?" Abbott demanded.

"It's just that we all feel connected to Stonehenge. If you're really selling it, it would be nice to know." Lucy either didn't see Abbott's growing frustration or didn't care.

"I have a question about the business," John said. "When are you making the announcement about shuttering the downtown store?"

Kate said, "After Denim and Diamonds." She glanced at Abbott for corroboration, but he was looking at the table, lips pressed tightly together, still fuming, she guessed.

"So, we're not telling the press about this until after the auction?" Lucy's tone suggested she didn't approve.

"No." That was Lyle.

"We prefer to keep everything business as usual until afterward," Kate helped him out.

Some of the wealthiest families and businessmen from the Greater Portland area would be in attendance, ready to hand over huge checks to restore so much of the area that had been devastated by the Eagle Creek fire, which had nearly destroyed the Multnomah Falls Lodge, decimated local businesses, and closed the historic Columbia Highway for months. It was also a chance to rub elbows with some of the Portland elite. Kate knew Abbott would want to keep up appearances, and she wanted Lyle to put his best foot forward as well. He'd been so morose lately. The shuttering of the store was getting to him even more than she'd expected it would.

Abbott said, "I would like my two daughters to represent the Crissman family that night. Entertain. Be happy. No political talk. No spilling secrets about the company. Just gracious hostesses."

Layla and Lucy exchanged a look. Kate was nearly bursting to remind Abbott that he'd asked her to play the crowd along as well, but Abbott went on, "Lyle and I will be greeting everyone as well. They don't have to know it's a final hurrah. It will be evident soon enough."

"Is Jerome Wolfe invited?" Lucy asked.

Abbott glowered and shook his head slightly, but Lyle answered, "Yes."

Kate could have beaned him. Couldn't he feel the nuances? Where the hell was he?

"He'll raze Stonehenge to the ground," Layla predicted. "Its value is in its age. It has history."

She was trying to hold Abbott's gaze, but he looked past her, focusing on John Linfield, and said, "My decisions are for the good of the business and the good of the family. That's all."

He abruptly stood, surprising everyone, including Kate, who'd expected the meeting to last longer than twenty minutes. But Abbott was nothing if not mercurial.

She scrambled to be one of the first by his side as he exited the meeting room.

Lyle, still seated, his expression slightly wild, gave her a look as she hurried past him. Kate wondered if he wanted an apology for pushing closer to Abbott than he was, but the words died on her tongue as he suddenly rose from his seat to join her, tucking his phone into his pocket. He'd been looking at it, she realized. Who had he been talking to? Immediately, she thought of those two long-legged women she'd caught him talking to the last time they'd been at Crissman & Wolfe together. Kate had wanted to scratch their eyes out. She'd hated the way Lyle joked and teased with them. Hated the way they simpered in the beam of his smile.

But he didn't look so happy now, so maybe she was overreacting. Whoever he'd been speaking with hadn't given him any pleasure.

"Bad news?" she asked him as they both hurried to catch up with Abbott, who was stalking away as fast as he could without breaking into a run.

"Huh? Oh. No."

"Did you get a text?"

"No," Lyle said shortly, and he, too, put on the afterburners as he hastened to catch up with his father. Kate had to speed up as well, especially when the elevator car opened and Abbott stepped inside, looking for all the world like he was going to engage the car before either Lyle or she got there.

Kate was almost breathless when she practically jumped inside behind Lyle and Abbott slammed his palm against the button for the ground floor.

Both Lyle and Kate turned to Abbott for an explanation for his hasty exodus.

He flushed and growled, "I won't be questioned about my company."

My company. Kate felt a spurt of anger, which she quickly quelled. She was sick of Abbott making a point about company ownership, but he only spoke the truth. If Lyle was ever going to get what was rightfully his, he was going to have to fight for it, and he needed her help.

Lyle looked away, focusing on the middle distance somewhere beyond the elevator car.

What was he thinking about?

"Was that text bad news?" she asked him outright.

He flicked a glance her way. She thought for a moment he would argue with her, having already said he hadn't gotten a text. But they both knew he'd lied about that. "No, it was just from Pat," he muttered.

"Is Pat a man or a woman?" she quipped back, thinking of that old *Saturday Night Live* shtick about a person whose gender couldn't be identified by either the way they dressed, looked, or were named. The whole gag was that no one knew whether Pat was a man or a woman. In other times, Lyle might have given her that sideways smile she'd loved so much and answered her question with, "Yes."

This time he answered, "A man."

Kate smiled fractionally. She didn't know if she believed him.

But she knew the code to unlock his phone and she could check it anytime she liked. Maybe tonight, when he was sleeping.

They left the elevator and followed Abbott as he strode outside toward the parking structure on the block opposite the store. Then, in unison, as if reading each other's mind, they stopped. There was no reason to keep following him, and it was clear he was in no mood for a rehash of the meeting. She and Lyle hesitated on the sidewalk. An awkward moment passed as they watched Abbott disappear into the parking structure. The traffic light changed. Cars and trucks moved along the street.

Finally, he asked, "You going back to the school?"

"This is my Friday off. I've just got to pick up Daphne later."

"Oh. Right." Lyle moved off toward the west end of the building.

"Where are you going?"

"My car."

She saw the lights flash on his black Mercedes, parked at a meter. Lyle climbed in the driver's side, started the engine, tossed her a brief wave, then drove off. She wondered if he was meeting this "Pat" and doubled down on her intention to break into his phone.

Lucy picked up Evie from school. Her daughter chattered away about someone in her class who'd puked up a "whole lot of Gummy Bears" on the playground. Evie said, "She shouldn't have had them. It's against the rules at school. And it was really, really gross when she went 'bleeaaahhh' and it came out into the dirt!"

"Gross," Lucy concurred, though she'd barely heard a word. She'd left work early again, but no one cared today. Her father and brother weren't around, and she wasn't sure Miranda knew of the coming change to her job. Lucy sure didn't want to be the one to tell her. Or maybe she did know, and that's why she'd been so supportive earlier. That didn't seem like Miranda, but who knew? All day long she'd been thinking about how her father had basically ripped her job out from under her. Her father and her brother.

If she complained, would she be heard?

And what happens when the store closes? Do you even have a job?

In the meeting, she hadn't been able to stop herself from glancing over at John, whose brows had been knit into a frown. *Maybe he cares that I'm being treated so badly*, she'd thought at the time. Hoped, actually. They hadn't made eye contact, but it had seemed like he was on her side. Forced her to rethink her own actions over the last few days. Maybe there was a chance for them after all. They were married. Husband and wife. Things weren't perfect, but what marriage was?

"I'm going to stop at the store," she told Evie.

"Can I come in, too?"

"Sure."

They walked down the aisles together, and Lucy bought

flank steak, the makings for scalloped potatoes with Gruyère cheese and nutmeg, a Martha Stewart recipe John just loved, and an Asian chopped salad in a bag. Okay, the salad was kind of a cheat, but it was really good, and she was going to have her hands full trying to get it all done in time. She assumed her husband had gone back to the office after the meeting. They hadn't spoken on the way out.

At the house, Lucy dropped the groceries on the counter and texted John, asking when he'd be home. Then she set about peeling the potatoes and slicing them super thin with her mandolin. John hadn't gotten back to her by the time they were ready for the oven, so she texted him again: Making dinner. Just want to know when you'll be home. Damn AutoCorrect tried to make something else of it, and she had to fight a bit to get the text the way she wanted it.

She heard the ding of the oven telling her it was preheated at almost the same moment her cell's swoosh sound said she had a text.

She checked the phone's screen: Not coming home for a while.

Annoyed, she responded: Can I have a closer ETA?

When he didn't immediately respond, she put the potatoes in the oven and thought, *Screw it*. Then, she immediately told herself to stop being such a bitch. How was he supposed to know she'd chosen this day to offer an olive branch? She would just cook the potatoes and see what happened by the time they were done.

Her cell rang. Well, good. He finally chose to call. But when she glanced at the screen, she saw it was Layla.

"A call instead of a text. Has the end of the world arrived and no one told me?"

"Hey, Luce. I was just thinking about stuff. Kinda thought I'd call."

"Ah. Yeah. There's no talking to Dad and Lyle. Their minds are made up. If we're going to have to find another way to hang on to Stonehenge, we're going to have to come up with a plan that leaves them out of it."

"I know."

"I'm waiting for John to come home. We haven't really seen eye to eye on all this. We've hardly even talked about it. But now that I have a new job . . ."

"That was shitty," she said suddenly. "Absolutely shitty."

"You got that right."

Lucy's mind had wandered a bit. She was still thinking about the state of her marriage. But Layla's angry tone on her behalf bolstered her mood a little. "You know, maybe we should talk to Lyle about it. Kate said he was the one who wanted to sell the place, but I don't know if I believe her. If we got Lyle alone, he might listen to us. We could remind him of all the good times we had at Stonehenge as children."

"The *only* good times we had," Layla reminded her.

"Remember that nature girl he called Nell, like the Jodie Foster movie? She was always in the woods."

"Brianne. But she wasn't like Nell at all. She just knew all about plants and wild animals."

"That's right. Brianne Kilgore. And she knew about insects, too. Creepy things."

"She was just so focused that Lyle thought she was autistic or something and was really mean about her."

Lucy nodded, even though her sister couldn't see her. Layla wasn't wrong, and she tended to be the one of the three of them who was the kindest. "Only in the beginning. He got over it and apologized, and Brianne's family was really nice to us. They knew Lyle was just being a stupid kid. He was kind of taken with Brianne, the way she knew things. We all used to go see the Kilgores whenever we were at Stonehenge, remember? They were about the only people close to Stonehenge, unless you went into Glenn River.

Maybe Lyle just needs to kind of go back there, see them, and remember how great it was."

"It's been a long time. And it wasn't ever that great."

"You got a better idea?" Lucy asked, growing impatient with Layla's foot dragging.

"No."

"You think I'm just grasping at straws."

"I just don't think Lyle cares anymore and we can't make him," Layla said. "We care. You and I care. But he doesn't."

"Well, maybe we can make him care," Lucy said stubbornly. "If he was just away from Kate, just for a little while, we could have a real conversation. But she's always there. The gatekeeper. Maybe Lyle is a lost cause. I don't know. I'd just like something to work out, and I don't want to lose Stone—"

"Lucy, sorry. I gotta interrupt you. I need to talk to you about something else."

"Oh. Okay . . ." Lucy heard the tension in her sister's voice.

"It's about the baby. My baby."

"Is everything okay?" Lucy asking, her heart clutching.

"Oh, yes, yes. Absolutely. Baby's fine."

"Okay."

"It's that Neil and I aren't getting along too well. We're not on the same page at all. He's . . . well, I did something, and I'm afraid he wants to cut me out now."

"He can't do that. You're the mother."

"I'm the egg donor."

"Same thing." She paused, hearing the grave tone in Layla's voice. "What did you do?"

"I need to tell you the whole thing, but there are some things that happened . . . I made a big mistake, and I went to a lawyer today about it. I didn't tell you before that Neil is Neil Grassley."

"Grassley?"

"Yes."

"Oh, whoa. Of the steel company Grassleys? He's *that* Neil?"

"Yes," she said tiredly. "And I signed a contract, giving over my eggs."

"*What?*"

"I took money for my eggs, but I haven't spent it."

"Well, that can't be legal, can it? How much money?" This was sounding very bad.

"The attorney I saw was recommended to me by a gallery owner. He's someone she knows. He's a criminal defense attorney, but he's going to try to help me, I think. Or find me someone who will. I need to break that contract because I can't have Neil steal my baby away from me."

"Who's this lawyer?"

"You know him, I think. His name's Dallas Denton. I've been placating Neil, but that hasn't worked. I just learned he has a new girlfriend, and I'm not going to let them raise my child."

You know him, I think . . .

"I'm going on the attack," Layla went on rapidly, as if afraid she might be derailed. "I'm hoping by the time we go to that Denim and Diamonds event at Stonehenge I'll be able to say I'm going to have split custody. That's my marker. That day. Now, I can't wait for it to get here. . . ."

Kate listened to Lyle's even breathing. It had taken him a long time to get to sleep. He'd fussed around with his phone, watching short videos and news articles, then had turned on the television, switching channels, never landing on anything. Kate had pretended to read a romance novel that made her absolutely crazy because she wanted Lyle to be that guy.

The way the hero of the book took his woman and made her feel like he couldn't live without her.

Kate had switched to feigning sleep, but Lyle had finally settled, and so she searched a toe out from under the covers. Slowly, she got up, freezing when he suddenly snorted and turned over. Now he was facing her, but his eyes were closed. Weren't they? Hard to tell, it was so shadowy on this side of the room. Over by the drapes, some light showed through from the neighbors' outside lamp pole. Annoying really, the way they kept putting security lights in it that shone into their bedroom like a searchlight. Eventually, Lyle had been forced to have a talk with them about changing out the bulb, and they'd acquiesced, so now it was just a light. Still too bright, but more bearable.

She eased to her feet and slowly padded away, her bare feet barely making a sound as she headed to the dresser where Lyle had plugged in his cell to charge. It was a chest of drawers that held only Lyle's clothes, so hanging around it would be suspicious if he woke. Kate simply unplugged the cell, holding it close to her body as the light came on as soon as she did, then moved like a wraith to the hallway. She slipped past Daphne's room to the spare bedroom, which was still a toy room even though Daphne was rapidly losing interest in everything except her one teddy bear, Horace.

Quickly, Kate punched in Lyle's access code, only to have the numbers jiggle and return to the keypad. She tried a second time, and a third, before realizing he'd changed the code.

Pat.

She would bet it was a woman's name. Patti. Patricia. She could see her. Long black hair and olive skin. Onyx eyes and supple limbs. Oh, she knew his tastes. All her life, her own blond hair had been her asset. Even Lyle had been attracted to it . . . or had pretended to be.

She wanted to throw the cell across the room and scream

and rip at her hair. She could see Lyle on top of the witch, could hear him moan as he slid in and out of her, could see him rear his head back and stiffen as he came inside her.

Well, he wasn't going to get away with it.

She'd rather see him dead than with another woman.

And this Pat wasn't going to get away with it either.

PART TWO

Chapter Nine

September Rafferty Westerly squinted at her new husband. "How much are the tickets for this thing?"

He looked over at her, buttoning up his white shirt, his grin somewhat sheepish, she thought. "More than you'd ever pay."

"And why are we going to this event?"

"Because a number of my clients will be there, and it's for charity."

"Who are these clients?" September asked, but she knew. Jake had rattled off their names a number of times already. An investment broker and adviser, Jake had nearly chucked his whole career at one time, but his clients had been unwilling to let him go. Since that time, September had lost her job with the Laurelton Police Department—budget cuts—and Jake had completely turned around, throwing himself back in the business, increasing his clientele and profit margin, readying both September and himself for the launch of their married life together.

Which was just peachy, she thought sourly, considering she now was jobless and dependent on him. It made her half crazy. Jake, of course, didn't see it that way, but she sure did, and though her wealthy father had offered to help her out, she'd rather die a death of a trillion paper cuts than depend on him or any of her dysfunctional family. She loved them, sometimes wanted to throw her fists into the air and rail at the heavens over them, but she wanted nothing from them.

What she needed was a job.

"William Ogden wants to introduce me to some of his friends, and he suggested the Denim and Diamonds benefit for fire damage to the Gorge," said Jake.

The Eagle Creek fire in the Gorge, which had jumped the Columbia River into Washington and burned over fifty thousand acres, closing I-84 for weeks and the old Columbia River Highway for months, was a memory now, but the cost of repairs was still increasing. Businesses in the area had suffered loss of tourism, and people had lost their jobs and livelihoods. The Crissman family was using their annual benefit and auction to raise funds for the reparations. They'd opened their sprawling compound, once called Wolfe Lodge—Wolfe being the name of an ex-business partner, though apparently the current Crissman patriarch never referred to it by that name—so Jake had told her. September knew little of the Crissman family's history apart from the name of their downtown Portland department store, Crissman & Wolfe. There, apparently, the Wolfe name was still considered okay.

September had been sitting on the edge of their bed, but now she flopped backward, wishing she could say something like, "Can't we just send money?" but unable to let those words pass her lips. It was Jake's money, not hers. He would argue the point if she denied his funds had anything to do with her, but it was the plain truth. She wasn't bringing in a second income, and at times like this, she felt useless.

"I have nothing to wear," she grumbled.

"Those jeans fit pretty well."

She glanced down at her clothes, her uniform these days:

jeans and a black V-necked ribbed sweater, of which she'd bought three because she liked them so well.

"I'm not wearing jeans," she muttered.

"That's the denim part of it."

Denim and Diamonds . . . She lifted her left hand, gazing at the extravagant, glittering solo diamond with a rush of pleasure and anxiety. She loved the ring. Wore it when Jake was around. But she had this irrational fear of either losing it, or having it stolen, and the damn thing felt awkward on her hand. She'd purchased a ring holder and placed it by the kitchen sink, but if she took off the ring and set it there for safekeeping, half the time she forgot to put it back on, and the other half she obsessed about finding it missing from the holder. The wedding band was plain silver. That, she could handle. More often than not, she left the engagement ring, with its ostentatious diamond, in a case in the bank of drawers in their closet for safekeeping and just wore the band.

"Well, I kind of like that idea," she admitted. Jeans, her ubiquitous sweater, and her diamond ring. She could do that.

Jake sat down on the bench at the end of the bed to put on his shoes. He was heading to the office and September was faced with another day with nothing to do. Recently, she'd visited her sister July and baby Junie, then stopped in to see her twin brother, Auggie—or, more accurately, August Rafferty—and his wife, Liv. Auggie had told September that Portland PD was hiring, which September already knew, but she was torn. Unlike her brother, who'd been recruited from Laurelton PD and made a lateral move to Portland as a detective, September would be starting at the bottom once more. She'd had an unprecedented rise at Laurelton PD from newbie to detective, and then, being the last hire, was the first unemployed.

Jake didn't want her to be a beat cop for Portland PD. If he had his way, she wouldn't be in law enforcement at all, so he wasn't the best person to complain to about her plight.

Now, he leaned over and kissed her lightly as she still lay on her back.

"Wanna little morning delight?" she asked.

"Yes. Always," he agreed heartily, even while he was pulling away. "But I have a meeting I can't miss." He waggled his eyebrows in a thoroughly cartoonish way. "I could maybe get away early?"

"I'm here for you anytime." She sighed.

He grinned at her, ignoring her melancholy completely. "A nooner, then." He leaned back in to kiss her a little more thoroughly, and September wrapped her arms around his neck and nibbled at his ear.

"You're pretty damn tempting. Maybe I should let this multimillion-dollar account go somewhere else."

She pushed him away. "Fine. Go to your meeting. I'll just turn on the TV and watch cooking shows. Maybe I'll learn something."

He slid her a look that said *Fat chance*, but wisely didn't comment on her culinary skills. She was half-inclined to prove him wrong. Find some fabulous recipe and whip together something incredible. It couldn't be that hard, could it? All she had to do was put her mind to it, and maybe a little trial and error?

She sighed again. But she didn't have the energy.

She heard Jake leave the little rambler house he'd already owned before their marriage and she'd moved into from her apartment. They were in the process of planning a new kitchen. Specs had been given to the city for a building permit and they were just waiting for the okay.

She picked up her cell phone and scrolled through several job apps, wishing Laurelton PD was looking to hire again. Her old partner, Gretchen Sanders, kept September informed, but nothing had turned up yet.

How long are you going to wait for one job? It's already been months.

Climbing to her feet, she refused to feel sorry for herself. When she'd first been let go she'd focused on her upcoming wedding, which had originally been slated for April and been pushed to the previous December, allowing about a month's preparation. It had been her idea and Jake had gone with it. She suddenly hadn't wanted to wait, and she needed something to do. The low-grade depression over the loss of her job had been pushed aside while she threw herself into plans for the small gathering at the Westerly family's winery, jumping into the arrangements in a way she never would have believed possible. She'd been reluctant to even set the date during their engagement, uncomfortable in taking the final step in a way that had had her family and her fiancé scratching their heads. She hadn't been able to explain it completely either. She loved Jake. Had loved him a long time before she'd even admitted it to herself. Hadn't even managed any other serious romance in her thirtysomething years on the planet. But she'd balked at the idea of that walk down the aisle, had been almost pathologically afraid of losing her independence. Still, she'd pushed the date, half afraid she might chicken out entirely if she waited too long.

The day of the wedding, she'd felt almost drunk, barely aware of her street-length white satin dress, the auburn wisps of hair curving down to her chin from the artfully messy bun atop her head, moving in her own blurry world with people sliding around the periphery of her vision, guiding her, talking to her, excited for her and Jake. She'd made it through the ceremony with no major faux pas, apparently, as no one had said anything to the contrary, and she'd danced at the reception and accepted everyone's gracious congratulations. She'd drunk one glass of champagne, though it felt like a dozen, and she couldn't remember the meal at all. When she and Jake were finally alone, back in his rambler home—theirs now, he constantly reminded her—getting ready for the trip the next day to Hawaii, where they island-hopped for ten days, seeing Oahu, Maui, Kaui, and the Big Island of Hawaii, she'd curled up in the comfort of his arms and wanted to weep. She wasn't unhappy. She was glad they were married. Glad it was over and they could get on with their lives. But she was scared of the future. Unsure what her role was without the job that had defined her far more than she would have credited.

It was an effort to push down her rocketing emotions and force herself to enjoy the honeymoon, though throughout the trip her chest was heavy with a kind of dark apprehension she couldn't completely shake. But she refused to let Jake know. *Fake it till you make it* was her mantra, and those words ran through her mind daily.

Of course, she hadn't fooled him. Not completely. He was pretty good at reading her. Maybe not as good as he thought he was, but pretty good. And after three months of marriage, though she was starting to feel comfortable with being his wife, she still fought to keep her panic about the future at bay. She almost dreaded the mornings. Her idleness. All those times during her career that she'd longed for a vacation seemed like someone else's life. A cruel joke.

But you've only been waiting for one job.

With a growl of impatience directed solely at herself, she grabbed up her laptop and searched the web for job opportunities in local law enforcement. There were a number of openings, but nothing she was interested in or felt she was qualified for. She checked farther afield, but the only position that was even close to what she might want was in Battleground, Washington, a commute far outside her targeted area and state.

Maybe something will just fall in my lap, she told herself as she headed for her morning shower.

Lucy examined the red dress, turning to see if it was too snug across her derriere. Nope. Looked pretty good. She touched the diamond stud in her right ear, watching its reflection shine in the overhead bathroom light. No denim for her. Straight on diamonds and a showstopping dress she'd bought with her store discount. Another perk that would soon be taken away. Except that it was too early to wear now, so she pulled it back off and hung it on a hanger, slipping it into a plastic garment bag. She, John, and Layla were arriving hours early, per her father's request, in order to ready Stonehenge for the Denim and Diamonds benefit auction. She would put the dress on at the last minute, so she smoothed on her gray slacks and a blue T-shirt for the preliminaries.

But some personal prep needed to be done now, so she pulled her hair into a tight bun, then threaded some curls away to curve by her ears and cut the severity. It would be nice to have a necklace to go with the earrings, but she didn't possess one. Great-grandmother Edwina had disappeared with all her jewels, and neither Junior nor Abbott had seen fit to drape their wives in "expensive baubles"—Junior's words, apparently, and ones Abbott also crowed at any given opportunity. Lyle had bought Kate that pearl necklace, but he'd probably been henpecked into it, and maybe the pearls weren't even real. She didn't see how he could afford them otherwise.

Sixty thousand dollars is still unaccounted for at work. . . .

Nope. She slammed her mind shut on that thought. Her father and brother had dismissed it as an error, told her to overlook it, assured her it would be straightened out by year's end by the firm's accountants.

Is that why you're losing your job . . . ?

Lucy closed her eyes and shook her head. She was too suspicious, and these people were her own family. *That's* why she was losing her job. She wasn't a team player.

Pushing those traitorous thoughts from her head, she carried the garment bag to her bedroom closet and slipped into a pair of silver sandals with tiny diamond-like gems embedded in the straps. No one expected anything but costume jewelry on your shoes, so she figured she was okay with just the diamond earrings. She looked at herself in the full-length mirror on the back of the closet door, examined the earrings, thought about that night at the Pembroke Inn with Mark, and shuddered. It was embarrassing, and well, creepy. Made her skin crawl. Yet she had a strange desire to go back to him, meet him outside the place again and screw him standing up. She'd seen a therapist on a daytime talk show describing how women who'd been sexually harassed or abused felt the way she did. To take the misdeed to its conclusion. It was a way to take back power. To say, *I did this. My choice, not yours.*

Though she suspected she wouldn't really feel any better when it was done.

She heard John coming up the stairs, and a few moments later, he entered the bedroom. He was in a black jacket, black shirt, and pressed denim jeans. He looked really good, his dark hair gleaming under the recessed lights in the ceiling above the entrance to the closet.

"I like your hair," he said after a moment of them staring at each other.

"Thank you."

The moment spun out uncomfortably. Finally, John lightly shrugged his shoulders and went to his nightstand for his phone and wallet, which he'd left there when he'd taken his shower.

Lucy walked back to the bathroom. There had been no improvement in their relationship over the last month. They were two people who spoke to each other only when necessary, and now that he had migrated to the Crissman & Wolfe offices at the warehouse, she rarely saw him during the day. She was alone in the empty offices at the store except for a couple of women who worked in customer service. Occasionally, there was a small problem in one of the departments, but the employees usually managed to right the ship without her help, so her being employed was pretty much super-fluous.

At home, she and John were polite strangers. No argu-ments, just quiet, though she sometimes felt like she was on the edge of a gathering storm. If Evie sensed the tension, she kept those thoughts to herself. Lucy suspected she was just happy they weren't openly fighting.

Bella was sitting today, though she'd tried to weasel out of it when something better had cropped up for later in the evening. Lucy would have just found someone else, but John had walked to her house and talked with her parents and Bella was back on duty. She was already downstairs with Evie, a bit of resentment in her eyes. They were watch-ing TV as she and John did their final prep for the benefit.

"You ready?" John asked her as she turned to her closet again for a coat as well as the garment bag. The rain had let up, but the temperature had taken a steep dive.

"Just about."

Five minutes later, they were heading out the door. Bella barely acknowledged them as they left, which could have been an improvement because Evie had told her Bella was currently into extolling the virtues of eating organically. Lucy didn't think she could suffer through Bella's enthusi-asm for non-GMO foods, kale, and tofu with John standing beside her in that remote way of his.

She climbed in his Audi, tucking the bottom of her long black coat around her legs. Her sandals sparkled a bit in the car's overhead light before John climbed in and closed the driver's door behind him. It was the first time they'd driven in the same vehicle since those last fights after she'd had her eye on Mark.

"It's a ways out to Stonehenge," he remarked as he pulled away from the curb.

"Yes, it is."

Though it was barely afternoon, the day was cloudy and gray, a light drizzle collecting on the windshield. Abbott had said he wanted them all at the lodge early, well before the festivities began. There was a cocktail hour scheduled, and then the dinner and finally the auction. Just to attend was a high fee per plate, and more contributions from expensive donations in both a silent and oral auction the crowd would hopefully bid up. There was a general desire to rebuild structures that were lost in the fire and help struggling businesses still trying to get their customers back. The hopeful expectations were that the benefit would raise a lot of money for the Friends of the Columbia River Gorge because people believed deeply in putting back what the fire had destroyed.

"Evie asked if we were still going to Stonehenge for Easter," said John.

"She mentioned it to me, too."

"What did you say?"

"That I didn't know. Maybe we won't even own it anymore."

John's lips tightened. Lucy wasn't exactly sure which side of that argument he'd landed on.

They drove in silence for a while; then John finally said, "How is Layla getting there?"

Lucy's heart made an uncomfortable flip. She'd seen very little of her sister over the last month. Layla was meeting with lawyers and notices had been written, a lawsuit filed, she believed. Layla had called her a number of times, laying out her plans. She was energized and primed for battle, though it sounded as if Neil had turned from vaguely threatening to out-and-out combatant. He'd warned that he would break her if she chose to follow through on her attempts for shared custody, but she had managed to record his threats, which would be helpful in her lawsuit.

Layla had explained, "I was trying to follow Neil around, find something out about him, but Dallas Denton told me to stay away from him. He's hired a private investigator. No one wants to tell me anything. I think they think I'll go off the rails. But so far, all I think he's found out is that Neil's new girlfriend seems to have moved in with him. . . ."

Lucy's stomach had clenched at Dallas's name, but she'd managed to keep Layla from noticing. "I hope it all works out for you," she'd managed to utter, and Layla had been too immersed in her own problems to notice her sister's discomfiture.

Lucy felt John looking at her, so she half-turned his way. "Layla's heading there in a Black Swan Gallery van. One of her paintings is up for bid, but it's large and she promised to bring it with her. She did ask for a ride back, though."

"Okay."

Lucy looked out her window as the populated area changed to denser foliage along the two-lane highway that wound toward Stonehenge. She could remember looking up through the moon roof of the wagon her mother had owned and watching the canopy of green leaves reach out and touch one another as the road narrowed onto a paved road barely able to handle two cars passing each other.

After her conversation with Layla about Brianne Kilgore, Lucy had tried to talk to her brother. She'd reminded him how much they had all loved Stonehenge, but Lyle had been distracted and disinterested. "What do you really want, Lucy?" he'd asked her, and she'd heard Kate's voice in his tone.

So, she'd answered him with the truth. "I want to save Stonehenge. Those are our family's happiest memories, and it's our heritage. Don't you feel that?"

"All I know is that we're bleeding money," he'd said repressively, "and if it takes selling Wolfe Lodge, then so be it. None of us wants to be a pauper."

"Do you call it Wolfe Lodge in front of Dad?" she'd asked, so surprised she'd been momentarily diverted.

"I don't talk to Dad about it much at all. It's a matter of economics, Lucy. I thought you were the one who understood that."

"I understand a lot." Her temper had started to rise at that point and she knew she should end the conversation before she said something unforgivable. Something she would regret later and be unable to walk back. Talking to Lyle was a lost cause anyway. But she couldn't stop herself from adding, "I'm going to find out whose idea this was and why we're in such dire straits. What happened to the Crissman fortune? All I've ever heard was that it was squandered. Who squandered it? Junior? Dad? You?"

"Oh, for God's sake, Luce. Times have changed. The world's different. Digital. Maybe if you woke up and became a part of it, you'd understand that."

"I am a part of it. I know profits are down. I even get why we're closing the store. But I want to know why we have to sell *Wolfe Lodge*. Why now? Why can't we wait until we've restructured the company? See what the profit and loss is? Kate said it was your idea to sell. Is that true?"

And that's when he'd hung up on her.

She'd taken that as a yes.

Now, as she and John reached the blacktop lane that led to the final bends toward Stonehenge, she pushed the button to recline her seat and looked through the moon roof as the budding lime-green leaves and forest-green fir needles swept across the screen above her.

Chapter Ten

Lyle pulled the car up in front of the lodge's sprawling structure with its two jutting wings, like arms reaching out to greet them. Kate knew that behind the lodge were some haphazard cabins, designed around twisting trails, forgotten bungalows with mossy, leaking roofs and beetle-devoured siding, smelling of mildew and damp and uninviting. She supposed they'd been nice once, at least during the summer months. They were a complete disaster now, however.

The lodge itself had aged as well, but the bedrooms hidden along the wings behind the main greeting rooms were in far better shape than the cabins. The roof of the massive building had been recently repaired, thank God, and Kate could grudgingly admit there was something somewhat enchanting about the lodge's cavernous rooms. The grand chandeliers were out of place within the building's rustic charm, but Lyle's great-grandfather's gifts to his wife were rich and beautiful, teardrop crystals glittering brightly. It was the chandeliers' juxtaposition with the weathered wood floors and pine walls that had inspired Kate to come up with the Denim and Diamonds theme. She was rather proud of herself, but though she'd brought up how great her idea had turned out several times, hoping Lyle would agree with her brilliance and thank her for it, to date he hadn't even noticed.

Now, Lyle pulled around the north wing of the lodge to park in a spot away from the main parking area but close to a side door where the catering trucks were already collecting. He turned the key, then sat for a moment, his arms resting on the steering wheel. She could see the grim set to his mouth.

She said gently, "You look handsome."

He didn't respond. Didn't look at her. He'd gotten a haircut a few days earlier and it was a little shorter than Kate liked, but he looked groomed and pressed, his gray slacks and white shirt with the black jacket professional but casual. He'd worn black alligator cowboy boots and a bolo tie. Okay, maybe it wasn't denim, but it was western wear, and that fell into Kate's definition for the night.

She'd donned a black dress, short and tight, for tonight's event. Initially, she'd been alarmed at the slight pooch of her abdomen when she'd tried on the dress last week. When had that happened? To make the dress work, she'd cut down her calories to less than a thousand a day, and today, the pooch was decidedly down. For good measure, she'd taken a laxative this morning, which had done the trick, and now her stomach was flat. She'd thought about bringing a change of clothes because the event was still hours away, but she'd decided she would just be careful. Besides, she liked the way she looked.

She, too, was wearing black alligator boots. She'd picked up both hers and Lyle's at a store that sold strictly western gear, which was attached to what was basically a tack room full of saddles, bridles, blankets, oats and feed, and God knew what else. She'd never been one of those horsey girls. She could count the times she'd ridden one: zero.

She'd thought about wearing the pearls Lyle had bought her, but she really needed diamonds. Her engagement and wedding rings were nice, but, though she'd never told Lyle—wouldn't dream of it!—she'd always been a little bit disappointed in the stones. Ah, well. She'd decided on the silver disc earrings with the three teensy diamonds along the edge for tonight. With her rings, she supposed she had enough diamonds. It just felt like she, of all people, should have something big and expensive. She'd hinted a bit to Lyle over the years, but he seemed singularly deaf to any of her suggestions, except for the pearls.

But when this creaking lodge sells . . .

She tried to calculate how much the real estate was worth. Millions. Lots of millions. She'd like to ask Layla what she thought. Layla wasn't an agent, but she was in the real estate world, and for all her artiness, she could be really clear on some things, real estate being one of them. But if Kate brought up the sensitive subject, Layla would cut her dead. Neither of Lyle's sisters had any true grasp on the realities of life.

"I'm going in to see if the caterer is here yet," Kate said, wondering what the hell was wrong with Lyle. She'd been cagily watching him whenever he opened his phone, hoping to catch his code, but the security release used his thumbprint and he rarely opened it with the required four digits. However, three days earlier there had been an update, and he'd had to shut down the phone and then use his code to open it. She was pretty sure it was five, three, nine, something. Maybe seven. She hadn't had a chance to use it yet; Lyle's phone was never more than a few inches away from him.

He roused himself from his torpor and opened the driver's door, stepping outside. Kate waited a moment, but he didn't come around to her side, so she let herself out, irked at him. She watched him walk off, heading around the wing of the building to the front door, while she stepped carefully down slate slabs surrounded by moss that led to the side door.

Could he say something? Talk to me? Whatever the hell's wrong, could he just tell me?

She realized she was muttering beneath her breath and stopped herself as she stepped inside the short hallway that led to the kitchen. She could hear the caterers clattering pans and talking among themselves, and she entered the room with a smile pasted on her lips. Her hair was pulled back in a French braid, and in lieu of a diamond necklace, she'd tied a red kerchief jauntily around her neck.

She glanced around the interior and smiled at the gleaming wood, freshly cleaned carpets and drapes, glittering mullioned windows reflecting the chandeliers' lights. A cellist was already setting up in one of the nooks—Kate's idea again—soft classical music to be an undertone to what she hoped was plenty of conversation and laughter.

"Is Jean-Luc here yet?" she asked a young Asian woman wearing a white apron over a black dress.

"Right here, madam," came Jean-Luc's smooth baritone.

Kate's smile widened. She was so pleased she'd gotten the chef. He hadn't been her first choice—or her second, for that matter—but she hadn't been able to pay the exorbitant amount required for them, and she'd worked her negotiating magic to get Jean-Luc. Of course, Jean-Luc wasn't cheap either, but he'd quickly understood the press he would receive for this elite event, and they'd come to an agreement that had worked for them both. Kate had bragged a bit to Lyle about that, too, and Abbott as well, but what had she gotten for her efforts? A grimace from her husband about the cost and a resigned remark from Abbott: "Well, we can't have some diner cook, I suppose."

They just didn't understand the complexities of the situation; but then, they were men . . . what could she seriously expect?

"You're here early," she said to Jean-Luc as she walked past the man warming up the grill.

"Yes, madam. There is a lot to do."

That was true. Beyond the sumptuous food the catering company was providing, there were nearly three hundred people attending and the dining room—which hadn't been much more than three rows of basic metal tables—needed serious prettying up by Jean-Luc's staff, and it was happening. Just as she'd planned. Kate couldn't help but feel more than a little bit of pride that it was coming together so perfectly.

"Madam, we will be ready by six. Champagne with berries. Strawberry, Cambozola, and honey on baguettes to start. Crudités. Skewered prawns. Candied bacon . . ." He sniffed. The bacon had been Abbott's personal request, and Jean-Luc apparently felt it was rather pedestrian. Then a lobster bisque for the first course, with attendant almond flax crackers. "It will all be beautiful," the chef assured her.

"I'm sure it will," Kate said.

"Leave it to me, chérie."

She left him to find Lyle's father. Because he was the one who'd demanded they come hours early, she was certain he must have already arrived. She ran into Lyle, who was standing in the foyer, gazing up at the gallery and the circles of white tablecloths draped over tables of eight with their centerpieces of stargazer lilies, Kate's personal favorite. She was surprised to see Layla, wearing what looked like a denim jumpsuit, standing at the edge of one of the auction tables that ran around the perimeter of the massive central hall, beneath the gallery. She realized, then, that Layla was positioned near a large painting of a river, somewhat crudely done in Layla's own distinctive style. Ah. The Columbia River painting she'd offered to donate. Kate inwardly sniffed. She preferred the impressionistic style. There was a modern tone to Layla's work that she found childlike but other people seemed to enjoy. And well, someone might just jump on a painting of the river, given that they were here to raise money for the whole area.

Her surrogate's got to be closing in on her last month.

A clutch to Kate's heart. She could feel her face set and stretched her jaw before pinning on another smile. "Hi, Layla," she greeted her.

Her sister-in-law had been staring into the middle distance but now focused on Kate. *She's lost weight* was Kate's first thought, which gave her a pang because that hollowed-out look looked good on her. Her second: only Layla could get away with that jumpsuit. All denim with a rhinestone belt, it was straight out of the 1980s, about as corny and tacky as could be, but . . . it suited her somehow. With her hair clipped back on one side by a matching rhinestone barrette that sparkled amid the light brown strands, she looked fetching. Her eyes were huge with her weight loss.

Immediately, Kate did a mental inventory of her own appearance, glad she hadn't come dressed down like Layla had.

"Hi, Kate," Layla greeted her. "The painting should really be under a light."

"Oh. Well, no one's going to care. I'm sure it's fine."

"We have time before the guests arrive. I'll figure something out," Layla said.

Kate bristled at her proprietary tone. "I'll take care of it," she said curtly. She examined Layla's ashen coloring. "Is everything okay?"

She immediately pulled in on herself. "What do you mean?"

"Well, you're a little pale . . ." She couldn't bring herself to compliment her on her weight loss. Not that she had anything to worry about herself. She'd gotten rid of the little stomach pooch. It was just that Layla looked like a model, and Kate would have dearly loved if Lyle's sister had a wart or two, figuratively speaking . . . maybe literally, too.

"No, I'm fine. Where's Lyle?"

"Oh, around," she said vaguely.

Where the hell was he?

She left Layla and stepped quickly back across the expansive foyer. There was a podium just inside the massive fifteen-foot-high double doors that would lead the guests inside, where a staff member would check off names. An anteroom lay on the south side, which they'd turned into a spacious coat closet.

"Lyle?" Kate called. Her voice echoed back at her, and she shot a glance toward Layla, who was once again staring into the middle distance. Kate could have been on the moon for all the attention she gave her. "Lyle," she said again, this time with an edge to her voice.

No answer.

She pulled back one of the double doors, intending to get some fresh air, only to find him pacing across the slate entryway. He was, unsurprisingly, on his phone. His back was to her and he was talking tersely.

". . . told you not to call me," he snapped. Then, "You know why!" Another pause, and then, "Not till Monday." He then yanked the phone from his ear, and for a moment, she thought he was actually going to hurl it down the drive. Maybe things weren't going all that well with *Pat* these days.

Sensing her behind him, he whipped around. "What are you doing?" he demanded.

"Actually, I was looking for you."

"Well, you found me."

"Lyle, for Pete's sake, what's wrong? You've been acting weird for days."

He started to say something, then looked past her, back at the rambling lodge. A moment later, he asked, "Did you ever think I might have some feelings for this place? Sure, we need to sell it. But it's hard."

That was it? "I know you have feelings for this place."

"I grew up here. The best times I ever had were here. We

used to play in the woods. Hide and seek. Layla and Lucy never found me unless I wanted to be found."

Kate nodded, preparing herself for one of his speeches. She'd learned that Lyle waxed rhapsodic whenever cued by the right word, one you might not even know you were providing. It was like stepping into quicksand with no way out once you started. Nevertheless, she tried. "I know all about it. The lodge is more home to you than anywhere else."

He wasn't to be deterred. "We spent the summers here. Made friends. We would go into Glenn River and get ice cream, watch the windsurfers on the river."

Kate had heard this same thing said the same way half a dozen times or more, a memorized speech. She'd never questioned him, but she knew he wasn't really feeling anything. It was all just words. And deflection.

"Who were your friends?" she interjected.

It brought him up short, managed to cut into the stream of consciousness he was relating. "What?" He gazed at her blankly.

"Your friends. You said you made friends. Who were they?"

"Oh. Just some people who lived nearby, in the woods." He waved toward the northeast.

He'd forgotten he'd already told her about them, a family with a daughter who was odd in some way, maybe autistic, maybe just painfully shy. He'd never said. He didn't like talking specifics about his past to Kate, only in generalities, and now he moved abruptly away from her, which she had expected, physically putting distance between them so she wouldn't poke too close to his memory.

"Who was on the phone?" she asked a little loudly as he was almost out of earshot. A bold move on her part, because she never pried into his business . . . that he knew of.

"It was just work."

"You're meeting with them on Monday."

Lyle turned to her, unable to hide the flare of surprise in his eyes. "Yes, that's right. And while you're eavesdropping, you want to know what the meeting's about?"

"I sure do." She smiled.

He blinked, unused to Kate showing him her steely side. But she was fed up with whatever deal he had going with *Pat*. Maybe this wasn't it. Maybe this was something else he was keeping from her.

"We have . . . several suppliers who want us to keep them on the floor. They can sell online themselves, they say, and I'm meeting with one of them Monday to try to stop their fears."

That almost sounded like the truth. Was Lyle that good at dissembling? Maybe. Whatever the case, Kate didn't for a minute believe he was feeling much regret over selling the lodge. That was just a convenient excuse to give his wife, who was suddenly asking too many questions.

Lyle went back inside without another word.

Kate inhaled a long breath and let it out slowly.

Sometimes . . . not often, but sometimes . . . she wondered what it would be like if Abbott were gone and Lyle inherited, and then maybe something happened to *him*, an accident of some kind . . . and she ended up with control of Crissman & Wolfe and maybe the proceeds from the lodge . . . sometimes that scenario crossed her mind. . . .

She fingered the red kerchief she'd tied around her neck as a nod to the "denim" side of the event. If that happened, she would be wise with her money, careful . . . apart from a diamond necklace and maybe a pair of matching earrings, that is.

Layla pretended to be staring off into space just as long as it took for Kate to lose interest in her; then she brought her attention back to her painting with a bang. It was good, she thought. Pretty good. She wanted to gnaw at her fingernail and obsess about it, but she wouldn't let herself go that far.

What the hell are we doing here so early? Another of Dad's commands we all comply with.

The auction items were spread out beneath the upper gallery, where the attendees would gather to eat. She was hovering near her own painting for reasons she couldn't quite explain. It was familiar, a part of herself. She wanted to do the same thing at galleries whenever her work was displayed, but she forced herself to stand apart. It just felt too much like begging. *Come look at me! Aren't I beautiful? Take me home! Buy me! Love me!*

That wasn't what she felt about other artists when they stood near their work at galleries and events, but she couldn't dissociate from herself.

Crazy, she told herself. She'd been told it often enough, or overheard her father speaking in hushed terms about her. Yes, she'd been odd as a child. She'd grown to depend on Lucy, who was stronger and mentally sturdier, though whenever Layla remarked about it, Lucy fervently denied it. "We're different, that's all," Lucy always said, but it was Lucy who ended up making all the difficult decisions, and Layla was grateful she did.

However . . . something had changed when Layla met Neil. Okay, maybe actually before she met him. After a lifetime of following her muse, Layla woke up one day and suddenly longed for a regular life. Nine to five. A suburban, or maybe urban, life, if the neighborhood was upscale. A husband and 2.5 children. Was that still the median number in American families? She'd heard that once, but it could be old school. A dog, or maybe a cat. A home with at least two bathrooms. A yard. Double car garage.

She'd had to shake herself back to reality. What? Hell

no! She'd been happy living her strangely fulfilling life in apartments with eclectic furniture and semiworking appliances. She loved painting in a way she couldn't describe. Lost in her art was what Ian had said to her, when they'd been so in lust at the beginning of their relationship. But after a few years with Ian she'd lost that edge and had found working at Easy Street a soothing, possibly mind-numbing, antidote to her restless artistic muse, and she'd spent more and more time at the bistro and less time at home with Ian and her easel. Even Easy Street's parsimonious owners had become more favored than an evening with Ian and a smoke-filled bong.

And then Neil . . . A door cracking open to that other world. And he was rich. Not the first thing she looked for in a relationship, but she certainly hadn't been opposed to being wined, dined, and wooed. Yes, wooed. That was the word. He'd set out to find a surrogate and had zeroed in on her because she was reasonably attractive and intelligent, and because she was a Crissman. She'd been swept into his world, willingly, and hadn't cared. She'd wanted to be in love. She'd wanted the whole enchilada: love, marriage, and a family. Well, okay, she'd told him marriage was an anti-quated institution and she really couldn't see herself as someone's wife, but that had been only partially true, a mantra she'd lived by for so many years she hadn't been able to give it up completely.

And Neil had played along, made her believe in her own fantasy. Looking back, she was aware he'd played her like the proverbial fiddle. She'd wanted what she'd wanted—or wanted what she *believed* she wanted, which amounted to the same thing in the moment—and so she'd ignored every warning sign that maybe he wasn't on the up-and-up. She'd thought he wanted the same thing. She should have recog-nized how he seemed to calculate everything. How he'd taken her blithe dismissal of marriage as a way to have their child and keep himself unbound to her, giving himself full custody of Eddie in the process.

She was interrupted in her musings by a young woman in black slacks and shirt setting down a plate of sandwiches near her. Oh, good. Her father hadn't forgotten they were bound to be here for hours and getting any kind of food would require a trip off the ridge into Glenn River or an hour back the way they'd come.

The catering staff girl left, and Layla looked over the assortment of sandwiches. The top several were vegetarian: tomatoes, mushrooms, basil, and cheese. The ones beneath looked to be chicken salad with butter lettuce.

She reached a hand out, but then dropped her arm. She should eat, but she couldn't. She was strung so tightly, she felt almost ill, and she was belted in tighter than she'd expected. Her last meetings with her lawyer hadn't been encouraging either. He just kept telling her to sit tight and wait, and that thought chased away any appetite she might have had.

And then . . . to top it all off, she'd heard from Ian about an hour earlier. She'd answered her phone tentatively when she hadn't recognized the caller, only to find it was her ex-boyfriend with a new phone. "Hey, lovely lady," he'd said in his drawl, the one she'd found so delightful in the beginning, so frustratingly slllooowww in the end. Those last few months she'd wanted to reach in and yank the words out of his mouth.

"Ian," she'd answered.

"I was wondering what you were up to."

She'd suddenly felt tears threaten, her nose uncomfortably stinging. She'd had to wait several long seconds to get herself under control.

"Hullo? You there?" Ian asked.

"I've been working at Easy Street. Painting some." *And another woman's pregnant with my child.*

"Same old, same old," he said, sounding slightly sad.

His tone brought her up short. Ian could manipulate in his own way; not as masterfully as Neil, certainly, but he knew how to play games, too.

And she found she missed him, a little . . .

But not enough.

"I'm busy, Ian," she said, her mind already moving past him.

"Can you spare me some time? I want to come over to talk."

"I'm not home right now."

"Where are you?"

"Stonehenge."

"Stonehenge. What are you doing there?"

"Family stuff," she said.

"You'll be back tonight?"

"Yes. I've gotta go."

"Okay. I'll call you later." And he'd clicked off.

She'd told herself that she didn't want to ever see him again, but she found herself looking forward to doing just that.

Don't let yourself believe in him, she warned herself. *He's not dependable.*

She saw John walking across the large expanse of the foyer in her direction and decided she didn't want to talk to him right then. She felt too raw and unstable. She turned and slipped around the tables of items to be auctioned, down a short hallway, and stepped outside. Green leaves glistening with perfect ovals of sparkling water from the last short downpour and the trunks of fir trees and a copse of oaks met her vision. She gulped in air as if she'd been suffocated. She remembered running through the trees, zigzagging, chasing after Lucy and being chased by their little brother, whom they'd labeled the Monster, a game she and her sister loved and caused Lyle to cry.

Maybe that's why he wanted to sell.

Chapter Eleven

Lucy stepped out of Stonehenge's largest suite on the second floor in her red dress and heels. The place was going to seed. The rooms smelled musty, the atmosphere close. They needed a good airing out, and she'd opened the windows for a while and just sat on a dusty bedroom chair for what felt like hours before she'd changed her clothes. However long she'd been gone, it was as long as she dared wait. Someone was sure to be looking for her soon.

She carried her now-empty garment bag and another smaller duffel that held her slacks, T-shirt, and makeup case. She was intent on finding John and the keys to the Audi to put her things in the car. Then she would be ready to play hostess to all the attendees.

Step right up, see the Crissman children dance atten-dance on their father. Abbott Crissman's every wish is their command. Do you like the lodge? Guess what? It's for sale, too!

As she whisked down the grand stairway to the lower floor, she saw Lyle and her father on the upper gallery, locked in an intense conversation. They didn't see her as she hurried down.

You should confront them. Make them include you.

She'd learned that neither her father nor her brother liked their new offices, which gave her a small, spiteful rush of pleasure. Served them both right. They'd made all kinds of decisions without notifying her until after the fact. They'd told John about whatever plans they'd cooked up before they told her, and she sensed a whole lot of unspoken misogyny fueled their choice to leave her and Layla out of the family loop.

They could just live with their decisions.

Maybe she was just mad at men in general. She'd suffered through her share of assholes. Like a well-oiled machine, her mind again cast back to that night at the fraternity house where she'd slept with the one guy she'd thought was different. She'd willingly had sex with him. Had wanted to make love with him. Had maybe . . . maybe . . . even initiated it, because he really hadn't been as interested as she was?

She slammed her mind shut on that one, unwilling to go that far. That choice had changed her life so drastically, she couldn't throw blame on herself. Not completely. And she'd been castigated so much by her father for getting pregnant that she'd been forced to defend herself as if she were totally blameless, which she could admit to herself wasn't the truth, but she sure as hell wasn't going to tell her father that. It was all part of the farce she'd played throughout Evie's life. Someday she would tell Evie about her father. Someday she might even tell Evie's father about his daughter.

Someday she might even tell John the truth about that one-night stand.

Picturing herself opening up to John left her feeling vulnerable. She shivered. Had they drifted too far apart to make that even a possibility? She saw herself trying to explain:

It was one drunken night at a fraternity party.

I knew his name, but I didn't really know him.

He wasn't one of the fraternity brothers. He was older.

I kind of crushed on him, and we had sex.

He seemed nice, but afterward he never called, and I realized he hadn't asked my name and maybe didn't care to know it. . . .

No, she couldn't tell him any of that. She could barely tell herself that. She'd been mad at Evie's father—and herself—for their complete recklessness, and John would never understand. He was too judgmental, though he prided himself on being fair and compassionate—total bullshit—and a part of Lucy had always sensed he would punish her for the truth.

So, no. He didn't get to know.

Members of the catering staff and the Friends of the Columbia River Gorge had arrived and were putting the final touches to the setup. Lucy circled around a group of them and nearly ran into her husband. "I need the keys to the Audi to put my stuff in the car," she said.

"I'll do it."

"No, I'll do it," she said mulishly. He made an exasperated noise and snapped the keys into her palm. She walked back outside, cast an eye to the heavens—the rain was still holding off—folded the garment bag onto the backseat of the car, and put the duffel in the footwell behind the passenger seat. Then she returned to the lodge through the front door. One of the young women dressed all in black looked at her askance, but Lucy didn't stop to explain that she was a Crissman and therefore working the room as much as she was.

The place was filling up. Waiters balanced trays as they eased between knots of guests on the main floor. Conversation buzzed, drowning out the notes of a lone cellist. Layla had wandered around aimlessly for what felt like hours but now was back at her chosen station near her painting. Abbott hadn't called a meeting of all of them. After demanding they all come early, he'd practically ignored her. Probably the same for Lucy, though she'd seen her father in deep conversation with Lyle. Those two were like coconspirators sometimes.

The main crush of the benefit guests was currently arriving. People were waiting by the front door, standing in groups. She recognized a voice, turned to it, and saw Cathie Hyatt. Neil's friend.

Oh . . . shit. Neil wouldn't be here, would he?

She eyed the room wildly, heart racing.

Cathie was chattering, but Layla was deaf to everything but the surf in her ear created by her roaring pulse. She'd never considered she might see Neil at the event. He knew it was her family putting it on.

Her gaze raked back and forth. There was Lucy in a red dress, just reentering from outside, sweeping up a glass of champagne from a server, then holding it in a death grip. John was saying something to her. They didn't look happy with each other. There was Lyle, standing by their father, both looking grim with Kate on one side, seeming to try to be listening in. A man Layla didn't recognize was talking to them, thrusting his champagne glass forward in sharp, staccato motions, making some kind of point. Cathie's husband, Rand, tried to catch Layla's eye with a smile, but she was too anxious to acknowledge him. There were several people from the Black Swan Gallery. No one else she recognized. No one. No Neil, as far as she could tell. She blinked, coming back to the present in time to see Cathie approaching, saying something to her . . .

"What?" Layla asked faintly, but Cathie was still talking.

". . . your brother looks so much like him, don't you think? More than your father does."

"My brother?" Layla repeated.

"Lyle's really the spitting image of Junior at the same age. Rand has a picture of them at a golf tournament. He and

Lyle could be twins, except for a few generations." She smiled, showing off dimples in a face growing full of creases. She and her husband had been friends of Neil's father before his death but considered Neil a good friend, too.

"Is Neil . . . coming?"

"Oh no, dear. I doubt it very much." She paused, apparently thinking of how to go on, then added, "We heard about your breakup. I'm so sorry."

"Ah . . . yes . . . thank you."

"Did you ever go see Dallas Denton?"

Her pulse made another uncomfortable spike. "Sorry?"

"I thought you were going to meet with him after our talk?"

Layla cast about wildly and finally remembered her conversation with Cathie. She'd been testing the waters a little bit. She and Neil hadn't quite fallen apart yet, but she'd sensed something was up. Cathie had been doing the talking, as usual, and mentioned a "good lawyer" one of her friends was using.

"She got into drug trouble, you know, and the prosecutor wanted to make an example of her," Cathie had confided. "It was just a prescription she had to refill a few more times, and I don't know what happened, but she called on Dallas Denton to represent her."

"For being overprescribed?" Layla wasn't tracking.

"Oh, I think there was a little something more. Maybe she . . . well, let's be honest. She sold a few pills to some friends. Drug trafficking is very serious, you know, and even though it was small and anyway . . . she ended up with community service, and now she talks to other people my age who don't think it could happen to them." Now, she eyed Layla consideringly. "I never really thought you had a . . . criminal problem. You just seemed, interested."

"Just talking, I guess." That was a complete lie, but she couldn't very well turn around now and admit she was suing

Neil for joint custody of Eddie, using the very lawyer Cathie had recommended, should Layla ever need a criminal defense lawyer.

Rand stepped up to them. "Would you like a glass of champagne, Layla?"

"Oh, no, thanks." Actually, she would like a glass of champagne. She felt like having a drink, and champagne was always her weakness. But she wanted to separate herself from the Hyatts. Nice people that they were, they were Neil's friends, and that was enough to put her on edge. They didn't appear to know about the raging custody battle as yet, and she didn't want to get in to it. Better just to excuse herself from them.

It was at that moment that a woman separated herself from the crowd at the door, handing over her black coat to an attendant who was using the closest room to the massive double doors as a coat closet. She turned toward Layla, and Layla was pierced by a serious déjà vu. *Who?* she thought, before realizing she looked a great deal like an actress in one of those superhero movie franchises. Not as pretty, she saw now, and probably a bit heavier. But her dark hair was the same, and some of her facial bone structure.

As Layla watched, she looked back to the man handing over his tickets. He was smiling at the young woman taking the tickets. Neil.

He came forward, and the dark-haired woman linked her arm through his. Layla could scarcely breathe. This was Neil's new girlfriend? Not only had he shown up, but he'd brought her as a companion?

Shock swept through her, so intense it left her shaking. She looked around for Lucy and found her sister staring coldly into her husband's eyes, her mouth grim, and John was glaring back at her as well, his whole posture suggesting he wanted to wring her neck.

". . . you okay?"

Layla realized dully that Cathie Hyatt was still beside her, still chattering. At that very minute, Cathie looked up and said, "Oh, there's Neil!" and then she sucked in a little breath as she saw Neil's guest.

Courtney, Layla remembered. Neil's girlfriend's name was Courtney.

"Excuse me," she said to Cathie and walked away.

Lucy waited for John to explode. Grab her and shake her. Scream at her. Drag her out by one arm.

Her transgressions had found her.

She had watched transfixed, frozen in place, as the white-haired gentleman from the Pembroke Inn worked his way over to her. She'd seen him coming as if from a long way away. Armageddon. End of days. He greeted her with pleasure. "My, my. You look wonderful in that dress, dear. I didn't expect to see you here. Are you with Mark?"

John had been turned toward the hors d'oeuvres tray of tiny bruschetta with strawberries atop a thin melt of cheese. Overhearing, he'd looked back quickly at Lucy and then the older man. "Mr. Carlin," he greeted him. "Do you know my wife?"

"*Your* wife?" Mr. Carlin's snowy brows damn near lifted off his face.

"Mr. Carlin and I met at the Pembroke," Lucy told John in a squeaky voice, her breath coming fast. She was hyperventilating. She had to appear normal. Carlin had seen her sneaking around the building to meet Mark. He *knew*.

"Oh, that other night?" John bit into the bruschetta, his eyes lasered on Lucy.

Lucy nodded.

"Who's Mark?" John asked, deceptively mild.

Carlin swept in his crinkled lips as if afraid to speak. It was Lucy who said through a dry throat, "The bartender."

"Lucy."

Lucy turned like an automaton to see Layla approaching rapidly, her skin ashen. She'd been standing nearby, then left, but now she was back and paler than ever.

She really is too thin, Lucy thought. She felt dissociated from the moment.

John saw Layla and said tightly, "Just a minute." Then he grabbed Lucy's arm and pulled her to one side. Lucy was aware of guests turning their way, a kaleidoscope of color in their gowns. She felt dizzy. Like falling through a vortex.

"The *bartender*?" he hissed. John was nothing if not perceptive.

She wanted to lie. To defend herself. To say that Mr. Carlin had gotten it wrong. But Carlin was about twenty feet behind John and she caught eyes with him. He was looking flustered, embarrassed by the scene unfolding before him.

"Lucy." John's grip on her forearm was hard.

"Ow," she said.

"*Lucy*." Layla again. Lucy turned to her. Layla looked desperate.

John leaned close. "If I learn you've fucked him, I'll kill you."

She shook herself free. Instead of scaring her, he'd filled her with outrage. "When did you get so dramatic? You're usually a block of ice." She turned and stalked away, aware of eyes following her as she moved blindly through the crowd, seeking an exit.

She glanced back. Layla was still standing by John. She gazed after Lucy, then looked to a woman in a black dress who was clutched onto a man in a suit with a Rolex watch and a black cowboy hat before turning her eyes soulfully back to Lucy.

Neil Grassley. Had to be.

Lucy felt a pang for her but couldn't stop. She pushed through the crowd and a back door and hadn't realized she was holding her breath until she was gulping fresh air.

September held her champagne glass and listened with half an ear to Jake and William Ogden discussing investments, specifically some of the better buys Ogden had made in the stock market. The man was puffed up with a certain amount of self-importance, though he did credit Jake with guiding him in the right direction. Ogden had called out to two other couples already, whom he'd then introduced to Jake, singing Jake's praises like a proud father. September had done her duty, smiling, shaking hands, making small talk. She'd caught her husband giving her a sideways smile. He knew she detested this networking and appreciated her cooperation.

She took a sip of champagne and caught a tense confrontation out of the corner of her eye. A guy in a black jacket and jeans was gripping the forearm of a woman in a red dress. September's attention sharpened. She'd been in law enforcement long enough to have seen a number of those moments. Sometimes they dissolved. Sometimes they turned into an ugly fight.

But the woman shook him off and stalked away. Another woman in a denim jumpsuit looked for a moment like she was going to go crashing after the first one, but she stood rooted to the spot. An hors d'oeuvres tray came September's way, and she selected a skewer of prawns that smelled of ginger and honey. She looked up again to see another tray, this one loaded with glasses of champagne, being set on a sideboard by a harried server near the man of the originally fighting couple. The server took several steps away, as if she

were planning on grabbing the attention of a blond woman
in a black dress, black cowboy boots, and a red neckerchief.
The tray of champagne was immediately raided by a number
of guests, some taking two or more glasses at a time. The
harried server never made contact with the blonde and returned a few moments later . . . staring at the tray a moment
before making a beeline to the kitchen.

September considered joining the fray for the champagne. So far, the waiters had been pretty stingy with the
bubbly, and with the price of the tickets, it was kind of a low
move. She was all for donating but give the people what they
asked for.

The woman in the red dress returned a few moments later
and said something to the man who'd held on to her forearm.
A note of reconciliation, maybe? He leaned back to the un-
supervised tray and grabbed up the last three glasses of
champagne, handing them to the woman in red, the woman
in the denim jumpsuit, and a female passerby who'd been
heading to the tray only to find it empty. The passerby
thanked the man profusely but shook her head, refusing the
drink. Then she waited near the sideboard, looking expectantly in the direction of the kitchen.

At least I got one, September thought, draining her glass.
She would have liked one of the bruschetta, but she could
never quite get her hand on those trays as they squeezed by,
though the man who'd held on to the woman's forearm
seemed never to miss. She watched him snag what looked
like a mushroom cap enveloped in cheese and wondered
if she could excuse herself and track down one of those
trays herself.

Kate surveyed the guests grabbing their own glasses of
champagne and trailed after the too-few servers with their

large faux silver trays of hors d'oeuvres. She had a mind to
have a word with Jean-Luc. Crissman & Wolfe was paying
a handsome price for this event—it wasn't entirely subsidized
by the patrons—and the guests deserved bountiful plates of
all kinds of goodies. Yes, the main course was the star of the
evening, and yes, that's what everyone expected, but this
would not do. Just would not do.

"Where are you going?" Lyle demanded as she moved off.

"To push the chef."

"For what?"

"The hors d'oeuvres. Honestly, Lyle. Open your eyes!"

He jerked back at her tone. Kate shot a glance to Abbott
to see if he was witnessing their argument, but he was staring across the room with laser intensity. Kate immediately
followed his gaze and drew in a harsh breath.

"You don't have to be such a bitch about it," Lyle declared,
but she wasn't hearing him.

Jerome Wolfe.

She felt a full-body shiver at the silver fox with the warm
smile and charming manner. He had a couple of older women
nearly swooning, and there were some younger ones eyeing
him with unabashed hunger. The man was gray before his
time, but in a way that only made him more appealing. *Silver
like money.* The words ran through her mind before she
could stop them.

But he was a predator. She knew that. He was trying to
get Stonehenge—*fuck! She never called it that!*—for a song.
Wolfe Lodge, she reminded herself sternly. It already possessed his name, though no Crissman would ever admit it.

She wanted to go over to introduce herself, but she felt
overcome with a shyness she rarely felt. *Get on with it, Kate.
For the family. You need to make the introduction.*

But an older man whose own gray hair was getting white
around the temples called Jerome over to introduce him to

a handsome younger man she felt she should know. The younger man was introducing Jerome to an auburn-haired woman in denim jeans and a black turtleneck. Kate inwardly sniffed. She certainly had taken the Denim and Diamonds theme to its lowest common denominator. Then she saw the rock on her finger and her heart flipped uncomfortably. Nice ring, she thought.

". . . do you hear me?" Lyle hissed in her ear.

"Yes, I hear you," she answered smartly. "Now, excuse me. I have work to do."

"Thought you were going to the kitchen," he reminded as she headed in Jerome Wolfe's direction.

"I am." She almost reversed herself, but then added, "In a moment."

Jake was spreading his hands and smiling ruefully at the praise William Ogden was laying on him. It amused September and made her inordinately proud, as if it were her doing instead of his. She was uncomfortable, too. Narcissism at its worst, she supposed, because she couldn't help thinking about herself, the loss of a job more acute. She shook the latest newcomer's hand, a good-looking man in his early forties.

"Jerome Wolfe," Ogden introduced for September's benefit.

"My wife, September Westerly," Jake told Wolfe, throwing her a warm look.

"Pleased to meet you," he said.

"Thank you. Are you the Wolfe of Crissman and Wolfe?" she asked.

"The current generation's latest version," he agreed. "My father died several years ago, so I'm it. Although my great-grandfather sold his half of the store to the Crissmans before my time."

William Ogden's eyes sparkled with an impish light. "Bad blood for a long time. Glad to see you've buried the hatchet with the current Crissmans."

"Have I?" Jerome Wolfe drawled, drawing a guffaw from Ogden. He turned to Jake, who was wisely staying far out of that conversation. "William wants me to meet with you to talk over my financial portfolio. I told him I would even before I met you. But I have a question for you first."

Jake lifted his brows, waiting. September sensed a certain tension in Wolfe.

"What do you think of this place as an investment opportunity?"

"This . . . Wolfe Lodge?" Jake said, sounding a bit surprised.

"It's already got my name." ·

"Are the Crissmans selling?" Jake's glance slid over to where a man in his late fifties with iron-gray hair and an equally austere manner was just coming down the stairs and glaring over at Jerome.

Lyle Abbott Crissman III or IV, September realized. Jake had given her a short history of the Crissman family, and she knew enough about them from casual conversation from her own father to know of their social standing. "Current patriarch is called Abbott," Jake had told her. "And his son is Lyle. One of those families that can't name any firstborn son anything but the same as his father."

"Look who you're talking to about strange naming procedures," September had reminded him. Her own father, Braden Rafferty, had named his children for the months in which they were born, which included September and her twin brother, August, who'd been born on either side of midnight of August 31. She and Auggie were fourth and fifth in the birth order after their brother March, and their sisters, May, now deceased, and July. To add insult to injury, their stepmother, Rosamund, had named her baby daughter January . . . yes, for the month in which she was born. And well, the truth was, July had named her daughter, June, though she'd sworn to high heaven she would never follow that crazy tradition and then had fallen into the same deep, dark pit.

Jake had said he wanted to have a boy in April. See how the family reacted to that. He'd sounded so serious that after September had laughed, her heart had clutched, and then he'd broken into a grin and she'd jumped on his back and pretended to strangle him for scaring her so much, and they'd ended up falling onto the bed and making love.

"What?" she asked with a start, realizing Jerome had asked her a question.

"I asked if you worked with your husband."

"Oh, no. I'm currently unemployed."

He seemed to sense there was more, because he asked, "And what do you do?"

"She was a detective with the Laurelton Police Department," Jake said.

Jerome looked surprised, then leaned in to peer at her closely. "I know you. You were on television. Their spokesperson."

"Once or twice," September said quickly. "Not that much."

"I saw Pauline Kirby interview you."

September managed a smile and nodded. She hadn't liked being interviewed by the newswoman, but now even those uncomfortable moments had a sheen of nostalgia. *You really are pathetic.*

Layla was nearly faint with anxiety. She'd spent the last month making plans on how to combat Neil and now here he was, with Courtney, and she could feel his cool gaze skating over her, could see the triumphant smile he didn't try to hide.

Why did you want me in the first place? she wanted to cry. There were many other respected families in the Portland area. Why her, why the Crissmans?

But if he'd chosen someone else, there would be no Eddie.

"Here," John Linfield said to the woman who'd initially refused his glass of champagne and who was now gazing expectantly toward the kitchen. "It may be awhile."

Layla had yet to take a sip from the glass he'd handed to her. "I need to go find Lucy," she said.

"She'll be back," he answered dismissively.

He turned from her, and she took a step in the direction in which Lucy had disappeared, and suddenly Neil was right in front of her. She stared at his bow tie and cummerbund, both made of denim and imprinted with spurs and branding irons. The diamond ring on his right hand had been in his family for years.

"Hello, Layla," he said. He was holding two glasses of champagne. "I picked you up a glass, but I see someone beat me to the punch." He gave John's back a long look.

"My brother-in-law," Layla said, then could have kicked herself for being too forthcoming. It didn't work with Neil. He played a game of wits and she needed to be sharp and careful.

"Ah," he said thoughtfully.

And then Courtney was there, filling the space beside him, her smile a challenge. Layla knew the type. She'd always deplored those kinds of female games, but now, finding herself in the midst of one whether she liked it or not, she wanted to fight.

But that would be a bad, bad idea. She had a lawsuit coming up. No drama. Nothing that might hit the papers, and let's face it, a skirmish at a social event of this prominence was a nonstarter.

All this flitted through her brain a half second before she thrust out her free hand to Courtney, tacking on a smile of her own, and said, "I don't believe we've met. I'm Layla Crissman."

"Courtney Mayfield."

Layla turned to Neil. "I didn't expect you at my family's event."

"It's a benefit for the Friends of the Columbia River Gorge," he reminded her, his smile widening. He loved a game of one-upmanship. She should have seen that from the get-go. "Not really your family's event."

"The Crissmans are hosting," Courtney said with a kind of false sweetness that set Layla's teeth on edge.

"Should I make anything of this?" Layla asked Neil. How had she ever thought he was attractive? He looked like a troll. Short, squatty, and smug.

"Of what?"

"That you came. That you're here, when you and I . . . are on opposite sides."

"I came to donate money to a worthy cause. We all have to do our part, don't we? Save the beauty of the area. Help the businesses that suffered. I noticed your painting over there." He nodded his head in the direction where Layla had placed her art. "Think I should buy it?"

Layla struggled to keep her expression neutral. "Sure. Maybe you could make it a gift for Ed—ah, our baby."

"Edda?" His eyes darkened.

She hadn't meant to give away her nickname, but there it was. "I call our baby Eddie."

Courtney sucked in a breath.

"Eddie," he repeated softly. "You don't have a right to name him."

"Not yet," Layla answered, even more softly.

Courtney blurted out, "I'm pregnant, too. Neil and I just found out!"

Layla's lips parted. She stared at Neil's girlfriend in shock.

Neil turned to Courtney, so angry he looked like he might hit her.

"It's a boy," Courtney said, though her voice sounded a bit uncertain, like she was seriously regretting saying anything.

"How do you know?" Layla looked at her flat stomach.

But Courtney had been hushed to silence, and Neil was stonily infuriated.

Layla gazed at him, hurt and angry. He was trying to steal her baby even while he was having one of his own.

She sure as hell was going to use that against him.

Chapter Twelve

Lucy walked out the back door and in through the front again. The pert young girl greeting guests had been too inundated with questions and confusion to ask for Lucy's ticket when she'd reentered after returning from the Audi, but this time she stood like a wall, demanding proof that Lucy was a paid guest. For a moment, Lucy was flummoxed, her head full of the memory of those embarrassing and revolting moments with Mark, the bartender, and the realization that John knew everything he needed to get the picture already.

"I'm Lucy Crissman," she stated firmly. "My family's putting on this benefit."

"Oh." The girl blinked. "Everybody has a ticket to prove they paid."

"Well, I don't have a ticket," Lucy said patiently. "I was already inside and went out through a back door. I could have gone back in that way, but I came to the front."

"I need to ask Roger. . . ."

"I'm sorry," Lucy said, brushing past her. She couldn't take any more of the regulations. She wanted to cry or stomp her foot in anger or shriek at the heavens or bang her head against a wall.

Kate was the first person who crossed into Lucy's line of vision and she groaned inwardly. Spying her sister-in-law, Kate turned toward her. "Lucy, where have you been?"

"Why? Have I been missed?" she was surprised into asking back.

"Jerome Wolfe has been asking for you and Layla and Lyle. I think he . . . well, I don't exactly know what he has in mind."

"Lucy!"

Layla's voice rang out, a small note of hysteria in it. Lucy left Kate and walked to where Layla was talking to a man and a woman. John was directly behind them, engaged in a conversation with someone else.

"Lucy, this is Neil Grassley and Courtney Mayfield. This is my sister, Lucy Linfield."

Lucy shook hands with Neil, momentarily jarred from her own problems to examine the man in front of her. Neil was shorter than Layla and looked Lucy right in the eye. He had a softness to him that was also evidenced in the plump grip of his handshake. He had a nice enough face, but Lucy thought she detected a coldness there. Courtney Mayfield didn't bother to shake her hand; in fact, she barely met Lucy's eyes as she gazed around the room with that look of hoping someone better would walk through the door.

"Lucy, Layla . . ." Kate's voice had a note of reprimand. Both sisters turned to regard her. "Lyle's over there with Jerome Wolfe. Do you see?"

Lucy swiveled her attention and first noticed how tense and uptight her brother looked. At that moment, a tray of grilled shrimp passed by, too far for her to grab a skewer. Just as well, she thought dourly. Her earlier hunger had vanished. She felt completely clenched up.

Tiny mushroom caps stuffed with crabmeat wafted past on a tray. Neil tried to grab one, but the small Asian server whisked them away, homing toward an empty tray that had been set down and once held champagne glasses. Another server with new champagne glasses hesitated a moment, then set down her tray and looked after the disappearing Asian woman, as if asking if it was the right thing to do.

Guests swarmed the tray and the girl backed away as if she'd left food out for dangerous beasts.

Kate said in sudden fury, "I told Jean-Luc the size of the crowd!"

John knocked back his champagne and reached for another glass. The Asian server came flying out of the kitchen and stopped short in dismay. Neil and Courtney were each helping themselves to a flute, which was sending Kate into conniptions. She rushed over and had a talk with the Asian woman. The other server was nowhere to be seen.

John asked, "Anyone want another?"

Layla said, "I'm still working on this one."

He gave Lucy a hard look.

"Sure, then, why not? I feel like drowning myself," Lucy said, meeting his gaze. She was determined not to let her problems with John eclipse the rest of the evening. What was done was done. Might as well drink too much and think about something else.

But before he could get her the glass, Kate implored, "Lucy, Layla . . ." And shooed them toward Lyle, who was regarding all of them with a strange look on his face.

"What?" Lucy asked him as they drew near. She realized he was turned slightly away from the handsome and evil Jerome Wolfe.

"Thought I saw someone . . . I knew . . ." Lyle grimaced and looked to Wolfe, who was staring straight at Lucy.

"Lucy Crissman," Jerome said.

"Linfield," she corrected. She'd met him a couple of times before, but he'd always seemed so chilly. There was something a bit austere about him, like John, like . . . he who would not be named. . . . She seemed to attract men of a particular type, though she wasn't attracted to Jerome Wolfe, the thief who would buy Stonehenge out from under them.

She glanced back at John and found him staring at her. As soon as they made eye contact, he turned away. It hurt. She couldn't deny that.

"And you must be Layla . . ." Jerome eyed Layla up and down, taking in the way she looked in the denim pantsuit.

"Welcome to the eighties," Layla said, reading him correctly.

"Ha." He grinned at her, but Layla only managed a sick smile in return. Lucy gazed at her sister sharply. Layla was miles away.

Kate said brightly, "Okay, Jerome. I've rounded them all up."

Wolfe glanced from Layla to Lyle and then back to Lucy. He addressed them all, but he kept his gaze centered on Lucy. "I've been in discussions with your father and Lyle . . ." Lucy slid her brother a look, but he was peering over the crowd, though she sensed it was for effect, as if he'd removed himself from the moment. "I've also been talking to an investment adviser about this lodge."

"Stonehenge should be on the historical registry," Layla said somewhat distractedly.

Jerome smiled at her but went on. "The investment adviser said buying the lodge likely wouldn't make me any money."

Lucy's attention had been wavering, but now it crashed back to the moment. She felt a spurt of hope. "That sounds promising."

"It's not," said Lyle, as if the words were ripped out of him.

"But I'm buying it anyway," Jerome finished, his smile almost a grimace, as if he were feeling pain. "Be assured your father and brother drove a hard bargain." He grinned more easily at Lyle, who didn't even act like he'd heard him.

"I just know you two girls have been against the sale and I hope there are no hard feelings."

Bullshit. Bull. Shit. Lucy glared at her brother, wanting to slap both of his two lying faces. And the same for Jerome Wolfe. Acting so warm and understanding while he was stabbing both Layla and her in the back. *Girls?* She hadn't been called a girl since the first years of college, and even then she'd been insulted.

"We *girls* don't want to sell, that's true," said Lucy. "We want Stonehenge to stay in the family. That's true, too. And though we may be fighting a losing battle, we'll continue to fight you."

Wolfe looked amused. "It's pretty much a done deal."

Lyle interjected, "It *is* a done deal. Lucy, could I talk to you?"

He glanced back at Wolfe and gave him a curt nod, then grabbed Lucy by the elbow and steered her away.

"Hey!" Lucy shouted, but Lyle's grip was firm. She twisted to glance over her shoulder and saw Layla move in John's direction once more, away from Neil and Courtney, who'd drifted closer to them and Jerome during their conversation. Perhaps Neil had hopes of overhearing what Jerome Wolfe and Abbott's three children were talking about. All the while, Kate was standing by awkwardly, as if she didn't know which way to turn.

Lyle led her to a spot under the gallery near Layla's painting, with Wolfe strolling toward them. "What do you think you're doing?" Lucy yanked back her arm and glared at her brother. "Have you lost your mind?"

He said, "Jerome would like to talk to you alone."

"So? You don't have to manhandle me," Lucy snapped, both annoyed and infuriated. Rubbing her arm, she threw a glance at Wolfe but said to her brother, "I'm not going to change my mind."

What was wrong with him?

He stared at her for a second, as if deciding how he could make her see his point of view, then snorted and shook his head. "Do whatever you need to," Lyle muttered, stalking away. In his hurry, he jostled an older woman. Her arm flew upward to catch her balance. Luckily, the champagne glass she was holding was empty; otherwise her drink would have spilled down the front of her dress.

Wolfe didn't waste time with niceties. "I want this lodge for the same reasons you do, Lucy. Family history. You Crissmans pushed us out long ago and we didn't want to be pushed out."

"Okay."

"I'm righting that wrong. You can either obstruct or facilitate the transaction. It's all the same to me. I'd just rather we worked together instead of against each other."

Lucy wished she'd gotten that last glass of champagne before she had to go toe-to-toe with Wolfe. She was resentful that she was the one who'd been appointed, apparently, to deal with Wolfe. "The main reason you want the lodge is to get back at us?"

"I wouldn't put it quite that way."

"What way would you put it?"

He shrugged and smiled, showing even teeth. She just bet he got by on his charm, but he was a snake in the grass.

"The lodge is cursed, you know," Lucy told him. "Bad things happen here."

His grin widened. "I do know that," he agreed. "Inexplicable deaths. Your grandmother . . . no, great-grandmother," he corrected himself before Lucy could do that for him. "And a number of people who worked at the lodge. Some near deaths. And the family that lives closest to the lodge, the ones with the nature girl, lost their son to mysterious circumstances."

"The Kilgores."

"Yes, the Kilgores."

The way he said it, with that trace of amusement, made her realize he knew all about the family whose property abutted Stonehenge. She corrected him. "Their son died of suffocation in his crib. A terrible accident."

"Have you talked to them lately?"

Lucy felt like there was some kind of one-upmanship going on here that she didn't understand. "Mr. Kilgore died last year, but I haven't talked to Mona since then. I think Lyle has, though." Lyle was closest to the Kilgore family.

"Daniel Kilgore died of heart failure and Mona is very frail. Their daughter—"

"The nature girl," Lucy cut in coolly.

"Yes, the nature girl, Brianne, is interested in selling. She knows I'm buying Stonehenge and so . . . after Mona dies, we're going to talk over a deal."

"I don't believe it. No way! Brianne loves that property. She's *in tune* with it. When we were kids, she would take all of us out into the forest. She knew every plant, every sign of animal life. She loved the woods. She couldn't have changed that much."

"I've talked to her, and she's ready to sell. That's all I know."

Lucy was flabbergasted. Her memory of Brianne was of someone almost otherworldly. She couldn't picture her making any financial decisions. But then, how many years had it been since she'd seen her?

"Lucy, I don't want to be on bad terms with you. I know your brother and father want us to come to an agreement that we can all live with."

"If you actually purchase Stonehenge, that won't happen."

"Wolfe Lodge," he corrected.

"Okay, *Wolfe Lodge*. I don't know how many ways I can say it. I'm not behind this sale, so . . . I choose to obstruct."

His demeanor grew harder. "Lyle felt I could appeal to you. Maybe he picked the wrong sister."

"Why don't you go talk to Layla and find out?"

"You really don't want to make an enemy of me," he said.

"I'll take my chances."

At that moment, someone came up and touched his arm. He held her gaze for a moment, a silent battle cry that chilled her inside, before turning around to talk to a woman she didn't recognize. Lucy couldn't think of one good reason to prolong their conversation, so she walked back toward the center of the room.

Her brother had moved toward the now-empty champagne tray along with Kate, John, and Layla. Lucy had lost sight of Neil and Courtney, which was probably a good thing.

As she headed straight for Lyle, she saw one of the staff press a last bruschetta in front of Layla's nose. Lucy lost sight of her sister as she circled around a group of six who were hovering near a table of crystal vases. The silent auction was about to close, and they apparently wanted to make certain they were the last signature and therefore the purchasers. When she finally got around the cluster of bodies she saw Layla had plucked up the bruschetta, but it was still between her fingers. She said something to John and then passed the hors d'oeuvre to him. John bit into the toast, holding up a hand to catch some of the tomato topping just as he saw Lucy approaching. Immediately, his expression darkened. Lucy's stomach clenched, but by then she'd caught up with Lyle, who was standing stiffly, watching Kate as she headed in the direction of the kitchen.

"Thanks for that," she told him coldly.

Lyle drew his attention back from his wife. "Jerome asked to talk to you. I just facilitated."

"And I obstructed. He tried to bully me. You shouldn't even consider him as a buyer. It's some kind of revenge with him. And he brought up the Kilgores."

Lyle made a sharp move away from her, but she followed.

"He said Brianne wants to sell to them," Lucy said. "Is that true?"

"How should I know?"

"Because *you know*," she shot back. "You've been working this deal behind my back and Layla's, and it involves the Kilgores' land, too. When was the last time you saw Brianne?"

"Years ago."

"Really? How many?"

"I don't know. What does it matter?"

"Did you convince her to sell?"

"The last I heard, her mother's still alive. She can't sell until Mona dies, and it's not our problem anyway."

"Wolfe also acted like there was some mystery about the son's death. Where did he get that?"

"I don't know anything, Lucy. Okay?"

But he did. He was hiding something. She could tell.

"There's no mystery about his death," Lyle added. "It was a tragedy."

"I know. But why would he say that?"

"I don't know."

"Lyle!" This was always the way it was with her brother. Pulling the truth out of him made her want to throttle him.

He made a gesture of frustration. "Okay, maybe . . . maybe they thought it was Brianne's fault."

Lucy pounced on that. "What? What do you mean? Have you talked to Mona?"

"I talked to Daniel. Brianne's a little unstable, and he . . . always wondered about it."

Lucy stared at her brother. Lyle had been enamored with Brianne when they were kids. They'd all been a little in awe of her. "I don't believe it. She was always into saving animals and trees and the fish . . . remember how worried she was about the salmon dying because they couldn't get past the dam?"

"That's why we have fish ladders," he said abruptly.

"But that's not how Brianne felt. I just can't believe she would want to sell."

"Whatever the Kilgores decide, it's nothing to do with us. If Wolfe has a whole plan for this area, good for him. It's his money to waste. There's nothing here, Lucy. It'll be decades, centuries, before any property around here turns a profit. It's too remote."

"We're only an hour or so outside of Portland," she protested.

"Far enough," he said bitterly. "You know about money, or you're supposed to anyway. This area is a bad investment. Feeling nostalgia for it doesn't make it valuable, except as an asset for sale."

"What's Wolfe's offer?"

"It's a good offer."

"Well, that doesn't answer the question. You said I know about money; why don't you give me the particulars?"

"I don't know the figures off the top of my head."

Lucy almost laughed, it was so ridiculous. "Of course you know the figures. I'm only asking for an estimate."

"Well, I can't give it to you," he snapped, his face flushing. He gazed in the direction Kate had gone and appeared to consider charging after his wife.

"Well, maybe you can tell me where the sixty thousand went, then. The company money you and Dad said not to worry about."

"Jesus, Lucy. Enough. Okay? Enough!" Lyle stalked away from her without another word.

Lucy exhaled slowly, unaware she'd even been holding her breath. She'd never called him out on the missing funds before. She'd let her father and brother do their little financial dance because it was Abbott's company, and maybe Lyle's, and whatever was going on it was their decision, not hers. It just hurt that they didn't trust her. What were they hiding?

"Lucy . . ." John gasped from somewhere behind her.

She turned and gave him a hard look. "Yes?"

He stumbled toward her and gripped her arm, looking around wildly. Slightly alarmed, Lucy glanced around, too. She noticed the Asian server talking rapid-fire, ordering the other server who'd left the last tray of champagne to the kitchen. She saw Kate regarding both of them with a piqued look. Then John, shockingly pale, was dragging Lucy toward the anteroom, stumbling around a heavyset woman, knocking her into the man next to her.

"I'm so sorry," Lucy murmured apologetically. She was irked at John and tired of men grabbing onto her. She tried to yank her arm free, but John held her in a death grip. "I'm not going in there! What's wrong with you? *Let go of me!*" she ordered in a taut whisper.

He was nearly bowling over some of the guests.

God, he looked ghastly. What was wrong with him?

"John, I—"

They were three steps away from the anteroom when John leaned over and threw up all over her shoes.

Chapter Thirteen

The stir across the room caught September's attention. She'd wandered away from Jake and now saw a portly woman being propped up by an elderly man who had been surprised by her sudden weight on him and looked like he might fold. She hurried forward. To her right, a hunched-over man was dragging a woman in a red dress toward the cloakroom when he suddenly leaned over and upchucked.

Not exactly what you want at a thousand-dollar-a-plate-plus dinner.

The elderly man managed to right the woman, who was loudly exclaiming her displeasure.

A pretty Asian server took one look at the pool of vomit outside the cloakroom door and ran for the kitchen.

"He pushed me! Just pushed me!" the heavyset woman cried, the quivering folds of her neck threatening to engulf her diamond choker.

The sour, pungent smell of bile and stomach acid filled the foyer.

"Oh!" The woman covered her nose with her hand, and several other guests quickly moved farther away. Even the cellist had stopped playing until someone whispered into his ear and he nodded, starting up again.

September circled around to the cloakroom door and was about to rap on the panels and offer help when she was nearly pushed aside by an older man in black slacks, a white shirt with black cowboy arrows delineating chest-high pockets, cowboy style, and a white felt cowboy hat. Abbott Crissman, their host, September knew; Jake had pointed him out to her earlier.

Crissman swept into the cloakroom, sending another waft of sour air outward as the man inside was throwing up again.

The door slammed in her face.

"John," Lucy said with real concern. She'd kicked off her shoes and was following her husband barefooted as he staggered toward the only chair in the room. White-faced and sweating, he yanked at his collar, loosening his tie, his breathing ragged.

"God . . ." he muttered.

He sank into the chair and held his head in his hands.

"You okay? Do you need something?" she asked, looking back anxiously at the door.

It suddenly flew inward, as if she'd said, "Open sesame," and Abbott stalked through, slamming it behind him. He stopped short upon seeing the puddle of vomit on the floor. "You're sick?" he demanded.

"Yes." John didn't look up.

"The flu? What?" Abbott asked, glaring at Lucy.

Knowing what they were all thinking, she was cautious when she put their fear into words. "Food poisoning?"

Abbott pressed his lips together, color riding up his neck. "It doesn't happen that fast," he dismissed.

"I think it can," said Lucy.

"No one else is sick."

Yet.

Lucy asked her husband, "John, do you want to lie down?"

He groaned. "I want to leave."

"There are beds in all the bedrooms," Abbott said. "Take him to the master on the gallery floor."

Lucy started, "I don't know if—"

"Take me home," John interrupted. His skin was white and he kept spitting onto the floor.

"Did you talk to Jerome Wolfe?" Abbott asked Lucy.

She threw her father an exasperated glance. "Yes."

"And?"

"Dad, I don't know. He wants to buy. You want to sell. I'm not even in the conversation."

"He wanted to talk to you, make his case. He wants to talk to Layla, too."

"Well, great," Lucy said, her eyes on her husband. His hands hung limply between his legs, his head bowed. "He can talk to Layla now. I think I'd better take John home."

"We haven't eaten dinner and the silent auction hasn't closed yet," Abbott argued. "The oral auction's just warming up."

"I think you're going to have to soldier on without me." Lucy's mind was turning toward the problem at hand: getting John somewhere he could be more comfortable and away from the benefit.

"I'm going to be sick again," John rushed out. He leaned forward and spewed up more vomit.

Abbott recoiled. "I'll get someone to clean this up. Don't step in it."

He paused at the door. "If Wolfe feels he needs your okay—"

"I don't give a rat's ass, Dad."

Abbott looked blankly at Lucy, as if he'd never seen her before. He seemed to want to keep on arguing, but in the end, he yanked open the door and headed out.

John spit some more and groaned again. Beads of sweat stood out on his forehead.

"Maybe we should go to a doctor," said Lucy.

"Where?" he gasped.

"Glenn River?"

"No. I want to go home."

"Okay." She hesitated a moment. "Can you make it to the car?"

He didn't answer, and Lucy saw that he was thinking that over. Several minutes passed, excruciating minutes while Lucy ran over what she should do. It sure seemed like John could use a doctor, but he was nothing if not stubborn.

She waited until she couldn't stand it, then asked again, "Do you want me to bring the car around?" He swallowed convulsively, clearly miserable. "John?"

"For God's sakes, give me a minute."

More time passed, and then there was a knock on the door. John groaned and muttered, "Get rid of them."

Lucy crossed the room and pulled open the door. An auburn-haired woman, one of the guests, she remembered seeing, was on the other side.

"Could you use some help?" she asked.

There was something efficient and no-nonsense about her that reached toward Lucy's heart like the support of a good friend. She didn't know her, but she didn't care. "I might," she admitted.

The woman stepped into the room. Lucy recognized that she was someone used to responsibility.

John snapped, "We don't need any help."

"I was going to get the car . . ." Lucy said.

"I'll stay here with him," she said, clearly not put off by John's rudeness or the pool of vomit on the floor.

"Thank you."

Lucy didn't wait to hear any further complaints from

John. She slipped out of the room, closed the door behind her, then hurried past the few milling guests who were still in the entry hall and out to the Audi.

September had watched Abbott Crissman enter the cloakroom only to exit a few moments later. He'd torn through the crowd toward the kitchen area. Soon after, a man and a woman with a bucket full of cleaning supplies and a mop were coming her way, while Crissman aimed toward the main stairway, where the last of the guests were slowly making their way toward the artfully placed tables that filled the gallery above. Those that were vaguely aware of the sick man had dallied, but they were mostly on the stairway now.

One couple, however, had stayed back with September. "Poor man," the woman said. She'd been standing nearby when the heavyset woman had lost her balance, and she was there still, her gaze on the closed cloakroom door. The portly woman was gone, as was her companion, who'd saved her from falling, but this woman, in a short denim skirt and jacket and her male companion, wearing jeans in a matching shade of light blue, were all that remained in the entry apart from the wide-eyed young hostess, who still had a look of repugnant horror on her face.

"Glad they're cleaning it up so fast," the man said as the cleaning crew mopped up the mess outside the anteroom door.

He and his date both looked at September. "Are you with them?" the woman asked.

"No, I just thought I could help," September responded.

"Yes . . . hmmm . . ." His gaze moved to the line of guests climbing the stairs. "We'd better go on up."

"I don't know if we should just abandon them . . . ?" Clearly, the man's companion had more of an empathetic streak than he did.

But there was no reason for them to miss the rest of the evening, so September said, "Oh, I'd go to dinner. And the oral auction. I've got this."

"Okay . . ." the woman said.

At that moment, the younger woman who'd been manning the door abruptly left her post, apparently thinking September's advice was meant for her, too. She beelined for the kitchen. September then saw Jake at the top of the stairs, looking around, and she lifted an arm to catch his attention. He connected with her, correctly interpreted that he couldn't really head back downstairs without creating a traffic problem, and simply lifted his chin in acknowledgment. September signaled that she would be up soon, and he nodded again, pointing toward the north end of the building, which was apparently where their seats were.

As the couple moved off, a thirtysomething blond woman marched from the direction of the kitchen, her mouth set, her eyes sweeping up the stairs after the guests.

Kate, September guessed, married to Lyle Crissman. The blonde darted a glance toward the cloakroom, then stopped the two workers who'd cleaned up the mess in the hallway, a young man in his twenties and a woman who looked to be about thirty, but who was prematurely gray, who'd been heading outside.

"Just wait here for a moment," she told them, chewing on her lip for a second before she realized she was doing so and stopped suddenly. "Then, I want you to clean the room." She hitched her chin toward the closed doors of the anteroom. "I think there's another . . . area that needs attention." Her eyebrows raised. "Okay?"

"Got it," the man said.

Next, her gaze settled on September. "Detective, can I help you?" she asked.

September was slightly surprised this woman was aware of her previous job. "Is the chef ill, too?"

"No. He's just . . . excitable. Is Lucy in there?" She hitched her chin at the closed door.

"If she's the woman in the red dress, then yes."

"Okay. You might as well go on to dinner. I'll take care of things." She held out one arm toward September and gestured to the stairs with her other.

"Are you Mrs. Crissman?" September asked, confirming what she'd already deduced from seeing the blonde buzzing around the event, a woman on a mission.

She offered a fleeting smile of surprise. "Yes, I'm Kate. But please, let's all move upstairs now."

"I will in a minute."

"It's probably the flu," Kate Crissman told her flatly.

"Or food poisoning," September said, responding to her officiousness.

"No one else is sick," Kate said quickly. "The chef's fine."

So far, September thought. "Do you need help getting him to the car?"

"Kate!"

A male voice called from above, and September saw Abbott Crissman had made it upstairs and leaned over the railing, signaling Kate Crissman with sharp gestures to march up to the gallery. Kate threw September a look, then expelled a breath in frustration and headed for the stairs.

September moved past the two workers, knocked on the cloakroom door, and Lucy Crissman answered.

Layla felt overwhelmed at the blur of faces around the tables. Neil and Courtney were having a baby . . . another boy. She couldn't believe it. How could that be? How could that be happening? Could she use it to her advantage? She certainly hoped so. Was it even true? Neil hadn't denied it, and he was really upset Courtney had let the cat out of the bag. How many weeks along was she? Enough to know she was having a boy . . . unless that was a lie, although again, Neil hadn't denied her words.

She'd attempted to follow Lucy and John, but her father had muscled his way past her and hissed that he would handle the situation. All he needed to keep the benefit from devolving into chaos after John's sudden illness was Layla to help her brother in keeping up family appearances, so she'd let herself be carried by the crowd to the second floor.

Now she felt lost, marooned, islanded. Into her field of vision came Jerome Wolfe. He seemed to be considering where he wanted to sit. She knew there was a seating arrangement, but she didn't feel like fighting her way through the tables to find where Kate had positioned her. It wouldn't be anywhere with anyone important, which was fine, but she suspected she might be placed somewhere in the back, because Kate wouldn't want Layla's hosting to interfere with her own, and there was no doubt Kate and Lyle would be near the central podium.

"Where are you supposed to be?" Wolfe asked her, inclining his head toward the tables.

"I don't know."

"I'm right over there," he said, holding out a hand toward one of the larger tables that could be considered the front of the room. "Care to join me?"

"I have a place reserved somewhere."

"Well, I have a plus-one who didn't show. Why don't you take her seat?"

The last thing Layla wanted was to get embroiled in a conversation with Jerome Wolfe. Her head was filled with Neil and Courtney and their baby and she didn't like Wolfe; he probably felt much the same about her. "I don't think so."

"Why not? Dad might not approve?"

She glanced to where she knew her father would be seated. It was the largest table, right next to where Jerome

Wolfe's two seats were. Lyle and the still-empty spot reserved for Kate were on one side of Wolfe's two. Lyle kept looking sideways toward Wolfe, now and then at Layla, then his gaze would slide to the crowd, almost as if he were searching for a particular face. Probably Kate's.

"Don't let me be all alone in between your father and brother," Wolfe pressed.

She was about to turn him down, but then her gaze fell on Neil and Courtney. Pregnant Courtney . . .

"Sure, why not?" she agreed.

Wolfe jauntily extended his elbow to her, but Layla wasn't about to go that far. She ignored the offer and preceded him to the seat next to her brother.

"What are you doing here?" Lyle demanded sharply.

"Accepting an invitation."

"From who?"

"Me." Wolfe laid one hand on Lyle's shoulder before taking the chair on the opposite side of her.

Lyle looked like he wanted to say something more. His lips moved, and the skin stretched over his eyes. Instead, he jerked his gaze from both Layla and Jerome and glared straight ahead.

Layla's eyes wanted to stray back toward Neil and his girlfriend, but she forced herself to focus on Lyle. "Isn't this what Dad wants?" she asked softly, out of the side of her mouth. "Us to be entertaining the enemy?"

"You changing your mind about Stonehenge?"

"Not even close."

Abbott appeared, looking slightly flushed. He did a double-take on Layla seated beside Wolfe, opened his mouth as if to object, then, he, too, clamped his lips into a tight line. Like son, like father.

Kate showed up moments later as the din of the crowd filled the area. All around Layla, people were reaching for the bottles of wine in the center of the table and pouring glasses, passing them around as the salad course was delivered.

Lyle hadn't touched the bottle on their table, but the couple next to him asked if he minded if they poured. He shook his head as Kate took her seat. She shot a frown Layla's way.

"You have a place at a different table," she said. "We're all supposed to host separate tables."

"I asked her to sit by me," Wolfe said, looking past Layla and Lyle to meet Kate's surprised eyes.

"How's John?" Layla asked Kate.

"I think Lucy's taking him home." She muttered, "Another table without a host."

Taking him home . . . If Lucy and John left, she would be facing another conundrum: no ride home. She ignored the glass of wine Wolfe poured her and pushed back from the table. "I think I'll check on them."

"They're bringing our entrées right now," Kate said tightly.

Sure enough, the catering staff were carrying up trays laden with plates of salmon atop beds of creamy risotto.

"Layla."

Neil's voice sent a sudden shiver down her spine. He'd gotten up from his table to come to hers. She'd seen him scoot his chair back as soon as she did, but she'd hoped it was just a coincidence. Of course not. But she couldn't talk to him. Not now. Not ever. She was still reeling from Courtney's blurt about the baby, and beyond that she was afraid she could say something that would hurt her case. Or maybe Neil would engage her in a battle of words, twisting everything out of proportion.

"I wanted to explain about what Courtney said."

"I think I got it."

"I'm not . . . we're not really together."

Layla keyed in on him. Her heart was still racing from too much adrenaline. "But you're having a baby together."

"It's complicated."

His expression was earnest, but she didn't trust it for a nanosecond. That much, she'd learned.

Courtney was looking over at them like she was just bursting with further news. Neil shot her a dark look that made her face fall.

"Does she know you're not together?" Layla asked.

"I've made my position clear."

"Really? Like you did with me? Oh, wait, no . . ." She lifted a hand to stop him before he began. "I signed the papers you sent me. I'm just not sure I understood the terms completely."

"You and I could work things out better between us."

She lifted her brows. "There's nothing to work out. We're done."

"You're not going to win that lawsuit," he said in a rush.

"I think I might," she lied. She knew it was a long shot. But Neil seemed to be harboring doubts, so she was going to go with it.

"We're not going into court." He was adamant. "If it's money you want, let's talk."

"I want Eddie. Period. I don't want money."

"We could settle for say . . . another twenty thousand more than I already gave you."

Layla blinked at him, speechless. She had no intention of taking the money, but it was his attitude that resonated. He sounded almost . . . afraid.

Misinterpreting, he doubled down. "I could write you a check tonight."

"I'm not taking your money. I'm trying to give you back what you gave me. I could write *you* a check tonight!"

"That's ridiculous."

Courtney had been hovering in the background, undoubtedly at Neil's direction, because she was antsy and jittery and staring over at them the whole time. She finally couldn't stand it. She hurried over to Neil's side, though the chill he sent her kept her a person's length away.

"Neil was just telling me about the deal he made with you," Layla said.

"You know about the baby?" she burst out.

"There is no deal!" he bellowed at the same moment.

"What about the baby?" Layla asked her.

She opened and shut her mouth twice, looking like the proverbial fish, glancing at Neil, whose face had reddened.

Neil gritted, "There's nothing to tell. Layla, this doesn't have to be this hard between us."

"I think it does. What's going on?"

"Nothing!" Courtney burst out, then looked like she wanted to clap her hand over her mouth, rolling worried eyes Neil's way.

"What about the baby?" Layla repeated. She was missing something and couldn't put her finger on it, but . . . suddenly, she understood. "Ah . . . your pregnancy. To make sure you had a *son*, you must have used in vitro to pick the embryo." Was that the big secret?

Courtney swallowed, still gazing fearfully at Neil, who ignored her. He was focused on Layla with laser intent.

"Okay," Layla said, turning away from him. She couldn't look at him. Didn't understand his obsession with having a male heir. Was soul sick that she'd become a part of his planned dynasty.

"You're trying to turn this into a war," he accused.

Layla trained her gaze down the stairs to the entry hall. Several workers with buckets and mops and an array of cleaning supplies were just finishing the grand entryway. One of them was staring at the closed anteroom door, her gray hair pulled back into a ponytail at her nape.

"All right," he hissed through his teeth. "Thirty thousand. That's the end of it."

She jerked around to stare at him. "I don't want one cent of your money! Where's this coming from?"

"You sure did before. What happened? Dad finally loosen the purse strings? Give you some power?"

"No." She regretted ever telling him anything about herself and her family. "See you in court," she said, heading toward the stairs.

"Is this where I say 'over my dead body'?" he tossed back.

She wisely declined to answer.

Chapter Fourteen

Kate watched Layla leave her seat at almost the same moment the waitstaff began bringing in trays of entrées and delivering them to the surrounding tables. She kept her eye on Layla, who was in a conversation with Neil Grassley. Moments later, Layla fled to the grand stairway and disappeared.

Inside her head, Kate ran through a series of increasingly pungent swear words. Damn Layla. Damn Lucy and John. Damn everyone who had *no respect* for what she was trying to accomplish here!

Someone asked Kate a question and she answered with a smile, trying to appear attentive as her own plate was laid in front of her. But her mind cast back to what had transpired moments before. Jean-Luc had fallen down in dramatic reaction to the news that John was puking but then had staggered upward, hand on his heart.

"Do you see this?" he'd screeched. Kate had glanced around. The poached pear and blue cheese salads were lined up on trays, ready to serve, and the salmon and risotto was nearly ready.

"It looks good," she'd said.

"But a guest has collapsed!" he practically screamed.

"Yes, and it better not be what it appears."

"You think this is *my* fault? *My food?*"

"It's unacceptable. Just unacceptable."

"Well, it's not my food," he snarled. "Maybe the gentleman is ill. The flu. Whatever."

"One of our guests is throwing up. If it turns out to be food poisoning . . ."

"It's not my—"

"If you and your staff brought this on—"

At that precise moment, Abbott had barreled into the kitchen, stopping short on seeing Kate. Jean-Luc had drawn himself up, his face turning a dark crimson. Kate had swallowed back her anger, taken Jean-Luc's last explanation and run with it, explaining to her father-in-law that all was well, that John had apparently come down with a form of the flu.

Jean-Luc had turned away to make sure the food was coming out perfectly, and Kate had thought she'd heard him mutter something about him knowing better than to give rich people a discount. Or had that been what she'd thought he'd said, because Abbott had taken her at her word, his own face revealing relief.

"Lucy's taking him home," Abbott said. "Everything's fine here, then?"

"Yes," Kate said.

"We will continue," Jean-Luc answered stiffly.

Abbott had disappeared, returning to the guests, and Kate had looked at Jean-Luc, who'd warned her quite rudely, "Keep your cleanup staff out of my kitchen."

"They won't come in here. They are just trying to help with the cleanup. The maintenance room and laundry are down the hall." Kate had flushed with annoyance.

"Hmph." He'd then turned to one of the waitresses, the

pretty Asian girl who looked scared of Jean-Luc, and barked, "Serve the wine, and don't leave the glasses unattended!"

Hoping against hope that disaster would be averted, Kate left the kitchen, face burning, and beelined for the cloakroom, where the man and woman who'd finished cleaning up John's mess were standing outside the door. She suspected they'd peeked into the kitchen to see what was going on, or maybe they'd thought that's where the problem was, and Jean-Luc had seen them. Whatever the case, their actions had earned her a talking-to by an overrated, narcissistic chef whose food wasn't even half as good as rated!

She'd slowed down in the foyer, aware of the noise from the diners above as the last of them headed up the stairs. Their voices rose in swells of laughter and upbeat chatter, the sounds of people having a good time. For a moment, she'd wanted to cry. Maybe they all didn't know yet, but they would, and when they learned about John vomiting, it would be all they remembered. And Jean-Luc? He could talk all he wanted, but it sure as hell looked like food poisoning to her. What if someone else got sick? It would be the legacy of her Denim and Diamonds event.

She'd been all set to have it out with the maintenance staff when she'd run into that detective, planted in the center of the foyer. And then Lucy had come back in, wearing sneakers. Kate had almost commented on her change of footwear, but with that detective trying to take charge, and Lucy letting her—didn't anyone have any sense of order and protocol any longer?—Kate had been forced to let them work it out and join the party upstairs.

She'd marched upward, crushed and angry. This event was supposed to be a jewel in the crown of her expertise tiara. A fine showing, the one where Abbott realized how important she was to the Crissman empire. But it had all gone so wrong and there was still so much night left. Her stomach was still clenched, and it was all she could do to force a bite of fish into her mouth.

Could John just be ill? Could it be that easily explained? She hoped to hell Lucy got him out of here tout de suite. Maybe . . . maybe then she could avoid the complete catastrophe this whole night was becoming, although she suspected it wouldn't be any better when she sneaked Lyle's phone away from him after he was asleep and she found out about *Pat*.

With that in mind, she poured her husband another glass of wine. It would be better if he was a little bit drunk. Maybe a lot drunk. She could drive them home. Put him to bed. Sneak his phone away . . .

"Thank you," Lucy said to the woman who'd put her arm around one side of John while she'd been on the other, together helping him out of the cloakroom and into the Audi. He'd slumped against the passenger seat, head back, eyes closed, and Lucy had hurried around to the driver's door, yanking it open, giving a wave to the woman, who stood to one side, watching Lucy drive away.

She'd introduced herself as September Westerly, and she had that capable, calm-in-a-crisis demeanor Lucy hadn't known how much she needed until it was offered.

"No trouble," September had assured her. Now, she stood outside Stonehenge's front doors and watched Lucy drive away into a misting rain. Lucy threw a last glance in her rearview, seeing the woman turn back to the door now that Lucy and John were on their way. She wondered if she would be as good at helping strangers.

"So, how was your fuck with the bartender?" John asked.

Lucy's whole body jerked in shock. She glanced over at him, but his eyes were still closed. "I didn't—that's not what happened," she stammered.

"Don't lie."

"I'm not lying."

Silence.

Finally, "Are you going to tell me what happened?"

"I can . . . but are you sure you don't want to see a doctor?"

"No doctor."

More silence. Lucy felt indescribably uncomfortable. She knew she'd hurt John, and she felt bad about that, and a little resentful, but she was consumed with getting him better. Was it food poisoning? Should somebody be doing something? Something to stop the people eating? Someone like Kate?

"How long have you known him?"

"Who? Oh."

John cracked a bloodshot eye at her. "Come on, Lucy."

"I'm thinking about *you*. Maybe we should go to an emergency room."

"Take me there and I'll walk home."

"It wouldn't hurt to be looked at."

"No."

"Fine."

"Did he have a big dick? Did he make you scream in that way you do, 'uh, uh, *uhhh*'?"

"Stop it, John," she said, horrified.

"Where'd you do it?"

"We didn't *do it*." She was starting to get mad, and it was better than feeling like such a heel. "He came on too strong, and I . . . left."

"At the bar? At a motel? His place?"

"Outside the bar."

"*Outside* the bar," he repeated, then lapsed into silence once more. Too late, Lucy realized she shouldn't have said that much because John suddenly inhaled through his nose in disdain. "The night I was there and you came around from the parking lot."

She wasn't going to correct him that she'd been on the other side of the building, locked in an embrace. She just kept her eyes on the road ahead.

John coughed, then coughed again, then leaned forward and puked up a small puddle of bile and liquid.

A roar went up from the crowd, and Kate surfaced to see that Abbott had climbed to his feet, got behind the podium, and was giving a speech. In her peripheral vision, she noticed that the female detective from the foyer had now reached the top of the stairs. As Abbott launched into introductions, the detective looped around the gallery rail to find her table. Kate could just see a lifted hand and figured the woman's handsome husband was signaling her.

She turned her attention back to Abbott, who was rhapsodizing about the rich beauty of the Columbia River Gorge and how all the attendees were making such a huge contribution in putting it back to its former glory. That generated a round of applause.

But Kate's mind wandered . . . Lucy and John must be on their way. Good. She wanted to forget about that unfortunate event and concentrate on the rest of the evening, hope the benefit could be salvaged. It didn't seem like people had been put off by John's vomiting. That was a miracle in itself.

She stole a sideways look at Lyle, whose hand was wrapped around the stem of a glass of red wine, the liquid glinting like rubies under the lights. Lyle was staring at a woman in a black dress with diamond-shaped cutouts down its front, huge holes that showed off fake boobs and smooth skin. Those were her diamonds? The little bitch probably thought that was funny.

At that moment, the woman got up from her chair, tugging at the hem of her short skirt—it hugged her butt like it was Velcroed on and barely kept her hoohaw from showing—as she wandered around the tables and down the aisle toward the ladies' room. Feeling someone's eyes on her, Kate turned back and found Jerome Wolfe regarding her. He lifted his own glass of Cabernet at her, and she, in turn, lifted her glass of Chardonnay. Then she lowered her eyes, feeling breathless and discouraged. He was handsome and successful, and he was going to make them rich with cash.

When she looked up, she saw Lyle was gazing at her in a way that caused her heart to seize for a moment. Had he caught her eyes on Jerome Wolfe? Luckily, he couldn't read her thoughts, though why should she care? Black diamond dress had certainly given him something to ogle.

He's your husband. Get him in bed tonight. You're close to ovulating. Maybe this time you'll get pregnant. Why not?

Movement caught her eye, and she saw that Layla, who'd headed downstairs, had returned, this time trying to stay out of the way of the trays of pear tarte tatin and blue cheese. Kate's stomach awakened, but she squelched her appetite. Not if she intended to keep wearing this dress. She hadn't eaten her meal. She sure as hell wasn't going to start with dessert.

Though she knew Abbott would consider it a transgression, she set down her napkin and got to her feet, working her way to where Layla had stopped near the top of the stairs.

"You need to get out of the way," Kate told her, gesturing to the members of the waitstaff who were ducking about with their trays.

"Don't worry. I'm about to head out," she said.

"You're not leaving yet." Kate glanced at her father-in-law, appearing to hold the crowd in thrall. Abbott was most comfortable when he was on stage in front of hundreds of people.

"I think I've done enough hosting to satisfy my father," Layla said in a flat voice. She almost acted as if her father's edicts were Kate's fault, somehow. For the love of Pete, she just couldn't win with Lyle's sisters.

"We should still make a unified showing."

"You can handle it, Kate."

Kate heard the condescension and burned inside. "Well, it's not my fault John got sick."

"No one said it was. I'll wait till Dad's finished speaking, then I'll tell him that I'm leaving."

Layla headed down the stairs, keeping to one side to avoid one of the young women who was carefully bringing up a tray of drinks.

Frustrated, Kate determinedly made her way back to Lyle's side. She saw he had his cell phone out, though he wasn't looking at it. That would piss off Abbott in a way neither of them could afford.

"Put that away," she said, sotto voce, as she took her seat.

"Where've you been?" he asked.

"Trying to talk Layla out of leaving."

"She's grossed out like the rest of the women."

"People are grossed out?" Kate's heart clutched with concern.

"Some can't eat." He threw a glance to a woman at a table about three over from them. She was as still as a statue and very, very thin. The plate in front of her looked like it hadn't been touched, though as Kate watched, the woman moved bits of salmon around with her fork.

"Anorexia," Kate said.

"What?"

"Well, look at her. If she's grossed out, it's just a convenient excuse for her not to eat."

"She's got nice boobs," Lyle observed.

"Those can be bought," Kate snapped. She wanted to slap him upside the head. He was such a *man* sometimes! Honestly, it was hell being the only grown-up all the time.

Abbott had finished, and now a heavyset woman wearing a denim jacket decorated with rhinestones and a straw cowboy hat, its band made of peacock feathers, had taken his place and was telling them all about the recent travails of the Gorge and the measures they were all taking to improve its viability once more. Kate listened to the drone, but it was just words, words, words, blah, blah, blah.

She let herself fall into a kind of self-imposed fugue to keep herself from being bored to death and heard the ripple of a joke sliding from attendee to attendee, something about a man losing his gorge while trying to save the Gorge. John . . . she realized. This then, was what they would all remember from the benefit.

Lyle heard the joke and snickered. She almost kicked him under the table.

Could the night be worse? she asked herself.

September stopped by the restroom and thoroughly washed her hands before heading back to the dining area, where she spied Jake, who signaled her to their table. He was standing by her chair as she wended her way toward him, and he guided her to a seat next to William Ogden. He was on her right, and on her left was the woman in the diamond choker.

Jake seated himself across from her and behind him, directly in September's line of vision, she could see Jerome Wolfe helping a young woman in a black dress with diamond-shape cutouts running between her breasts to her waist to a chair. She'd stumbled, and now she clung onto his arm for dear life. Clearly, she'd had a few too many. Behind them, a woman was speaking at a podium, her cheery voice reminding them all to have a wonderful time and get ready to bid, bid, bid on the items in the oral auction.

"Everything okay?" Jake asked September.

"Yeah."

The woman in the choker assured her, "We were just served, so the food's still hot. Sometimes it pays to be seated away from the action." She didn't look like she felt that way, however.

"Were you with the sick man?" Ogden asked her.

"Uh, yes. He and his wife are on their way to a doctor now, I believe."

"Food poisoning?" The woman held a hand to her chest. "Should we be eating?" This was a moot point; her plate was clean.

September picked up her fork. "I think we're okay. And, well, I'm starved," she said, and that, apparently, relaxed them a little.

She glanced over the rail to see another of Abbott's children—Layla, she believed—standing in the massive foyer, alone.

Chapter Fifteen

Layla felt a headache coming on. Could be a rager if she didn't get herself under control. She would have liked to blame it on the fact that she'd had a glass of champagne, maybe a glass and a half, but it had more to do with her tense arguments with Neil, and that she hadn't eaten enough to sustain herself today.

Her mind went to the auto accident that had left her barren and had taken another woman's life. Just like it always did when she felt low and a little out of control. She couldn't completely dissuade herself of the guilt, but it was at these times that she did her best painting, a strange development resulting from that terrible event. She felt like painting now. Getting out of here. Running away.

But she would have to literally run; she had no way home.

She heard the oral auction begin. Dessert had been served. Speeches were over. Time to break out the pocketbooks.

Did she want to stick around to see what her painting went for? No. Definitely not. She just wanted to go home. Kate and Lyle were the most likely candidates to give her a ride, but they would stay to the bitter end. Same with her father.

You could ask Neil.

Ha, ha. You're just so funny, Layla.

She wandered toward the kitchen but was met by the Asian server who guarded the door like a sentry. "Chef wants no one in the kitchen but staff."

Layla nodded and moved away. Fine; she didn't care anyway. Aimless, she strolled across the grand entry, listening to the rapid-fire patter of the auctioneer. She reached the door to the cloakroom and pushed it open, and was immediately hit by the sharp, head-clearing scents of chemical products. The cleaning staff had left the room spotless.

She felt almost envious that Lucy had gotten to leave early.

She stood in the cloakroom for a good twenty minutes. The din of noise from the guests was a low roar of talk and laughter, which was lifting by degrees as the night wore on. She could hear the auctioneer. Whatever was being currently auctioned off was creating a wave of raucous conversation that almost sounded like shouting. The volume of the crowd was becoming ever louder, a by-product of the temporary deafness that occurred when people overimbibed.

She walked back into the foyer and was hit by a wave of noise.

". . . going once, going twice . . . *sold* for twelve thousand dollars!" the auctioneer screeched to be heard.

The noise level fell off. Dropped into a collective gasp.

Holy guacamole . . . not her painting . . . not purchased by Neil! Did he think he could buy her off this way?

No . . . He'd offered her thirty thousand. *Thirty thousand!* He clearly thought she had a case, was a threat to his plans. What did he think she could do?

"Thank you, Mr. Wolfe," the auctioneer declared to a rousing handclapping.

Wolfe? *Wolfe?*

Then her father's voice through the microphone. "Layla? Where are you? Come on up and thank Jerome for his generous gift to the Friends of the Columbia River Gorge. . . ."

* * *

It was Neil Layla saw first as she mounted the stairs to the gallery, a smile pinned on her face. A sick smile, she suspected, though she tried hard to appear grateful and happy. Neil seemed a bit shaken. By the sale of her painting to Wolfe, or something else? She realized he'd been one of the bidders in a lively back-and-forth she'd nearly blocked while she was in the cloakroom. So, he'd battled with Jerome Wolfe for her painting.

What did either of them hope to achieve?

Wolfe was regarding her with lazy amusement as she greeted him. She shook his hand, the diners all watching, then the last item was placed up for bid, a trip to a donor's vacation home on Hawaii, the Big Island. As the bidders began again, Wolfe inclined his head to the hallway leading away from the gallery toward the west bedrooms. Thankfully, the corridor was empty; no guests to overhear them, the hum of conversation barely audible.

"Why did you pay that much?" she asked as she followed him.

"Why shouldn't I? You don't think it's worth it?"

Word games. Just like Neil. Layla answered flatly, "No."

"You're denigrating your own work. Why, I'd—"

"Shut up. Excuse me for saying it, but shut . . . up."

Surprised, he stared at her, silver eyebrows twin peaks over dark eyes.

Layla held up her hands. "Do you want my support in the sale? Buying my painting isn't going to change my opinion."

"Maybe I paid too much."

"You did. I just said so."

He leaned back a little, assessing her. "They said you were the easy one."

"Who are *they*?" she bristled.

"I was told Lucy was the tough one."

"My father or brother, or both? Doesn't matter. You're wasting your time trying to curry favor with either one of us. Lucy and I don't want you buying Stonehenge. We want to keep it in the family."

"There's nothing I can do to sway you?"

He was a little smoother than Neil, but they were cut from the same cloth. She said with a shrug, "You don't have to quit trying, of course. Up to you."

"What if I said I enjoy your company?"

"All five minutes of it that we've had?"

"More than five minutes, at the table. And I do enjoy your company."

"Okay. Fine. That enjoyment's about to come to an end." She glanced back the way they'd come. The event was beginning to break up and she would be able to say her good-byes to her father, collect her coat, and leave.

"Maybe we could extend it?"

She was growing really tired of his banter, clearly something that usually worked for him. But then she considered. "You came here alone?"

"My date canceled at the last minute."

"So there's room in your car for a passenger?"

"Maybe."

"I could use a ride home."

He looked pleased. "Will giving you a ride help my case?"

"No." If she hadn't been so desperate to leave, she would have walked away right then. The prospect of several captive hours with the man wasn't something she looked forward to. But . . . "You'll have the entire trip to try to convince me."

His slow smile was fitting. So like his name: wolfish.

"I'm going to find my father. I'll meet you in the entry."

She nearly ran into Neil and Courtney as she left Wolfe and walked back toward the crowd. Courtney was being shunned by Neil. He was really icing her out. Because of her bomb about being pregnant? Or maybe that she was so excited she couldn't be trusted to keep their secret. Her words had made Layla realize Courtney and Neil had selected a male embryo to assure they were getting a boy. When had all this come down? It hadn't been that many months since Neil and Layla were still considered a couple.

Unless he'd been seeing Courtney, planning this, at the same time he was dating Layla.

Naomi's words flitted across her mind. Courtney being *very interested* in Neil and Layla's coming baby.

"There you are," Neil said, his gaze moving past Layla to where Jerome was coming up behind her.

Jerome said, "Sorry about outbidding you."

Courtney answered, "Oh, Neil wasn't serious. He was just trying to run you up!"

"That right?" Wolfe asked Neil.

Neil was almost apoplectic, furious with Courtney. Layla felt a small glow of happiness. *Schadenfreude.* There was something to be said for feeling joy at someone else's expense.

"I think your father's looking for you," Neil said to Layla, his jaw vise tight.

"I'll go tell him good-bye."

And because she could, she shot a glance back toward Jerome Wolfe and said, "I'll only be a few minutes."

"Take your time," he said expansively, looking at Neil. "My chariot awaits. . . ."

Neil gamely tried to hide his stunned reaction, but Courtney just gaped at Layla, the flash of competitive anger in her gaze saying clearer than words how she felt about Layla leaving with Jerome Wolfe.

"Jesus Christ, Lucy. I'm not going in there."

"Come on, John," Lucy muttered, fighting her growing anger.

"I'm fine!"

"You're not fine. You're sick. You've been sick all over the floor this whole ride."

She'd pulled beneath the emergency room portico at Laurelton General. Now she yanked on the emergency brake and glared at him, torn between real concern and frustration. She didn't know what to do for him. His stubbornness had no place here.

"I just want to go home and go to bed. Is that so impossible for you to do?"

"It's possible. But why won't you let someone look at you, now that we're here?"

"No one else came down with food poisoning," he said, referring to the fact that recent texts from Abbott and Kate had revealed that, at least so far, no one else was sick.

"It could be something else," Lucy said.

"It's probably the fucking norovirus. That's what it feels like. Why should I go in there and infect everyone else?" He glared back at her, pale and sweating.

"Fine. But all I know to do is give you lots of fluids and Aleve or ibuprofen or something."

"Good enough," he grunted.

One of the emergency room staff, a male nurse or orderly, came out the door and looked at her. Lucy heard a distant siren and realized she was in the way. The man called to her, "Are you bringing someone in?"

She rolled down the window. "No. I'll move my car." She sent the window back up and pulled through the portico and back onto the street.

John sighed heavily. "I'm going to sue that fucking caterer."

"So, it's not the norovirus."

He leaned his head against the window and coughed.

You should be nicer. He's really sick.

"Or maybe you did this. You and your bartender boyfriend."

"Oh, John."

They drove the rest of the way in silence.

* * *

Layla's buoyant mood lasted for about ten minutes into the ride inside Jerome Wolfe's charcoal Mercedes before she started feeling both awkward and weary. He'd paid far too much for her painting and she didn't know how to feel about that. And she wasn't going to change her mind about Stonehenge, so she'd really cadged a ride from him on false pretenses. And it hadn't helped that when she'd said good-bye to her father, Abbott had been so clearly delighted that she was leaving with him. He was reading far too much into it, and Layla hadn't been able to set him straight with Wolfe standing right there.

"I really appreciate this," she said now, for about the third time.

"My pleasure," he said, also for about the third time. But then he slid her a look and said, "I'll find a way to get payment back."

"For the ride?"

"For the ride . . . and the painting. I did overpay, didn't I?" He slid her a grin.

"I told you you did. But it's for a good cause."

"I wanted that prick, Grassley, to sweat. For all his supposed money, he's a cheap son of a bitch."

"You bought the painting to show him up?"

"Well, like you said, it's for a good cause. Also, maybe this'll give you a little more . . . I don't know, *cachet*, as an artist. Overspending could be good for you."

"It doesn't work that way," she said.

"Doesn't it?"

"No."

"If I pay enough for your work, and then talk you up among the people I know, some of them pretty heavy hitters in the local art scene, it'll make a difference."

Layla dropped her gaze from his, her heart starting a slow drumbeat. She didn't like his words or his tone.

"You don't think so?" he asked.

"I prefer to think someone would appreciate my work on its own merits."

"You do have nice . . . merits." Again, that sideways glance.

Layla had been propositioned enough times to recognize the beginnings of a pass. A pretty heavy-handed one. "Does that line actually work for you?"

"First time I've tried it."

"Well, I—" She sucked in a surprised breath when he dropped a hand to her jean-clad knee and ran it up the inside of her thigh. She clamped her legs together and grabbed his hand before it reached her crotch, but just barely. Mutely, she stared at him, hoping she looked angry and determined instead of horrified.

He kept his hand where it was, held by hers.

"I don't like Neil, but he said you were a good lay . . . Lay . . . la . . ." he whispered.

Her pulse jumped. No. That was a lie. Had to be. Neil would do many things, but she didn't think spilling their sex life to the likes of Jerome Wolfe was one of them.

"I think you'd better move your hand," said Layla.

"Which way?" He pushed against hers.

She held him back and stated coldly, "This your way to win me over about Stonehenge?"

He chuckled. "I don't really care what you think about selling *Wolfe Lodge* to me. You and your sister think you have so much power, and the deal's done. I was just being polite, acting like I cared what you thought."

"Why did you buy the painting?" she sputtered.

"Your father thinks I'm a savior. Your brother, too. I figured why not add to that cred. And Grassley was so obviously eager to prove something to you, or maybe your family, by buying it that I had to shut him down."

"You had to," she repeated.

"So, now I'm thinking a little fifty-fifty here," he suggested. "I do something nice for you, you do something nice for me."

She very deliberately picked up his hand and shoved it away from her. For half a second, she thought he was going to grab at her again, but instead he shrugged.

When she set her jaw and stared through the windshield, calculating how long it would be before they reached her home, he tsk-tsked with his tongue, then said, long-suffering, "Now you're going to be mad, right?"

She could feel tears burning behind her eyes, but she'd be damned if she let him see. Why did she always pick the wrong guys? *Even for a ride home.* It was humiliating how good she'd felt in those few moments when she'd thought she had some power over Neil and Courtney.

She stopped talking. He hadn't made his move on her until they were over an hour into the ride. Somehow, she managed to hold it together until he pulled up in front of the coffee shop below her condo. She jumped out, having to pull at the handle twice in her haste, fearing for a wild moment that he'd locked her in, but finally the door opened, and he chuckled at her terror.

Face burning, she managed a tight, "Thank you," racing to the door with the steps that led to the second floor.

"My pleasure . . ." were the words that followed her.

Ducking her head against a light drizzle, feeling exposed and vulnerable, she used her key fob and pushed through the door, hurrying inside. She closed the door behind her and took the stairs to the second floor. She half-screamed at finding a man standing outside her door, a backpack slung over one shoulder and slumped against the wall.

"Oh, shit. Ian," she said, recognizing him belatedly.

"Hey, babe."

She collected herself with an effort. "How'd you get in the outside door?"

"Had to stand in the rain till someone took pity on me." She saw then that his man bun had been drenched. "That old guy on three recognized me." His eyes slid over her. "You look good."

She was so discombobulated, all she could do was nod jerkily. Pulling out her keys, she slid the one for her condo into the lock, pushing the door open. She didn't want to deal with Ian. She wanted to be alone.

But she couldn't just slam the door in his face. "What are you doing here?" she asked.

"Well, I wanted to see you. I just . . . missed you."

"Yeah?" She stood in the doorway, looking out at him.

"Yeah."

He had a bedraggled-cat-in-the-rain quality that got to her even when she knew it shouldn't. "Why now?"

"Can I come in for a little while?"

It was after ten o'clock, climbing to eleven. Not horribly late for a Saturday night, but Layla felt like she'd been on a marathon of keeping up appearances. All she wanted to do was lock herself in and think over the events of the evening, try to pick through what had really happened.

But Ian had never been a guy who made her feel small, or scared, or a pawn in some larger game. She opened the door wider.

"Thanks," he said in relief, dropping the backpack near her couch. He was sporting a new blondish goatee that was also dewed with rain.

She had a feeling he was looking for a place to crash and she was an easy mark. "I'm going to bed. You can have the foldout," she said, pointing to the couch.

He lifted his hands. "Thanks, Lay. I mean it."

Sure thing.

"You look great in that, by the way." He indicated her jumpsuit. "You dieting?"

"Just not able to eat."

She left him sorting out the hide-a-bed, and fifteen minutes later, she lay in her own bed, staring at the ceiling. She grabbed the extra pillow and placed it over her own face, fighting back the urge to emit a primal scream.

Kate listened to Lyle's breathing, which was uneven at best. He was on the edge of wakefulness and she didn't dare grab his phone until he was fast asleep.

Though the Denim and Diamonds benefit hadn't been the debacle she'd feared after John had gotten sick—she'd expected his possible food poisoning to ripple through the crowd at some point and scare them all silly, which hadn't happened, thank you, God!—neither had it been a rousing success. While no one else came down with the same symptoms of whatever he'd caught—undoubtedly some bad germ—the crowd seemed fairly restrained, enjoying themselves but not with the energy she'd hoped for.

The auction had proved a success, though, and Kate was still reeling over the fact that Jerome Wolfe had purchased Layla's painting for *twelve thousand dollars*! For God's sake, was the man made of money? Layla had seemed more stricken than happy at first, though maybe that had to do with the fact that Neil Grassley seemed to be squiring around a new woman. Kate couldn't decide what she felt about that. The new woman was pretty enough, but she didn't hold a candle to Layla, especially since her weight loss. Or maybe it was just that Layla looked like a country western star in that getup.

Maybe she should have gotten Naomi, the surrogate's, number from Layla when she'd first offered it to her. Because Lyle had given her the cold shoulder almost as soon as Kate had slipped beneath the covers. No sex tonight, although she'd tried her damnedest, squeezing close, cuddling, massaging his limp penis for all she was worth. She'd had a mental picture of her fertility falling from a tap and circling the drain as Lyle ignored every desperate attempt she made to get his juices flowing. But she'd lost that battle. The wine she'd purposely plied him with—which, yes, she should have thought through more—had won out. Alcohol had never been Lyle's friend in the bedroom.

Kate stewed on that a moment or two longer, feeling low and miserable, until she kicked herself back to reality. Why should she expect to get pregnant this time, when they'd had oodles of earlier chances that hadn't panned out?

She thought back to the benefit, reminding herself that John's illness hadn't completely derailed its success. All the same, that didn't mean Kate was out of the woods just yet. She shuddered at the possible headlines she could see over the next few days. As much as she'd looked forward to the event, now she wanted it to pass through the news cycle in a hurry.

As she fretted, Lyle rolled onto his side. His breathing slowed, began evening out. Okay, well. The night wasn't a complete bust if she could get into his text and email lists. His cell was on the nightstand, inches from his hand.

Kate eased out of bed and stood for a moment in the semidarkness. Faint illumination from their outdoor lighting slipped through a crack in the curtains that covered the French doors leading to their back deck and yard. The house was Craftsman style, small but recently updated. In fact, that renovation had brought the taxman around and, of course, he'd noticed their new kitchen at once. The man's weasely, prying eyes had led to him scratching out some numbers, even though Kate had tried hard not to give him too much information. Didn't matter. He'd ended up calculating their renovation costs on the high end, and their property taxes had zoomed up. Highway robbery, that's what it was. Everybody with their hand out. Lyle had shrugged and said it was the price of living in an area with good schools. She'd nearly had a conniption fit right then and there. Good schools? Good *schools*? What was he thinking? She worked at a *private school*, for Pete's sake. Where was the tax break for *them*?

Her breath started coming faster at the thought, and she took a couple of moments to calm herself down. Wouldn't do to wake Lyle up. Wouldn't do at all. She tiptoed around the bed and gently lifted the phone. She then let herself out of the bedroom as quietly as she could and moved down the hall to the main bathroom, tucked herself inside.

Switching on the light, she tried a few last numbers and suddenly *voilà*, the screen showed all the icons for his apps. Yes! She pressed the little cartoon bubble that indicated texts and the screen opened to his list of last messages. She recognized many of the names and was curious about what he'd texted with Abbott and John, but she was more interested in what he'd sent to Pat.

Pat.

Kate unconsciously ground her teeth together. This person—this *evil* person—was at the root of her problems with Lyle.

Not problems, she reminded herself immediately. This was just a momentary speed bump along the highway of her marriage. It was nothing. A little slowdown she was going to fix.

Unfortunately, a quick scan didn't list any Pat. There were several messages that were listed from just initials, so she looked for a "P," but, again, there was nothing. Well, of course. That had been their little joke—way back when. She sorted through the texts from most recent to further back, her hands growing a little slippery as she sweated from tension. If Lyle should wake up and see his phone was gone . . .

But that didn't bear thinking about.

She checked several text chains from people he seemed to know through business. She tried to see if any of them could be Pat, but it didn't seem so. A text chain with the initials LP was likely from a woman—there was a reference to a pink scarf sometime back, which put new meaning to the meeting Lyle and *she* had scheduled for Monday at two p.m. at, of all places, the Pembroke Inn.

Jealousy ran through Kate's veins like green poison, but though she read that text chain three times, trying to absorb the tone, she couldn't rightly say it was romantic. It appeared to be a series of meetings, the pink scarf being a clue to LP's identity. Maybe they hadn't known each other that well. Or maybe that was the way they made it look on purpose. To throw anyone off who happened to view it.

Or maybe it was a blind assignation, a quick fuck with a stranger.

"Mom?"

The phone squirted from her fingers at the sound of her name from behind the bathroom door. She juggled frantically, trying to catch it. *Oh shit. Oh shit. Oh shit.* She managed to catch it by her fingertips before it got completely away, and she drew it in to her chest like a wide receiver cradled a football, her heart pounding so hard it hurt.

"What?" she whispered through the panels to Daphne.

"I don't feel good."

Kate set the phone on the counter and cracked open the door. "What's wrong?" she asked, trying not to sound impatient. She had to get the phone back before Lyle woke up.

"My stomach hurts."

Kate's own stomach clenched. Oh no. Was this the same

thing John came down with? Maybe something Daphne had gotten from Evie? Please no.

"Well, come in here," she said, drawing Daphne inside. "If you have to throw up, just go ahead. I'll be right back." She swept up the phone and headed down the hall.

"But you'll come back?" she called, as if she needed reassurance.

Kate nodded, waving at Daphne to keep quiet.

Slipping inside the bedroom once more, she listened for Lyle's breathing, barely able to hear it over her thundering heart. She realized he was still fast asleep, and she tiptoed back to his nightstand, replaced the phone, then softly retraced her footsteps to the hallway, willing her heart rate to decelerate.

When she got back to the bathroom, Daphne was lying on the bath mat in the fetal position.

"Oh, sweetie," Kate said, brushing back her child's hair. Now that the phone was safely away, she could concentrate on her daughter, though her mind was racing along its own course. Could the Monday meeting at the Pembroke be with Pat? And could Pat be Patricia, who'd once worked at Crissman & Wolfe? Why would the initials be LP? Was it a middle name, something like Linda Pat?

It would be easy enough to find out if she could figure out a way to be at the Pembroke in disguise and see who showed up.

"I don't think I'm gonna throw up," Daphne said.

"Oh, honey. Okay."

Daphne shuffled to the toilet but curled up on the floor again.

After several moments, Kate asked, "Do you want to go back to your room? I can bring you a bucket, just in case."

"Okay."

Daphne slowly got to her feet and walked back to her bed. Kate tucked her in, then hurried to the kitchen, finding the white plastic bucket she kept under the sink. She quickly brought it back to her daughter, who was still lying down.

When upchucking didn't seem imminent, Kate moved to the door. "If you need me, just call. I'll leave both your door and mine open."

"Okay."

As Kate turned to leave, Daphne asked, "Mom? What were you doing with Dad's phone?"

Chapter Sixteen

Lucy sat at the dining room table, her chin propped on her hand, regarding the remains of breakfast after she'd rushed out to take Evie to school, leaving John in bed. This norovirus was much worse than she'd initially imagined—coming out of both ends, as it were—and yes, she believed it was the norovirus, because no one else had gotten sick at Saturday night's benefit and it had been practically a week. Of course, someone could come down with the norovirus at any time—it was highly contagious—but as far as she knew, that hadn't happened yet. Kate had said Daphne had been ill on Saturday, but she hadn't thrown up or shown other symptoms, so that didn't seem to be part of the equation. John had gotten better for a few days, so she'd thought maybe the worst had passed, but now he didn't want to get out of bed.

Maybe John had picked up the germ somewhere else. Lucy had quizzed him about his whereabouts and who he was with prior to the benefit, but he was too sick to do much more than wave her off . . . or make another snide comment about "the bartender." She was really getting tired of that. He didn't even know what had really transpired, and Lucy had zero motivation to tell him. She had no defense for her actions, and she certainly regretted them, but did they need a total postmortem? He knew she'd done something and for the moment, that was good enough for both of them. She'd made a poor choice. If he wanted a full accounting when he was well, she'd see about it then. For now, she just wanted him better. If it was the norovirus, three days was usually the worst of it. She was counting the minutes.

Picking up several dirty plates, she carried them to the sink, her mind moving on to her next problem. She was going to have to quit her job. There was nothing for her there any longer. Her father and brother had begun treating her like an outsider even before this downsizing of the company and the pending sale of Stonehenge. So, fine, she would be the outsider. Layla had made herself a life away from the family business; so would she.

Layla.

Lucy felt guilty about ditching Layla to face Neil and his new girlfriend alone, but criminy—that was her new word; old-fashioned but expressing just the right amount of mild frustration to get the point across without hitting the bitch range—she had enough problems of her own. And anyway, Layla had seemed fine when Lucy called to apologize. She said she'd gotten a ride home with someone at the benefit but hadn't elaborated when Lucy had said she was sorry for running out on her, even though she'd had a good reason.

Layla had told her not to worry. Everything had worked out, which had eased Lucy's guilt, but there was something odd in her sister's tone, something she'd asked about but Layla had brushed off.

"I'm going back to Dallas Denton on Wednesday," Layla had said, changing the subject. "I want to move ahead with the lawsuit full-bore. Neil is trying to be nice, and that's almost worse than when he puts his cards on the table."

Dallas Denton. Lucy had winced at the name. With everything else going on, she had pushed that piece aside, but every time Layla mentioned Dallas's name it was like microphone feedback, screeching in her ears. She wanted to clap her hands over her ears and moan.

Dallas Denton. He whose name could never be mentioned.

But now he had entered her circle of acquaintances and friends. Her sister's lawyer no less. She tried speaking his name as she put soap in the dishwasher and hit the Start button. "Dallas Denton."

It wasn't so bad . . . was it so bad? No. It was a long time ago, and she had other worries now.

And let's face it, he'd given her Evie.

Walking to the bathroom, she looked at herself in the mirror. She squinched up her face, examining the lines around her eyes. Not too many. She had to work pretty hard to make them appear, thank God. Still, she'd barely been more than a kid when she'd connected with Dallas. A freshman at Oregon State University. Over ten years ago. At a fraternity party no less.

She'd gone to the party reluctantly, attending with a long-ago friend who'd begged her to go, though in truth that friend had only wanted to be with her boyfriend. She'd promised Lucy she wouldn't just lock herself in a room with him, which is exactly what ended up happening. So, Lucy had wandered through the house, alone and somewhat morose, ready to leave and walk back to the dorm alone. That's when she noticed Dallas Denton, who apparently wasn't a fraternity brother, but she hadn't learned that till later. She knew he was older—quite a bit older, as it turned out—and she'd learned later that he'd been there, much like she had, at the behest of a friend who was trying to corral his younger brother, a frat boy who loved every bad thing there was about being a frat boy. Dallas had agreed to try to help the friend with his brother, only it hadn't worked out that way as, not so many months later, said brother ended up getting in trouble for hazing and was subsequently kicked out of the fraternity and the university.

What Lucy noticed that night was that Dallas Denton was tall, dark, handsome, and serious. The seriousness was something she prized in a man, and it was in short supply among the first-year boys she met on campus. Dallas's sense of gravitas even while he smiled and joked with the other guys drew her to him. He was having a beer from the tapped keg, drinking from a plastic cup. He wasn't guzzling it. He wasn't acting crude or rude or dumb. A number of girls came up to him and tried to win his attention, but though he was polite, he didn't give them any encouragement, so most of them drifted away, looking back hopefully to see if he might notice them, but he never did.

After a time, he headed upstairs to a game room, and Lucy moseyed up there herself a short time later. Dallas was watching a couple of guys compete in a video game matchup . . . and he was taking shit from a shorter, muscular guy who thought he was God's gift, in Lucy's biased opinion.

"C'mon, man. Loosen up. Your brother knew how to loosen up. There are stories to be told . . . stories to be told, to be sure."

"Long-ago stories," Dallas answered agreeably enough. "He's a cop now."

"But he's still a brother." He held out his arms and shifted around to encompass the mostly shitty decor of the older building that housed their fraternity. "You never were a brother here."

"Nope."

The shorter man was called Jimbo, which was a short form for his name, Jim Borden. No matter that Dallas clearly had no interest in the whole fraternity scene, Jimbo wouldn't give up on him. He kept invoking Dallas's younger brother's name, Lucas, who was several years out of school already. Lucy learned later that Dallas himself was through law school and in practice at a well-respected Portland firm, but at the time she hadn't been interested in much more than getting to know him.

"C'mon, man," Jimbo encouraged. "Chugalug! Take a little walk on the wild side for once in your life. We got shots of everything you could want downstairs. Jell-O shots for the ladies, too." He leered around, his gaze briefly settling on Lucy, who was standing to one side.

"I'm fine," Dallas told him.

Dallas's friend was somewhere in the fraternity house with his little brother, hanging with him as a way to monitor him, from what Lucy picked up from the conversations around her, and it left Dallas in much the same boat as Lucy, waiting on their friends.

Lucy was also drinking from the keg, and eventually Jimbo noticed her hanging around and suddenly decided she was the one he would dangle in front of Dallas as bait. She laughingly tried to call him off, but he was loud and persuasive and, well, she did want to meet Dallas, so she let herself go along with Jimbo. Though she wasn't really thinking of it in those terms that night, Dallas was everything she was looking for in a man. Jimbo was just a means to an end for her, and he was kind of amusing in his let's-all-get-drunk-and-naked—apparently, one of his favorite sayings—way.

She tried to talk a bit to Dallas, but he barely looked at her.

And then . . . there was a gap of time she couldn't quite recall. In vague flashes of remembrance, she recalled being in Dallas's arms on a bed somewhere. They were kissing, and then making love. Or, rather, having sex, because she couldn't really credit that to lovemaking when she could barely remember it, and he didn't seem to recall it much either.

He fell asleep almost immediately afterward, and Lucy lay beside him. She slowly sobered up, naked and surprised and somehow . . . happy? She'd wanted him, and well, she'd gotten him, sort of. She was thrilled to be in his arms. She liked feeling his muscular back and his legs tangled with hers. She hadn't experimented much sexually. It all seemed too messy and problematic, and yet she'd gone to bed with a man she barely knew and had no regrets . . . at least then. . . .

She could barely credit that attitude now. What had she been thinking? Nothing, apparently, past that moment.

She wasn't on the pill. Wasn't prepared in any way. Hadn't even thought it through! It was so unlike her, that it took her a long time to admit that maybe, just maybe, she'd been roofied. There was that gap and then they were in bed . . . She wasn't sure who had initiated their coupling, but she kind of thought it was her. She could recall kissing him, standing up, reaching on her tiptoes . . . and then they were in the bedroom . . .

Criminy . . . no, that wasn't good enough. *Catastrophe*, like the Parisian dog/rabbits in that cartoon. That was the word. Catastrophe. She'd finished out the year and then had Evie, and then studied online and took night classes, working for her father during the day.

Dallas Denton never called, and when she called him, he pretended he didn't even know her name. Or maybe he didn't. She thought about telling him they were having a child, but the words stuck in her throat. He was so politely distant and disinterested and basically waiting for her to get to the reason for her call, which she declared was a lawsuit she still had to think about. When he asked her her name again, she lied and said she was Lucia Rochet, a fake name she'd sometimes used in her youth, when she'd wanted to make herself sound more exotic.

Over the years, she'd worked up a grievance that had hardened into resentment against him. She wouldn't tell anyone the truth, not even Layla, who only knew Evie's conception was the product of a one-night stand. Layla had asked carefully, "And you didn't use birth control?"

Lucy had thought about excusing herself with the roofie theory, but instead she just shook her head and let the story die. Her father questioned her mercilessly about Evie's mysterious father, but Lucy would never tell. Whatever she thought about Dallas Denton, she didn't need her father coming after him, barrels loaded. She knew Abbott would chase Dallas down, guns blazing. Not that he really gave a damn about Lucy, but the blemish on the family name . . . a granddaughter without a father . . . that he would defend like a warrior.

So, Lucy had Evie and it was pretty wonderful, mostly, even though being a single parent was a challenge. And then she'd met John . . . John was another guy she'd been attracted to because of his seriousness. It felt a little like déjà vu. She was attracted to a strong man, who, in this case, was attracted to her, too.

What she'd neglected to realize until it was too late was that John's sense of responsibility came from a need to control.

Ah, well . . .

One of these days, she was going to have to tell Evie the truth, but that was a ways off. More immediately, she might have to tell Layla. She'd mentioned she knew Dallas Denton to her sister, once upon a time, but she hadn't specifically said he was Evie's father. All she'd said about that was that she'd tried to call Evie's father shortly after learning she was pregnant, but he hadn't been interested in her or her child. This was a stretching of the truth, but it was as far as she'd wanted to go. She was so embarrassed and yes, ashamed, roofie or no, that she'd slept with a man who cared so little for her that he couldn't even pretend he liked her the next morning. He had, in fact, gotten up and left while Lucy was trying to search out a safe ladies' room in the fraternity—and it had taken her a hell of a long time to find said safe place. When she finally came back to the room, the only part of him that was still there was the faint scent of a man's cologne, a familiar aroma she still caught once in a while—in a mall, or an airport, or once at their own store—that reminded her of him.

Layla had timidly questioned her once, asking whether she felt any guilt about not letting Evie's father know, and she'd answered, quite truthfully, "No."

But now Dallas Denton was Layla's attorney, although how that had happened was a complete mystery. The man was a defense attorney. He represented criminals, for God's sake. Okay, or maybe innocent people charged with crimes; Lucy preferred to think of him as the bad guy. And how had Layla even met him? Lucy wanted to know, but she didn't want to ask, didn't want to give herself away in any way, and Layla, for all her flightiness, could be very intuitive. When Layla had first announced that Dallas was her attorney, Lucy, after the initial shock, had hoped it would all sort of go away. Maybe that could still happen. Though she absolutely wanted Layla to gain joint custody, couldn't some other lawyer, one more versed in custody suits, take over? Lucy didn't want to be any part of the lawsuit with Dallas in charge. What if he needed a character witness and she was put on the stand and made to tell the truth? She couldn't imagine looking into his eyes and talking about custody rights of a child.

Her whole body shivered at the thought.

Heading back to the kitchen, she shoved thoughts of Dallas aside with an almost physical effort. Grabbing herself a bottle of club soda, she poured a tall glass over ice. Maybe John would like one, too, she thought. He'd scarcely eaten anything in the past two days—most of it had come right back up—though he'd gulped water like he'd just walked out of a scorching desert.

Pouring a second glass, she carried them both to the bedroom, the ice cubes clinking in a friendly fashion. It gave her a bit of a lift. It was no good dwelling on the past. She needed to keep herself in the here and now. And maybe, if she tried harder, she could make things work with John. They were married and just going through a rough patch. Even the best of couples had them.

But first he had to get well.

"Hey," she said, setting his glass on the nightstand, glancing around for something to use as a coaster. "I brought you something."

He was lying quietly in the bed, turned away from her. There was a paperback book on her side of the bed. She circled the footboard, picked up the book, brought it back to John's side, lifted the glass again, and wiped the condensation on her sleeve before setting it down on the Agatha Christie novel she'd been rereading.

She straightened up and looked down at him, sipping from her glass. He was on his back and his pallor was pale and waxy. "John?"

When he didn't answer, she tried to set down her own glass, not caring about a coaster. But she missed the edge of the nightstand. The glass dropped to the carpet and liquid spilled out.

"John!"

She leaned over him, checked his breathing. Thready. She put a hand on his shoulder and shook him lightly. "John . . . John? Wake up. Wake up!" She shook him harder. No response. He was out cold.

A coma?

Panicked, she glanced around. Her phone. Where was her phone? In her purse . . . somewhere. She reached instead for the landline handset and dialed.

"Nine-one-one. What is the nature of your emergency?"

"My husband's ill. He's been sick and now he's . . . I don't know? Maybe in a coma, I think? He's in bed. Really sick and I can't wake him. You need to . . ."

Lucy dashed into the ER a few minutes after John's ambulance arrived at the hospital. She'd called Bella for emergency babysitting, but she wasn't home. However, Bella's mother, Maureen, heard the barely controlled panic in Lucy's voice and offered to come over herself. As soon as she arrived, Lucy jumped into John's Audi and, disregarding the speed limits, raced to Laurelton General.

Now she strode straight to the only manned desk in Emergency, little more than a cubicle with Formica walls separating it from two other similar arrangements. The woman behind the desk was in a roller chair, and she slid from a long credenza covered with files to where Lucy was now standing in front of her.

"I'm here for John Linfield. I'm his wife. He just arrived by ambulance," Lucy told her. She had trouble quelling the panic in her voice. John had to be all right. He had to.

"Just a moment." The receptionist smiled congenially. She picked up a handset. Lucy still stood in front of her, so she said, "Go ahead and take a seat in the waiting room."

"But my husband—"

The receptionist had already turned to the conversation on the phone. Lucy turned around blindly, then walked stiffly to one of the chairs, vaguely aware of a young man sitting forward in his seat, his hands hanging limply between his knees, his eyes glued to the double doors that led to the inner workings of the emergency room. Near the windows, an elderly man and woman were cuddled into two chairs. The man's left hand was gripping her right one hard. Closer to Lucy, a mother was cradling a toddler who was sucking her thumb, eyes closed, oblivious to her mother's tension.

Dear God.

John . . .

Lucy was sick with shock. She hadn't paid enough attention to how ill John was. *How ill is he?* She shouldn't have listened when he refused the doctor that first night at the benefit. She should have made him go into Emergency right then and there. She shouldn't have gotten annoyed and frustrated and pissed. She shouldn't have believed he could shake it off, man up, figure it out.

No one said the norovirus was this deadly for a healthy young man. It had been over a week, and in that time he'd never once shown signs of improvement, just insisted he didn't need medical attention.

He'd been wrong.

And now . . . and now . . .

He'll be all right. He will. He's strong . . . he's . . .

She looked down to realize she was wringing her hands.

The minutes dragged on, rain peppering the huge wall of windows, fluorescent lights shimmering over the couches and chairs of the waiting area. Sometime later, after a howling child had been brought in and hustled into an examination room, a woman in a white lab coat came through the double doors. A doctor. She stopped short, looking around the room. The young man, the elderly man, and the young mother all stared at her expectantly, each lifting their heads.

The doctor's gaze fell on Lucy.

John. Oh. John.

Lucy got to her feet, her heart knocking in her chest.

Grim-faced, the doctor walked closer. Lucy read her name tag: Dr. Winstead. "Mrs. Linfield?" she said.

"Yes." Lucy could barely force the word out.

"I'm sorry, Mrs. Linfield." Her voice was soft. Hushed. Firm. "We couldn't save your husband."

Lucy stared at her, waiting for something more. "What?" she said. "What?"

Dr. Winstead gently led her back to her chair. Lucy sat down hard. She blinked several times. The doctor was talking in that same calm tone, explaining what had happened, but she didn't hear a word.

Couldn't save your husband . . . John was dead? Is that what she meant? *Dead?* "I don't . . . I don't know . . . I don't know what you mean. . . ."

More words. Lucy felt herself go into full body shock. She was cold. And shaking. Her vision blurred. Her ears roared.

". . . someone we can call?"

Was there someone they could call? That's what she'd been asked. Was there?

"My sister," Lucy whispered, feeling as if she were slipping into a void. Her voice sounded like it belonged to someone else. "I'll—I'll call her."

She pressed Layla's number on her cell with quivering fingers. Her heartbeat throbbed in her ears. She was dizzy.

"Hey, Luce," Layla answered.

Lucy opened her mouth to respond and nothing came out.

"Lucy?" Layla asked, her voice sober. "What is it?"

"It's John . . . he's . . . gone. . . ."

And then the world fell away.

Chapter Seventeen

September read the obituary of John Linfield with a distinct sense of shock. Deceased husband of Lucy Crissman Linfield. Deceased after a short illness. Deceased only a few days after the Denim and Diamonds Benefit and Auction. His illness had seemed a minor hiccup in the evening that most people hadn't even known was going on. And it had *killed* him?

Was that what they were saying?

She tossed down the paper, picked up her cell, and called Jake. His voice mail was all that greeted her. She remembered then that he had a meeting this morning with, by coincidence, the people William Ogden had introduced him to the night of the benefit. She would have to wait till this afternoon to get hold of him.

Her mind went back to Linfield. Dead. Lucy Linfield was now a widow.

Glancing at the clock, she swept up a messenger bag, dropped her cell phone inside, and grabbed her jacket from a peg by the back door. She texted her old partner, Gretchen Sanders, and asked her to meet her for coffee. Gretchen texted back that she was tied up at the station; could September meet her there? September made a face. It still bothered her to go back to her old job site. Shaking that off, she headed for the door and the dark gray Subaru Outback she'd recently purchased. She drove to the Laurelton police station, steeling herself as she headed inside to the reception desk. She almost felt like an intruder. Guy Urlacher, her onetime nemesis, who always hassled her about protocol, was no longer at the desk. It was oddly sad now that she was no longer employed.

The new hire, a young woman with short brown hair and a penchant for dark eyeliner and lots of it, looked up at her expectantly. September said, "Detective Sanders is expecting me. September Raff . . . Westerly." She was never going to get the hang of a new name.

"Okay, I'll let her know."

Gretchen buzzed herself out a few moments later. Slim, tough, with curly, near black hair and slanted blue cat eyes, she smiled at September in a way she'd never done when they were working together. Absence makes the heart grow fonder, apparently, September thought. In truth, she felt much the same way as Gretchen. Somewhere along the way, they'd become friends. When they'd first been partners, their relationship had been pretty rocky. Gretchen hadn't appreciated being saddled with a newbie, and September's sudden celebrity, though unwanted, had drawn Gretchen's derision.

"Come on back," Gretchen said, eyeing the receptionist with a hard eye in case she objected, as Guy would have. "I'm ready. I'll just get my things."

The girl hit the buzzer and September followed Gretchen into the squad room. She looked around for Wes Pelligree, one of the other detectives she'd worked with, but only George Thompkins was in sight. Overweight George, who rode his chair rather than do fieldwork. George, who'd been kept on at the station because he had seniority over September.

George, who now looked as if he'd shed thirty pounds.

September took in his new shape in a glance and tried not to look surprised. She'd seen him at the wedding and he hadn't looked smaller, but then, everything had been such a blur that day, anything was possible.

"What do you think of skinny over there?" Gretchen drawled as George looked up from his computer at September.

"Hey," he greeted her with a wan smile.

"You look great," September told him.

"Yeah, he's half the man he was," said Gretchen. She and George had always had a testy relationship.

"Jeannie's got me on a diet," he said, glancing away quickly, as if he'd given away some big, dark secret.

September glanced at Gretchen with questions in her eyes, and Gretchen jerked her head in the direction of the door, a silent signal that she would explain later. As she went toward the break room to pick up her jacket, September asked George, "Is Wes around?"

"He's working on a case." George had returned his attention to his computer, but she sensed he wasn't really paying attention to whatever was on the screen.

Once she and Gretchen were in her Outback, September asked, "What gives with George?"

"Jeannie dumped his ass months ago. She seemed to think he was a big-deal detective, and when she learned he basically sits on his ass all day, she moved on. She did have him on a diet, but the heartbreak is what's really done the job."

"He looks better," said September.

"You think so? Marginal improvement. You were at that benefit, weren't you?"

"You heard about John Linfield."

"Yeah . . . one of the Crissman daughters' husband."

"Kinda why I called you this morning. I helped him to his car. His wife drove him to the doctor, or away anyway."

"You helped him to his car," she repeated.

"The wife, Lucy Crissman, looked frazzled, and the benefit was going on, so I thought I'd facilitate. Get him on his way. It was a shock to see he died."

"I was going to call you, but you beat me to it. We got a call from the Wharton County sheriff. Told us to make sure we did an autopsy and look for poisoning. Angel of death mushroom poisoning. Didn't realize you were so personally involved."

"Angel of death mushroom? Wharton County, where the benefit was held?"

"Yep."

"What's the sheriff's deal? He thinks the poisoning happened there?"

"He's got his suspicions. Apparently, the angel of death grows all around the Pacific Northwest, associated with oak trees, mainly. Pops up at certain times of the year. Gotta be careful when you're picking mushrooms because it can look like one you'd eat. Anyway, that specific a request goes through the lab pretty fast."

September nodded. The lab could be backed up for weeks, but when you knew what you were looking for, processing was much faster. "So, it was poisoning?"

"Yep."

"And the sheriff thinks it happened at the benefit . . . ?"

"Takes a few hours before symptoms appear, so either right before he got there or while he was there."

"So, early in the day, then. Not while the guests were there." September's mind was racing. "Are you treating it like a homicide?"

"Wes's in contact with the sheriff. Apparently, a tip came in about the poisoning."

"I want to talk to Wes."

"And he wants to talk to you, because you were there. Glad you called for coffee, so I could give you a heads-up.

Think I could squeeze a scone out of you, too? I skipped breakfast."

"I'm buying?"

"Yes."

September slid her a look and realized with a pang how much she missed their camaraderie.

Lucy sat with Evie in front of the television. If you'd asked her what was playing on screen she wouldn't have been able to tell you. Evie had picked the show, but if you'd asked her what was on screen, she wouldn't have been able to tell you either. Evie's body was snuggled up against Lucy's, one of her arms slung around Lisa, the French rabbit/dog stuffed animal who was sporting a diamond ring on one of its toes. Costume jewelry that looked surprisingly real. Lucy had her arm around her daughter as well. It reminded her of the time before John, when it had been just the two of them. She'd been worried about money in those days, she remembered, but there had been joy in raising her daughter before her marriage.

Did you just marry him for security? she asked herself harshly. No . . . no . . . no, that wasn't true. She'd married him because she'd wanted a partnership. That's what she'd wanted. It hadn't turned out that way, really, but that had been her wish.

And now he was gone.

Her eyes burned. She'd been unable to shed tears, but her eyes had burned over and over again since she'd first learned about John. It was a blur. It was all a nightmarish blur. The past few days since his death, her father, brother, and sister had all come by to help her, and she'd tried to respond, but it hadn't worked.

The landline rang, and she lifted her head to look over at

it. Evie stirred and looked at Lucy, who sat in place. "Mom?" Evie asked.

"Okay."

Lucy rose heavily from the couch and walked to the phone. She wasn't surprised to see it was her mother calling. Normally, she would feel dispirited and annoyed, but these weren't normal times.

"I'm coming to you," her mother said by way of greeting.

Lucy's burning eyes finally shed tears. "Thanks, Mom," she choked out.

Kate watched through her window at April Academy at the children running around the playground, all of them appearing to be working hard at recess. She picked up her coffee cup by rote, never taking her eyes off the scene of joyous melee. Evie wasn't at school today, and Daphne had questioned whether she was sick. Kate had tried to explain about a death in the family, and though Daphne clearly understood the words, she didn't quite get how devastating it all was.

"What happened to her real daddy?" she'd asked when the news had first come down. Daphne apparently felt that John's death didn't count at the same level as a *real* father. Her attitude gave Kate disturbing insight into how she saw Lyle, so she'd doubled and redoubled her efforts to have Daphne see how terrible John Linfield's death was for Evie.

"John is like her real daddy," Kate started in, only to be immediately interrupted.

"But he's not. She doesn't know who her real dad is," Daphne assured her.

"Well, it doesn't matter. What matters is, her stepfather was like her real daddy."

"No. He's not. Evie doesn't like him that much."

"Daphne, he's gone." Kate's patience snapped. "Don't talk like that. It disrespects him."

"Who?" she asked, her brow furrowed.

"John Linfield!" she declared in exasperation. "He *died,* Daphne. He's not coming back!"

Daphne had reared back in the face of Kate's fury, her eyes wide. "I know that."

"Well, then, stop talking that way. It's not right, and people won't understand if they overhear you. And don't say anything like that to Evie, or Lucy. My God."

They were going to have to start seriously attending church, Kate thought. Somehow, Daphne was missing out on the basics of proper behavior and *feelings*. It didn't help that Lyle never wanted to do anything that included worship, even though some very important people went to the church Kate had zeroed in on.

Lyle . . . She loved him. *Loved* him. He was her other half. Her man. Her husband.

She'd followed Lyle on Monday, even though she'd been reeling in the aftermath of the Denim and Diamonds fiasco. Yes, people had put down their money at the auction and no one had seemed particularly upset about John's illness at the time, except the family, of course, and that ex-cop who'd been on television who was married to the wiz financial adviser, though, to be fair, no one had understood the severity of John's symptoms. She certainly hadn't.

Kate had pulled up to the Pembroke Inn wearing a brunette wig, oversize tortoiseshell glasses, and a bulky coat. She'd sneaked into the restaurant bar, shooting a quick glance around to see if Lyle had beaten her there. He hadn't, but then, she hadn't expected him to; she'd planned on getting there ahead of the assignation.

She'd taken a seat at a table that offered her a view of the door, and then kept the menu in front of her nose to cover most of her face. The waitress had asked her what she

wanted, and she'd purposely answered in a lower tone than
normal, so that if she had to speak when Lyle appeared, he
wouldn't recognize her voice. She had then ordered an iced
tea, her stomach too clenched with anxiety for her to even
think about food.

She'd been frightened, not sure what she would do if Lyle
found her out. He would be totally pissed and on to the fact
that she'd gotten into his phone. Yet she had to know what he
was up to.

Even so, she'd just about decided it was all too risky when
she saw him enter. She immediately pretended to be searching in her purse, though she dared a quick look his way,
relieved to see him stride directly to the bar and take a seat
at one end. He was almost out of her range of vision. She
could only see his hands. But the seat to his left remained
open for whoever he was meeting, and it was directly in
Kate's line of sight.

Okay, okay, she'd warned herself. So far, so good. She'd
sent Daphne home with Evie after school; quid pro quo for
Kate taking Evie the week before. To leave work early, Kate
had complained of a headache and then made good her disappearance before April could question her too thoroughly.
This, of course, had been before John collapsed into a coma.
He was ill at that time, and Lucy had been somewhat reluctant to have Daphne at her house, but Kate had pushed,
needing Daphne to be somewhere else because she hadn't
known how long she would need to be. Of course, none of
them had known John was fatally ill. Kate had thankfully
picked Daphne up before he'd gone into his coma.

But anyway, she'd been surprised when the woman who
took the seat next to Lyle was middle-aged and hard-edged.
No, this was not Patricia who'd once worked at Crissman &
Wolfe. This *Pat* had sat stiffly on the barstool next to Lyle and
had seemed cold and unforgiving. *Looks like a ballbuster,*

Kate had thought, put off by Lyle's choice, a bit baffled and also somewhat relieved. She tried to imagine this dried-up witch in the bedroom and failed completely. The woman looked like she'd opt for arm wrestling as her preferred choice of physical contact.

Kate had waited in a kind of suspended horror to see if Lyle would put his hand on her or draw her near, but it didn't happen. Gradually, she began to think this was a business meeting of some kind, though she couldn't see what the hell it could be about. It seemed clandestine. There was just something about both Pat's posture and Lyle's stiffness, and the way Pat looked around a time or two, as if scoping out the other patrons, that made it appear like an assignation. Whenever she saw Pat glance to her side, Kate made sure she herself was focused elsewhere. She didn't *think* she'd been seen, and Lyle hadn't said anything in the days since, so she felt she was safe.

While they were at the bar, neither Pat nor Lyle ordered anything to eat or drink other than water, and it was only because Kate was looking at them so hard from her peripheral vision that she noticed when Lyle slid Pat a flat packet wrapped in brown paper. Drugs? Oh my *God*. Was it drugs? Kate still had no idea.

Shortly after the transfer, Pat got up from her stool and prepared to leave. Her coat flipped open a bit as she headed out, and Kate realized she was wearing some kind of uniform beneath it—blue scrubs—like she was in the medical profession. A nurse, maybe? Why was Lyle giving drugs to a nurse? Or maybe a doctor . . . ? Kate didn't see how that was likely. Pat just looked too . . . unimportant. Some other medical job perhaps?

It was all a mystery, one Kate hadn't had time to unravel because then John had gone into a coma and to the hospital later that night, and here they all were days later, living in a state of shock.

Kate had tried to be supportive to Lucy, but her sister-in-law was unreachable. Totally undone. Kate guessed she would feel the same way if anything happened to Lyle, but she somehow hadn't expected it of Lucy. Everyone knew about the fight they'd had at Stonehenge. God. *Wolfe Lodge.* How many times was she going to mess that up?

"Kate?"

Kate jerked as if cattle-prodded and turned toward the voice. "What?" she asked stridently, spying April standing in the doorway.

"Daphne apparently would like to go home."

Kate glanced at her desk clock. "It's barely one."

"I'm just the messenger." April sniffed, clearly offended by Kate's tone, but Kate couldn't seem to rustle up the energy to apologize. She found she was pissed at everybody, John Linfield included. He shouldn't have died! And now Lyle and Abbott had practically shut her out as they went about their business. Yes, they, too, had tried to comfort Lucy, and she'd seemed to respond to them more than Kate, but everyone—all of the Crissmans—were keeping her at arm's length, like she didn't count.

"Okay," Kate said to April, whose lips thinned before she turned away.

Kate closed her desk and walked to Daphne's room. There was a young mother holding a baby boy of about nine months in the hall. He was squirming to get down and she set him on the ground as Kate knocked lightly on Daphne's door. The little boy held on to his mother's fingers and balanced on wobbly legs. He grinned at Kate, showing two little bottom teeth, his blue eyes mirthful.

The sight of him, the wanting, made her almost physically ill. The teacher came to the door and Kate practically pushed her way inside.

As soon as her daughter saw her, she grabbed up her backpack and ran to meet her, practically throwing herself into Kate's arms. Kate squeezed her eyes closed, then opened them again, in control once more.

"What is it, honey?" she asked.

"I wanna go home!" Daphne wailed.

"Did something happen? Sure. We can go. Did someone hurt you?" She threw a hard look around the classroom.

"Evie's dead!" she cried.

"*What?* Oh, no no no. That's not true. It's her stepfather that—"

"I want to see *Evie!*"

Kate grabbed Daphne's arm and hurried her down the hall, away from her classroom and all the wide-eyed stares. She yanked her phone from her purse as soon as they were out of earshot. "Evie's not dead. For goodness' sake, I'll call Lucy and Evie right now. Maybe we can stop by to see them."

"*Nowww!*"

Kate scrolled to Lucy's number and depressed the Call button.

Lucy answered dully, "Hi, Kate."

"Sorry to bother you at this terrible time, Lucy, but Daphne would really like to see Evie. She wants to make sure she's all right."

"Ummm . . ." Kate heard her ask her daughter if Daphne could stop by. "Fine," Lucy said when she came back on the phone, her voice a monotone.

"We'll be over soon."

Kate followed Daphne out to the car. Her daughter had subsided, and she was mostly silent as they drove from the school to the Linfield house in Laurelton. Kate had barely pulled into the drive when Daphne jumped from the car and ran to the front door, pressing the bell over and over again.

"Hey!" Kate scolded, hurrying after her, which took a

few moments because she'd accidentally trapped the strap of her purse between the driver's seat and the console and had almost jerked herself off her own feet for a moment. "Give them a chance, for God's sake!"

Lucy answered the door at that moment, while Daphne was pushing the button again. Daphne dashed past her without a hello.

"Sorry," Kate apologized to her wan sister-in-law.

"My mother's coming," Lucy said, more to herself than Kate. "They're doing an autopsy on John to determine what killed him."

"Oh, an autopsy. I guess they would . . . do they know what it was?"

"No one's told me anything. It feels . . . strange."

"How do you mean?"

"I don't know." She shivered. "I just feel like the other shoe hasn't dropped yet."

PART THREE

Chapter Eighteen

Dallas Denton was tired of lies. Tall ones, whoppers, little white ones, teasing ones . . . he'd had his fill. If someone couldn't own up to their own behavior—good, bad, or indifferent—he could no longer abide it.

This was problematic; Dallas was a defense attorney and the number-one action taken by his clients, when they didn't like the hard questions, was to lie. He'd heard it all. They were innocent of all wrongdoing. Inordinately persecuted by the police, the prosecuting lawyers, the world in general. It was all a terrible mistake. No one understood them. They'd come to him to put the world right again.

And he had . . . first for a firm he'd slowly decided was venal at its core. Now, on his own.

Currently, he was trying to appear attentive to the woman seated on the opposite side of his desk, not be too judgmental. Joanna Creighton was rambling away. She'd been going on for about fifteen minutes on the attributes of her teenage son, a young miscreant who dabbled in criminal behavior as if he were determined to try everything in the goody bag. He seemed to be fulfilling his bucket list for breaking laws. Thievery, drug dealing and/or using, robbery, burglary, even a bit of extortion on his supposed friends . . . you name it, he'd tried it. He was a bad apple whose good looks and charm had bamboozled everyone in his orbit, especially his mother. That was until the DA had pressed charges. Now she wanted Dallas to defend the boy. She'd brought him in the week before so Dallas could get a look at him, but all the kid had done was examine him resentfully from beneath a swath of blond hair that covered half his face. Dallas had wanted to tell him to straighten up before it was too late, but he'd been in similar situations enough times to learn that if the parents didn't discipline their children, he was done before he even started.

"Alastair wanted to come again," Joanna told him earnestly now. "But I thought it would be best if I came alone this time."

She was smart enough to see that Dallas had been unimpressed with her son's supposed remorse for his crimes. Alastair had managed a mumbled, "I guess it's against the law," when Dallas had reviewed the charges against him. The friend wouldn't go after him on the extortion charges, and most of the rest of his crimes had been viewed as penny-ante . . . except the drug dealing. To date, Alastair had managed to escape the burglary, robbery, and theft felonies, but that was if—and this was the big *if*—he pleaded guilty to the drug dealing. This was the stalemate they found themselves at, because Joanna wanted him off scot-free. Dallas had tried to explain that the kid, being only sixteen, would likely be charged as a juvenile. It was a miracle he hadn't been caught before. But Joanna was having none of it.

She said for about the fifth time, "He should never have been hanging out with those other boys. He got talked into trying that awful stuff. Opioids; you hear about them all the time. He wasn't selling them. He admitted he tried some pills, but his friends talked him into it, and you know how easy it is to get hooked. He should never have tried it. And his father and I are going to make certain that never happens again, I can tell you."

"Mrs. Creighton—"

"Joanna," she insisted.

"Your son was caught in th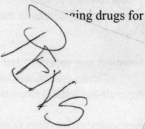ing drugs for money."

"It was a setup. I told yo

"It was a sting," Dallas and caught selling opioid

"Whose side are you for court?"

Dallas said patiently will probably have to reduced sentence is

"He's not going to ja   for delinquents, or whatever it is!

"The evidence is too strong against

"I came here for help and all I hear is negativ   re you going to defend him or not?"

"Only if you understand that he'll likely be convicted and we can work on the sentenc—"

She threw up a hand and jumped to her feet. "Stop. Just stop. People who matter gave me your name, and if you won't help him, I'm going to tell them what a disappointment you are. We'll find someone else who will actually *defend* him, if you won't."

"That's certainly your prerogative, Mrs. Creighton."

"*Joanna.*"

"If you want me to stop working on your son's case, I will immediately. I understand how hard this is for you. It's uncharted territory for parents, a really foreign, inhospitable place to find yourself. Your child is in the system. The forces of law and order are coming at you like a steamroller. There's no escaping them."

"You don't know that!" Tears sprang to her eyes.

"If I could give you one piece of advice, it's to change your focus. Start planning a defense instead of a denial. That's where you are. That's reality."

She wanted to scream at him. It was in her taut face and angry stance. She wanted to blame him for her son's perfidy. Dallas had been here before. Transference. It was sometimes his lot.

She seemed about to say something more, but in the end, she turned on her heel and stalked out. The door remained open until Billie, his receptionist-cum-secretary-cum-girl Friday—his only employee—came to shut it. She sent him a commiserating smile and slowly closed it.

Dallas sat back in his chair and stared at the ceiling. He'd been a defense attorney a long time and he'd learned to advise his clients not to tell him whether they were guilty of the crimes they were accused of. He needed to believe they were innocent to give them the representation they deserved. But if their guilt was self-evident—proven, really—there needed to be a come-to-Jesus meeting between him and his client. Dallas couldn't defend someone he knew was guilty, even if they claimed they weren't. He was honest with clients about that.

"If you want me to get the best sentence for you, I will. If you want me to defend the case as if you're innocent, I'll try to the best of my ability, but you may be better served with a different attorney."

The result was, sometimes they stayed with him, sometimes they didn't. He was lucky in that most of his would-be clients understood what he was saying.

That was his rule, and if it lost him clients, so be it.

Or maybe he'd just become jaded over the years. Lately, he'd moved away from criminal defense and taken on other types of cases, his next client a case in point.

Thinking of Layla Crissman, he glanced over at *The Oregonian*, lying on his desk. One headline grabbed him:

ANGEL OF DEATH KILLS LOCAL HEIRESS'S HUSBAND. Layla's sister, Lucretia Crissman Linfield, was the local heiress and the victim was her husband, John Linfield. The headline almost made it sound like Lucretia was the angel of death, but apparently, Linfield had consumed enough of the Amanita ocreata mushroom, sometimes called by other names, such as the angel of death, the destroying angel, or the death angel, whether accurate or not, to shut down his organs and kill him.

Fifteen minutes later, Billie buzzed him and said, "I'm sending in Layla Crissman."

"All right."

Layla walked inside his office wearing a long, flowing black coat over a pair of black slacks and a red blouse. She withdrew a paisley red, yellow, and blue scarf from around her neck.

"Let me take your coat," Dallas said as she shrugged out of it. He hung it on the antique wooden coatrack in the corner of his office, a gift from his ex-fiancée, who'd complained about how sterile everything in his life was.

"It's like winter out there. Hard to believe April's around the corner," Layla said.

"Hopefully, one of these days soon the temperature will rise about forty-five degrees," Dallas agreed.

There was something charmingly untidy about Layla. That artistic, bohemian thing he normally found a turnoff but that came so naturally to her that it made him smile. She'd signed a document she was now regretting signing, and he was in negotiations with the other party, Neil Grassley, a man Dallas had met on more than one occasion—and had never been impressed by—and he was trying to help her out. He'd done a bit of surface investigation into the man when Layla had come back to him with a new wrinkle— more like a crevasse—in the pending lawsuit.

Now, she leaned forward in her chair and asked, "What's going on with Neil?"

"Still working that out."

"How long will it take?"

"Hopefully, we'll have some answers soon."

Dallas had hired his younger brother, Lucas, an ex-cop, a guy with a colorful look at life, so colorful that Dallas had encouraged him to become a novelist when he had shown an aptitude for writing but who'd chosen to become a private investigator instead, to look deeply into Neil Grassley's life. Lucas had already given Dallas a preliminary study on the man, but after Grassley had offered thirty thousand for his and Layla's baby, Dallas had turned to his brother for more help.

Grassley had been fighting Layla tooth and nail for full custody, and legally, he had the upper hand, so it was strange that he'd offered her so much money, even if it was a blurted comment with no serious follow-through, as it seemed to be. Since the benefit where this had taken place—and Layla had learned his new girlfriend was pregnant as well—Grassley had ramped up both his attacks and his coercion to get what he wanted . . . which was currently in question, as he had done an about-face and was now, as they would say in an earlier century or two, wooing her.

"Grassley is still proposing marriage to you?" he asked.

She flushed, shook her head, then said, "Yes."

"And he's not involved with the pregnant girlfriend anymore, as far as you know?"

"Says it's over. And he knows I wasn't involved with Ian."

Initially, Grassley had caught Ian living with Layla and had shouted that he was going to use that against her, that she would be an unfit parent, living with a man who made no bones about the fact he used recreational drugs. But he'd had a swift change of heart, apparently, and now seemed to believe Layla's contention that Ian was couch surfing. Grassley had become a suitor, a swain, practically begging her to come back to him. Ian, apparently understanding that he was a liability, had reluctantly moved on.

When asked what happened to the pregnant girlfriend, Courtney Mayfield, Grassley had said he'd made a mistake with her and it was over. Layla had asked about the baby to come, and Neil had said he and Courtney were "working it out."

Layla had pressed him on that issue, but he hadn't fully explained. She wanted to know what was really going on, and she'd come to Dallas for help. Dallas, too, was interested in Grassley's motives. The man was all over the place . . . and his decision-making was erratic, to say the least.

"Where are you on the marriage proposal?"

"I told him I needed more answers about Courtney and the baby. He said there wasn't anything more to tell. I was going to deny him and keep on fighting for split custody of Eddie, but now things are getting weird. Did you see about my sister?" She glanced at the newspaper.

"I did."

"She thinks she's going to be accused of murder."

"Of poisoning her husband?"

"Which is crazy! There's no way. Everything feels . . . out of control. And Neil . . . came by last night and demanded an answer. After all this time, all the terrible things he's threatened . . . How can anyone have that kind of change of heart?"

"It's not usually the case," Dallas agreed.

"He told me he doesn't even want a prenup. He just wants to marry me, have our child, and live happily ever after. He actually used that term. *Happily ever after*. He's up to something."

"What do you think it is?"

"I don't know. Some kind of trickery that I can't see? Doesn't make sense, except . . ."

"Except?" he asked, when she stopped herself.

"I want to say it's just to beat out Jerome Wolfe . . . but that's too childish and bizarre to really consider, isn't it?" She peered over at him.

She had told him that some kind of verbal pissing match between Wolfe and Grassley had occurred at the benefit for the Friends of the Columbia River Gorge, held at the Crissman family's lodge in Wharton County. It hadn't sounded like the kind of thing that would generate such a strong reaction, but he was always surprised at what humans could get up to and their reasons for it.

"I don't know," he answered honestly.

"He's kind of pressuring me," she said. "He *is* pressuring me," she corrected herself. "And . . . even though I don't trust him, it makes me kind of happy. It's lots better than fighting and heading for court."

He wanted to tell her it was no reason to say yes to him, but he kept his lips closed. She was working through Grassley's abrupt about-face in her own way.

To that end, she mused, "If I actually say yes . . . maybe I could use the money for my sister's defense . . . and I would get my child."

"Kind of drastic." For all his good advice to himself to steer clear of her decision-making, Dallas couldn't contain himself.

"I don't love Neil. I don't really like him that much," Layla admitted. "And I've never been totally practical. That's more like my sister. But I think we're going to need money for my sister's defense. I need to help her, and I'd be helping myself, too."

"You don't know that she'll be accused of any crime in relation to her husband's death."

"No. I don't." She half-smiled. "Do you ever just know something, though? Kind of, you know, feel it? Like you can see it happening, even though you think it's maybe not plausible? That's the story of my life."

Dallas nodded. He was still formulating a response when she popped out with, "So, will you represent her? I'll find a way to pay you. She didn't kill her husband."

"Let's talk about investigating Neil before we go on to your sister. You need to know what's driving him. Also, what's in his contract with Courtney Mayfield, if there is one. I'll have Luke check it out, and I'll have him look into Jerome Wolfe, too."

"No. I know all about him." Her voice was cold.

Dallas considered. Layla had alluded to something that had happened between them when she'd taken a ride home with Wolfe after the benefit, but she hadn't been specific. What she'd said was that she had a nose for loser men. She'd also noted that Wolfe was in negotiations to buy the lodge and Layla was against the sale.

Now, he told her, "If Grassley gives you a deadline, let it expire. I want to see how this plays out a bit."

"I don't want to fight Neil anymore. I just want my child. And I want to help my sister."

"Just give Luke some time to look into everything. I'll get back to you as soon as I know anything."

"Will you meet with my sister?"

"We can certainly schedule something. I need to talk to her, personally, if this is her case, not yours."

"Well, um . . ." She glanced at the clock above Dallas's head, between the two windows that today were looking out on a cold, blustery day. "I told her to give me twenty minutes, and then to show up."

"Here? Today?"

At that moment, Billie buzzed him and said, "Uh . . . Ms. Crissman's sister is here? Lucretia Linfield?"

Dallas didn't have another meeting scheduled this afternoon. Layla's was the last of the day. But he almost wanted to protest on principle when he registered the tension on Layla's face.

But . . . what the hell.

"Send her in," he told Billie.

The door opened, and Dallas's first impression was that the slim woman who walked so tentatively through the door was a pale copy of herself. Her skin was blanched and her hair lay straight, as if brushed down and forgotten. Her hazel eyes sober and a bit unfocused. She had a black purse slung over her shoulder and one arm kept it clamped hard to her torso. Her dress was black, too. Unrelenting black, which only washed her out further. There was a delicateness to her that appealed to his own sense of chivalry. He was always fighting his personal need to help damsels in distress.

He thought: *This is the practical sister?*

She reminded him of someone he'd once known, but he couldn't quite put his finger on it.

"Hello," he said, coming around the desk and extending his hand to her. He saw Layla's eyes stray to her while she hesitated briefly, then carefully clasped his hand. She stared down at that union as if there were something fascinating and just a little bit horrifying about their two hands meeting.

"Dallas Denton," he said.

And she said, after a hard swallow, "Lucy Linfield."

"I don't know if it's knowing Layla or if you just seem really familiar. Have we met before?"

She looked up at him, searching his eyes, and said, "I would have remembered."

Lucy was living in an alternative universe. Or a nightmare. Or some kind of dark comedy where she was the central joke. Had to be.

He didn't know her. He wasn't acting. He didn't remember her at all.

He didn't remember you right after it happened, so why did you think he would now?

And John was dead. Her husband gone. Just . . . gone. She couldn't get that into her brain yet, into her memory. And now this investigation . . . It was all so surreal, but it was happening. Her life was changing, as her mother, Sandra, who was still here, kept reminding her. Sandra had learned of John's death and was still here, thinking she was helping, but was she?

Layla was talking. ". . . hoped you would take her case. They're trying to say on the news that she's a black widow. Killing him for his money. But she wouldn't hurt a fly, right, Luce?"

She was being called on to corroborate Layla's plea.

"That's right," she said, barely able to get the words out.

Layla had browbeat her into meeting with Dallas Denton. Lucy had done everything she could think of to put her off, then had broken down and confessed that Dallas was Evie's father. She was too dispirited to lie about that when John was dead and the authorities were building a case against her. No one had said as much, but she could tell. And it was just terrible. Awful. She couldn't believe this was happening.

And then Layla had said, quietly, just so Lucy could hear, "I always knew it was Dallas. That's why I went to him in the first place."

"How? How did you know?" she'd cried.

"Because you told me about that night right after it happened."

"I didn't name names!"

"You did enough for me to piece it together. Whenever his name came up on a case, you asked a lot of questions. Lucy, you're not sly. You go in feet first every time."

"But that's a leap, to think he was Evie's father."

"I'm good at leaps," she'd answered.

And she was. Layla was intuitive in a spooky way. Had always been. Lucy knew it for a fact, and oh hell, what did it matter anyway? Layla had known the truth and set her up with Dallas, and here she was and he didn't remember her.

You should just walk out. Turn around and head out the door.

She should never have listened to Layla. She should never have held onto a strange hope that he might help her. What had she been thinking?

"Tell me what happened," Dallas said. He'd walked back around his desk but was still standing, waiting for her to take her seat.

"At the benefit?" Her voice was dry and raspy.

"And before, if you think it's pertinent. Give me a snapshot of your marriage and why the police think you could have had anything to do with your husband's death."

Lucy turned blankly to Layla.

Dallas said, "Layla, maybe you should step outside? Attorney-client privilege."

"Oh." Layla, who'd taken a seat, slowly stood up, her eyes on Lucy. "You okay?"

Lucy nodded jerkily, and Layla, after another long moment of consideration—maybe she was rethinking this crazy idea—left the room with a "I'll be right outside."

And then she was alone with Dallas. *He looks even better now*, she thought. Dark hair with faint gray traces at the temples. Something knowledgeable about his eyes, like he'd seen things that had created the gravitas she recalled so vividly. Mouth that looked capable of smiling, although he was regarding her pretty seriously now. She recalled making love to him, sort of, and it made her uncomfortable. All of it was hazy, unreal.

"How did you meet your husband?" he asked as they both sat down.

"Oh. We're going way back?"

"Only if you want to."

He was just trying to get her going, she realized. Giving her an opening. He knew nothing about her. Nothing about Evie. Whereas she'd surreptitiously followed his life: knew there was no wife, no kids, although he'd recently been engaged . . . maybe still was.

"I was a single mother," she said. "It was hard."

He waited.

"I met John and he seemed . . . he was . . . what I was looking for, and I guess he felt the same." Actually, he'd known she was a Crissman. She'd always suspected that played into his interest in her. The money. The prestige. What a laugh that was now. "We were good together. . . ." Mostly.

"Your husband was poisoned the day of the benefit?"

"That's what they say. Those mushrooms, I . . ." She sensed his sharpened interest. "I didn't kill him. I wouldn't. I couldn't. But I know of those mushrooms."

"How?"

Why had she said that? She was sorry she had. She'd kept that from the police detective. Had only responded to his questions with yes or no answers. But there was no going back now. "When Layla, Lyle, and I were kids, we saw them. Not that far from Stonehenge. The local nature girl pointed them out to us."

"The local nature girl?"

Lucy told him about Brianne Kilgore—it was much easier than talking about more personal topics—and how Brianne had introduced them to the sights and sounds of the forest in a way that was mesmerizing. ". . . she knew about the mushrooms. That wasn't surprising; she knew about a lot of stuff about nature. Plants, animals, the watershed. Whatever. She even had a pet squirrel family that would come to their back door that she could pet. She would make tea out of pine needles and it was awful, but we didn't want to disappoint her, so we drank it. Animals were drawn to her. It was weird and kind of magical, in our eyes. She was also . . . on the spectrum of autism, or Asperger's, I think . . . not completely, but sort of. My brother was enamored with her, but she wasn't interested in him that way. He hung out with her the most."

"When you were told what caused your husband's death, did you tell the police you had knowledge of the angel of death mushroom, as did your sister and brother?"

"No. I was . . . I didn't . . . None of us would ever have used the mushrooms on anyone or anything living! They were pointed out to us, that's all. I just think John's death has to be a mistake. I don't know how he ingested the stuff, but it's . . . but no one would intentionally kill him."

"Who did you talk to with the . . . is it the Laurelton PD?"

"Yes. Detective Pelligree. He showed me the autopsy report that listed poisoning as the cause of John's death. When the news people got hold of the story . . ." She couldn't hold back a shudder at the lurid headlines that had followed.

"But the police? What do they think? Do you have any idea?"

"I don't know. I don't think . . . they think it was an accident." She drew a breath, aware her heart was thundering as if she'd run a mile race. "Should I have told them that I knew about the mushrooms?"

"It would be a good idea. Full disclosure."

She closed her eyes and groaned, envisioning the types of future headlines.

Dallas said, "I understand that it takes a few hours before symptoms arise, could even be a day or two."

"Yeah, I Googled it after John . . . after they told me what killed him. Poisoning by Amanita ocreata, commonly known as the angel of death mushroom."

There was a moment where Dallas seemed to take that in and Lucy had another wave of feeling like she was in a dream. Then he asked, "How do you think he ingested it?"

Lucy was starting to feel uncomfortable. Asked herself again what she was doing here. But she needed an ally. Maybe a defense attorney. Someone on her side, and well, she'd listened to Layla and here she was, so . . .

"I don't have a clue," she admitted.

"Do you think it was the day of the benefit, or sometime before?"

"I think it was at the benefit. The day before the benefit was Friday, and Lyle left work early and came home. I was there, too. We both were . . . having some problems at work, and so we ate what was in the house. I mixed some tuna fish with mayonnaise and we had sandwiches. The next morning it was oatmeal. We pretty much shared from the same food until we got to the lodge."

"What time did you get there?"

"Early. My father wanted us there before noon to help get the place ready. Kate, my sister-in-law, had hired a company to prepare the place, but Dad decided we should all be there way ahead of the guests. Way ahead. We were there before the sandwiches and salads were brought in. I didn't eat any. But everyone else did, I think."

"Everyone else, meaning?"

"My father, brother, maybe Kate and Layla, the staff that was there . . . We were there for a lot of hours. Maybe Lyle drove into Glenn River? There was talk of that. I don't know."

"Anything to drink?"

"Water. I think there were some sodas earlier in the day."

"Then nothing till the benefit?"

"Till the hors d'oeuvres. Actually, I didn't eat any of them either. I just couldn't get one. The trays were never where I was. John managed to try everything, but a lot of people did."

Dallas nodded. She could practically see the wheels turning in his mind. "Was there some reason anyone might think you were guilty?"

"I don't think so."

"You and your husband were getting along. Happy. Nothing anyone could see to say otherwise?"

Lucy's mouth was dry. She thought of Mr. Carlin, who'd seen her with Mark, the bartender, and who'd given her away to John at the benefit. "We had our problems."

He hesitated, his eyes on her, and Lucy felt almost naked. "Big problems?"

"No . . . but we weren't in a great place when he died."

"The police are looking for answers, and to that end they'll follow lines of questioning, interview anyone who might have information. As the deceased's spouse, you're in the center of the investigative circle. You'll be interviewed multiple times, but from what you've just told me, at this point I don't see a strong case against you. If you're leaving something out, now's the time to say so."

Her assignation with Mark weighed on her mind, but she couldn't bring herself to bring it up. Not to *him*. Not to Dallas Denton.

Now, she suddenly couldn't take talking about it anymore. The walls were crashing in. "I didn't kill my husband. I would never harm anyone. I couldn't. If I wanted out of the marriage, I would have divorced him. I thought about it," she added defensively. "Our marriage hasn't been great for a while, but I could never hurt him physically. Never."

Her words echoed back at her, heartfelt, sincere, and somewhat challenging. Okay, their marriage hadn't been perfect, and she'd been unhappy, but murder? No one could think she could murder him. It was ludicrous.

"All right," he said, as if he'd come to a decision.

"You'll . . . take my case?"

He nodded. "The next time the police want to interview you, refer them to me. I'll be there with you, Mrs. Linfield."

Her throat was hot and dry. "Okay. And it's Lucy, not Mrs. Linfield."

"Lucy," he repeated thoughtfully, causing her heart to flutter.

She thought for a moment he was remembering, but he simply got up to see her to the door.

Chapter Nineteen

Layla was waiting for her right outside his office door. She practically grabbed Lucy by the elbow and steered her through his outer offices, down the elevator, and out the front door to where they were standing on Third Street in downtown Portland under gray skies. Traffic moved sluggishly, tires humming against streets that shimmered with rainwater.

"He didn't know me," Lucy said, turning her collar against the drizzle. "I don't think it was an act."

"What did he say about John's death?"

"He's going to be there the next time the police interview me, and they *will* interview me. I don't know how I let you talk me into this. I don't know what's wrong with me. It's been a nightmare since John died. I feel like I'm walking in a fun house. I'm making bad decisions."

"Dallas Denton is a good decision. He's one of the best criminal attorneys around."

"Criminal attorneys . . ." She half-laughed, half-hiccupped, shook her head. "How did we get here?"

"Somebody poisoned John," Layla said, answering her literally.

"Maybe it was an accident. I don't see how . . ." Lucy

drew a deep breath and pulled herself together. She'd had enough of falling apart and forced her attention away from herself and her problems for the moment and onto her sister's emotional situation. Her mother was right. Layla needed to be taken in hand. Lucy gazed at her sister hard. "Whatever happens, you aren't marrying Neil. I don't know what the hell's going on with him, but you know better. Something's nuts there."

"Yeah, I know. I gotta figure it out. But right now, this is about you."

"It's not just about me," she argued. "You need to seriously get your head on straight. And I know you want your baby. I want you to have your baby. But marrying Neil . . . ? That isn't in the cards."

"I know."

"Do you? Bad things happen when you make bad decisions, Layla. Really bad things."

"I'm not going to talk about this now." She flipped the hood of her jacket over her head as the drizzle turned to rain. "I've got to go help Mary Jo restage a house."

"Are you kidding?"

"It's no big deal. I'm cutting back at the bistro and concentrating on staging and my art. I'm okay, Luce."

Are you? Lucy silently asked, and, as if hearing her, Layla sketched a good-bye—or maybe she was just warding her off—and headed up the street. "You want a ride?" she called after her.

"No, I'll Uber it," she yelled over her shoulder and sidestepped a woman walking a tiny terrier wearing a raincoat.

Well, fine. Lucy headed to her car and drove to Crissman's, walking up the stairs to her office rather than taking the elevator, the exercise mostly to get her tired brain to think. When she made it to her desk, she realized there was no one else in the offices. Miranda's office was locked up tight. Lucy had been in and out a couple of times since John's death, but she hadn't been able to concentrate and had only done the tasks that absolutely required her attention. After sliding into her chair, she tried to log on to her computer and found she was locked out.

"What?" she whispered.

She immediately picked up her cell phone, checking her last emails. She had two accounts, one for personal and one for business. The business account hadn't logged any incoming messages for twenty-four hours. The last message that showed was from one of the vendors. It had come in two days before. The vendor asked Lucy to phone her. Lucy plugged the number into her cell but got no answer. She gave that up and called Lyle but got his voice mail.

"Forget that," she said under her breath and phoned her father.

"Abbott Crissman," he answered stiffly on the fourth ring, though he had to know who was calling.

"I'm locked out of the office computer and I haven't been receiving messages. There's no one in the office either. What's going on?"

"We're moving everything to the warehouse, just like we said we were."

"But the store's still here. Some office staff need to be here. Where's Miranda? With you?"

"The inventory's already been moved," he said impatiently, not answering her directly about Miranda but adding with annoyance, "We're closing shop, Lucy."

"I know that," she said impatiently.

"I don't know why this is so hard for you."

"You don't know why it's so hard for me?" she practically shouted.

He backed off. "We're all shocked at losing John. You know that. But we're on a time line."

"You said the store wasn't moving till summer!"

"Well, it's moving now," he said angrily, giving up all pretense of understanding.

"What the hell is going on? I mean really, Dad. What's really going on?"

"We're saving the store."

"Are we?"

"Who have you been talking to?" he asked suspiciously.

My mother, she thought, but said, "Do I have a job, Dad? Do I?"

"Of course you do. But don't come in until you're better. We can handle it. I told you that at the memorial service."

Yes, he had said as much at the service, but she hadn't really been listening. Lucy had held Evie's hand throughout and greeted the large turnout of guests as best she could. Layla had run a certain amount of interference and her mother had been in her element, directing the show, deflecting the crowd away from Lucy whenever she sensed it was becoming too overwhelming for her. Evie had stood beside Lucy, clutching her stuffed animal, Lisa, in her other hand as if she'd reverted to childhood, which she likely had. Evie had wrapped strands of silvery beads around both her own neck and Lisa's, the stuffed rabbit/dog. Oh hell. She was going to think of it as a dog from here on out. Jesus. Why was everything so hard?

"I'll be there tomorrow," she told her father and ended the call. She'd almost said today, but she needed to see her daughter, and even though her mother was picking Evie up from school, Lucy wanted to go back home and hold Evie close. And her mother, who had been great in the immediate aftermath of John's death, was becoming a problem, too. Sandra had reverted to her carelessly bossy ways and had started to seriously get on Lucy's nerves, Layla's, too, for that matter. She just couldn't stay out of their business.

Lucy got back to her house at half past four and walked

in on her mother and Evie in the kitchen, making Rice Krispies Treats. Lucy was glad to see her daughter involved in some activity, and happy to see that the *dog*, Lisa, was seated in a chair across the room, apparently forgotten in the moment, still wearing her "jewels."

"That looks great," Lucy said, plucking up one of the Rice Krispies Treats, wondering if she could manage to choke it down, also wondering just how much of an ingrate she could be. She was past ready for her mother to go back to her own home. In fact, it suddenly felt like an imperative.

"It is good," Evie said, flashing a smile. Something else that had been missing since John's death.

"Evie tells me you guys are going to stay at Stonehenge for Easter," said Sandra, drying her hands on a striped towel, her blond hair shimmering beneath the kitchen lights. Slim and tanned, Sandra folded the towel neatly. "Is that right?"

Lucy had been nibbling on the confection and now she nearly choked on a piece as she sucked in a breath. "Well, I don't think that's really in the cards, given everything."

"You said we could go! You told me we could go!" Evie stared at Lucy in horror, tears jumping to her eyes.

"I said maybe. I don't know, honey. We need to check with Grandpa and Uncle Lyle. . . ."

"I'd say it's unlikely, because your father's selling that place to that man who bought Layla's painting." Sandra's voice was ice.

"Mom!" Evie looked in horror from her grandmother to her mother.

"The sale hasn't gone through yet," Lucy stated firmly, giving her mother the eye. "I'll talk to Dad. I just can't think about it now, Evie."

"Daphne wants to go. We have *plans*!" Evie cried.

"I'll do my best! That's all I can promise!" Lucy could feel herself teetering on the edge of a meltdown.

Shaking her head, Sandra said, "It's a shame. Your father took all his money out of the company and now has to sell off the last pieces. He's always been a shit businessman."

"Language, Mom," Lucy protested. "Dad made the decision because the store's moving to online sales."

She sniffed. "You know better. I just hope there's some kind of inheritance left for Evie."

"I'm going to the new offices tomorrow," Lucy said with determination.

"The warehouse? Do your best, Lucretia. I hope it's enough. You know what your father's like. Junior was a good man, but Abbott isn't."

"Stop." Lucy moved her gaze meaningfully to Evie. "We all have our faults."

"Is he really selling Stonehenge?" Evie asked, her voice quavering.

"It hasn't happened yet." Lucy turned to her mother. "Dad wasn't alone in his . . . decisions. Junior was part of the problem, too."

"You only know what you've been fed by your father. Don't blame Junior for Abbott's faults." She shook her head. "What did I ever see in Abbott Crissman? Oh, that's right, good looks and money, which he pissed away. He had a lot of it in those days, but he ran through it." She sighed audibly and rolled her eyes. "Of course, Lyle's been no help."

"Dad's keeping the most profitable part of the business," Lucy defended.

"And squeezing you out . . . the one and only person who actually cares about it."

"Mom . . ." Lucy warned.

Silence fell between them. Lucy was both angry and scared. Her mother was hitting all her own worries right in the bull's-eye and she didn't want to hear it.

"I'm sorry," Sandra said shortly.

"I don't want to talk about this." Lucy's chin was tight.

"Okay." Her mother leaned back against the counter, surveying her daughter, chin thrust outward. "Maybe you'd rather I left."

"No! Grandma, don't leave!" Evie cried.

"Your mother wants me to—"

"Mom! God," Lucy cut in. She was so tired of Sandra's games. "Do whatever you want!" Furious, she stalked out of the room, up the stairs to her bedroom, and flung herself on the bed, hating herself for acting like a teen drama queen, unable to stop herself. Her mother's passive-aggressiveness drove her insane.

She lay there for a moment, hot face buried in her pillow, knowing she was racked with fear over the future and that it was making her irrational, crazy, nothing like her usual self, yet she couldn't contain her emotions. She wanted to have a complete shit fit, and with that in mind, she lifted her head and thumped her pillow furiously with her fist.

And Dallas Denton . . . didn't . . . even . . . remember . . . her.

Was that it? Was that the cherry on top of this whole awful sundae? She couldn't get him out of her head. Yes, she'd wanted to go see him. Had let Layla's crazy plan unfurl with a certain amount of hope. Had looked forward to the meeting, even while she was frightened to the soles of her feet. She'd had some insane idea that seeing him again would help. A bright spot in the otherwise dark void that had become her world.

Not. So.

Knock, knock.

Lucy inwardly groaned but sat up on the bed, pressing her palms to her hot cheeks for a moment before saying, "It's open."

Her mother looked in. "I shouldn't have pushed. You're

under a lot of stress, and I'm stressed, too. That policeman asked so many questions. . . ."

"Detective Pelligree. He just wanted to know what happened."

"It's worrisome."

Lucy nodded. She knew even better than her mother how it felt to be interviewed like you were a suspect. Not that Pelligree, a good-looking black man in cowboy boots with a pleasant demeanor, had done anything to intimate that the questions were more than routine, it was just . . . John had been *poisoned.*

"But I am going to leave," Sandra added. "You need it. I need it. We all need to get back to normal somehow, and now that you have a lawyer to defend you, you'll be taken care of. But I'm not sorry for what I said about your father. And watch Lyle. He's under Abbott's influence, and that's not good."

"You've never liked Lyle."

"Untrue. I don't like his mother. Lyle's fine."

That was debatable, but Lucy let it pass. "I know Lyle and Dad aren't being totally transparent."

"I just want what's best for you, Evie, and Layla. Watch out for your sister. I know that right now everyone's trying to help you, and they should, but you're the strong one, Lucy, you know that. You always have been. And—" Her brow furrowed a little. "And Layla's . . . flighty."

"I don't feel like the strong one."

"Oh, you are. You just don't know it." Her lips twitched a bit, a smile fleeting. "Even the strong have bad days . . . or weeks."

"Or months? Or years?"

"Yes. Look, you know Layla's not that great at decision-making. Right?"

"Yeah—I guess." Lucy nodded.

"Don't let her do something stupid for the greater good."

"She knows better than to marry Neil."

"Does she?"

Catastrophe, Lucy thought, keeping that thought to herself under her mother's sharp eye.

Layla looked at the staging of the house in Portland's West Hills and thought, *Cold*. Everything was in grays and dark browns and whites. It was one of the newer homes, a midcentury modern built in the 1960s, and it had been completely renovated, but there wasn't a pop of color anywhere. Layla hadn't been asked to do the original staging, but Mary Jo wanted her "magic" now.

"That couch has got to go," Layla said. "And the bedrooms need a theme. They're just so blah. They would be better if one leaned feminine and one leaned masculine. Teenage boy. Young miss . . ."

"We wanted it to be swank, like the sixties," Mary Jo defended herself.

"I see that." Layla wisely said nothing more. She rarely defined rooms by gender herself, but this house needed warmth, a family to view themselves in it. What the original stager had put in place clearly wasn't working. "I'll come up with something."

"Do it fast. Tomorrow's another broker's open house and I want it to pop!"

"I'll get you a few pillows and some art, but that's about all I can do on that short notice."

"Fine," Mary Jo sniffed.

Half an hour later, Uber dropped Layla off outside Easy Street Bistro. She went inside and ordered a cup of coffee from a friend. Though she tried to concentrate on adding pops of color to the house being staged. She needed to find the right items because she needed to be paid for her work. More than ever, she could use the money.

And if you marry Neil, money won't be an issue. . . .

She slammed her mind shut on that thought. She'd never been particularly motivated by money and she didn't intend to be now. But if marrying Neil could get her both Eddie and a way to help Lucy . . .

Layla walked the few blocks to her apartment, hurrying up the stairs to her floor. There just weren't enough hours in the day any longer. Time had sped up since the benefit and everything in her life was moving at warp speed.

She'd barely closed the apartment door behind her when her cell jingled, the ringtone she'd selected for Neil because it was slightly annoying. Yes, his change of direction toward her was too fast. Something had clearly happened. Something she didn't understand. But she was rolling with it, waiting for clarity while she pretended to go along. She'd told Dallas Denton she intended to marry Neil. She'd let Lucy think the same thing. She wanted Eddie, and if that was what it took to have him, maybe she *would* marry Neil; she didn't know for sure at this point. But what she did know was that she didn't *want* to marry him. It was just an option.

She slid the scarf from her neck, tossing it over her coat, which she'd hung by the front door. Her mind skidded around another thought, one she didn't want to even have in her head, but there it was: *Did Jerome Wolfe scare you so much that marrying Neil seems like a safe option?*

Scare wasn't quite the right word. She'd been disgusted and alarmed at his actions, understanding even though she didn't like it that she was some kind of pawn in both his dealings with her father and in some undefined battle with Neil. A hand-over-the-end-of-the-bat thing.

But, along with all that, there was the vista of dating nothing but trolls like Wolfe for years and years. Guys who were just waiting to take advantage of her, and that was truly frightening. Seeing Ian after her encounter with Wolfe had somehow only made the whole thing worse. Ian was a nice guy at heart, but he was a slacker. If she were yoked to him in marriage he would be a dead weight.

What do you really want?

She'd asked herself that question so many times, she had a mental vision of it written on a ragged piece of paper with one word: Eddie. She wanted Eddie, and beyond that, nothing else.

Her cell rang, those annoying notes again, and she yanked it from her purse to examine the caller ID. Sure enough: Neil. She sent the call directly to voice mail. She wasn't ready to make decisions about him just yet. She wondered what Courtney had done to so thoroughly turn him off her. Something to do with the baby?

Layla made herself a cup of tea. Her apartment had a lingering scent of vanilla from the candle she'd lit that morning, after her breakfast of a piece of buttered toast. She hadn't eaten anything since and she was hungry. She'd lost weight, enough that people had commented on it, and she'd wondered briefly if there was something wrong with her. To that end, she'd had a complete physical and learned what she'd already known: she was stressed out. And that was before John died. She couldn't imagine what Lucy was going through, what her stress level must be.

She glanced at the blank black screen of her cell. Jerome Wolfe had called her twice since that lovely ride home. She'd ignored him as well. She'd told anyone who would listen about what he'd done, how he'd come on to her, how he'd kind of frightened her, believing in full transparency. True to form, her father had been put off and a little angry with her.

Really? Well, of course. Abbott was Abbott.

Her brother had stared at her blankly, maybe with a little bit of fear in his eyes. What the hell was his problem anyway?

And then there had been her sister-in-law. Kate hadn't been able to believe Layla's accusations about the wonderful Jerome Wolfe, but then, she was always dazzled by money and good looks.

Only Lucy had understood.

The phone rang. She glanced at the screen, though she knew it was Neil again. *Calm, Layla. Be calm.* She drew in a slow breath, exhaled even more slowly, then answered. "Hi, there."

"Are you at home?" he asked.

"Just got here, but I'm going out." Not that it was the truth, but she just couldn't stand being at his beck and call.

"I wondered if you wanted to see Naomi."

Not what she'd expected. Layla sank onto one of the two barstools around her small counter. Yes, she wanted to see Naomi. She'd called her twice, but Naomi was always busy, breathless, couldn't talk. She'd wondered if that was because of something Neil had said to her about Layla, but maybe it was simply the truth.

"Right now?" she asked.

"I could come pick you up."

"It's dinnertime. You sure it would be all right?"

"I've talked to her, Layla. I'm in your neighborhood. I'll be up in a minute."

He clicked off, and she was left with the feeling this was a setup. Another Neil trick.

He knows Eddie's your weakness.

She braced herself.

When the knock came, Layla almost didn't answer it. She sensed she was on a dark path. She shook that off and answered the door. Neil was bundled up against the rain. He wore a dark hat and a raincoat, and for a moment, she inwardly panicked, but then he smiled and swept off the hat, placing it and his coat on the rack beside Layla's.

He looked . . . odd, she thought. A bit shrunken?

"What's wrong?" she asked him.

He laughed, a short, bitter bark. "I should never have gotten mixed up with Courtney. She's a fucking nutcase."

"What happened?"

He waved that away. "She's gone. Back home, or wherever she came from."

"What about the baby?"

"There is no baby. She lost it."

Is that what this is about? Layla wondered.

He gazed at her tenderly, in a way he never had before. Almost apologetically. She had the distinct desire to run. Run away. Get away from him.

"You need to eat something," he said. "I'm taking you to dinner, and then we'll go see Naomi."

"I can't marry you," she heard herself say. "I've thought about it, and I want Eddie, but I just can't do it."

"I don't want to share custody. I don't want to shuttle back and forth between my home and your apartment. If you won't marry me, move in with me."

Was that worse or better? Layla didn't like either option. "If we're living together, you won't fight me for custody?"

"I don't want to fight you at all. I've done this all wrong. When I saw you at the gallery, I just . . . fell for you. Layla Crissman. I should have offered to marry you then. Right at the start."

He sounded nostalgic and sad, not like Neil at all. She peered closely at him, almost to make sure he was the same man. "What happened, Neil?" she asked him. "Something's happened. You're not yourself."

She saw his eyes were red-rimmed when they looked up at her. "I have an empire for my son and no woman. Without you, he'll be raised by nannies, other women, like I was, and I don't want that."

You should have thought of that before. "I don't understand how you can have such an about-face. You get that, right?"

"You and I started fighting about things. It just wasn't working."

"We were always supposed to share custody," she reminded him. Neil was the one who'd turned it into a war.

"We were supposed to be together," he corrected. "We still could be. I want that. Don't you? Don't you want to be a family?"

The pull was great. The family part. But with Neil as the centerpiece? "I want my baby more than anything," she admitted.

"Then let's give it a try. No prenup. Everything I have is yours."

Layla exhaled slowly. "You make it sound very attractive, but . . . there's something you're not telling me."

"I'm being completely honest."

"Honest, maybe. I can believe that. But completely? No. Tell me what the big turnaround is, Neil."

"I made a big mistake with Courtney. I was angry with you. You wanted to fight all the time."

"You wanted to control every aspect of my life," she reminded him.

"I got involved with her and we decided to have a kid, but she's nuts."

"You brought her to the benefit."

"She met me there. Knew I was going. Came in her own car and waited for me. I just let her because . . ." He trailed off.

"You wanted to hurt me," she realized. He was embarrassed to tell the truth.

"When I saw you there, in that jumpsuit . . ." He smiled faintly at the memory. "I don't know . . . I just wanted to start over. But you were cold, and Courtney was there, and I said some things I didn't mean. I've thought about it ever since. I don't want it to be this way between us. Let's start over."

He looked up at her, his face pale.

"What did Courtney do?" Layla asked, aware she was digging to the heart of it, also aware he was holding something back.

But Neil just shook his head. "Come on. Let's go put some meat on your bones and see Naomi."

Chapter Twenty

September pulled up in front of the Linfield house and watched the rain fall in sheets. April showers in the last few days of March.

She had no business being here, yet she was going for it.

Earlier, Wes Pelligree had called her about the Linfield case and asked her about the benefit. She'd told him the little she knew, and he, in turn, had explained about the Wharton County sheriff's call, the results of the autopsy, and the fact that he'd followed up with the sheriff to find out who the tipster had been about the poisoning.

"An unidentified caller reached one of the deputies and told him to tell the sheriff that it was Amanita ocreata poisoning. Call was traced to a burner cell bought for cash at a convenience store in Glenn River. Cameras in the store are pretty much for show, not actually working, so there's no video record of the sale."

"The caller knew that," said September.

"That's my guess."

"What's your theory on that?"

"Someone knows something. Whether it's the poisoner or someone else, don't know yet. The call was made from the Portland area."

He went on to tell her that if John Linfield had ingested the mushrooms at the benefit, it likely would have been early on, not long after he'd arrived. "Either that or he ate them before he got there." Just before the end of the conversation, he added, "His wife drove him to Laurelton General's ER that night, but she didn't bring him in. One of the orderlies thought they were arguing. He asked her if she was coming in, but she drove off. His feeling was Linfield wanted to see a doctor, but the wife wasn't interested."

It was that comment that convinced September she needed to do something, for she had a very different view of Lucy Linfield. "I don't think that's accurate," she told Wes.

September had just about decided to do some investigating of her own when Gretchen had called, sounding rather stressed, which was totally unlike her, and demanding they meet. So, two nights earlier, September had met her at Lucille's, a diner not all that far from the station, sliding into the red faux-leather booth opposite her.

Gretchen looked harassed, her tightly curled black hair wilder than usual, her blue cat eyes serious.

"What?" September asked.

"D'Annibal's out. Transferred, maybe. No one knows. And his replacement's a woman, a captain. The chief's basically retired. He's been old since forever, you know that, so now we have *her*."

Gretchen struggled with women. Actually, she struggled with everyone. "Okay, well, maybe give her a chance."

"Pelligree's quitting. Got a job with Portland PD."

"What? When? I just talked to him."

"Next week, or the week after next. Maybe he'll get to work with your brother."

"What about the Linfield case?"

"What about all Pelligree's cases? He's got two other ones he's working on. You think Skinny's going to step up?"

Skinny was a much nicer nickname than lard-ass, one

of Gretchen's favorites for George, though George still had
a ways to go to fit the moniker. But she was right. No way
George was taking on more work. "What are you saying?"

"Put your damn résumé in. Maybe she'll hire you. We're
going to have a spot open. Unless she wants her own people,"
Gretchen added darkly. "Maybe I should leave, too."

Gretchen handled adversity so well most of the time, and
she was known for liking the weird, wacko cases, especially
the bloody ones, that September had a hard time digesting
this new persona.

"What's her name?"

"Captain Boob Shelf."

"What is it really?"

"Captain Calvetti. But I'm not kidding about the boob
shelf. She comes in the door and all you see are breasts, and
not in a good way. She could lose a few pounds. Not as many
as George, but definitely some. She's got all kinds of *ideas*.
Wants us to clock in and out when we go in the field. Not a
problem for George. He just rides his chair, although with
the Jeannie thing, he's been on the phone more and moodier.
Maybe Calvetti will get after him about it." A slow grin
spread across her lips. "Now that would be something to
look forward to."

September let that one slide. "So, who's taking over the
Linfield case?"

"You're looking at her, I suppose."

"Need some help?"

Gretchen surfaced from her funk to eye September spec-
ulatively. "What'd you have in mind?"

"I don't think Lucy Linfield killed her husband. I want to
talk to her, see if there's anything else there. Wes told me
about the burner phone from Glenn River and the orderly at
Laurelton General. I want to see what she has to say about
both of those."

"Pelligree was going to go to Wharton County and talk to the deputy."

"I can do that."

"That might piss *her* off. This is 'police work.'" Gretchen slid September a faint smile.

"I'll take that as a yes."

"You and I never had this conversation."

So now she was outside the Linfield home. Whether she was going to apply for her old job back at the Laurelton PD was still up for debate, but she was determined to find out the truth about John Linfield in the meantime.

Kate narrowed her eyes across the table at Lyle wolfing down his evening meal without tasting it. She'd tried hard with the dish, one of his favorites, a beef stroganoff she'd always declared was one of her family recipes when she'd actually pulled it off the internet's "All-Timey" Best Recipes, one of those homespun sites that specialized in doing everything by hand. Kate had substituted mushroom soup for the sauce with a little Worcestershire. Lyle never knew the difference.

Mushroom soup . . .

She shuddered a little. She'd decided after John's death that she would never eat another mushroom, but that wasn't exactly practical. Still, she'd never liked those little caps of fungi anyway, and now when she saw them in the grocery store they looked evil. And if they were open? Those gills? She'd looked up Amanita ocreata online and had seen words like *volva* and *veil* and thought it all sounded slightly sexual and creepy.

So, no. She wasn't personally going to eat mushrooms, but a can of mushroom soup was benign enough. She'd tasted the stroganoff and forced herself to eat some, though

Daphne had loved it before she ran off to her room, and now Lyle was forking it in like it could be his last meal.

It *was* John's last meal. . . .

Kate swallowed, pushing that thought aside. She needed to be a perfect wife tonight. She needed to talk to Lyle about a few things, and he'd become harder and harder to communicate with since the benefit and, well, before that, too.

She'd sneaked his phone a few more times. Nothing for a couple of weeks and then wham-o, another mention of the pink scarf. There'd been no exchange of a scarf at the Pembroke the day she'd spied on him and *Pat*, so maybe it meant something else? Some kind of code?

They were meeting again tomorrow afternoon, and now that she knew what Pat looked like, Kate intended to follow her after the meeting with Lyle, find out more about her. She had her wig and a whole lot of questions.

But there were other topics she wanted to discuss with her husband first.

Lyle looked over, caught her staring at him. He didn't say anything. Just went back to eating, which kind of pissed her off.

"You know, Layla's surrogate is going to have her little boy in a month or so."

Lyle paused to take a healthy drink of water. He glanced over at his wineglass, which was empty. Kate got up and reached for the bottle of Cabernet on the kitchen counter, refilled his glass.

What the hell? He didn't seem to have any interest in sex anymore, so she plunged in and said, "What do you think about using her, or another surrogate, to have a boy?"

Lyle clacked in the back of his throat. "Like we could afford that."

She was taken aback. "We can afford it."

"Not unless Stonehenge sells. Even downsizing the

company takes a lot of money. Dad's not sparing any until we get settled."

"Well, Stonehenge is selling. And you said you've eliminated positions already, and with John's death . . . I mean, that's one less employee. . . ."

"Dad finally let Miranda go." He said this with a certain amount of satisfaction, and though Kate had always championed her husband against the old biddy, this time she felt a tweak of worry at his tone.

"What about Lucy?" she asked, the words just popping out of her mouth.

"She's been too distraught to come in." He dismissed his sister as he reached for his wineglass, but Kate saw the way his eyes stared into nothingness as he drank. Something wrong there.

"But she'll be back soon."

"Sure."

He went back for the stroganoff, ignoring the green salad and raw, cut-up carrot sticks, which she'd mainly put out for Daphne's benefit, about the only vegetable she would eat.

"I'd really like another child," she said.

"It's a bad time."

"When would be a better time?"

"I don't know. Never?" He glowered up at her.

"Lyle, we've always wanted to have—"

"You've wanted it," he cut her off. "You're the one who says we have to have a boy, an heir for the 'Crissman fortune.' That's all you talk about. Just talk, talk, talk. Whine, really. Whine that all of this isn't enough." He threw out an arm to encompass their house.

"Lyle . . ."

"Kate, I need a break, okay? I need a big break."

She was stunned. Didn't know what to say. *She* was the problem? She'd given her all to this marriage, above and beyond the call of marital duty. For him. For them.

Daphne strolled in at that moment, clutching her American Girl doll, which she'd named Maddy after a long-ago friend, though the doll had come with some other name. Daphne hadn't played with Maddy in so long that it caught Kate's attention, and she nearly screamed when she saw Daphne had wrapped Kate's pearls around the doll's neck.

"Jesus, Mary, and Joseph!" Kate declared, jumping from her seat. "What are you doing with my pearls?"

"I just wanted Maddy to look nice."

"Those are expensive. You know how expensive they are? You don't go into my room and steal my things!"

"Oh, relax," Lyle muttered.

"No. No!" Kate practically yanked the doll out of Daphne's arms and gently removed the pearls.

Daphne blinked back tears. "Evie has jewels for Lisa."

"Who's Lisa?" Kate asked, not really caring. She thrust the doll back to Daphne and kept the pearls.

"Her stuffed animal. Her dog, from *Lisa and Gaspard*."

"I don't know what you're talking about," said Kate.

"Neither do I," said Lyle.

"It's a cartoon! It's about these dogs and they live in Paris!" She was sucking in air like she was going to cry. She whirled around and slammed Maddy into the couch, then stomped out of the room, yelling back, "I want to go to Stonehenge for Easter with Evie!"

"I'm sick of hearing that," Lyle muttered, knocking back the rest of his wine like it was a shot. Then he got up from the table, managing to pick up his plate and clatter it into the sink before he left the room.

Kate looked down at the pearls clutched in her hand and noticed that the clasp was giving way. "Oh, for fuck's sake," she muttered, enraged. She wanted to yell at Daphne and she wanted to yell at Lyle. She wanted to yell.

Instead, she went back to the bedroom and said to Lyle,

"I'm going to need the receipt on the pearls to take them in and have the clasp fixed."

"What?" he muttered. He was in the bathroom and the door was nearly closed.

She pushed in and found him standing at the sink, staring at his reflection. His eyes met hers in the mirror. "I need the receipt for the pearls. The clasp is—"

"I'll take care of it."

"—broken. I can take care of it."

"No."

She thought about it a moment and said softly, "You don't want me to see the price, do you? I think I can handle it." She smiled broadly.

"I don't want you to see the price," he agreed, giving her a tense smile.

"What jeweler did you go to?" He'd dropped the pearls into her palm while her eyes were closed. They'd nestled into her palm, and when she'd opened her eyes, she'd gasped.

"I'll take them to get fixed."

"Lyle, I can—"

"I'll take them. Okay?"

His glare was enough to stifle her, so she just nodded and said, "I'll leave them on your nightstand?"

"Fine."

Kate pooled the pearls on Lyle's nightstand, looked at them for a moment, then returned to the kitchen and family room. Maddy was sitting on the couch, staring at her with glassy eyes that were kind of creepy, but Kate looked past her, concentrating on an inner vision of Lyle at Crissman's jewelry counter, purchasing a strand of cheap pearls for under a hundred dollars to fob off as something expensive on his unsuspecting wife.

Chapter Twenty-One

When the doorbell rang, Lucy was slowly chewing on the last bite of a grilled cheese sandwich—Evie's choice—while Evie sat at the kitchen table and worked on a homework assignment with Lisa the bejeweled dog seated on a chair beside her.

Lucy glanced at the clock. Seven p.m. She looked through the window to the heavy rainfall that had plagued them all day.

"I'll get it!" Evie yelled, nearly knocking over her chair in her haste to answer the door.

"Wait." Lucy followed her. God knew who it could be. The police, maybe. No, the police *probably*, Lucy decided, with a fearful nosedive of mood.

She was right. Peeking through the sidelight, she saw the woman detective who'd helped her wrestle John into the Audi at the benefit standing on the porch. Oh. Dear. God. "Hello," Lucy said carefully as she opened the door. What was her name? Something unusual, Lucy thought, but couldn't call it up.

"Mrs. Linfield, I'm sorry to bother you. I just wanted

to talk to you. I'm . . . interested in what happened to your husband."

"I have an attorney now. Dallas Denton. He told me not to talk to the police unless he was with me."

The young detective's interest sharpened on her. "I'm not with the police."

Lucy blinked. She sensed Evie beside her, taking it all in, and shooed her back to the kitchen and her homework. "I saw you on TV," Lucy said, eyeing her.

"Yeah. I imagine you did. But since then, I was let go by the Laurelton Police Department because I was the last hire and they were cutting expenses." She flashed a smile. "So, I'm here on my own."

"Why?" Lucy asked. She didn't really believe her. Not with everything that was happening.

"Because I want to know what happened. Why someone anonymously called the Wharton County Sheriff's Department and told them to look for the angel of death mushroom poison as the cause of death, someone who obviously knew what would be found."

"And you think I did it?" Lucy asked, feeling dizzy. She clutched the doorjamb and fought the sensation.

"No. I don't. But someone did, and I'd like to know who that someone is. The police are still following your husband's case. It appears to be a homicide. I know some of the things they've learned, but I . . . want to help."

"I don't understand."

She chuckled ironically and shook her head. "Call it the need to find a criminal. Or maybe it's boredom from not having a job. Either way, would you mind talking with me? You can certainly call your lawyer. I've heard of him but never met him. I have met his brother, Luke Denton. We ended up working a case together just before I left the department."

Lucy looked into her face. September, she remembered.

Her name was September. She opened the door wider and let her in, aware that she might be making a huge mistake, equally aware that she needed help.

And though she had Dallas's card and could call his work number, and maybe he would get the message tonight, she didn't think she would place the call. Layla ran on instinct, and this time Lucy did, too.

Naomi appeared pleased to see Layla with Neil. Pleased and relieved. She led them into her house, which was comfortably messy, with a few dirty dishes left on the counter from dinner. Her husband was home, but he slid his plate into the sink and disappeared from the living room, shooing their children ahead of him. "Come on, kids, let's see what's on," he said, stepping into a TV room while Layla and Neil talked to Naomi.

"I'm big as a house," Naomi half-apologized, but it was an out-and-out lie. She'd gained weight since Layla had last seen her, but it was all concentrated in her belly. Her face actually looked thinner.

"You look great," Layla said.

"I guess it's no surprise I'm happy to see you together," said Naomi.

Neil dropped in, "I've asked Layla to marry me."

Naomi brightened so much that Layla didn't have the heart to disabuse her. And being here, in the warmth of her home, the scents of tomato sauce and garlic lingering around them, Layla could almost picture herself in the same loving picture.

Almost . . .

Neil asked all kinds of questions, ones Layla felt she should be posing, but she'd never really felt comfortable about it. She sensed it wouldn't be okay, like Neil would never accept those questions coming from her, which was ridiculous. Still, she kept her mouth shut for the most part and noticed there was something yearning about Neil that hadn't been there before. Is this what impending father-hood had done?

What happened with Courtney's baby?

Was it even ever real?

And why had Neil offered an additional thirty thousand dollars for Eddie, only to turn around and become *this* . . . ?

Layla examined Neil while he was talking, really taking him in. He was earnestly interested in the baby, in Naomi's health and ergo the baby's. He truly, desperately wanted to be a father . . . to a son. That irked her a bit. His insistence on a male heir had bothered her all along, but she'd let it slide. Now, though, Eddie was a fact, and so, here they were.

Here. They. Were.

On the ride home, Neil was pensive, which was just fine with Layla because she felt the same way. They'd shared a nearly silent meal at an expensive restaurant in the Pearl District, one of Portland's chichiest areas, neither of them eating much of the sumptuous meals that had been laid in front of them by the renowned chef of a much-lauded French restaurant. The only discussion they'd had was a sober reflection on John Linfield's death, which had ended with Neil musing, "Your sister doesn't seem like she would kill anyone," which, though she agreed with him whole-heartedly, had pissed Layla off to no end. Maybe everything Neil said or did pissed her off these days. Besides, she hadn't wanted to turn the conversation away from their situation with Eddie's upcoming birth, not even to Lucy. To that end, Layla hadn't snapped, had kept her cool and tried to ask Neil more questions about what was motivating him. She'd wanted to get inside his head, but he'd closed himself off. Apparently, he wasn't going to give her anything further after his profession of love, if that's what you could call it, when he'd admitted he'd fallen for her. Maybe she was reading more into that than was there, but nothing about the new Neil made any sense.

Once they returned to her apartment and he pulled up to the curb, she invited him in, but he declined, his vehicle idling, while she climbed out onto a rain-drenched street, though the rain itself had stopped for the moment. She slammed the door shut and was about to walk inside when he rolled down the passenger window.

Before she could turn away, he said, "Wait."

"For what?"

"I just want you to know. I'm making provisions. For the baby, and for you, if you want to be a part of his life."

She leaned in, regarded him soberly. "You know I do."

"I've been accused of being greedy. It's true, I am. I've got some things to work out, but I want you to seriously think about committing yourself to me and the baby."

"Neil, I am committed to Eddie. I've never—"

"You know what I mean. I want us to be a family. Under one roof. Think you can do that?"

Yes. *Yes!* She wanted to tell him yes, if that would get her Eddie. And the means to help her sister, if it came to that, which she sensed it might. Still, rational thought prevailed. "It's all I'll think about," was all she said.

"Okay." He half-smiled, and she remembered why she'd trusted him in the beginning. "I'm going out of town for about a week. When I get back, I'll ask for your decision."

Lucy poured herself a second glass of wine while September covered her own glass with her hand to keep from having a refill. Lucy had ushered the ex-detective into her home as if she were a long-lost friend, and had poured out her heart about John, her marriage, raising Evie together, the closing of Crissman & Wolfe, and the uncertain state of her employment within her own family. It had all rushed out of her as if a dam had broken, though she had yet to tell the ex-detective anything about John's death . . . homicide . . . nor the true state of the Crissman family finances, which was shit, if Lucy was reading the signs right, which she was.

"What about you?" Lucy asked. "I mean, what are you really doing here?"

"I thought I'd explained: I want to know what happened."

"I know, I know. But really . . . why this? Why me? You've gotta have a reason."

Lucy squinted at her glass. Was it already half empty? When was the last time she'd even drank? At Denim and Diamonds . . . ? She'd hardly had anything then.

"I don't like people getting away with things," September answered slowly, as if testing every word for its veracity.

Lucy forced herself to focus. She had a point to make, and she was going to make it, by God . . . if she could just remember what it was. Oh yes. "Okay . . . so why are you here? It's not your job. You said so." She was having a little trouble tracking. "You know, I probably shouldn't talk to you," she decided, then couldn't help asking, "Are you telling me the truth?"

"Yes. Of course," September said, then added, "Listen, I admit I don't know exactly why I'm here, but it feels like there's been some kind of a setup." She frowned a little, thinking. "Is it? I don't know. But I want to know. And I don't have a job. Not right now, and I want to . . . this is going to sound wrong, I can already tell. . . ."

"What?" Lucy asked, not following.

"I want to make a difference, I guess. Does that sound corny?"

It did, but Lucy had the presence of mind not to say so.

"I guess I want to fill my time making a difference." September set down her wineglass and exhaled.

Lucy finished her wine and studied the bottom of the empty glass. She felt kind of sad because she didn't know if she wanted to make a difference, and you should; you should want to make a difference. All she wanted right now was . . .

Dallas Denton.

Nope. No. That wasn't true. Well, it was a little true, but she really wanted peace. Relief. For the horrible last month to go away and never return, God, everything was such a mess. She eyed the bottle and said, "I'm gonna have another glass of wine. I shouldn't," she wagged her finger at the detective, "but I will."

Hours later, Lucy woke up on a gasp, dry-mouthed, every cell in her body screaming for water.

Where was she?

The family room couch.

She lifted her head and squinted at the television, which was on low, flickering images and mumbling voices. Her mouth tasted gross and her head was heavy and starting to ache.

She got up slowly and walked carefully to the kitchen, dragging down a glass from the cabinet, filling it with tap water, gulping it down.

September Westerly. What had she told her?

Her heart started pounding and she leaned against the cabinets for support, setting down the near-empty glass with a clatter. Oh. Shit.

". . . if the police come, call me. I want to be there when they interview you. . . ."

She'd gone against everything Dallas had warned about. She'd talked to the police. Okay, the *ex*-police, but was there really a difference? Once a cop, always a cop?

What had September said?

I want to make a difference.

Well, okay. That was okay. That sounded okay. . . .

Yeah, but what if she finds something that makes it look

like you're guilty? What if she gets on the wrong track? What if she's really undercover, lying to you, trying to entrap you?

Lucy moaned and tried to talk herself out of the irrational fears that were gripping her. *What time is it?* she wondered, glancing at the clock. One thirty-seven. Had Evie found her way to bed? She'd been in her room when September and Lucy were talking, but had she stayed there?

She turned out the lights and checked the doors, glad to see she'd had the presence of mind to lock everything up after September left. She kind of remembered the detective leaving, but the three—or was it four? Or, God forbid, five?—glasses of wine had definitely done their job. Carefully, she headed up the stairs, holding on to the rail, turned in to every step because it sure felt like she could stumble.

Evie was fast asleep, a book teetering on the edge of her bed. Lucy scooped it up before it fell to the ground and placed it on her dresser before heading to her own bedroom.

The bathroom light was on and she drifted toward it, looking at herself in the mirror. Shit. Scary. She looked pale and wide-eyed, like, yes, like she'd seen a ghost.

Fear. Fear for her own safety and that of her daughter, because if anything happened to her, what would happen to *Evie*?

Where was her cell phone? Downstairs.

She stumbled back down and found it on the kitchen counter, next to her purse. She yanked out her wallet and the business card she'd stuffed inside it. Dallas Denton, Attorney. She called the office number, which invited her to leave a message.

"This is Lucy Linfield. I may have . . . I made a mistake . . . I talked to September Westerly. . . . She was with the Laurelton PD and she came by . . . and I probably shouldn't have talked to her, but I did. . . ." She left her cell number and then hung up.

In bed, she reviewed what she'd just done and started feeling stupid.

She fell asleep with her arm flung over her face, warding off the world.

Dallas jogged along the edge of the small man-made lake near his Laurelton home. The whole area was a developer's vision: healthy living with homes nestled into the hillside on one side, the lake on the other, though it was really little more than a large pond. Didn't matter. It did the trick. A clubhouse with an indoor pool and an exercise room was situated near the gates to the exclusive community. Dallas had purchased the house when he and Monica had gotten engaged. It was only after he'd looked inside himself and realized the knot building in his stomach was more than pre-marital jitters, it was actually from a growing dread about marriage to a woman he had relatively little in common with, that he'd pulled the plug on the engagement.

But he had the house.

The air was still thick with moisture, but it wasn't falling from the sky. It dewed on his face as he ran. To the east, there was a crack of gray light, opening to dull amber surrounded by lines of clouds. He inhaled the sharp spring air, felt its coldness in his lungs. Winter hadn't lessened its grip yet, even though it was almost April. He didn't much care. He almost welcomed the icy bite in the back of his throat, the wet cold that made him feel like he was alive.

Back at the house—two stories, three bedrooms up, a den down, stainless-steel appliances in the kitchen, a laundry room off the double car garage—he took the stairs two at a time, breathing hard from his exertion, stripped down and stepped under the shower, letting steaming hot water run over his skin.

Twenty minutes later, he was heading out of the house to his office. Billie would already be there. She seemed to think it was expected of her to beat him to work and was appalled when he showed up early and got there before she did. He'd taken to stopping at a local diner, Lucille's, that was near the Laurelton police station, to collect breakfast and give her time to get to the office. The diner had the added advantage, sometimes disadvantage, of allowing him to see some of the city's finest and exchanging a few words with them. He was often on the opposite side of the police in the courtroom, so he tried to make friends with them when he could. Not that it always worked. As a rule, they thought he defended scumbags, and yeah, he did. No question. But less and less. He'd grown intolerant of miscreants and liars, and if that meant he was having a crisis of conscience job-wise, well, fine.

He walked into Lucille's, greeted by the *bong-bung* of an annoying arrival bell. He swept into a booth and waited for a server to drop a mug and a menu in front of him. It didn't take long. One of the oldest old-timers, a woman who looked like she'd spent decades in a yellow uniform holding a pot of coffee, came by, upended a mug, dropped a perfect pour of coffee into it, slapped a menu down, and moved on. He'd thought she might be Lucille, except everyone called her Del, short for Delores.

The menu stared up at him. Lucille's name was written in a large, flowing, and curly scroll.

Lucille . . . Lucretia . . . Lucy . . .

He drank his coffee black and thought about Lucy Linfield. He knew her. He'd met her. He just wasn't sure where. Or, for that matter, when. Was she one of Luke's friends? His brother had had lots of girlfriends, romantic and otherwise, during his growing-up years, whereas Dallas had made self less approachable.

"My friends call you Grandpa. You know that, righ Luke had said to him once.

"Yes," he'd answered, though it had kind of taken him aback.

"You gotta loosen up, man."

Luke, who'd become a cop and had quit his job in solidarity with his mentor when the older man had been accused of

wrongdoing. Luke, whose own sense of responsibility had
waxed while Dallas's had waned a bit. Well, maybe that was
pushing it too far. It was more like he was tired of wearing
the mantle of respectability, while at the same time being
treated like dirt on someone's shoe for defending people
accused of crimes.

"The Only Omelet," he ordered, when Del swept by again.

"You got it, hon."

The Only Omelet was, in fact, the only omelet on the
menu. It was fully loaded, and if you wanted something
different, you had to take away from the ham, sausage,
cheddar and cotija cheeses, tomatoes, onions, spinach,
and mushrooms. The only extra you could ask for were
jalapeños. That was a bridge too far in Dallas's mind.

The Only came fast, and Dallas was finished with breakfast by eight o'clock. The restaurant was filling up with
patrons and the noise that came with them. Conversation
waxed and waned over the clatter of silverware. The entrance door opened and closed, musical notes over the
shuffle of feet and the rush of a breeze that slipped inside,
where the smell of brewing coffee and sizzling bacon filled
the interior. He let his mind wander some more on the mystery that was Lucy Linfield. Had he seen a picture of her
with Layla? Something to do with the Crissmans?

He had a strange sense about her, a tickling of memory
that was both intriguing and unsettling. She wasn't the
one who . . .

"Mr. Denton?"

He looked up to see an attractive young woman in
jeans and a rain jacket. She pulled a hood from her auburn
hair and thrust out a hand. "September Westerly, formerly
Rafferty, formerly of the Laurelton PD."

"You worked with Luke on the Wren case," Dallas recognized.

"That's right. I'm just heading to the station to meet
someone. Thought I'd get a coffee."

"But you're no longer with the police?" He gestured for her to sit down and she slid into the booth opposite him.

"Not currently." She gazed at him through squinted eyes.

"What?"

"I . . . well . . . it's fortuitous that I ran into you because I wanted to talk to you."

Dallas lifted his brows. "Huh. Okay."

"I'm looking into the Linfield poisoning and I met with Lucy Linfield last night, at her house. She said you were her attorney."

"I told her not to talk to the police unless I was with her." He could feel a knot of anger forming in his chest. One more time a client hadn't listened to him.

"She said that, too. I'm not the police. That's not what I'm trying to do. But I want to follow their investigation. I plan to go to see the Wharton County sheriff and follow up on that tip they got."

"Are you friends with Lucy?" His voice was clipped, and he glanced around to ensure that no one in a nearby table was listening in. The only person nearby was a young mother with a three-year-old who was refusing to take one bite from the stack of pancakes she'd ordered.

"I met Lucy at the benefit," September was saying. "I helped her husband to their car after he was sick. If John Linfield was poisoned at the benefit, then it happened early. Only a few people were there. Somebody brought in the mushrooms and doctored his food. I also plan to look into Linfield's background. Does he have an enemy? I just don't believe it's Lucy."

Dallas cooled off a bit. Was surprised how quickly he'd reacted to this news. Not like him. "You sound like you're doing police work."

"I am, in essence. But I guess I'm working your side on this."

"And you're doing this out of the goodness of your heart?"

She reacted to his sardonic tone by jerking to attention. "I'm not asking for a job, if that's what it looks like. I just wanted to be clear with you."

He wasn't sure what he thought of her. "My brother's coming to my office at nine. You have time to meet with us?"

She lifted her brows, thought a moment. "Okay."

They exchanged information. She gave him her cell phone number and he gave her the number of his office as she was ordering coffee from the server who'd cruised by. As he left, Dallas wasn't quite sure what to make of her, but he decided to give her the benefit of the doubt. Luke was actually showing up at eight-thirty, so he'd have a few moments to debrief him about September before she arrived.

A few minutes later, Dallas walked into his office. Glancing away from her computer screen, Billie looked at him over the top of her glasses and said, "There's a phone message for you from Mrs. Linfield."

Her careful tone suggested there was something Dallas definitely ought to hear, so he told her, "I'll check it out."

At his desk, he listened to Lucy's early morning message and decided September Westerly was right: It was fortuitous that she'd caught him at Lucille's. Lucy Linfield was unstable, and that made for a dangerous client.

What time was it?

Lucy shot straight up, glancing in panic at the alarm clock. *Eight!* Jesus! She threw back the covers, groaned at the thick feeling in her head, and stumbled toward her closet. She threw on a tan blouse and black slacks, pulled on a pair of black socks, and squinched her toes into black leather mules. Then she furiously brushed her teeth, shooting surreptitious glances at herself in the mirror, encouraged at least that she didn't look as bad as last night. She applied face makeup a little heavier than usual to give herself some color, a bit of eye shadow and mascara, and brushed her hair.

Back through the bedroom, she called, "Evie? You up? We gotta go."

"I made myself some toast," Evie called back from the kitchen.

Lucy could smell the peanut butter as she hurried down the stairs. "Oh, good. Good. How's the homework?"

"Done."

Lucy looked around for Evie's backpack, spied it on the couch with Lisa's ears sticking out. "You're not taking Lisa to school."

"Can't I?" she pleaded.

"No . . . no . . ." This was an ongoing battle, one Lucy had thought had ended the year before, but John's death had created a new normal.

Glowering, Evie bit into the uneaten half of her peanut butter toast.

Lucy realized she'd left her purse upstairs and trudged back up, finding it on the chair in her bedroom. At least she'd had the presence of mind to bring it upstairs, even if she hadn't charged her phone.

It was Friday. And she was determined to show up at the warehouse and find out what her job situation was, once and for all. Her father and Lyle had been so clandestine about the whole thing, she wasn't sure where she stood.

She dropped Evie off at April Academy, just making it before nine o'clock, very aware that this might be Evie's last year there. Two and a half months left of school she would pay for, by hook or by crook. Come fall, Evie would have to be enrolled in public school, which was just fine in Lucy's eyes, even though she knew Evie would howl about leaving her friends. Fine. Lucy understood her daughter's frustration. Lucy would've done the same thing when she was Evie's age.

As she drove to the new Crissman offices, she thought about her conversation with September. She hadn't said anything she shouldn't have . . . at least that she could remember. Vaguely, she recalled phoning Dallas's office and leaving a message. A semihysterical message, she thought, which made her growl low in her throat at herself.

Shake it off, she told herself as she pulled into one of the spots outside the complex of warehouses. The offices of Crissman & Wolfe were located in a glass-and-concrete building positioned close to the parking area and in the front of one of the warehouses. A cluster of structures behind the offices made up the whole of their operation.

CRISSMAN was posted in large white letters across the front and most visible warehouse. She glanced up at the letters as she pushed through the front door. No Wolfe any longer. A good thing, in her estimation.

A girl she'd never seen before was behind the counter. She looked up at Lucy expectantly.

"I'm Lucy Crissman Linfield," she said coolly.

"Oh. Yes. Of course. I'll call Mr. Crissman."

Lucy tried not to fume while she waited for the girl to phone either her brother or her father, which one she didn't know. Eventually, she was allowed to pass through the door and into the business offices, where four people she'd never met were seated at desks, behind computers.

She'd been completely disregarded. Forgotten. Kicked out.

She was angry, hurt, and humiliated, but she'd be damned if she'd let her father see.

Abbott came through one of the doors, looking at Lucy with some surprise. "I thought you weren't coming today."

"No," she countered, her eyes thinning. "I said I was coming in."

He frowned, as if about to disagree, then caught himself. "Well, come on back, then." He waved her to follow him. "We have a place for you, back here."

Did he? Why did she suspect he was lying? Something was definitely off. He led her through the door, and Lucy swallowed back the hot, angry words she wanted to shoot out at him through a flamethrower. When she saw the glassed-in cubicle next to her brother's, she calmed herself a bit. Maybe everything was okay. She'd almost convinced herself that she was imagining her father's surprise at her appearance, but when she closed the glass door behind her and sat down at the desk, she inhaled a familiar scent. John . . . her husband. His aftershave still lingered. This had been his office for the short time he'd been here before his death. Oh. God.

She felt her bones collapse and placed her hands over her face.

Damn it all!

Her cell phone rang. She squeezed her eyes shut tight and let it ring.

It finally went quiet, and then she heard the *bing* that meant she had a voice mail.

It took a few moments for her to pull herself together. Finally, she was able to stuff down her emotions. Sitting up, she squared her shoulders and picked up her cell. It wasn't a number she recognized, but she listened to the message anyway.

"Lucy, it is Babette," came the heavily accented voice of one of their local dress designers, a coup for Crissman & Wolfe, and now Crissman; Babette's styles were incredibly popular, so much so that it was only a matter of time until she left them for a national chain. "I am having much trouble being paid. I am owing more than ten thousand. So I cannot give more product, you see? Please take care of immediately."

Lucy's hot anger and hurt was immediately buried under a frigid avalanche of shock. What the hell was going on?

She went to look for her father and found him closeted with Lyle in another, larger glass office, Abbott's. She pushed open the door, and they stopped talking as if she'd pulled the plug. That added to her fury, but she ignored it for the moment and stated bluntly, "Why isn't Babette getting paid?"

Abbott frowned. "The dress designer?"

"Yes, the dress designer! Maybe our best designer. One who's been exclusive to us, although without a box store I don't see how we can possibly keep her!"

"Calm down," Abbott said, which sent her temper into the danger zone.

"How? How do I calm down?"

"How did you hear about Babette?" Lyle asked soberly.

"She just called me! Asked me why she hadn't been paid. Expects me to take care of it, but . . . is that even my job anymore? I don't know what my job is. Maybe you don't know what my job is," she said, sweeping a hand to include them both. "What is *going on*?"

Chapter Twenty-Two

"Rafferty seemed like a straight arrow. If she says she's working for the Linfield wife, she's probably telling the truth. She wants to follow up on Linfield's death, I'd say let her. Save me some time." Luke Denton was sprawled in one of Dallas's client chairs, his lanky frame spilling over the side. He delivered this pronouncement with spread hands. Luke's that's-all-I've-got posture.

"She's Westerly now. September Westerly."

"Got married, huh?" He smiled crookedly.

"Yep."

Luke had begun a relationship with a woman the year before and it appeared to be heading to the altar as well. Dallas could see the difference in his brother. A stilling of his basic restlessness. A happiness that had eluded him for most of his life. Had eluded them both, maybe.

"We've got a few minutes before she gets here. What about Grassley? Found out anything about what's going on there?"

"Neil Grassley wants an heir. A son. We know that."

Dallas nodded. It was the very reason Layla Crissman had appeared on his radar, according to Layla herself. "The surrogate they chose is due in about, I don't know, eight weeks? Six weeks? Coming right up anyway. But apparently, that wasn't enough. He used another surrogate, too. The Mayfield woman. Implanted an embryo in her, too. Looks like he got involved with her as well, to have a kid. Another son, but it seems like Neil and Courtney Mayfield no longer are together. Grassley told Layla that Courtney lost the baby."

"Huh. I'm not sure I'd believe it, if Grassley said it. He's an odd duck." Luke was scratching about a day's worth of beard stubble.

Dallas suggested, "Maybe losing the baby was the cause of the breakup."

"Haven't confirmed that yet." Luke shook his head. "Mayfield's a hard one to pin down. Has an apartment on the east side, but she's never there, as far as I can tell. She'd moved in with Grassley . . . maybe she hasn't moved out. Works at a data processing center Deep East."

Deep East was Luke's way of describing the eastern reaches of Portland, the sprawl that reached the edge of Gresham.

Luke went on. "But Grassley, he's different, easier to follow. He has a usual routine. Goes out for coffee in the morning. Walks to a place about a block from his condo. Doesn't talk to anybody, except on the phone. And he kind of shouts—you know how people do on a cell phone, to block out the surrounding noise, like traffic and other pedestrians—so I was able to piece together some of what he says. For the most part it sounds like he's talking with a stockbroker, or someone managing his assets. Once I heard him with an accountant, I think, by the conversation.

"Yesterday, though, he was on the phone with his lawyer, talking about that will of his. I was walking about two steps behind him and he was so engrossed in what he was saying, he was totally unaware of me or anyone else, for that matter. Almost walked into a man waiting for the next TriMet bus."

"What did he say?" Dallas asked.

"Well, he didn't mention Layla Crissman's name, but he indicated he was ready to sign on the dotted line." Luke glanced through the window and added, "The man's making plans."

"No idea on his sudden desire for matrimony?"

"Got a couple things to follow on that." Luke met his brother's eyes again. "He's got some kind of a doctor's appointment coming up, but I don't know what it's for. And it sounds like he's leaving town." Luke was frowning again, seeming to be trying to piece information together. "And that IVF clinic he and Layla used? It's the same one he used with Mayfield."

"You got that from eavesdropping."

"No. Hell, I've got other means," Luke said with a smile. "Anyway, I'm working on something there, but they're tight with their information. All that HIPAA stuff."

"HIPAA stuff is important," Dallas said.

"Yeah, yeah. I'm fully aware," Luke said with a grin. His insouciance was one of his best and worst traits.

"Nothing illegal. I don't want to have to defend my methods and yours in court."

"Hey, I'm an ex-cop," Luke protested.

"Yeah, right."

"There's something there, though. I think . . ." He trailed off.

"What?" Dallas asked.

"I'll do some more digging. I'll let you know when I've got something."

As if on cue, Billie buzzed Dallas and said, "September Westerly is here."

"Send her in," said Dallas.

* * *

Lucy had stalked out of the fight with her father and brother, infuriated and hurt, but her brother followed her to her office, closing the door behind them.

"What's wrong with you?" Lyle demanded.

"You know, you're really pissing me off. You and Dad both. You don't want me here, okay, fine, I'm not here. I'm leaving."

"Calm down."

"Oh, that's a good one. Calm down. Relax, Lucy, you're upset. Why don't you just say 'you're such a woman'? That'll go over big with me."

He actually rolled his eyes.

"You and Dad have been plotting ways to get rid of me. Well, congratulations, I'm gone. But first, why don't you tell me why Babette isn't being paid? Are there other people not being paid? What's the financial status of Crissman and Wolfe—I mean, Crissman?"

"Shhh . . ." He shot a glance toward the door that led to the central cubicle area.

"I doubt they can hear us in this hermetically sealed glass box."

"Would you stop being a bitch for just a second?"

"I'm not sure I know how. Once a bitch, always a bitch. What about all those new employees? Who are they?"

"Jesus, Luce. They're our online people. How do you think we're doing business?" he demanded.

"Hope you have a bigger online sales force than that or there won't be enough orders to sustain the business."

"We're just getting it together."

"What about the system we had . . . just last week? Or a couple of weeks ago?"

How long had they been "restructuring"? It felt like they'd been pulling the rug out from under the company far longer than she knew.

"It's all been changing. You just haven't paid attention."

"Oh. Right. I've been so in the loop all this time."

"You don't approve of anything, Luce. That's who you are."

"Who told you that? Dad? That isn't true!"

"You just want to be an obstructionist."

She took a step backward and really looked at her brother. "You and Dad have been talking about me a while, I see. That's your conclusion?"

His jaw set in a stubborn line.

"Tell the truth. Did you really plan for me to be here at all?"

"Of course we did. We just . . . know you're still getting over John's death. We thought it was better if you stayed home for a while."

"And if John had lived?"

He lifted his shoulders. "Absolutely. You'd be here." But he looked away.

"What about the missing sixty thousand?"

"I don't know about that, Lucy! How many times are you going to ask me?" he exploded.

"Shhh . . ." she whispered back at him.

"I don't have to take this." He grabbed for the door.

For reasons she would ask herself about later but didn't understand in the moment, she popped out with, "Did John know something about the business he shouldn't? Is that what happened?"

Lyle whipped around to stare at her. "What did you say?"

Immediately after the words were out, she heard how terrible the unspoken accusation was. "I'm sorry. That came out wrong." She lifted her hands. "I just . . . I don't know."

He said through his teeth, "We're having a hell of a time around here convincing people *you* didn't kill him and that's what you say?"

"I didn't mean it that way. . . ."

"Yeah. Fine. You're right. There is no job for you. You're not needed. John wasn't needed, but we gave him a job because Dad felt responsible for your family. Is that what you wanted to hear? Now there's not enough to justify either of you."

Having it so boldly thrown at her was a blow, even though she'd suspected it, and she was too tired and too hung over to be having this fight, but here it was. "There's not enough?"

"We're fighting for survival. What part of that don't you get?"

He yanked open the door with enough force that the glass quivered as he stalked away.

Lucy watched the door close behind him.

She suddenly couldn't breathe. Couldn't stand another moment of being here, of being lied to.

She grabbed her purse and walked out.

September's gaze fell on Luke as soon as she entered Dallas Denton's office. Luke rambled to his feet, greeted her warmly, shook her hand, and, grinning, commented on her new name before dropping into his chair once more.

They'd met over the Wren case, September's last case before she was let go from Laurelton PD, and it had taken a bit of time before they'd learned to trust each other. Luke was a PI, and even though he'd been with Portland PD, September had warned him not to get in the way of the investigation. A fat lot of good it had done; Luke had been on a path to protect Andi Wren from a stalker and killer and hadn't been interested in warnings from September or anyone else in law enforcement.

"So, you're an ex with the PD, too, now," Luke observed.

"Not by choice."

She'd stopped in at Laurelton PD before this meeting, her real focus of the morning ostensibly to check in with Gretchen but also to test the mettle of the new Captain Calvetti. She was slightly alarmed that Lieutenant Aubrey

D'Annibal had been . . . repositioned, which could mean anything. D'Annibal had been a fair man. More than fair. He'd been distraught that he'd had to let her go, even though he'd done a great job at hiding his feelings. She'd just suspected how he really felt from knowing him, and Gretchen had confirmed it.

As for Captain Dana Calvetti . . . she did possess the massive chest Gretchen had remarked on. It did enter the room before she did. But the jury was still out on whether she was the tyrant Gretchen called her. She'd seemed nice enough, and September didn't think there was anything sneaky underlying her comment, "Oh, you're the detective we've seen on TV." Maybe there'd been something snarky in there somewhere, but September was trying very hard to keep an open mind. She hated the thought that Wes Pelligree was leaving—she'd had a crush on the man when she'd first gotten the job with Laurelton PD and before reuniting with Jake, the boy she'd loved mostly from afar in high school and now was her husband—but she wasn't going to wait around to see if someone else was going to fill his position if there was any chance she could have it. She'd asked Calvetti about any openings and had received a "go ahead and turn in a résumé to HR." Not exactly a ringing endorsement, but it was likely Calvetti just wanted to dot every *i* and cross every *t*, making sure she wasn't accused of favoritism.

Now, Dallas invited her to take a seat and she sat down in the unoccupied chair. He asked her to lay out her plan to help Lucy.

"My client says you were a cop and now that you aren't, you just want to help her due to some need to . . . how did she put it? 'Do the right thing.'"

"I said I wanted to make a difference."

"Ah."

September could tell Dallas didn't quite believe her

motivation was altruistic, and well, maybe it wasn't. Maybe she had something to prove. Solve the case and head back to Calvetti with something that would demonstrate her worth.

If she could do it.

"I think I can help." September explained about her intention to follow Pelligree's work in Wharton County, interviewing the people he talked to again, elaborating on what she'd told Dallas at Lucille's earlier. She also revealed her feeling that John Linfield's homicide and his wife's apparent guilt seemed like a setup, finishing with, "I want to call the sheriff's office and ask about angel of death mushroom poisoning found in the autopsy. They have to know something. Maybe they're even on to the killer."

"What about Pelligree? He won't like you stepping on his toes," Luke said, and Dallas was staring at her hard, as if still trying to size up her intentions.

"He's taken a job with Portland PD. My ex-partner is probably getting this case, among others, until someone else is hired."

"All right," Dallas finally said, though he didn't seem totally convinced.

She flashed him a smile. She'd been half afraid he'd put his foot down, demand that she cease and desist, but of course he really couldn't. He had no authority over her, and neither did the police at this point.

"If you need help, let me know," Luke said as she stood.

Dallas's voice stopped her at the door. "Jerome Wolfe is set to buy Wolfe Lodge back from the Crissmans."

September hesitated, her hand on the knob. "I heard."

"Both of the Crissman daughters are against the sale, but their brother, Lyle Crissman, and father, Abbott Crissman, are pushing forward. Luke's done a bit of research and learned that there's an adjacent property Wolfe's looking in to, too."

"Who owns the property?"

"The Kilgores," Luke answered. "Daniel Kilgore's deceased. His surviving wife is Mona, and they have a grown daughter, Brianne. I've been trying to talk to them, but they don't want anything to do with me."

"So, what . . . You're thinking that maybe they'll talk to a woman?" September guessed.

Luke gave her a thumbs-up, and Dallas said, a bit reluctantly, "You might ask Lucy Linfield about them."

She turned her attention back to him, her eyebrows raised. "Are you giving me carte blanche to interview Lucy Linfield?"

"Well, why don't we find a time to talk to her together," he said, earning him a baffled look from Luke, who said, "Maybe after the trip to Wharton County?"

September appreciated that Luke understood she was anxious to get started. She'd been about to say the same, but Dallas took the hint and, holding up a finger, indicating she should wait, picked up his desk phone receiver with his free hand. A few moments later, he said, "Mrs. Linfield? It's Dallas Denton." His gaze was on September, still standing at the door. "I'm at the office with September Westerly. She said you and she spoke earlier. If possible, we'd like to meet with you later today to discuss the case and our plans. Is there a time that's good for you?"

Lucy clicked off her cell phone and stepped out of her car and into the teensy Easy Street Bistro parking lot, where she'd been lucky enough to grab a spot. She'd called Layla before she left the warehouse, found out her sister was working, and headed back across the Willamette River to the west side when Dallas Denton had phoned.

As always, whenever she talked with Dallas, her insides tightened, her heart beat a little faster, which she assumed was normal, considering her situation. She climbed out of her car, locked it, then headed, head bent against a gust of brisk air, into the warmth of the small café.

Layla was just finishing with an order at one of the tables when she spied Lucy. Her broad smile of greeting nearly did Lucy in. The one family member she thought she could count on. Layla pointed to an empty two-person table and Lucy moved toward it, feeling emotional enough to break into tears. The table sat in the northwest corner of the restaurant and was surrounded by windows that looked out on the drying street, a spate of rain having moved through, the wind scuttling down the sidewalk, cars moving steadily through the city street.

Inside, the scents of coffee and scones and maple sugar and bacon assailed her, making her feel slightly ill. She sank down at the table, her thoughts churning.

Layla cruised over. "You okay?" she asked.

"I've . . . well, I was going to say I've been fired, but I don't think I've had a job for a while; I just didn't know it."

Layla glanced around the small dining area, assessing her tables to see if any of her customers needed help. Another waitress was taking an order at the other end of the room, where a group of eight people had cobbled together a number of tables and was taking an inordinately long time to order. Apparently satisfied that she had a few seconds free, she turned back to Lucy. "I'm sorry. Fired? Really?"

Miserably, Lucy nodded.

"Why? What's their story? Dad and Lyle's, I mean."

Lucy gave her a short rundown of what had just occurred at the Crissman warehouse, finishing with, "It's not the same. Nothing about it's the same. It makes me . . . sad, and worried."

"Yeah, why hasn't Babette been paid?" Layla murmured. "I don't like the sound of that."

"I don't either. Not one bit."

"Maybe if you talked to Dad—"

"Not a chance. It won't work," she cut her off. "No one's listening to me. You'd probably have better luck."

"Yeah, don't bet on it." Her eyes restlessly moved around the room. "Hold on a sec." She hurried over to a table where a couple was obviously finished with their meal and quickly smiled and placed a check on their table before returning. "Sorry," she said to her sister.

"I'm serious," said Lucy. "About you talking to Dad and Lyle. They might listen to you."

"Oh, right. If I had a penis, maybe." Seeing another table was ready with their order, she slipped away again and, managing a smile, gave the family of three all her attention, even finding a coloring book and crayons for the child, who appeared to be three or maybe four, a girl with a big pink bow holding back her bangs.

Lucy watched her, thinking about what Layla had said. Was that it? Did you just need to be a man to be taken seriously in the Crissman family? She'd known her father was fairly misogynistic, but she'd never believed it applied to her. Or maybe she hadn't wanted to believe it.

When Layla returned, Lucy said, "I don't think they wanted John there either."

"He wasn't family."

"You're having a boy," Lucy said.

"Great. He can have a job at Crissman and Wolfe, if it even exists by the time he grows up." She shrugged.

"Crissman," Lucy corrected her. Her sister's so-what attitude improved Lucy's a bit. "Are they hiring at Easy Street?"

Layla smiled. "Wouldn't that just turn Dad's hair white? Both his daughters working as waitresses."

They both laughed, then Lucy sobered and said, "Actually, I don't know that he'd really care. For all of Dad's posturing, I don't know that he's even thinking about us.

Lyle told me they didn't need John, that Dad had felt he was just supporting me and John and now he doesn't care about that either. He made it sound like the company was going down the tubes."

"That's why they're so rabid to sell Stonehenge to Wolfe," Layla muttered.

"Maybe Kate knows something more about what's going on, but I sure don't."

"I won't let them sell Stonehenge to Jerome Wolfe," she stated positively, again scanning her tables.

"How are you going to stop them?"

"I don't know." Layla pursed her lips as she thought. "But I'm going there with you over Easter. Maybe I'll never leave. Stage a sit-in. Occupy the building. Make a land claim."

Lucy snorted. "Maybe I'll join you in that." She pulled out her phone and checked the time. "But for now, I'm going to see if Evie can go home with Daphne. I've got a meeting with my lawyer this afternoon at my house."

"Dallas?" Layla peered hard at her, even as she was signaled back to the counter by the other harassed waitress.

Lucy nodded, feeling her heart trip a bit.

"Let me know how that goes. I'm out of here in a few minutes. Have some minor changes to a staging I've got to take care of. Neil's out of town for a week, so I'm around if you need me."

"You can't marry him."

"I know."

Kate clicked off her cell phone, a little annoyed at Lucy's presumptuousness. Yes, okay, she had problems. Big problems, and she was meeting with her attorney, so that meant what? That she was about to be accused of murder? That was huge, and yet . . . Kate had problems of her own. This afternoon was the next meeting of Lyle and *Pat*, she of the pink scarf, whatever that meant. Not at the Pembroke Inn this time; at a different spot Kate had cruised by on her way to work this morning, which had earned her a barrage of questions from Daphne.

"What are we doing here? I thought we were getting Starbucks. Why are we going away from the school? You're not going to take me to some restaurant, are you?" she'd groaned as Kate had cruised through the parking lot of a Mexican restaurant that served happy hour from three to six. Lyle's appointment with Pat was set for four p.m., a couple of hours before he came home to his family.

Now, she didn't know quite how she was going to do everything. She'd gotten a sitter for this afternoon from an agency that demanded a four-hour minimum, which was highway robbery at their rates, and now with Evie added into the mix, it would be even more. But on the plus side, with Evie there, Daphne wouldn't ask too many questions, and even if Lyle reached home before she did, the extra people in the house would send him up to the bedroom to escape and Kate could say she was doing some shopping or something. He wouldn't look too closely at what she was doing. He never did. She'd put a Crock-Pot together with beef stew this morning, so dinner would be ready. Not that he seemed to really care about that these days either.

He'd swept up the pearl necklace while Kate was getting ready for work this morning; at least it was no longer on his nightstand when she'd hurried Daphne through her morning routine. The dawdling could drive her insane, and it was always worse when Kate had somewhere she had to be. It was like Daphne had radar that picked up the slightest vibe of her mother's anxiety.

But okay. She could get Daphne and Evie home, set up with the sitter, and still fly out of the house and head to a bathroom somewhere to change into her disguise and make it to Arriba by four . . . maybe . . . if the traffic wasn't too bad.

But the necklace . . . the necklace . . . She was so angry she could cry. She *had* shed a couple of tears into her pillow last might. Lyle was lying to her in all sorts of ways. What had she done to deserve this? Nothing! All she'd wanted was to be a good wife to him, to make his life easy and comfortable. All he needed to do in return was treat her with respect.

The day crept by. April came in and barked at her twice, and Kate had had to drag herself back from daymares about Lyle sweeping in the door and announcing it was over, he was in love with someone else, he'd been seeing her for months, they were eloping to the Seychelles and so he was going to need that divorce right away, okay, Katie?

Her anger coalesced inside her, a hard, dark rock in the center of her being. She would kill him first.

Chapter Twenty-Three

Layla took Uber to the Black Swan Gallery, where she met her friend, Matt, who was a struggling artist like herself but also worked at the gallery part-time. He had an eye for color and had half-partnered with Layla on the staging business, offering free storage space in the building behind the southwest suburban home he'd inherited from his parents. She told him, "I want to look to see what we have. I've got to buy some red pillows and cheap art, but I just want to dig through what's in storage before I add to my credit card debt."

He nodded. "There're some really good cerulean vases in there."

"Blue isn't going to work. This house is cold. Buyers are mentally shivering already."

He shrugged and said, "You got a key."

"All right. Thanks."

She took another Uber back to her apartment. She was going to have to drive her car to Matt's house, and to Home-Goods or Bed Bath & Beyond, or somewhere she could pick up what she needed without spending an arm and a leg. Mary Jo expected her to have whatever was required at a moment's notice, even though she was practically a one-woman operation, unlike the larger stagers around town who had their own warehouses full of furniture and house-hold décor; Mary Jo just liked Layla's more reasonable prices. Over the past several seasons, Layla had purchased some larger pieces of furniture and redone them, sanding down bedsteads and nightstands, restaining or painting them, buying old lamps and antique tchotchkes, massive picture frames that needed time and elbow grease to bring them back to life. She had a modest stockpile of items, and with Matt's goodwill, and sometimes the use of his truck and muscle, she'd managed to start her own small business, broadening her scope, though Mary Jo jealously guarded Layla as if she owned her.

This task meant she needed her own car to bring back items for the staging; therefore, she would have to take the used green Toyota Corolla she'd purchased on time and had paid off a year earlier, the one she rarely ever drove. She thought briefly of the woman who'd died in the car crash, and her husband, who'd continually threatened to sue Layla even though it had been decided in court that the accident wasn't her fault and he didn't have a case. Apparently, the truth didn't matter to him. Only his own truth, which was that someone should pay for his wife's death, and that some-one was Layla.

She hurried up the steps to her apartment, then practically skidded to a stop. In front of her, unwrapped and propped against her door, was her painting, the one Jerome Wolfe had purchased at the auction. A note had been carelessly taped right onto the painting itself, right on the canvas, and she carefully peeled it off as she read: *I overpaid, but it was for a good cause, right? Not really something I have any use for. If you resell it, send me a check. J.*

She could almost hear his sarcastic tone, see his evil grin. "Asshole," she muttered.

The man hated her, hated her family, and wanted to

provoke them any way he possibly could. She'd played right into his hands by asking for a ride.

She thrust open her door, frustrated and angry right down to the tips of her toes, wrestling the painting inside. It was large, too large for either her apartment or her car . . . but . . . it was full of brilliant oranges, reds, and golds. Just what the doctor ordered. She couldn't help but smile at the irony of the situation.

Yanking her cell phone from her purse, she called Matt and ordered the gallery truck and a worker to help her. "I've got a painting to move to an open house today. Think you can find someone to ferry it for me? Hang it on the wall . . . ?" She would have to pay them for the expense with what she made from the staging.

"Got it," Matt said.

"Thanks." She clicked off. Matt was the only man in her life she could depend on, she realized. Too bad he was gay and in a committed relationship.

She looked at the painting, said a few choice swear words in her mind about Jerome Wolfe, who loved twisting the knife, then decided she was the winner in this one. Hell if she was going to pay him a dime if she resold it.

Or maybe she would see if Neil wanted it after all. She didn't know if he'd been bidding on it at the benefit just to compete with Wolfe or to play with her like Wolfe had, but there was a chance he actually wanted it.

She wasn't going to marry him, in any case. She'd toyed with the idea, but Lucy was right. It wouldn't work. No matter how much she wanted Eddie, any marriage she would agree to would just be because of the baby. The whole thing would fall apart and could be even uglier than the last few months between them. But . . . she could work on making peace and getting what she wanted at the same time by offering the painting as an olive branch.

All courtesy of Jerome Wolfe, who loved to throw his

money around and make the point that his family had
prospered while hers had declined.

Lucy rinsed her sweating palms beneath the kitchen
faucet, then wiped them with a paper towel. Nerves. She'd
never particularly been a palm sweater, so why now?

*Like you really don't know. Dallas is coming to your
house. Better recheck your deodorant, too, because this
could become a full-fledged sweatathon.*

She took her own advice and hurried upstairs, applying
more Secret under her armpits. Then she surveyed her outfit.
Black slacks and a white fuzzy sweater with a cowl neck.
She tried a smile at herself in the bathroom mirror and decided she had on too much blush, the result of realizing she
was too pale and going full tilt into the beauty products.

*And what do you care anyway? You're not going to tell
him about Evie. He's just coming over as your attorney. You
shouldn't even really like him.*

She patted off some of the color on her cheeks, then
fussed with her hair for a few minutes, hating it, finally
snapping it back into a ponytail and adding small faux pearl
earrings, aware that her hands were trembling slightly . . .
and beginning to sweat again.

She blasted the room with another string of swear words
just as she heard the doorbell ring. Swiping her palms on her
slacks, she hurried downstairs, allowing herself an extra five
seconds at the door while she mentally composed herself.

Jesus Christ, what are you, fifteen?

Dallas looked at Lucy Linfield gazing up at him, her
smile a little unsure as she answered the door and invited
him in. Something there.

And then a forgotten memory tackled him like an NFL

linebacker. The ponytail . . . the curving lips . . . the slight insecurity . . . He *knew* her.

"Lucy," he said in a stranger's voice.

"Come on in. Is September with you, or is she coming separately?" Lucy glanced past him, unaware of his shock.

"No, she's on her own."

That night at the fraternity house. *She* was the girl. Wasn't she? *Wasn't she?* She didn't seem to know him, but that girl's name had been Lucy. He remembered that much, even if most of that night was a blank thanks to Jim Borden, Jimbo, who'd purposely roofied him, his specialty, apparently, according to some of Luke's fraternity brothers, a few of whom had suffered the same fate as he had. Jimbo had been indiscriminate, choosing whoever he felt like to drug, though only a fraction of those roofied had come forward as he had, or the jail time might have been a lot longer for his "pranks." The last Dallas had heard, he'd moved to Los Angeles, trying to break into the Hollywood scene at some level. Luke thought he'd broken into the drug scene instead, which would be no surprise. Dallas had never told Luke the total truth of what had occurred that night. He hadn't figured it out himself for quite a while, and he suspected his younger brother might do something rash and impulsive and life-altering, meaning Jimbo's own life might be altered for the worse. Beyond a still-smoldering anger over the shortness of Jimbo's jail term, and a belief that Borden's life would likely be taken care of by his own bad choices, Dallas had let the matter go.

But now . . . here . . . how?

He was following Lucy into the house, lost in memories, completely out of the moment. He had to drag his attention back, focus on his surroundings. Her place had the homey feel of a family. There were pictures on the mantel above the fireplace in the family room, afternoon light slanting on them: John Linfield and Lucy and a series of a young girl, aging from a baby to about eight, maybe nine.

The doorbell rang again. "There she is," Lucy said, walking past him as she went to the door again, circling around him as if she was afraid to touch him, a faint floral scent of perfume following in her wake.

He heard their voices. The two women greeted each other like old friends. From what they said, apparently, Lucy had drunk more wine than she intended the night before. Lucy's voice was bright and eager, almost manic, he thought. Did she know?

Lucy had walked September back to the family room and he greeted her, but his eyes followed Lucy. Did she know?

She was offering them water or sodas, beer or wine. September declined everything, but he said, "Water would be great."

She smiled and a few minutes later put a tall, cold glass in his hand, ice tinkling inside. He lifted it to his mouth and drank half of it down in a gulp.

Now September was talking to Lucy about Jerome Wolfe, about his wanting to purchase both Wolfe Lodge and the adjacent property, asking Lucy for her opinion on that news, to which Lucy gave her a scathing review of Wolfe himself. Was it his imagination, or did she seem almost eager to focus on September and ignore him?

She had to remember. No wonder she'd seemed so familiar. He'd spoken to her the night before . . . talked some . . . The night of the fraternity party, all he'd wanted to do was leave. How he'd gotten talked into going there was still a mystery to him. He normally actively avoided those kinds of events.

My friends call you Grandpa. You know that, right?

Okay, maybe he'd tried to prove he was something he wasn't that night. Maybe he'd wanted to show his younger brother he was cooler than he was, but Luke hadn't even been there that night. He'd stolen away with some girl he'd met, and he'd left Dallas at the fraternity with "brothers" years younger than Luke, ones he hadn't even known all that well.

Dallas thought of Joanna Creighton, who'd wanted him to represent her son who'd got caught selling drugs. Young adults sometimes made bad choices. He defended people who made those bad choices. He'd made some bad choices himself; case in point. What he couldn't handle these days was people not owning their mistakes, lying about them.

"What do you think?" Lucy asked him, her fine brows pulled into a line. It made him realize he'd been silent as a tomb throughout their discussion.

He had to cast his mind back to recall what they'd been going over. The Kilgore property. Should September follow up with them as long as she was going to be in Wharton County?

And he realized Lucy was also silently asking if she should bring up her knowledge of Amanita ocreata, which she'd brought up to him yesterday . . . was it just yesterday? . . . how Brianne Kilgore, the nature girl, had shown Lucy, Lyle, and Layla the deadly mushrooms that had killed her husband.

Dallas deliberated. It was a risk, talking about it, especially because Lucy hadn't told the police yet. If September decided to take that information back to them before Lucy brought it up on her own . . .

Lucy must have read something on his face and misinterpreted it as a yes, because she launched in with, "The Kilgores' daughter, Brianne—my brother used to call her Nell, after the movie with Jodie Foster? She knows all about nature, animals and plants and you name it . . . she pointed out the angel of death mushroom to us once. We all knew about it, my sister and brother and I, but of course, none of us ever dreamed of actually using it. It was just a fascinating fact, one of a number that Brianne revealed to us. . . ."

She told September much the same tale she'd told Dallas the day before, about visiting Stonehenge and visiting the Kilgores. When she was finished, she sent him a worried look, probably wondering what had robbed him of speech. With an effort, Dallas said to September, "She hasn't told the police this yet."

"You think I should?" Lucy asked anxiously.

"Maybe after September talks with the Kilgores." He looked to the ex-detective.

"Sure. I'd like to interview this Brianne Kilgore," September said. "You're going to want full transparency when you talk to them, though. You don't want the police to determine you're hiding something."

"I'm not hiding anything," Lucy shot right back. "It's just . . . I can't really believe this. Who would want to kill my husband? With *poison*?"

No one had an answer for that, so a few seconds later, September said, "I've got a few hours of daylight left. Maybe I'll go to Wharton County right now."

Dallas nodded. The sooner the better.

"Do you want a key to Stonehenge?" Lucy asked. "I still have one."

"Sure."

Lucy went to the kitchen, searched in a drawer, and pulled out a metal ring that had a number of keys on it. She twisted one off, then handed it to September, who tucked it into a zippered pocket. The ex-detective was wearing jeans, ankle boots, a sweater, and a short jacket with a hood, clearly ready for the outdoors.

She left a few moments later, and Dallas followed both Lucy and September to the door. After September left, Lucy turned to him, her eyes clouded. "You hardly said a word. Should I be worried?" There was a thread of panic to her voice.

"I was just listening, thinking things over."

"Are you worried about September? Do you think she'll go to the police?"

"No . . . Luke said she's a good investigator."

"She seems so nice. Maybe I shouldn't have talked so much." Lucy was clearly having second thoughts.

"I think it's okay."

"Well, what's wrong, then?" she asked. "Is it my case? I've got to say, you're scaring me a little."

"That's not why I was . . . disengaged."

"Well, what?" She held his gaze, her expression careful.

He decided to go for it. "Sorry. It's just that you've seemed so familiar and I was trying to place where we might have met."

"Oh." Color pinkened her cheeks.

She *did* remember. He would bet that was what caused the blush. "I think I've got it now," he said, watching her. "We met . . . you and I . . . about ten years ago at my brother's fraternity house. I was there for—"

"Oh, yes. That's right," she cut him off. "I remember."

"All of it? Because I don't. I woke up sick in the dark, and I . . ."

"You grabbed your clothes and left," she said flatly. "At least I assume that's what happened."

He was gut punched. "You were the girl in the bed, then . . . ?" He vaguely remembered a girl beside him, a flash of white skin. "I just remember talking to you downstairs."

"Okay." She nodded several times, wrapping her arms around her torso, clearly uncomfortable. "Yes . . . that was me."

"You knew it was me . . . you've known . . . ?"

"Did I know who I slept with? Yes," she snapped.

"I'm sorry. I don't . . . know what to say."

"Not my finest hour. Maybe we can leave it at that." She tried on a tight smile.

"One of the fraternity brothers, Jim Borden, spiked my drink."

"Jimbo."

"Yeah. He thought it was funny. A joke. I wasn't the only one, by a long shot, I'd say. He went to prison over it, for a time."

"Did he?" She sounded almost distracted.

"That's what I understand."

"Okay. . . ." She'd been looking past him, but now she glanced back. "So, you don't remember anything about that night? I mean, after we went upstairs . . . ?"

He didn't know what the right answer was. He didn't want to insult her, yet the few memories he had were indistinct enough to seem like a dream.

"Well, that's an interesting reason for not calling," she said lightly, taking his silence as answer enough.

"I don't think there's a Hallmark card for this," he said carefully.

Her bark of laughter was accompanied by tears standing in her eyes.

"Lucy, I'm sorry." He stepped forward, but his movement just caused her to step back.

"Don't be. You didn't know." She held up her hands. "It's years ago. Water under the bridge."

"Doesn't sound like it."

"No, truly, it is." She was nodding rapidly. "I thought about calling you, but when you didn't call me, I just let it go. It's silly to even care. I'm over it." She looked up at him brightly. "Can we just get back to the problems at hand?"

Holy shit. Holy mother of . . . oh, goddamn . . . shit . . .

Lucy could barely think. She wanted to run away, but where? To some other room of her own house? To another universe?

He didn't know . . . he didn't know!

All these years . . . the choices she'd made, all of them based on a wrong assumption. But what if she'd called him, reached him, told him the truth? What would have happened?

It was almost comical. Almost.

"Sure," he said, answering her last question, but then, "You knew this when you came to my office? You've known it all along?"

Was that an accusation? No. He was processing. Like she was processing. Oh, hell. *Oh hell!*

Her heart clutched. What if he did the addition, realized Evie was his? Her eyes shifted of their own volition to the photographs on the mantel. Immediately, she looked away, afraid he would follow her gaze, realize . . . or at least put the question in his head . . . about what the truth was.

"My sister told me to come see you after John died," she explained. Her ears were thundering. She couldn't *think*.

"Did Layla know?"

"I never told her everything . . . about that night." *Careful. Careful now. Think about what you're saying. Is this really the moment you want to blurt everything out? Should she? No . . . no . . . not yet.* She needed time. "But I must've said something, because she figured it out."

"So, she knew when she came to me?"

She wasn't sure where this was going, but there was nothing to say but the truth. She nodded jerkily.

"Huh . . . okay."

She sensed he wanted to ask more about it. All the questions she had answers to. *Yes, we made love. Yes, I was more than willing. Yes, I wanted to sleep with you. And yes, there were consequences. . . .*

What she did say, was, "Other people have one-night stands."

He inclined his head in agreement. "Still . . . wish I'd known. Coulda been a different outcome."

"Yeah, right?" Her laugh sounded fake to her own ears. "I'm glad we met again."

Aren't you engaged? she wanted to ask, but she couldn't find her tongue. After a few more awkward moments, Dallas told her he'd be calling her with an update on what September learned, then took his leave. As soon as he was gone, Lucy pressed her back against the door and shut her eyes. The effects of a sleep-deprived night and a long day had brought on the headache that had been hovering around the edges of her skull. Luckily, Evie could be at Kate's for another hour or two.

She went upstairs and dropped on the bed fully clothed, dragging the bedspread around herself, cocooning herself against the world.

Arriba was divided into a warren of rooms; therefore, it wasn't nearly as easy to see to the bar from the tables. The walls were splashed with bright primary colors, red, green, blue, and sunshine yellow, and dotted with sombreros, serapes. and maracas in every conceivable shape and size. Kate balked when the hostess, who was in black pants and a close-fitting black jacket, apparently having missed the color-scheme memo, tried to seat her too far away, without clear sight of the bar, which was where she expected Lyle and Pat to meet. She lobbied for a table in one of the rooms nearest to the entry area, one with a fairly in-line view of the bar if she sat just so. The hostess clearly disliked being thwarted, however, and marched back to her podium with her nose in the air. Little bitch. She wasn't fooling anyone with those "diamond" earrings.

Kate was in a fever of excitement. Her knee was shaking and her pulse raced. She took a deep breath and quickly reached up to adjust her wig, which itched and felt awkward and heavy. The big glasses made her want to rub her nose, but it was all a small price to pay.

She'd arrived forty minutes early, so she ordered a small plate of nachos that came in a huge mountain that made her certain they'd given her the large platter. A heated discussion ensued between her and her waiter, one the hostess tried to poke her nose into as well, which made perspiration collect under Kate's arms as time kept ticking by. She groaned when she saw the waiter confer with the manager, apparently, which the hostess avidly listened in on as well. Did these people have nothing more important to do? Wasn't there anyone else in need of a margarita or something?

She finally had to lift a hand and say the nachos were fine, fine, totally fine before their little cabal broke up, and by that time it was ten minutes to four and she felt wrung out. She was mad at Lyle. Deep-down mad. Ready-to-wring-his-neck mad. He was meeting Pat on the sly, lying about the pearls—she just knew it—and acting like he could barely stand Kate's touch anymore. What had happened to his sexual appetite? He sure could flirt with the cute young women around him, but could he give his wife a kind word? No way.

By the time Pat showed up a few minutes before four, Kate was horrified to see she had mowed through the nacho mountain until it looked more like a molehill. Lord, she was going to pay for this! She could practically feel her body ballooning with excess calories.

Zeroing in on Pat, Kate pretended she had laser eyes to burn a hole in the back of the woman's ugly gray raincoat. Pat seemed tense, too. Kate could see her toe wiggling as she sat on the barstool. Her purse was on the seat next to her and she took out her wallet to order a cup of coffee. No drink, even though it was happy hour. Well, Kate hadn't ordered one either, but then, she was on a mission and couldn't afford to dull her wits. Maybe Pat was, too?

Lyle brushed in about five minutes later.

There you are, you lying bastard, she fumed in her seat.

He pretended to look around and then finally decided to sit in the seat on the other side of Pat's purse. Lyle shot another glance around the room, checking to see if anyone was watching, and Kate's pulse spiked, even while she quickly ducked her head to look inside her own purse, which sat on the table in front of her, as if searching for something in its depths

A few moments later, she carefully peered over the rims of her glasses to note that Lyle had ordered a beer. He drank slowly and appeared to be scrolling through his phone. Pat had her phone in hand as well. Kate's waiter brought her the bill and Kate almost missed Lyle putting something in Pat's purse because the waiter was blocking her view. She had to dart a quick look around the man's right side, just in time to see Lyle pulling his hand away. The edge of an envelope peeked from the bag.

A few minutes later, Pat paid for her coffee, swept up her bag, and left. Kate was in a panic. She threw down a twenty . . . damn, was it more than that? She snatched out another five. Not worth that much, but she needed to sneak out.

Nerves stretched tight, Kate scurried toward the entry area, passing right behind Lyle's back on her way to the door. Luckily, he wasn't interested in anything but his phone. Hurrying, she reached her car in time to see Pat climbing into a black Volkswagen Passat. Good, okay. She slipped into her car and switched on her engine as the Passat sped out of the lot and onto the side street. Kate eased in behind her. Okay. Okay . . . she had enough gas to go over a hundred miles, so unless Pat was heading on a long-distance trip, Kate was okay.

She had a bad moment thinking about leaving Lyle at the bar by himself. That little hostess was just the kind of snippy bitch to catch his attention. Maybe she was the reason he'd chosen Arriba. Meet Pat for another pass off of God knew what, then hang out at the bar and see what kind of hot piece of ass shimmied by.

No. Stop it. She couldn't think that way. Not now. Not while she was chasing down Pat.

Still, her brain was in a froth of indecision as the Passat suddenly turned onto a side road, to a less commercial area. Kate followed, aware her and Pat's were the only two cars on a street that was a mix of small businesses and some tired-looking houses that were slowly being overtaken by new commercial buildings, an area becoming gentrified, which to Kate's way of thinking was a good thing. She couldn't understand these people who protested that their neighbor-hoods were being unalterably changed. Well, of course they were. For the better!

The Passat swung to the right and into what looked like a circular drive. Kate almost followed but stayed her course, a gasp in her throat. She'd thought the neighborhood looked familiar; she'd just never driven it before. A glance toward the building Pat had turned into: Cascade Place Assisted Care. The assisted living community where Junior, Lyle's grandfather, had spent his last days. Kate had visited the assisted care center with Lyle a couple of times but had always been a passenger in the car. The area was really start-ing to be much nicer now. Though Cascade Place was one of the highest-ranked care centers around, it was planted in the center of a dicey area.

Pat had eschewed the front portico and driven down the side of the building toward the rear parking lot. Kate wound around the block, coming to the lot from the other side. She pulled into the rear parking lot in time to see Pat huddled under a small awning, punching in the code for the back door into an electronic keypad. Kate didn't remember the code, and it probably had changed anyway in the months—almost a year now—since Junior's death. She couldn't catch the door before it closed, so she hurried around the sidewalk to the front of the building and was able to walk inside through the main doors without buzzing.

The woman at the reception desk smiled at her, but Kate just lifted a hand and marched forward, acting as if she owned the place. Always better to ask for forgiveness rather than permission. She almost missed the sign-in book as she passed. Maybe it was better to sign in. She picked up the pen and wrote in April's name, just to be on the safe side if anyone checked later, then headed down the main corridor.

She was concerned she'd missed Pat, but she needn't have worried. Pat was standing at a nurses' station at the juncture of the north/south and east/west corridors.

Kate had to stop short and pretend to be looking for the women's room.

She found the door and pushed through into the bathroom. She was breathing hard, her pulse racing, her mind whirling. Pat appeared to be one of the staff at Cascade Place. What did that mean?

After several moments of planning her next move, she headed back into the corridor and past the nurses' station. Pat was sitting behind the broad desk, reading a computer screen. Kate saw her name tag: Lauren Paulsen. Ah, LP. And as she glanced up at Kate with an inquiring look, Kate said, "Hello. I'm interested in having my aunt come to Cascade Place. Do you think I could look at any of the rooms?"

"We're full right now, so I don't know. Check at the office. Someone there can help you."

"Are you a . . . nurse?"

"I'm an administrator now." Her faint smile was chilly, as if she thought Kate had impugned her somehow. *Must be a new position or she wouldn't be so touchy*, Kate thought.

"Okay. Thank you."

She wanted to ask a thousand more questions but wasn't sure where to begin. And truthfully, she knew enough now about Lauren Paulsen to demand answers from Lyle. He was the one who owed her an explanation.

As she turned away, she caught sight of a picture of Lauren with a couple of other staff members, all in their scrubs, but Lauren was wearing a pink scarf tossed jauntily around her neck.

Chapter Twenty-Four

September fought traffic and made it to the Wharton County Sheriff's Department at around five p.m. She hurried up the front steps of the low concrete building, glad the rain had stopped, though she was wearing jeans and a raincoat, and when she entered, she strode to the desk where a young woman with upswept blond hair and a tan uniform smiled at her.

"I'd like to see the sheriff. I'm following up on the anonymous call you received about Amanita ocreata poisoning. The sheriff already spoke to Detective Wes Pelligree about it."

"Oh. Um . . . the sheriff's left for the day. . . ."

September had thrown out Wes's name to try to get around the front desk before she had to explain she wasn't with the police. That plan had apparently worked, at least for the moment, but her trip still looked like it might be for naught.

The girl said helpfully, "But Deputy Morant is still here. He's the one who actually took the call."

"Great. Would you tell him September Westerly's here to see him? I think Wes might have mentioned I would be following up." September held her breath. She wasn't used to having to explain her interest without the full support of the law behind her, but the call was put through and Deputy Morant appeared a few moments later, meeting September outside the front desk. He strode through with his chin lifted in self-importance, but he eyed September up and down and softened a bit. "Come on in," he invited, pushing back through the door from which he'd exited, September following. They entered a room with a couple of desks and chairs arranged tidily around the periphery. It was about half the size of the Laurelton Police squad room, with even less furniture. There was a topographical map of the county on the wall and September glanced at it, mentally gauging approximately where Stonehenge and the Kilgore properties were, checking their relationship to Glenn River, the closest town, and where the burner cell phone had been purchased from which the call was made.

Morant was about fifty, in good shape, with strong-looking arms and a new haircut that was shaved white above his ears. He shook hands with her and introduced himself, then said, "I can't tell you any more than I told Detective Pelligree. The call came in and we were told to look for angel of death poisoning in the . . . what's the vic's name?"

"John Linfield."

He grunted. "Right. Linfield's death."

"It was a woman's voice on the phone," prodded September.

"That's right. I told the sheriff about it, and he called you people at Laurelton PD to order the autopsy." He hesitated. "Pelligree didn't mention you."

She nodded crisply. "Wes is no longer on the investigation. He's moving to Portland PD." Morant made a sound of surprise as September went on glibly, "I know. Detective Sanders and I are going to miss him. So, I thought I'd meet with the sheriff and you personally. We really want to find this caller and learn how she knew what to look for." She

hadn't technically said she was still an officer, but she was
certainly skating on thin ice.

"The phone was from the StopGo shop by the Shell
station in Glenn River."

"I'm heading there next," September said. "The caller
gave the information directly to you. Do you remember her
exact words?"

"'The angel of death killed someone at the Stonehenge
auction. The autopsy will show you.' That's pretty close."

"She used the word 'Stonehenge'?"

"No . . . no . . . that was me. She said, 'at the Crissman
auction.'" He looked a bit sheepish. "I'm sure this time. That
place is just called Stonehenge around here by people."

"When you say people, you mean . . . ?"

"Oh, neighbors, really . . . the Kilgores for sure. I know
them pretty well. Daniel Kilgore died a while back, but
Mona and Brianne are there."

"The Kilgores own the property that abuts . . . Stonehenge."

He smiled. "That's right."

September asked a few more questions, but Morant had
nothing further. She took her leave, breathing a sigh of relief
that the deputy hadn't found her out. She drove directly to
the southern edge of Glenn River and found the StopGo convenience store near the Shell station and headed inside,
noting the rows of neatly arranged packaged goods: junk
food, auto supplies, a small dairy section, magazines, bat-
teries, phone chargers, everything to grab on the go. She
walked up to the counter. A middle-aged man with a sweeping gray mustache was at the register. His name tag read
Barry. She introduced herself. "I'm September Westerly
with Laurelton PD. Are you the person who sold the disposable phone that was sold from this store and used to phone
the sheriff's department about the Stonehenge poisoning?"

"The what?"

"Its real name is Wolfe Lodge."

Barry hesitated and looked over his shoulder. A woman about his age had appeared from behind a tan door near automotive supplies and was slowly walking their way. She had short, steel-gray hair and a stolid face that was focused on Barry. Her name tag read Rhonda.

"I talked to an officer," said Barry, as Rhonda reached the counter, eyes narrowing.

"Detective Pelligree. I talked to him about the phone sold from your store."

"We don't know anything," said Rhonda.

September wondered if they were married. There was something about her possessiveness that spoke of their being more than just co-workers.

"We're gonna get cameras now," Barry said.

"Shoulda done it a long time ago," Rhonda agreed.

"There's no paperwork for the sale?" September asked, knowing she was going to hit a dead end because Wes had already filled her in, but she wanted to hear what they had to say anyway.

"Just a cash sale. Lot of people want disposables for cash," said Rhonda.

"You don't remember a woman buying a phone?" September asked Barry, who had dropped his gaze to the counter.

"I should," he said.

"Can't remember everyone. We get a lot of customers," added Rhonda.

"Of course," September said agreeably, though she was the only one in the store on a Friday evening, when people would be getting off work.

"You have some ID?" Rhonda asked suspiciously.

Ah, the jig was up. Bound to happen. September swept in a breath, not quite sure what she was going to say, when Barry looked up and said, "It was over a year ago."

"You do remember her?" September asked, surprised.

"Nah. Just remembered doing the paperwork," Rhonda jumped in, glaring at Barry as if she wished he would stop talking.

"That's right," Barry agreed. He looked at September directly. "If we knew anything, we'd tell ya. We just don't remember."

Rhonda snapped, "That's for sure."

"Okay," September said, thanking them and taking her leave before Rhonda requested her ID again. She'd managed to bluff her way through better than she'd hoped, but she sensed she'd pushed as much as she dared. She was likely going to have to play it straight from here on out.

It was almost six o'clock by the time she reached the Kilgore home: a two-story farmhouse with a moss-covered roof, water dripping down a drooping corner and a fenced area with several goats staring out disinterestedly through wooden rails. The long, winding drive had led through a forest of Douglas firs. She figured the Crissman property, Wolfe Lodge, was to her west, but the forest was too dense to see the huge home. September mentally compared the well-tended Crissman grounds to the wild, nearly engulfed by vegetation Kilgore property and thought about Jerome Wolfe's apparently avid acquisition of both.

She parked the Outback to one side of a large mud puddle, stepping out cautiously, her ankle boots leaning toward the more decorative when faced with rough terrain. Knocking on the heavy oak door, she heard the deep bark of what sounded like a large dog. No immediate answer by a human. She tried a second time, got another bark, then took a step back, gazing up at the brown-stained board-and-batten siding. From the corner of her eye she glimpsed the goats, still staring, watching her.

Finally, she heard a slow thumping inside, someone approaching. A walker, she thought. Mona Kilgore, Daniel Kilgore's widow?

When the door opened, a woman with a cloud of white hair, stooped over a metal-framed walker, appeared. September's first impression was that the woman was in her eighties, but a closer look—and a mental calculation based on the age of her daughter, Brianne, late twenties—put her closer to sixty.

"Mrs. Kilgore, my name's September Westerly. I'm working with Lucy Crissman Linfield to—"

"I know who you are. Martin called me."

Martin? Before she could ask, Mrs. Kilgore lifted a hand and motioned to invite her in, then picked up the walker and began slowly thumping her way into the back of the house. September quickly closed the door, then followed her, passing two what looked like little-used front rooms down a hallway to a kitchen and a small sitting room with a lit gas fire. Through a window, September had a view of the propane tank that fed the house back-dropped by dark green firs.

"I'm not sure who Martin is," September said.

"Oh. Deputy Morant."

"Ah. He called you?" My, my, they were a tight-knit community.

The older woman sat down heavily in a recliner and swept a red, orange, and brown afghan over her knees. She wore a solid blue robe that snapped up the front, a pair of blue-and-green-striped pajama bottoms, and gray slipper socks that offered traction and looked as if they would stay on her feet.

"Cancer," she said to September's unasked question. "My husband died from his heart. Me, it's the big C."

September nodded.

"I don't know anything about that phone call, if that's why you're here."

"It's one of the reasons I drove your way," she admitted. She then explained that she was looking for background on the Crissmans and their deal with Jerome Wolfe.

"Jerome Wolfe," she said, her lips pulling back into a grimace. "You think there's a connection to him and the death of Lucy's husband?" Her skepticism filled the room. For all her infirmity, she was clearly sharp and opinionated.

"Just gathering information at this point."

"You're with the police?"

"I . . . was," she admitted.

"Was . . . that's not what Martin said."

"I'm working with Lucy Linfield's attorney on this case. The police are running their own investigation."

"They think she did it? Killed her husband?"

September assumed "they" were the police. "I'm not sure, but it isn't my theory."

"You got a theory?"

"Just trying to put things into focus at this point."

"Hmmm." Mona Kilgore looked past September, who was still standing near the kitchen, and said, "If you want something to drink, you'll have to help yourself. I could use some water. There's a pitcher in the fridge. Glasses in that cupboard." She pointed to one left of the sink.

September found the glasses and pulled out two, pouring them each a glass of water from the pitcher kept chilled in the refrigerator. She took Mona hers and kept one for herself.

"Sit down," Mona invited, and September settled on the couch. She heard heavy padding and turned to see a huge, older mixed-breed dog moving toward them from the front of the house. He came by and stared at September a moment, then moved toward Mona, easing himself down on the braided rug that filled the area, heaving a deep sigh as he settled.

Mona said, "Duke and I are quite a pair."

"How old is Duke?"

"About thirteen. Followed Brianne on her bike all the way from town, wouldn't let her go."

"Glenn River?"

"Yep. Twenty-two miles. She has a way with animals. You probably heard."

"She works at an animal shelter."

"Mmm-hmm. She'll be back soon. You can talk to her, if you want."

September thought it was time to get to the point. Maybe she would have time to talk with Brianne, maybe not. She'd gotten most of what she was looking for from Deputy Morant.

"I understand you're selling your property to Jerome Wolfe."

"Don't want to. Daniel never wanted to. But Mr. Wolfe turned Brianne's head, and she's the one who's gonna have this place after I'm gone, so what good does it do to fight? I'd like her to keep it. It's all she's ever known, but Brianne doesn't heed me or her father. Never has."

"When you say 'turned Brianne's head,' you mean romantically?"

"Yes, ma'am. The man's handsome, I'll give him that. Brianne's a looker herself. Don't know where she gets it."

September didn't like the idea that Wolfe might be using his charm to steal the Kilgore property. "Has he made an offer?"

"Yes, he has, and Brianne has accepted it. But we both have to sign, and I'm the holdout. I'm not leaving this place till I'm gone." She sighed. "And where will she go, once it's gone and so am I? Miss . . . what did you say your name was?"

"September."

"Like the month? Huh. Well, September, my daughter can't see past today. She'll sell, and then I'm afraid once the paperwork's done, Wolfe'll disappear, too. She'll try to come back, but there'll be nowhere to come back to. He'll put up a gate. Raze the house. Harvest the trees. It will kill her."

"If—"

"I've tried to tell her," Mona went on. "Believe me. I've

tried, but she doesn't listen." She shook her head. "Brianne understands death. She's seen it with all the animals and with her father, and she knows it's happening to me soon . . . but she doesn't understand people. She can't see that Wolfe is using her, and you can't tell her differently. The man's a snake in the grass, if you ask me, but Brianne won't hear of it."

"What's the nature of their relationship?"

"Are they doing it? That what you're asking?" She leveled a look at September.

"Well, I—"

"It's not sexual. I'm pretty sure. She tried that once and it didn't work. Maybe Wolfe could convince her otherwise, but I don't think he's even trying. He wants the land, and he's got Brianne's adoration already. He's the kind that wants what he can't have, y'know?"

The picture she was presenting was in keeping with what had been inferred about Jerome Wolfe. "Maybe your daughter needs a lawyer, to ensure she gets a fair price."

"Oh, she does. She needs one. But she won't do it. The price is fair. Maybe not top dollar, but it's close enough that no one's crying foul. I hear the Crissman daughters don't want to sell, but the son does."

"I believe the sale of Wolfe Lodge has been spearheaded by Abbott Crissman, Lucy, Layla, and Lyle's father."

She snorted. "Lyle Abbott Crissman the third. I know the man all right."

"You don't like him."

"None of us ever did. His father now, Junior, my Daniel liked him quite a bit. Said he was the best of the bunch, meaning the men in that family. I guess the old guy, Criss, was a terror. Killed his wife. Never found her body. Said she ran off, but Daniel's family never believed it." She pointed a trembling finger in the direction of the Crissman property. "They're all evil. Maybe not the girls, but you can't trust a Crissman man."

September took that in.

They heard the rumble of a truck's engine and Mona said, "Okay, there she is."

A few moments later, September heard a door open; a back door, through a storeroom off the kitchen. She heard someone taking off their boots, she believed, and then a slim, rawhide-tough-looking young woman walked in, sock-footed.

Nell, September thought in surprise. She looked a lot like Jodie Foster except that her hair, pulled back into a ponytail, was pure, unadulterated silvery gray.

"Runs in the family," Mona was saying, as if she'd read September's thoughts. "The hair. That's what she got from me. Cousin's the same way. We all gray early."

September just stared. Brianne Kilgore was the gray-haired woman from the cleaning crew at Wolfe Lodge the night of the benefit.

September had never really looked directly at the cleaning crew the night of the benefit. She'd been so focused on Lucy and John and everything that went with taking care of the problem of his illness that she'd barely given any of them a second thought. Now, however, she recognized her and said in surprise, "You were at the Denim and Diamonds, Friends of the Columbia River Gorge event."

"Who are you?" she asked. Her blue eyes slid over September and slid away.

"September Westerly. I'm here on behalf of Lucy—"

She cut her off. "I saw you talking to Jerome."

September took a moment to assess. "I . . . um . . . yes. I spoke to him that night. I spoke to a lot of people." She hesitated, and then added, "I was there with my husband."

"Brianne, sit down a moment," Mona said. "Talk to this nice woman. She wants to help."

"Help?" asked Brianne. She remained standing, her voice flat.

Mona went on. "She's an ex-cop, but now she's working for Lucy Crissman. She doesn't think Lucy killed her husband and she's here trying to figure out what happened to him . . . you said his name was John?" She looked to September.

"John Linfield."

"He's the man that died," said Brianne.

"That's right." Mona nodded. "And someone called the sheriff; actually, Martin, down at the station, took the call. Whoever it was said Mr. Linfield died from those mushrooms."

"The angel of death. Amanita ocreata." Her voice had little or no inflection. Duke struggled upward, his face turned toward her, and whined piteously. Absently, she walked over and leaned down to him, murmuring and rubbing the crown of his head.

"That's right," Mona said a little nervously.

September suspected she was worried that Brianne might have had something to do with Linfield's poisoning.

"We think he ingested the mushrooms sometime that day. It could have been the day before, but it seems unlikely," said September.

"You think the mushrooms were picked here," she said.

"Well, you can get them lots of places," Mona put in hurriedly.

"I think you're right," Brianne stated, staring at the dog.

"You do?" September asked, trying to get a feel for this girl, woman.

"The big oak's closest to their property." She was matter-of-fact.

"You don't know that's where they came from." Mona looked worried.

"Where is the big oak?" September asked carefully.

"I'll show you. Mushrooms grow around the roots in the spring. I've seen a lot of them. You have to be careful."

"Yes," September agreed.

"Come on, then."

With that, she stalked back across the kitchen and to the storeroom and her boots.

Mona said urgently, "She would never hurt anyone."

September didn't respond. She wasn't sure what she was seeing with Brianne Kilgore, but she knew she couldn't categorically make that same prediction.

They tromped through the woods. The goats had followed them to the edge of their pen, baaing loudly for Brianne, who'd stopped to reach through the fence rails, rub their heads, and tell them she would be right back. September tried to picture Brianne's life outside this home, sought to imagine her in another world, and failed. She understood Mona Kilgore's worry. Brianne might not prosper in the world outside. She had very little affect, and September suspected she didn't perceive social signals in the same way most people did.

"Jerome Wolfe wants to buy your property," September said as they walked. Her boots could very well be ruined after this, but ah, well. She should have been better prepared.

"He is buying it. As soon as Mom dies."

"How is your mother?"

"She takes medicine. She'll die before the end of the year."

Her way of being was a little disconcerting, but September had to go with it. "What about you? What will you do, after the property's sold? Where will you go?"

"Jerome showed me a good place to be in Glenn River. An apartment on the first floor. If Duke is still alive, he can come, too. I'll sell the goats. We had two horses, but they were sold when Dad died."

"This is your idea to move? Not Jerome's?"

"Yes . . . we made it together."

"He's a good friend to you."

"I love him," she said simply. "He always is nice. Not like those other ones."

"Other ones?"

"Lyle Crissman is not nice. He told my father I killed my little brother, but I didn't. He just died. I'm not to blame for that."

Mud and leaves were sticking to September's boots and a frigid plop of rain sneaked down her neck, sending a shiver along her spine. "Are you to blame for something else?" she asked carefully.

"John Linfield's death is not my fault."

"Whose fault is it?"

Brianne stopped short beneath the bows of a giant oak. September could see why she called it the "big oak" by virtue of its size. It was one of the few trees besides Douglas firs that grew on the Kilgore property. Brianne glanced down at the ground, where several groupings of little whitish caps glistened in the rain. September regarded the innocuous-looking mushroom tops, thought of John Linfield heaving and flushed, and fought a full-body shiver.

"They are symbiotic. The big oak is helped by them and they get nourishment in return. They make a trade."

September pulled her eyes from the gleaming caps and looked around the base of the tree. The ground had been tramped over. There were mushroom stalks without caps. "Someone's been here."

"I have," Brianne admitted. "I saw him throw up. I cleaned it up, but I knew what it was from. The angel of death. I came out to see if someone had been to my tree."

"Had they?" September asked, fascinated.

She thought about it for a long moment. "I don't know for sure."

"But you think, maybe?"

"If you had pieces of the mushroom you could check the DNA," she said reasonably. "Plants and animals have specific DNA."

"Makes sense. But we don't have any pieces. We just have a tox screen that shows the poison. A printout of the chemistry that—"

"I know what a tox screen is."

"Okay."

They were silent for a moment, then Brianne turned back the way they'd come. Night was falling as they approached the house again. September asked her again if she had any idea who might have picked mushrooms from the big oak, but Brianne had stopped answering her. She then tried a few more questions about Jerome Wolfe, searching for a connection, but Brianne wasn't interested in hearing anything remotely negative about the man she loved either.

"Do you think you'll still see Jerome after the sale?" September questioned as they stood outside the front door.

"Of course. He gave a lot of money to the shelter. He loves me back. I don't listen to my cousin or my mother anymore."

"Your family's probably just looking out for your best interests."

"They both thought Lyle Crissman was a nice man. I let him have sex with me, but he told my father I killed my little brother and I didn't."

September gazed into her wide blue eyes. Not a shred of makeup and she was very attractive. "You had sex with Lyle Crissman?"

"Four times. He used protection."

Her candor was breathtaking. "Recently?"

"When we were in school. He was nice then. Before he told my father I killed my brother."

"Do you have any idea who might have killed John Linfield?" she asked again.

"I think it was a mistake."

"Why do you say that?"

"He shouldn't have died," Brianne said simply.

September glanced at the door, hoping Mona was still in the back room and not huddled with an ear to the door. "Did you use the mushrooms that killed John Linfield?"

"I would have killed Lyle. He told my father I killed my brother and it wasn't true. I don't think people like him. That's what I think."

"Did you make that call to the sheriff?" September asked, half fearful, half certain she was getting to the truth.

"I knew it was Amanita ocreata. I knew it was the angel of death. That's what I knew. Good-bye, September Westerly."

She turned abruptly for the door.

PART FOUR

Chapter Twenty-Five

Kate sat at her desk, struggling to listen to April, who was gritting out a list of grievances against the school's parent organization, one family in particular, who'd had the gall to point out ways April herself could run the school better.

"They should pay attention to their own jobs. And, of course, they're the ones who are always late paying," she complained.

Pinning on a commiserating smile, Kate looked over at her. Since following Lauren Paulsen almost a week ago, she'd lived in a dull box of indecision. She'd planned to confront Lyle, who'd done just as she'd suspected that day, beating her home and going upstairs to closet himself in his room. Evie had still been at the house, so Kate had let the moment go, instead driving Evie back to Lucy's—who'd looked like she'd just rolled out of bed, though she'd said she had a meeting—and gone home to put together a meal of sorts, leftover chicken and rice that no one had eaten. Lyle hadn't even come downstairs.

Twice during the past week she'd had a brief opportunity alone with Lyle after Daphne had gone to sleep, but both times her husband had left the room when she'd tried to broach any kind of conversation. She was so mad at him, felt so betrayed, that she didn't care if he was having a break-down of some kind—which was sure what it seemed like—and so the problem had just lain in her consciousness, a dead weight that suffocated everything else.

But she was going to confront him soon. She couldn't live this way. Whatever he was hiding, she needed to know about it.

She collected Daphne at the end of the school day and headed out. Lucy was picking up Evie, and they waved at each other in the parking lot, neither of them offering much more than a lifted hand. Lyle had mentioned that Lucy wasn't coming to work anymore, which was annoying. How did Lucy think she was going to pay her bills? Was she ex-pecting some huge life insurance payoff?

That thought sent Kate digging through Lyle's and her own personal finances as soon as she and Daphne got back to the house. How much insurance was there on Lyle? They *had* life insurance, didn't they? Her heart clutched as she dug frantically through the file cabinet, which was part of Lyle's desk. Oh, yes. There it was. Three hundred thousand? *What?* That wouldn't even pay off their mortgage!

But the business . . . Crissman & Wolfe . . . no, *Crissman* now, was under Abbott's control and he was leaving it to Lyle. He maybe had some other minor assets to share with Layla and Lucy, but Lyle was his son and main heir.

She closed the file drawer, thinking. There were money problems at Crissman . . . something going on there that Lyle wasn't talking about. And what had he done with her neck-lace? She'd asked about it, but he'd just mumbled that it was being fixed, all the information he would give her.

And what about Lauren Paulsen and the pink scarf?

Daphne yelled from her room, "Are we getting me that new Easter dress today?"

Kate had promised. Now she wished she hadn't said anything. "Tomorrow, maybe."

"Are we going to Stonehenge right after church on Easter?"

Irritated, Kate yelled back, "No. If we go to Stonehenge"— *Jesus, Wolfe Lodge, Kate*—"it'll be before that. School's out the week before Easter."

"*If?*"

"I told you, I don't know if we're going yet! I don't think we are!" What the hell was the big deal with Wolfe Lodge anyway?

Silence.

Well, fine. Kate was sick of hearing about it. There were so many more things to worry about. She headed downstairs and saw Maddy flopped over on the couch. The doll was currently wearing costume jewelry, a necklace of green stones folded over several times around her neck and a matching bracelet elastic-wrapped twice around her arm. For some reason, Kate was filled with incredible rage. She snatched up the doll, intending to throw it against the wall, then was shocked at herself. With an effort, she counted backward from ten, carefully seating Maddy upright on the couch.

Get a grip. She couldn't afford to lose her cool or her perspective. She couldn't let Lyle's cheating ways ruin her life. She determined right then and there that she had to confront Lyle about Lauren Paulsen soon. Today. Tonight.

The rest of the day, Kate watched the clock, and when Lyle came home from work she was flipping pancakes in the kitchen with Daphne seated at the kitchen bar, working on her math homework. As soon as Lyle walked in, Daphne slid off her stool and ran to give him a big hug, shrieking, "Daddy!" Kate looked over at her daughter, wondering what was up because Daphne mostly ignored Lyle these days. Her first thought was, *she never does that;* her second, *the little suck-up.* Daphne wanted to go to Wolfe Lodge for Easter and she was using her wiles on Lyle to that end. Kate was almost proud of her.

But Lyle just smiled kind of sickly and said, "I'm going upstairs."

"We're having breakfast dinner!" Daphne exclaimed, clearly disappointed that he didn't see this for the treat it was.

"You're coming back down for dinner," Kate said.

"I ate late. I'm good."

And he disappeared.

Daphne stared after him. "What's wrong?"

"Sometimes dads have bad days," she said through her teeth, serving up the pancakes. She plopped down a bottle of maple syrup and slid a bowl of grapes, pineapple chunks, and slices of banana Daphne's way. Then she walked over to the television and clicked the remote till she found the Disney Channel.

"I can watch TV while I'm doing my homework?" Daphne asked in surprise.

"To your little heart's desire. I just need some time to talk to your dad."

"He's not my real dad, you know," she said tentatively, afraid her privilege might be taken away if she made waves.

"I'm aware," Kate said grimly.

She marched up the stairs and caught Lyle in their bedroom in his boxers. Her husband looked over at her in surprise, as if she'd violated his space somehow. A dark cloud crossed his face, but Kate was through with tiptoeing around.

"Who the fuck is Lauren Paulsen?" she demanded.

Lyle reared back as if she'd slapped him, then the color drained from his face. His lips moved like he was working up excuses, but his brain didn't seem to be coming up with anything.

They stared at each other for long seconds. Kate could hear her blood pounding in her ears and her chest was rising and falling rapidly with emotion. When he just stood there, she said, "What are you giving her?"

"I'm not—"

"Yes, you are," she said stonily.

"It's not. I can't . . ."

"Lyle, damn it, tell me what you're doing or I'll go to Abbott. I've seen the packages you hand her. What are they? Tell me, or I'll go to your father. So help me God, I will."

His mouth slackened, and he looked so miserable she almost went to him, but she was too furious, too hurt.

When he answered her, she was frozen in place by his reply. "Dad already knows . . ."

Jake drove September back to their home after a trip to a local steak house where they'd both ordered fish—salmon for her, halibut for him—and she'd let him talk about his work while she remained silent, working her way through her meal, barely tasting it, her mind running in the same hamster wheel it had ever since she'd gone to Wharton County.

"Want to talk about it?" he asked now as he hit the garage door and parked his car next to hers.

This was the same question he'd asked her all week, and she gave him the same answer, a shrug of her shoulders and, "It's Dallas Denton's move."

She'd told Dallas what she'd learned, which wasn't all that much, although Brianne Kilgore had flirted with both the fact that she might have an idea who'd used the mushrooms and that she didn't seem to think the poison was meant for John Linfield. September had also told Denton that Brianne was in love with Jerome Wolfe, or at least idolized him, and that she had no use for Lyle Crissman after a sexual relationship with him. So far, she hadn't mentioned that Lyle would have been Brianne's own target should she have been

overcome with the urge to poison someone. September was
still thinking that over.

To date, the Laurelton Police hadn't interviewed Lucy
again, so they were all kind of waiting to see what the next
move would be. Since reporting to Denton, September had
been sitting on her hands. Not that she was employed by
him . . . not that she was employed by anyone, for that
matter . . . she was on the team by her own volition. But
unlike working for the police, where there was generally
some other case to go over while she waited for develop-
ments on the current one, she was, for the moment, basically
stymied.

My work here is done. . . .

Even though he was a short-timer, she'd phoned Wes and
told him about her interviews with Deputy Morant and the
couple at StopGo. He'd been upfront with her about the investigation; she felt she owed him the same. After her report,
she'd also admitted, "I don't believe I was clear with them
about my current status with the police."

"Ah," was his response, a smile lurking in his voice.

She hadn't told him about her trip to the Kilgores, and she
felt a little guilty about that, but it hadn't been part of the original information he'd passed along about the case, so she let
their discussion move to the topic of his decision to leave
Laurelton PD. "I'd been toying with the idea, and when I
heard D'Annibal was leaving, I just said okay, time to go,"
he said.

"What happened with D'Annibal? Do you know?"

"Rumors. He had twenty years in and was flirting with a
change. Calvetti pushed for the job and got it."

They talked for a while more, September feeling a weight
on her chest. She'd had a thing for Wes when she was first
on the job at Laurelton PD, a hidden crush that never saw the
light of day but had evolved into a great friendship. The fact
that he wasn't going to be at the station, on the chance that
she might get back there herself, made her feel low.

The only good thing was that Wes didn't think there appeared to be a serious case against Lucy at this time, and he agreed with the assumption that Gretchen would undoubtedly be picking up the caseload he left behind. No one could count on George.

Now, as she and Jake entered their house, her thoughts skimmed back to her trip to Wharton County. "I just feel like I was lied to somewhere in there. Or maybe not exactly lied to but misled."

"By Brianne Kilgore?" Jake asked. He was the one person she'd told the extent of what she'd learned and the impressions she'd had.

"No, she was pretty clear, in her way."

"Who, then? Her mother? The deputy? The people at the convenience store?"

That tickled September's brain. Barry and Rhonda . . . neither had said anything to her, but Rhonda had been so grim and somehow locking down on Barry.

"Maybe. I don't know. I'm going to think on it."

"What does Abbott know?" Kate demanded for about the fifth time. Lyle had turned away from her and gone silent, as if giving her his back would somehow render her unable to communicate with him.

"I don't want to talk about this now," he finally said. He then lurched into the bathroom and slammed the door behind him.

Kate moved immediately to the door, slapping her palm against the panels until it stung. "What does he know, Lyle? What did you do? What are you giving that woman in those packs you're slipping into her bag?"

"You've been following me!" he accused, his voice muffled.

"Of course I've been following you. You deserved to be

followed." She rattled the bathroom doorknob. "Open the door, Lyle."

"Leave me alone."

Now that Lyle had recovered a bit from the shock of her accusation, he was trying to weasel out of the whole thing. She recognized the tactic. He was a master at it. But she was through playing that game.

"I'll take this door down with my bare hands if you don't open it," she ground out. "I mean it. I will. I will break it *down*!

She waited. Nothing.

She saw red. Distantly marveled that she actually did see red. Everything in her vision was bright, blood red.

Was he just standing frozen behind the door like the chickenshit he was?

She glanced around the room, searching for a weapon. All she could come up with were the lamps. Solid brass. Heavy.

She crossed the room and yanked the one on his side of the bed out of the wall. Thought about it. Unscrewed the finial. Removed the shade. Then she hefted it in her hand several times, testing its weight. Back across the room to the bathroom door, she brought it up to her shoulder in a base-ball stance.

"Hey, batta, batta," she whispered and swung—

Crash. The door panel splintered. She could see Lyle's shocked face in the small gap she'd opened and swung again.

Crash! The whole center panel broke open.

"Fuck, Kate! What the fuck?" he shrieked.

She reached through and unlocked the door from his side, then yanked it open.

She stood in the open doorway, shaking with fury and adrenaline.

His eyes strayed to the lamp she still held in her right

hand. She said evenly, "You tell me right now or I don't know what I'll do."

"You're out of your mind." He took a step back, bumping up against the counter.

"I am," she agreed.

"Mommy!" A scream from down the hall.

"It's all right, Daphne," Kate said, her voice surprisingly calm. "I dropped the lamp. Don't come in here. Go back to the Disney Channel. I'll be right there."

"Are you okay?" she asked, worried.

"Never. Better."

As soon as she heard Daphne's footsteps slowly receding, she turned her full attention back to Lyle. "I can see you're thinking up a lie," she said, surprising him with her hard tone. "It's time for the truth. Give it over or I'm going to Abbott with what I've observed. I don't care what he knows. I'm going to tell him what I know."

They stared at each other, both breathing hard.

"What was in the package, Lyle?" she asked again.

"Money." The word popped out through trembling lips.

Kate was trembling, too. Reaction. She could feel it in her thighs. "What for?"

"A . . . payoff."

"To Lauren Paulsen. A nurse . . . er . . . administrator or whatever at Cascade Place Assisted Living. Where Junior died?" The questions came hard and fast. She'd had a lot of time to come to her own conclusions. "What did you do to him?"

"Nothing! No, no!" He lifted his palms, horrified. "I didn't do anything to him. I miss him. I so miss him, you don't know. . . ."

"What was it for, then? The money."

"She was blackmailing me. . . ."

"What for? How?"

He stared miserably down at his toes.

"Lay it out, Lyle. Lay. It. Out. I can't just pull every fucking word out of your mouth!"

"It was the will. Junior's new will. Lauren was one of the witnesses. There was another witness at the place, too. Maura, or Maren, or something. But she was nice, whereas Lauren . . ." He inhaled and exhaled, girding himself. "She wormed her way into Junior's good graces. Always doting on him. She knew he had money. She was always looking for a way to get her hands on his money."

"Did she manage to do it?" Kate asked, alarmed.

"No . . . no . . ."

"What about this new will, then?"

"It's not the one we're using. Junior divided the new will into thirds for me and Layla and Lucy. He cut Dad out entirely. Asked me to take it to the lawyer, but Dad found out. He wanted to destroy it, and I told him I did, but it's in a safe-deposit box. Lauren knew what it said, and she figured out it wasn't being distributed to the rightful heirs and started demanding cash."

"How much cash?"

"Ten thousand at a time." His face twisted in pain. "When she needed more, she'd send me a pink-scarf message."

"I saw her in a picture wearing a pink scarf."

"Junior's last gift to her, for being such a great helper," he added bitterly. "He never knew what she was really like. She used the scarf as a signal to me that she needed more money."

Kate gulped down a deep breath, processing. She'd had so many terrible scenarios in her mind that this one almost didn't seem that bad. Except Lauren Paulsen was a blackmailer. . . . "She'll never stop asking for money."

"You think I don't know that?" He made a sound of disparagement. "I took sixty thousand out of the company. Lucy knows about it. Dad thinks Lucy just screwed up. He's never trusted her, but she's smart. She won't let up on me, but what am I supposed to tell her?"

"Jesus, Lyle. You stole from the company?" This, on the other hand, was damn near treasonous.

"Dad's been taking money from the company in a larger sense, moving it to 'investments,' but I think he's really bleeding the company dry. At this rate, there might not be anything left."

She'd always admired Abbott, but that admiration died a quick death. Now she was in survival mode. They both were.

"What should I do?" Lyle asked her after the moment between them stretched out into eternity.

"How should I know? You're the one that got into this mess!"

"Think of something, Kate," he pleaded.

He was weak. That's all there was to it. She'd known it and ignored it. Told herself she loved him, and maybe she had, maybe she still did. "If you want my help, you'll help me make a baby. No more turning your back on me. I mean it, Lyle."

"I haven't . . . I've been kind of . . . off. . . ."

"Well, figure out how to get on again," she snarled. "You need a magazine? A picture of some hot chick like the one you were ogling at the benefit? Go ahead. Whatever it takes."

"The cost of another child is so . . . much."

"Oh my God. Are you really turning me down?"

She was shivering from head to toe, from rage, from reaction, from the high of having all the power for once.

"No," he said. "I'm ready. I promise."

"It's not exactly conception time, but there's no harm tuning up," she said, stalking across the room and locking the bedroom door.

Chapter Twenty-Six

Lucy put on a pair of black slacks and a red sweater. Ripped them off. Tried on a pair of gray pants with a blue blouse. Ripped them off. Told herself she was an idiot. Found a pair of dark brown pants and a camel-colored sweater with a cowl neck . . . nearly ripped them off, then forced herself to keep them on.

She was meeting Dallas for a late breakfast at a diner. And it was a meeting with Layla, and about Layla, nothing really to do with her at all. It was sad, sad how terrifically she wanted to impress him.

He's not interested in you, she scolded herself. *He's engaged, or was, or . . . He's your lawyer, nothing more. Now you know why he couldn't remember you. It's a farce. A dark comedy. You shouldn't even be thinking about him because someone killed your husband. . . .*

Her blood chilled at the thought, and after a moment she took off the pants and sweater and put on her jeans, a black V-necked casual shirt, and a light gray rain jacket. She looked at herself in the mirror. Okay, maybe she had a little more makeup on than usual, but she looked ready for a diner.

She was dropping Evie off at a friend's. She'd tried to

reach Bella but had learned she'd spent the night with a friend from her cheerleading days—her mother was hopeful—so she'd frantically made a playdate for Evie. Lucy had been pushing those playdates since John's death. She was going to owe everyone big-time. Have to pay them back sometime in the future. Evie had suggested they all come next week to Stonehenge for Easter, but Lucy had put the kibosh on that. She hadn't even spoken to her brother or father in a week. Easter at Stonehenge was not anywhere on her horizon.

"You ready?" Lucy asked her daughter, who had been playing on her iPad.

"Yep." Evie put down the iPad, then ran to her room and returned with her stuffed dog.

"We're not taking Lisa," Lucy said.

"Yes, I am!" She clutched the dog closer.

"Evie . . ." She was about to berate her for dragging the stuffed toy, which was looking worse for wear, its fur matted, everywhere she went, but she knew better. It was too soon after John's death. They were all coping. Maybe she could wash the damn thing. "Fine. Bring it," she said.

"Her," Evie corrected. "Bring her." And they went to the car.

Half an hour later, Lucy entered Lucille's, the diner Dallas had suggested, spotted him in a booth in the back, and slipped into the seat opposite him as he stood up at her approach. Layla, naturally, wasn't there yet.

"How are you?" Dallas asked, reseating himself.

"Good. Well." She clasped her hands and put them on her lap. A young girl holding a coffeepot came by with a mug, but Lucy shook her head.

Dallas had called her and related what September Westerly had learned from her trip to Wharton County, which was just more of the same as far as Lucy could tell. The new information was that Lyle had apparently had some kind of relationship with Brianne Kilgore, whose affections had

turned to Jerome Wolfe, and she now considered Lyle a
liar because he'd allegedly told Brianne's father that Brianne
was responsible for her infant brother's death, which everyone knew was a lie.

But Brianne had shown September where the angel of
death mushroom was near at hand, and that seemed ominous.
Sure, the mushroom grew all over the Northwest, but these
were right next to Stonehenge at the "big oak." Lucy thought
she might even remember that tree. That couldn't be a coincidence.

Dallas had asked September if she felt Brianne was the
poisoner, but September hadn't been able to answer him.
The facts were that a woman had called into the sheriff's department on a disposable cell phone and told them to check
for angel of death poisoning in the death of John Linfield.
If it somehow had to do with Brianne Kilgore, it was unclear
what the motive was.

Lucy had pushed most of it aside. She was still consumed
with the bad feelings she had over her father and brother's
betrayal, and she was still trying to work out what she felt
about Dallas. Every time her mind touched on the lie she
was withholding from him, it bounced away. She was going
to have to tell him that he was Evie's real father if she hoped
for any kind of long-term relationship with him. What would
he do when he found out? She liked their reconnection and
she sensed he did, too. Was that built on guilt over what had
happened in the past? Maybe. Maybe not. Whatever the case,
she wanted to keep seeing him, and that meant she was going
to have to find a way to tell him about Evie.

"How's your daughter?" he asked now, causing her to
inhale sharply.

"I think okay," she answered, trying to smile. It was just
normal conversation. Small talk. Nothing to freak out about.

"She's kind of hanging on to a stuffed animal that she'd pretty much forgotten about. Regression, I guess."

He nodded. She realized he was struggling with conversation a bit, too. Their history was something they were both getting used to. "I asked Layla to come to my office, but she suggested a more informal meeting with you, too."

"I'm glad to come."

Layla blew through the door at that moment, her hair tamed into a ponytail for once, her cheeks flushed. She could have checked with Lucy about a uniform; their clothes were nearly identical, though Lucy had left her hair down. She squeezed into the seat next to Lucy and said, "Sorry I'm late. I just came from Neil's. He didn't answer my knock. He's been gone over a week and I haven't heard a word from him. He hasn't returned any of my texts."

"Is that weird?" Lucy asked.

"He's pretty good about responding, even when we were at our worst."

Dallas had been silent, listening. Now he looked around and said, "Maybe we should take this to my office."

"Why?" Layla asked, suddenly at attention. "Do you know something?"

"It would just be more private."

"I'm okay with this," Layla said, but she lowered her voice a bit.

Dallas hesitated, then said, "I decided to look over your contract with him again, now that the situation's changed. You gave him complete control over your embryos."

"Yes," she said, waiting.

Lucy leaned in a bit, wondering where this was going.

"I sent Neil's lawyer, Penelope Gaines, notice that we're suing for custody of the embryos, and she called me and said, basically, that you had legally turned them over to Neil, which was the truth."

"Which is why I hired you," Layla said.

The waitress came by to take their order. Layla asked for a cup of decaf and Lucy decided she'd have the same. Dallas asked if they wanted anything else, but they both shook their heads. He waved the woman off and as she left, Layla said tensely, "Where are you going with this?"

"Yeah," Lucy agreed. Something about his tone was making her nervous, too.

"Currently, Neil owns those embryos. How many were used and how many are left?"

"I don't know exactly," Layla said. "It took on the first try. Naomi's in her last month."

"So, make a guess," he pressed.

"Four, maybe?"

He leaned back in the booth. "Luke's been doing some re-search for me. He apparently found someone at the clinic who would talk to him about Neil and the embryos. My brother, the ex-cop who sometimes steps over the line . . ." Dallas shook his head. "It appears . . . possibly . . . that Neil used them on another surrogate."

"What?" Layla breathed. "*My* embryos?"

Lucy demanded, "Who?"

Layla's voice rose. "Is that even legal?"

"You gave him custody," Dallas reminded quietly.

Oh, shit . . . Lucy thought. "Courtney?"

They both looked at her, Dallas sober, obviously already twigged to that possibility, Layla confused, struggling to process.

"No, she lost her baby. Neil told me she lost the baby," Layla babbled. "He broke up with her. Maybe that's why."

"Luke's running Courtney down right now. She's been surprisingly hard to find," said Dallas.

"Oh my God." The color drained from Layla's face. "Oh my God."

"We don't know anything yet," Lucy said.

Layla moaned. "What if he lied? What if she's still pregnant with *my* baby?"

"Stop it," Lucy said. "Dallas is working on it."

"What if he's hiding her? Maybe he's not on a trip at all. Maybe he's with her and they're planning to steal Naomi's baby, too!" Layla's voice rose, and Lucy grabbed her hand, holding hard.

"Maybe we should have gone to your office after all," Lucy muttered to Dallas.

"We can go now," he said.

"No, no . . . let me think." Layla struggled to compose herself, waved him back down. "Oh my God."

"I've got a call in to Penelope. She hasn't called me back yet, but I'm going to find out what Neil's real plans are and—"

"*I'm* going to find out!" Layla declared, jumping to her feet. "I'm going to break down his door. He's got to be back by now. I know where the key is. I should have used it while he was gone!"

"Wait," Dallas said sternly.

"Courtney said she was having a boy. They did IVF. That's the only way she'd know so early," Layla said, her eyes moist.

Lucy said, "Just wait. Just . . . wait till there's more."

"Layla, we're working on it," Dallas said. "Don't do something that'll jeopardize your case."

"I won't. I'm not."

Lucy asked, "Are you sure?"

"Yes . . . yes." She turned to Dallas. "Thank you. I'm sorry I got into such a mess. Luce, I'll call you later."

"Don't go to Neil's," Lucy pleaded. "Stick around."

Layla shook her head and headed for the door. And she was gone.

"I don't like this," Dallas said, frowning.

"Neither do I."

"Will she be smart?" he asked.

Lucy choked out a half-laugh. "I think so. She won't do anything to lose a chance to have Eddie."

"If Grassley's playing around with her child's . . . possibly *children's* . . . lives . . ."

His words hammered into her. She felt almost dizzy.

"You okay?" he asked.

"I feel . . . tired."

"You need something to eat."

She did. He was right. But she didn't think she could eat a bite. But she didn't want to leave either.

She nodded, and he signaled for the waitress to return.

Layla waited for Uber. She should have asked Lucy for a ride. She should have pushed Neil for the truth. She should never have listened to him about anything! She'd gone to see Naomi twice this week, believing only good things for the future. Happy. She'd *believed* Neil!

She'd been planning to give him her painting, for God's sake!

It's a lie. It's all been a lie. He was never going to marry you. He was lulling you, needing time to pass so he could hide Courtney's baby. She blurted it out at the benefit and he tried to buy you off! He knew you would never allow it! He was trying to get you out of the way!

"Don't . . . don't . . ." Layla warned herself as the silver Prius appeared and she got in the back. She told herself to go home but gave the driver Neil's address, plugging it into the phone as well. She'd lied. She'd known she was going to his place as soon as she heard the truth about the embryos.

Don't go over the edge. Think it through.

Layla closed her eyes. But she knew there was truth in there somewhere. She had a knack for these kinds of things.

Neil lived in a condo in the Pearl, a converted warehouse where the units sprawled across one level, nearly three thousand square feet each. The exterior door required a key, but you could easily get someone to buzz you in. Once inside, there was a bank of elevators. Neil was on the eighth floor.

Layla had no trouble being buzzed in. She eschewed the elevators and went right for the stairs, clanging up the steps until she got to the eighth floor. Neil always left a spare key behind a fake electrical outlet at the top of the stairs when he was out of town, unless he'd changed his ways since Courtney, but no, there was the outlet.

Layla eased back the outlet cover and found the key. She crushed it into her fist, replacing the outlet, then pushed through the stairwell door to the eighth-floor foyer. Each floor had four units, one on each side of the building. She went to Neil's door and pressed the bell. Distantly, she could hear it ringing inside. She waited, counting to sixty, then pushed it again, listening to its muffled peal.

To hell with it.

Threading the key in the lock, she thrust open the door to his apartment. Straight ahead was a vista through floor-to-ceiling windows to the rest of the Pearl. Neil's view was east, toward the Willamette River and the Fremont Bridge. She could see the bridge's white suspension cables capped by two flags at the top of the arch, one on each side, framed in her sight.

She smelled something sour. Vomit?

She walked down the entry hall and turned into the kitchen.

Neil lay on the floor, eyes and mouth open, a small circle of throw up by his lips. Blood pooled beneath his head.

She didn't have to be told he was dead.

Chapter Twenty-Seven

Lucy's cell rang.

She had ordered two poached eggs and wheat toast and had managed to eat some of it. She and Dallas had put a discussion about Layla aside for a few moments, but then had devolved into carefully polite conversation that seemed to go nowhere and made her acutely aware that she was on an uphill climb if she thought they could be friends, somehow.

Friends . . .

The Evie secret.

They could never be friends.

She couldn't think about that now either. Too many other more pressing issues. No way to say: *There were consequences to that night, Dallas. Our daughter, Evie. She's wonderful. The best part of my life. I wish I would have told you. But now you can meet her, and I hope you love her as much as I do. . . .*

Her cell rang again, sounding almost more insistent.

Lucy plucked the phone from her purse. "It's Layla," she said, shoving the Evie situation to the back of her mind. She answered. "Hey, how are you doing? You okay now?"

"Lucy . . ." Layla's voice was strangled.

Her radar spun into high gear. "What's wrong?" she asked, her tone catching Dallas's attention.

"Neil's . . . dead. I'm at his condo . . . and he's dead."

"What? Jesus, Layla!" She half-rose, as if pulled up by an unseen string, banging her knee on the underside of the table. Now Dallas was on his feet, too.

"I've called nine-one-one. They're on their way. . . ."

"Okay, okay. I'll be right there." Out of the blur of her vision, she saw Dallas throw down some cash. She stepped out of the booth and headed blindly toward the door, Dallas on her heels.

"I think he's been dead a while," Layla said faintly.

"I'm coming. . . ."

"We're coming," Dallas corrected, sounding grim.

"Hurry," Layla whispered and clicked off.

In the blast of cool air outside, Lucy stopped short. Dallas put his arm over her shoulder and led her toward the parking lot. "What happened?" he asked.

"Neil's dead. He's . . . he's . . ." She couldn't seem to breathe. She had a vision of John in the bed, in a coma, just before he died. John . . . and now Neil . . .

He absorbed that news. "Is she at Neil's?"

"Yes. My . . . my car's over there. . . ."

They were walking in the opposite direction of her silver Escape.

"We're going in mine," he said, steering her in the direction of a black BMW SUV.

An officer from Portland PD was already in Neil's condominium by the time Lucy and Dallas arrived. Two detectives and the coroner were on their way. The officer hustled Layla, Lucy, and Dallas into the eighth-floor foyer. Layla was white as a sheet and seemed to have lost her voice. Lucy caught a quick glimpse of Neil's feet and then had a mental image of his waxy pallor and sightless eyes.

"What happened?" Lucy asked, though she didn't expect an answer.

Dallas warned, "Layla, don't say anything to the police. We'll give a full report later."

"I already told the officer I let myself in with the key and walked down the hall." Her voice was a scared whisper.

"Okay. Just don't volunteer anything further."

"Why?" She turned horror-filled blue eyes to him. "Maybe he fell . . . There was blood on the corner of the counter. I saw it."

"We don't know what happened yet."

It was the same nightmare Lucy had just lived through. "You think there's been foul play?" she asked.

"We don't know," he said again, his expression grim.

And then there were hours of a nightmare that didn't end, with gawking neighbors and questions from the two detectives who clearly found it suspicious that Layla's lawyer was already on the scene. Dallas explained to them the circumstances of what had occurred, but they just stared at him coldly, two men, one older and one fairly young, both wearing I've-seen-it-all expressions. Almost reluctantly, they allowed Layla to leave, but not before letting Dallas know she would likely be called into the station.

"Intimidation," Dallas said, when he, Lucy, and Layla were back in his SUV. Layla had insisted on the backseat, her arms wrapped around herself, her knees tucked in.

Lucy suggested she come back to her house and she agreed.

"My God, I'm cold inside," Layla said, shivering like she was afflicted with ague.

"I'll get you a brandy," Lucy said.

"I don't know . . ."

"You need it," she insisted more firmly. "You're not

driving. You're not going anywhere. But I've got to pick up Evie."

"Would you like me to do it?" Dallas asked. He'd followed them into Lucy's house.

"No." Her abruptness surprised him, and he turned to look at her. "No, thank you." She offered a tentative smile that abruptly fell away. "But I need my car. Can you take me back to Lucille's? I'll pick up Evie."

"All right. Sure."

"I'll be right back," she said to Layla, who was on the couch under a blanket, her teeth chattering. "Then we'll have that brandy."

As Lucy and Dallas headed back outside, the late afternoon sun was peeking through the clouds. Dallas pressed the buttons on his phone to call Luke, bringing him up-to-date on Neil's death and the fact that he needed to find Courtney Mayfield ASAP.

Once he was off the phone, Lucy asked him, "You think Courtney's involved somehow?"

"I don't know. I just find it hard to believe Grassley's death was a complete accident."

Lucy thought about that. About the vomit on the floor beside him. So much like John . . . What were the chances that Neil had died from poisoning? Was that reaching? Could it be just an accident?

No. That was too unlikely.

Could it be someone who'd targeted both John and Neil? Lucy's husband and the father of Layla's child?

Was that just as unlikely?

It was the question that followed her the whole time it took to drive to her car, say good-bye to Dallas, pick up Evie, then down a snifter of brandy with Layla, who barely touched hers no matter what medicinal purposes it offered, and fall into bed, consumed with exhaustion.

She woke up the next morning with it still all on her mind, and no closer to an answer.

"Let go of my hand," Daphne whispered loudly into the expectant quiet of the church.

Kate jerked as if stuck by a pin, then released her tense grip on her daughter's fingers as the organ music swelled and people all around her began singing a hymn she didn't know.

Palm Sunday. Kate had dressed with care. Her hand drifted to her bare neck, where the pearls should have been. Fake pearls, okay. He'd used the money he'd stolen to pay off Lauren Paulsen and had bought her an imitation. But the necklace had looked real. Lyle had yet to give it back to her.

Lyle. They'd made love twice yesterday and once this morning. If you could call it making love. It was a little soul-destroying, knowing he didn't really want to, that he was just going through the motions. But he owed her. What he'd done . . .

Daphne yanked at the collar of her dress, a sweet A-line covered in a print of tiny pink roses. She'd balked at the dress when Kate had pulled it out for her. Lately she'd balked at a lot of things. In fact, she'd decided for inexplicable reasons that she only wanted to wear pants. "No dresses," she'd declared belligerently this morning, crossing her arms over her chest.

Kate had had it. "You're wearing a dress to church."

"Why?"

"Because you just do."

"Isn't *Dad* coming?"

Another sample of her new annoying behavior. Daphne had taken to stressing *Dad* every time she said Lyle's name, suddenly needing to make it clear he wasn't her biological father at any chance she got. Oh, sure, she'd called him

Daddy last night, when she'd wanted to go to Stonehenge, but that daughterlike attitude had lasted about two seconds. Had Daphne overheard more of their fight than she acted like? She'd stared at the ruined bathroom door this morning and then at Lyle with solemn eyes, not saying a word. Did she blame him for it? Had that crystallized her negative feelings?

"Dad isn't coming today," Kate had told her, and Daphne had harrumphed in a way that infuriated Kate. She'd had to let that one go, however, as her daughter had then, somewhat reluctantly, slumped over in acquiescence, arms hanging down as if she were heading to the gallows, and deigned to let Kate help her change her clothes. So, now Daphne could just yank on her collar till kingdom come. Fine. Just how many battles was Kate supposed to fight?

Now Kate picked up one of the hymnals—opened to a random page because she couldn't really tell which song it was, and who cared anyway?—holding it so tightly her knuckles showed white.

What should she do about what Lyle had told her? What if that Lauren bitch asked for more money? Lyle had admitted later that he was tapped out. He thought his dad had money squirreled away somewhere, but it wasn't in the company.

Maybe she should go to Abbott, let him know she knew the truth?

But if you confront him, he'll cut you dead . . .

But if you don't, and this comes out later . . .

But it won't come out. The will's hidden. Safe and secure . . .

But Lauren knows . . . she's a blackmailer. . . .

And God knows what Abbott is doing with the money . . . Lyle's money . . .

The last note of the hymn ended on a crescendo, voices raised in song. Emotion swelled inside Kate's chest, nearly bursting. She closed her eyes, felt tears star her lashes. Generally, she loved church. Loved walking in and seeing the parishioners dressed in their best clothes; well, except for some of the teenage boys who looked like they had no idea what a comb was and those jeans and *T-shirts*? What kind of parent would allow that? Still, today, she just felt sick at heart.

She had to do something.

She couldn't let this fester and become worse.

Besides, who was to say that Abbott might not arbitrarily change his mind about his own will? What if he got mad at Lyle in the future and cut him out? Wasn't a third portion of the true will better than nothing?

Kate opened her eyes. The minister was droning on about something. Oh, yeah. Giving . . . That's what it was. Giving. She had to be more giving. Sharing. Like in sharing with Lyle's sisters.

Daphne squirmed beside her. "I have to go to the bathroom."

"Can't you hold it?"

"How long are we going to be here?"

"Not much longer."

"I'll try," she said dubiously.

Kate looked over at the teenage boy with the uncombed hair. Okay, maybe that was a nicer shirt than she'd originally thought. It just didn't have a collar, which was still too casual for church, but he did have a jacket he'd tossed over the pew because the room was hot today, the body heat adding to the discomfort. People were fanning themselves with today's program leaflet. Spring had finally arrived.

Tomorrow she would confront Abbott with the truth, she decided.

"Mommy, I can't hold it," Daphne whimpered.

"Okay, let's go."

She clasped her daughter's hand again and left by the side aisle, waiting outside the bathroom, her thoughts churning.

Maybe she would confront him today. Or maybe next week, or next year . . .

Maybe she wouldn't have to face him at all, but it was dangerous to wait.

After you get pregnant, she told herself, aware it might never happen. What was the name of that surrogate? Naomi. She was due to pop anytime now, so maybe she'd be ready for another trip to the IVF clinic soon.

Lyle was going to be on board this time. That, at least, was something she could count on.

Neil's death was on the front page of *The Oregonian*.

Lucy snatched the paper from her front porch, then hurried back inside the house, shutting the door and shooting a look down the hall to where Layla had moved to the guest room. It was late. Evie was up and outside, playing some imaginary game on the back patio, enjoying the watery sunshine.

There wasn't much more in the article than she already knew, but she found herself breathing hard by the omission of Neil's death being an accident. They weren't saying homicide yet, but it was implied, and though there was no mention of cause beyond head trauma, Lucy sensed there was something more to come.

That other shoe she'd been expecting to drop.

She pulled in her shoulders as if protecting herself. And she did feel the need, as unnamed fear assailed her. "Someone's out there," she said softly. "Someone's got a plan."

Her cell rang, and she jumped a foot at the sudden sound. Glancing around, she caught a glimpse of her phone on the kitchen counter. She swept it up. Dallas.

Seeing his name made her feel giddy with trepidation.

Was it always going to be this way? No matter what else was happening in her life, anything to do with Dallas Denton shot through her like an electric current?

No time for that now.

"Hello there," she greeted him.

"Hi. Is Layla still there?"

"Yeah, but she's still in bed."

"Okay." He paused a moment, and she could visualize him thinking hard. She'd seen that intense look on his face. "I'm putting both my brother, Luke, and September Westerly on this. I want to know as much as the police do, as soon as they can find out anything about Grassley."

"Have you heard anything more?" Lucy asked.

"Nothing specific. But I want to get ahead of this thing. What do you think?"

"I don't know." She was trying hard not to think about Neil Grassley's body again . . . the blood . . . the vomit . . . the fixed eyes . . . with limited success. "What do you need me to do?"

"Keep the press away. They'll likely figure out where Layla is, so expect them. They're going to want to talk to her and Courtney Mayfield. Luke is searching for her. We just need to keep Layla buttoned up."

"Okay."

"I'll check in later."

He clicked off and Lucy did the same, placing her phone back on the counter. She called Dallas's image to mind, holding it close. It was the one positive she wanted to cling to through all this.

Pulling herself together, she heaved a sigh. Couldn't daydream like a sap about nice things all day. She needed to keep moving forward.

Deciding it was time to get Layla up, she tapped lightly on the bedroom door, opening it at the same time. "Do you know what time it is?" she asked as the door swung open, revealing an empty bed, remade.

What? Damn!

Evie had come inside and skipped down the hall after her, and she, too, peered inside the empty room. "Where's Aunt Layla?" she asked.

Lucy pushed down her concern and smiled at her daughter. "Oh, she probably had to get going early."

"So, you don't know either?"

Lucy sighed. "That's about right," she admitted.

Chapter Twenty-Eight

On the Uber ride back to her apartment, Layla had realized she had four messages. She'd turned her cell ringer off on Friday afternoon when she'd met with a small group of Realtors about doing their home staging for them and forgotten to turn it back on by the time she met Layla and Dallas at the diner, and then she'd discovered Neil and she'd practically gone into a trance. So now it was Sunday morning. She'd sneaked out of Lucy's home early, not wanting to disturb her, and waited in a crisp, quiet dawn, the air cold in her lungs, dew glistening on the leaves of the shrubs lining Lucy's driveway.

Her head had cleared and she felt calmer. Scared shitless, really, deep inside, but less frantic. Neil was gone. That was a fact. And Naomi was still pregnant with Neil and her child . . .

Naomi. Layla's mind had fluttered to her in the past eighteen hours or so, but she'd been too distraught to do more than let the thought slip in and then out of her consciousness. Now she realized Naomi was one of the four calls and she'd left a message. Layla listened to it as the driver dropped her off outside the Starbucks on the first floor of her building. The scent of coffee followed her up the steps and through the door. Once inside, she had a moment of weakness, a wave of horror and grief. Neil was gone . . . killed?

She listened to Naomi's call, basically a sober message for Layla to please call her. It had come in the night before, probably shortly after the first news of Neil's death. Naomi had also sent her a text about the same time: Layla, can you call me? I saw the terrible news. I'm stunned.

It was still too early to contact Naomi, but in an hour or so, she would phone her.

Another call was from Mary Jo, who clearly hadn't seen the news at that point. She'd been cheerfully thrilled about an offer coming in on the cold house, and the people had asked about the painting, wanting it thrown into the deal. That would be a way to ignore Jerome Wolfe's suggestion that she pay him half, but now that she'd had some time to feel ownership of the painting again, she wasn't sure that's what she wanted to do.

The third call was from Jerome Wolfe himself, and it chilled her blood. "I thought your sister was supposed to be the killer, but maybe it runs in the family . . ." came his mocking voice. She immediately deleted that voice mail.

The fourth message was from Neil's attorney, Penelope Gaines, whom Dallas had just mentioned yesterday. She saw that, in reality, it had come in first, on Friday afternoon. The attorney had introduced herself, then said, "Mr. Grassley has made a change in his will that he wanted me to discuss with you. He asked that a meeting be set up for early next week, when he's available as well. Would sometime Monday or Tuesday work? I'm putting this in an email to you as well. Thank you."

Changed his will . . . maybe to include Eddie?

She made a pot of decaf coffee, watching the brown liquid puddle into the carafe as the sun rose higher in a cool gray sky.

She picked up her phone again, searching the internet for

local news. It didn't take long . . . and there she was. A
picture of her, not a great one, from the Black Swan Gallery.
But it was the stories that were coming out that made her
throat close in fear, words leaping off the page:

> ". . . wealthy Neil Grassley with baby on the way found
> dead on his kitchen floor . . . police not ruling out
> homicide . . . Layla Crissman, daughter of Crissman &
> Wolfe's Abbott Crissman, first at the scene . . . Grassley
> and Crissman purported in custody fight . . . Crissman &
> Wolfe brick-and-mortar store shuttered over increasing
> losses . . . Crissman's sister, Lucretia Linfield, in the news
> after husband's poisoning . . . black widow sisters? . . . IVF
> at the center of Grassley's life . . . second baby on the way
> with Grassley girlfriend . . ."

Layla, who'd been feeling like she was having an out-
of-body experience, reading all the clips, zeroed in on that
last article. An interview with Courtney, who was very clear
that Neil and Layla's relationship had ended months before
and that she was the new woman in his life. "We are having
a baby together," she added, going on, then, about how devastated she was, hinting that maybe the police should look
into Layla's motivations as Neil had told her Layla was
suing him. . . .

Was it true? Was Courtney really still pregnant, and if so,
was the baby really hers?

Thoughts swimming, Layla sank down on the couch,
switched on the television, and watched mindless programs
and infomercials. She must have fallen asleep with her
phone in her hand because when it rang she jerked awake,
her cell slipping to the floor.

She saw it was Lucy and hesitated before refusing the
call. She didn't want to talk right now. Lucy then texted: You
at home?? OK?? Please let me know.

Layla heaved a sigh. She felt gritty and exhausted. She texted back: Home and OK. Don't worry. Taking a shower and staying in. Not talking to the press. Will call later.

Lucy responded: OK. Here if you need me.

Layla sank back on the couch, then checked the local news on her phone again. More of the same, and now a new interview with Steven Berkhauser, the man whose wife died in that fateful accident, baldly claiming that Neil Grassley wasn't the first person Layla Crissman had killed. "My wife's gone and it's Layla Crissman's fault. Maybe this time she'll get what's coming to her. . . ."

"What are you talking about?" Kate practically shrieked when she got home and Lyle, standing near the sliding door to the deck, hit her with the news that Neil Grassley was dead, probably murdered.

She couldn't fathom it. First John and now *Neil* . . . ?

He said, "I tried to call Layla, but I think her phone's off. I texted Lucy and she texted back that Layla was fine."

Kate shook her head. "Maybe I should go see her. . . ."

"What about Dad and . . ." He glanced around, as if looking for Daphne, who'd run upstairs to change her clothes. "Have you thought about the will?"

"We have to bring the new will to light. We have to."

"Dad'll fight it," he said nervously, glancing outside to where a few empty, forlorn pots were waiting for spring plantings.

"What if all his 'new investments' don't pan out?" Kate demanded. "What about all that money, Lyle? Your money."

"Well, and Lucy and Layla's."

"What about Stonehenge?" she suddenly asked. "Goddamn it, I mean *Wolfe Lodge*?"

"The sale's going through. We need the cash," Lyle said by rote, like someone had pulled a string.

"When? *When*?"

"We're supposed to sign this week. Well, Dad's supposed to sign. It's really his, outside of the company."

"You've been his proxy."

"Well, *yeah*," he snarled with a return of some spunk. "What did you want me to do, say 'Oh, no, Dad, you can't do that. You might spend all our money?' You sure as hell were on board."

"I didn't have all the facts!" She wanted to hit him, he was so dense. "God, Neil Grassley . . . and John . . . and *this*! Jesus H. Christ. I could just scream!" She grabbed her purse, nearly blinded by rage. "We've got to get that will and take it to your lawyer . . . no, he's your father's lawyer, too. I'll find a different one. We need to do it tomorrow, as soon as we can." She smacked her palm against his chest.

"What about today?" he asked.

"It's Sunday," she snapped.

"I mean, what about the dinner we're supposed to have with Abbott and Ainsley?"

Ainsley Hershey-Smith was Abbott's "friend." Someone close enough to Kate's age who, though she claimed to have a boyfriend she was living with, went out to dinner with Abbott occasionally by herself. Kate wasn't certain they were sleeping together, but she was pretty sure what was on Ainsley's mind: money. The kind Abbott was taking out for "investments."

She and Lyle had been at two excruciating dinners with Ainsley before. The woman pretended she and Abbott were just such good friends. She even talked about the mythical boyfriend enthusiastically.

"Maybe we should cancel. We should see Layla and Lucy, not Ainsley. Hopefully, Abbott will cancel first."

* * *

". . . Courtney just got back last night," Luke said. "Something fishy there, Dallas. She was all set up to talk to the press."

"Like she knew about Grassley already?" Dallas asked. He was looking out through his window in the direction of the clubhouse.

"Or she's a very cagey opportunist. I tried to connect with her, but she won't talk. I'm working on the theory that she might have been staying with her parents. Get this: they live in Glenn River."

That woke him up. "That's . . . coincidental."

"I thought so, too. Want me to check with the folks to find out if she's been there?"

"Let's pass this one to September, if she's willing. She's got history with Wharton County already."

"I'll call her," Luke said.

Dallas turned away from the view and dumped the rest of his cold coffee into the sink. It was getting on in the afternoon and he was sick of being in this house. A lot of stuff coming out of Wharton County . . . John Linfield's death . . . a woman calling the police to steer the investigation to Amanita ocreata poisoning . . . those same mushrooms on the Kilgore property. Was Courtney Mayfield somehow involved? Had Grassley pulled the same about-face on her that he had on Layla? Pretending they were a couple and then just using her for the child she could give him? The son?

IVF . . . Luke was half-convinced Neil had used some of Neil and Layla's embryos and possibly implanted them in Courtney. His source said there were none left, so they'd either been destroyed or used. . . .

In listening to the news, he'd gleaned Courtney was acting like she was still pregnant. If that were true, was it really her baby, or was it Layla's? DNA would tell. And with Grassley gone, the baby would legally be Layla's.

He had a bad feeling about that. He knew Layla hadn't killed Grassley, but there was a circumstantial case building against her that was even stronger than the one against Lucy for Linfield's death. Layla had been in the process of suing Grassley for joint custody of their upcoming child after being paid to give up all rights. She and Grassley's relationship had fallen apart and he'd taken up with another woman, Courtney Mayfield. Mayfield was, or had been, pregnant with another son, according to Mayfield—that still needed verification—and there was a possibility that that child was also Layla and Grassley's. The surrogate having the original child, a boy, was due very soon and if Neil Grassley were gone, that child would be Layla's.

Dallas had been lied to by the best of them, had fallen for those lies a few times, but Dallas sensed Layla Crissman didn't have it in her. She wasn't the calculating mastermind who was being created by people who were angry and/or jealous of her.

His thoughts turned from Layla to Lucy. Like Layla, he didn't believe Lucy capable of doing harm to anyone, but again, a circumstantial case against her could be put together. She and her husband had been fighting at the benefit. She hadn't taken John into the ER, even though they'd gone there, which was easily explained by Linfield's refusal to enter, but the orderly who'd talked to Lucy seemed to want to place the blame on her. Possibly worse yet, the consensus among people who knew the Linfields, according to Luke's reporting, believed the marriage was nearing a crisis point just before the poisoning.

Still . . . Dallas couldn't seem to get Lucy Linfield out of his mind. Was it because of their past history? Partly. But she'd also reached him in a way he'd wondered if he could still be reached. He sensed she felt the same way.

He shook his head, mentally kicking himself. She was a

recent widow and a client, two good reasons to steer clear of
any personal relationship.

Walking into the living room of her home, September
clicked off her phone and looked at the time. Four o'clock.
Did she have time to drive to Wharton County again? Luke
had given her the address of Courtney Mayfield's parents
and she was glad to be back in the investigation, thankful
Dallas had suggested she be the one to check it out.

Neil Grassley's death was being handled by Portland PD,
and though she'd called Wes Pelligree and Gretchen *and* her
brother, Auggie, who should have been the best source of information because he worked for Portland PD, no one knew
anything yet. They'd promised to pass anything along they
learned, and fortunately, each had asked for, and received,
approval from their superiors.

She was still finding it hard to believe Grassley was dead.
It had been a distinct shock when she'd heard the news earlier that morning. She'd wondered at the interviews that had
followed. Trouble, dire trouble, seemed to circle the Crissman women. Was there something else at play?

If she went back to Wharton County, she could head over
to the StopGo again, see if Rhonda and/or Barry were
around, press them a bit. And she could check on Brianne
Kilgore. She'd had a churning feeling about Brianne, and not
a good one, since their meeting. She'd liked Brianne, but
could she trust that the odd woman wasn't involved in the
mushroom poisoning somehow? Brianne seemed to believe
John Linfield wasn't the killer's target. Had Lyle Crissman
been the intended victim? September had been chewing on
that possibility and not come up with any clear answer.

And what about Courtney Mayfield? She'd come from
the same area. That seemed more than coincidental, but
was it?

You need to know what definitively killed Neil Grassley.
Was it a blow to the head or was it something else?

Jake was outside on the deck, cleaning off the barbecue. It was still cold enough that he was wearing a jacket and the wind was blowing his hair. September pulled open the sliding glass door, came up behind him, and wrapped her arms around his waist, snuggling close.

"Uh-oh," he said.

"What, uh-oh?"

"You're hugging me. Something's happened." He turned around, holding out one arm to keep the scraper away from her, wrapping his other arm around her.

"Can't I just hug you? I hug you a lot!"

"I can feel the difference." He was smiling, teasing her.

"Okay, I'm thinking of going back to Wharton County, so I might miss dinner. . . ."

His eyes probed hers. "This about Grassley's death?"

"That was Luke Denton on the phone. Courtney Mayfield's parents live in Glenn River. Gives me an opportunity to check in with Brianne Kilgore again." He opened his mouth to say something, but she cut him off before he could utter the first syllable. "I'm fine. You don't have to accompany me. Just don't burn the steaks and save me one."

"I never burn the steaks," he said, affronted, turning back to put down the scraper on the grill.

"Yeah . . . well . . ."

Jake had always had an uneasy relationship with her job, but after months of September moping around, he seemed to finally be kind of getting it. At least she hoped so.

"Quick interviews. Nothing too dangerous," she promised.

"I'll wait till I see the whites of your eyes before I put your steak on the grill."

She kissed him. "I'll text you when I'm on my way back," she said, then hurried out before he could change his mind.

* * *

Lucy debated calling Dallas. Touched open her phone three times and let the screen die to black again. She didn't have any reason to call . . . well, she didn't have any reason that didn't have to do with Evie, and she didn't want to deal with that subject. Not yet. Especially with her daughter wandering in and out wherever Lucy was, claiming to be bored. Though this was probably a good sign, based on all the terrible upheaval in their lives, Lucy found it annoying. She tried not to feel that way. Evie hadn't known Neil Grassley, so his death wasn't something she could process, and though John's death had deeply affected her, she seemed to have turned a corner. Good. Great.

"Maybe we should go out for pizza?" Evie suggested hopefully.

Why not? "Good idea," Lucy said. "Grab a jacket."

Evie ran up the stairs and was just coming back down when the landline rang. Lucy inwardly groaned, wanted to just vamoose for a while, but Evie was already beelining for the phone.

"It's Grandpa," she called, reading the caller ID.

"Don't pick up—"

"Hi, Grandpa."

Lucy closed her eyes. He'd called earlier today, as had Lyle. She'd texted them both back that Layla was fine. Her father had said he wanted to talk to her and she'd ignored that. Now she'd been had.

"Hi, Dad," she said, taking the handset Evie was holding out to her.

He didn't waste time with pleasantries. "I'm having dinner tonight with Kate and Lyle . . . and Ainsley. I want you and Layla to be there."

"Layla's out, and so am I. Evie and I are just heading out

for pizza." She almost asked, "Who's Ainsley?" before remembering Kate had once mentioned Abbott's friend. She believed Kate's description had included the phrase "grasping bitch." Lucy had written that off to Kate's basic insecurity when it came to her place in the family, but now she wondered.

"Cancel the pizza. We'll be at the Pembroke Inn."

Oh, great. The Pembroke. "I'm not canceling the pizza, and you can call Layla, but—"

"She's not answering."

"—she won't answer. But she'll text you, and I can guarantee what her answer will be: no. If you have something important to say, just say it."

"I just want a family dinner," he said petulantly.

She rolled her eyes. "Dad, we all need a little more lead time, and that's on a good day."

Evie had heard a lot of this and was vehemently shaking her head. *Pizza*, she mouthed, hooking a thumb toward the garage.

"I know you're upset about your job. I'm not saying it's over. If we get turned around soon, you can have it back."

"Can I? Gee, thanks."

"Lucy . . ."

"I gotta go, Dad. Really. Have a nice dinner. Oh, and did you ever pay Babette what you owed her?"

"I don't know what you're talking about."

"The designer. The one the store owes money to."

"We're up to date on all our accounts," he snapped.

"Good . . . and good-bye."

She hung up and walked briskly toward the garage, catching up to Evie and passing her, so that Evie hovered at her heels.

In the garage, she climbed in the Escape and Evie jumped

in the passenger seat. "You're not old enough," Lucy said, hooking a thumb to the back.

"I think I am," Evie said but reluctantly obeyed. "You were kinda mean to Grandpa."

"'As ye sow, so shall ye reap . . .'"

"What's that mean?"

"What goes around, comes around, only in biblical style, it being Palm Sunday and all."

"You're kinda acting weird, Mom."

"Yeah, well . . ."

It kind of runs in the family. . . .

September reached the StopGo convenience store at around five-thirty, only able to arrive that quickly because it was Sunday and the traffic was light. She planned to go to the Mayfields' house next, which was on the far side of Glenn River, almost in a straight line east. There were a couple of people wandering around the store, two kids poring over the candy section, a man carrying a six-pack to the counter, while a woman was buying lottery tickets. Barry was at the register. There was no sign of Rhonda.

The guy with the beer was in a suit, although with his full beard, fuller belly, tattoos, and general beefiness, September thought it might be his Sunday best. He paid for his purchases after the woman pocketed her lottery tickets. Next, it was September's turn to stand in front of Barry.

"Remember me?" she asked.

He shot a glance toward the tan door. "Yep."

"You sure you don't recall the woman who bought the disposable phone?"

The kids with the candy, two boys around eleven, were behind September, pushing and shoving each other, giggling.

Barry looked down at the counter. "Rhonda doesn't want to be involved."

"It's a homicide, Barry," September reminded him soberly. "Keeping something back, anything, isn't going to play well."

He mumbled something under his breath, but she couldn't catch it with the boys roughhousing behind her. Their giggling had turned to laughter, which sounded like it could escalate into fighting.

"What?" she asked.

"She had gray hair," he said.

One of the boys fell into September, and she turned around and gave him the evil eye. They both straightened, as if someone had put a rod up their backs, but she barely noticed. *Gray hair.*

She turned back to Barry. "Was she young or old?"

"She didn't look old in the face."

Brianne.

"Thanks," September said, and turned to leave with a final stern look toward the boys. They watched her, but one of them elbowed his friend. The friend elbowed back. September half-expected the pack of Skittles clutched in the first boy's hand to drop and spill across the floor, and as another elbow was thrown, that was exactly what happened, multicolored candies scattering across the floor. Barry yelled and Rhonda charged through the tan door, but September was already in the parking lot and striding to her car.

Six-thirty p.m. at the Pembroke Inn. Kate sat in frigid silence while Abbott made the grand gesture of buying a bottle of champagne—the cheapest on the menu, Kate noted—and Ainsley chuckled at everything he said, as if he were the most entertaining man alive, which made Kate dig her nails into her palms. Ainsley was blond, but Kate could see her dark roots. Kate was barely blond herself these days. Took a lot to keep her hair looking good, so she understood the work that went into it, but Kate didn't really believe Ainsley had ever been anything more than dishwater.

Beside her, Lyle was as rigid as Kate, although his knee was bobbing again. His tell. Abbott had apparently tried to get both Lucy and Layla to join them, but it hadn't happened. That had alarmed Kate. Not that the sisters couldn't make it, but that Abbott wanted to gather the whole family together. She had the terrible feeling it had something to do with Ainsley . . . and in that she was proved right moments later.

"I've asked Ainsley to marry me," Abbott said with a proud grin.

Kate was half-prepared, but Lyle apparently wasn't. "What?" he demanded, in shock.

"She's been unhappy in her relationship—"

"Very unhappy," Ainsley put in.

"—and we've been kind of talking about it for a while now." Abbott looked tenderly into Ainsley's face and Kate felt bile rise in her throat. "We just realized we wanted to be together."

"Love can be so unexpected," Ainsley agreed, blinking away tears.

Oh my Lord . . .

Lyle was on his feet. "You're getting married? To *her?*"

"Yes, son." Color crept up Abbott's neck, suffusing his face.

"You can't." Lyle's expression faltered, and he paled as his father's face reddened.

At that moment, the waiter brought the champagne, asking everyone how the evening was going as he popped the cork and quickly filled four glasses. He grew aware of the explosive silence that had rendered them all mute, unaware how to deal with it. With a mumbled, "Let me know if you need anything else," he hurried away.

Kate reached for her glass. Everyone else slowly followed suit, looking around as if caught in some kind of trap.

"To the happy couple," Kate said flatly, raising the flute. "Good thing you're so in love, because you won't have any money now that the real will of Lyle Abbott Crissman Jr. has surfaced. Hope you have a little nest egg of your own, Ainsley, because Lyle Abbott Crissman III"—she nodded to her father-in-law—"was cut right out of it."

Chapter Twenty-Nine

September had traveled to Glenn River to talk to the Mayfields, so she quickly drove to their home, a gray-shingled, two-bedroom post–WWII bungalow that looked in need of a new roof, a new paint job, and a new garage door. The existing door bore a car-size dent in its center and didn't seem to be on the frame correctly, leaving an angled gap at the bottom. She hoped to make this visit quick because she felt an urgency to hightail over to the Kilgores again. Brianne was at the center of the poisoning somehow. September didn't want to think of her as the poisoner, but the investigation kept circling back to her. It stood to reason she was the one who bought the cell phone and made the call to the sheriff's department. September wanted to know why, and she was anxious to find out Brianne's reasons.

She knocked on the Mayfields' front door in the fading light, a cold, moaning wind sweeping around the corners of the house. She could smell the dank, earthy scent of the river the town was named for and shivered inside her light jacket.

A porch light flared and the door opened. Behind a tattered screen, a middle-aged man with horn-rimmed glasses peered out at her. "Yes?" he asked suspiciously.

"Hello, Mr. Mayfield. My name's September Westerly

and I'd like to talk to you about your daughter, Courtney."
September had considered calling first but had learned that
often forewarning was forearming.

"You with the press?"

He almost sounded amenable to that idea, so September
said, truthfully, "I've been on television a number of times."

Nodding, he said, "Courtney said you might come by.
She's been interviewed a lot today." He opened the screen
door, inviting her in. "I'm Bob and this is Jan." He nodded
toward a woman with hennaed hair, the bright red suggesting
she'd just had it done. September slipped inside and he
closed the door behind her.

"What do you want to know?" Jan asked. She was seated
in a high-backed chair, her arms folded over her chest, as if
she'd been just waiting for an interview. Behind her, on a desk
set up in a corner of a dining room, was a rather sophisticated-
looking computer monitor and wireless setup, which seemed
a bit out of place in the small space that was stuffed with
well-used mismatched furniture.

Bob caught her look and said, "Courtney sometimes
works from home. She's a data inputter."

"Until she and Neil fell in love," Jan said.

"Has she been staying with you the last week or so?"
September asked.

"Well, yes . . . she didn't feel safe at her apartment with
that Crissman woman on the rampage, and look what happened!" Jan said, her expression aghast.

"You're referring to Neil Grassley's death." September
didn't want to put words in their mouths, but she didn't want
to assume anything either.

Bob said, "Courtney knew he was in danger, and that she
was, too. That Crissman woman was after his money, and
she would do anything for it."

"She had a story to tell," Jan said. "And she told it. I pray it was enough to keep her safe. We didn't want her to go back, but she knew it was her duty to get the truth out there."

September nodded. Both parents seemed to think their daughter could do no wrong. She tried a couple more questions about Courtney's relationship with Neil but was met by more glowing reports of their daughter's loving relationship with a man cut down in the prime of his life by the terrible Layla Crissman.

"You wait. More's coming out about her," Jan said with a knowing nod of her head. "She killed him. Like her sister killed her husband."

"We don't know that one for sure," Bob said, "but it sure looks like it. The police'll get 'er, if it's true."

"Don't be so sure," Jan said crisply. "Crissmans have gotten away with murder for too long! You know the history of that lodge, don't you? People dying. The old man that built that place killed his wife, mark my words. Courtney knows all about all of them."

"How did your daughter meet Neil Grassley?" September asked.

They looked at each other. "At a coffee shop," Jan said, but Bob overrode her.

"No, through work. Courtney was a freelancer and he hired her."

"But they met first at that coffee shop," Jan insisted.

"Courtney claimed she was pregnant on the news today," September said.

"Yes," Jan said after a moment.

"With Neil Grassley's child?"

"That's what she said," Bob answered.

"And . . . hers . . . ?"

"What do you mean?" Bob looked at her as if she'd lost her mind.

"Neil and Layla Crissman used a surrogate for a baby with one of the embryos they created at an IVF clinic. It's been theorized that your daughter was a surrogate for them with one of their other frozen embryos."

The Mayfields turned to each other.

"That's a dirty, downright lie," Bob said.

"Someone is defaming our Courtney, and I guess we know who that is," Jan agreed hotly.

After that, they didn't want to talk to September any further. The clock on the far wall was climbing toward seven o'clock, so September thanked them and left. The Mayfields were locked and loaded to sing their daughter's praises and denigrate the Crissmans, no matter what.

Thirty minutes later, she came through the stand of Douglas firs that led to the Kilgore property, dying sunlight flickering through the thick branches, and pulled up to the house. There was a new dark gray Mercedes in the driveway parked beside the beat-up truck Brianne had arrived in the last time September was here.

Her stomach growled, and she texted Jake and told him she'd just arrived at the Kilgores and to forget the steak. He texted back: **Be careful.** To which she returned: **Always.**

Then she headed to the door.

Kate's bald announcement about the will caused Ainsley's brow to pucker and Lyle to gasp out, "Kate!" in a strangled voice.

But the greatest impression was on Abbott, whose already red face grew scarlet as he growled furiously, "You don't know what you're talking about!"

Kate drank her champagne, aware she'd stepped over a line and starting to feel she'd maybe made a mistake.

Abbott noisily scooted back his chair and leaned forward, shaking a finger at her. "I always knew Lyle married his mother! You're just like her! Out for yourself and what you can get!" He slapped his hand at her several times, as if to wipe her away. "You're not getting anything from the Crissmans! You can't . . ." He suddenly gasped and fell forward onto his elbows.

"Dad?" Lyle said, scared.

"You all right?" Kate asked, also getting to her feet as people at nearby tables turned to stare.

Ainsley mewed, "Abbott?"

Abbott tried to stand, then his whole body slumped, and Lyle jumped up and managed to catch him before he toppled onto the floor.

Now frantic, Kate clawed her phone out of her purse and punched 9-1-1. Though her fingers trembled, she was in control. She had to be. She didn't want Lyle's father to die, but if he was going to leave this world, she was sure glad he hadn't gotten married first.

The Kilgores' door was answered by Brianne. She stared at September as if she'd never seen her before.

"Hi," September said uncertainly from the porch. "I wanted to talk—"

"You're the ex-cop," Brianne said in her flat way. She was holding on to the door as if she might slam it shut.

"Yes, that's right." September hadn't really said she was an ex-cop to Mona or Brianne, so someone else had informed her.

And then Jerome Wolfe's tall form appeared in the back room, standing in about the same spot September had on her previous visit. "Mrs. Westerly," he said in his trademark mocking tone. "How nice of you to drop by."

Brianne turned toward him, smiling slightly, as much emotion as September had ever seen on her face.

"Were you just in the neighborhood?" Wolfe asked her.

September felt herself still inside, and she silently warned herself to be wary. Wolfe walked down the hall toward her, his face in shadow, until he was standing beside Brianne, who looked somewhere past his left ear, still smiling, about as close to eye contact as September had seen her make as well.

"I was following up on some information in Wharton County," September said, thinking hard. She didn't want to talk in front of Wolfe, yet she suspected whatever was said would be related to him by Brianne, no matter if September asked her to keep it private or not.

"Trying to clear Lucy Crissman's name, or is it Layla now?" Wolfe asked. His demeanor was friendly, but September had to step carefully.

"Lucy Linfield," Brianne said.

"I stand corrected. Lucy Linfield." He smiled down at Brianne, whose eyes were momentarily all over him before she threw a look at September.

The dog, Duke, made his way slowly toward them, toenails clicking on the old hardwood floor.

"Could I talk to you alone, Brianne?" September asked.

"What do you want?" she asked, frowning slightly.

"I'll just mosey back down the hall," Wolfe said.

September watched him leave, thinking he'd dropped all pretense of the polished businessman he'd projected at the benefit. He wanted Stonehenge and the Kilgores' property and he didn't care what anyone thought any longer. And she'd learned from Lucy that his animosity toward the Crissmans ran deep.

Brianne acted like she was going to follow after him, but September said, "I know you made that call to the sheriff's station. I have a witness."

Brianne's eyes flew all over the place, searching for something to land on. She was half-turned away from

September, who went on, "You know who poisoned John Linfield."

"No, I didn't see them."

"Did you bring the mushrooms to the benefit?"

"No."

"Did you bring them for someone else?"

"No." Brianne was squirming, now facing down the hall to where Jerome Wolfe stood, feet apart, arms over his chest, waiting for September to leave.

"But you know who had them there?"

"I didn't see who harvested them. I don't want to talk to you."

September seized on that. "But you know who harvested them . . . from the big oak?"

"You're trying to trap me. Jerome is right."

She turned away, and September said a bit louder, "You need to tell someone, Brianne. Deputy Morant . . . Martin? He's a friend of yours? Tell him who took the mushrooms from the big oak. It's not safe to keep that secret. Brianne . . . ?"

Duke whined at September, his head swiveling to watch his mistress head down the hall. Jerome Wolfe said something softly to Brianne that September couldn't hear, then he came to the door again, blocking her view of the interior. September told him, "Tell her to talk to Deputy Morant about the angel of death mushrooms."

"You think she poisoned John Linfield." His tone was skeptical.

"I think what she knows is dangerous, and she should tell everything to the police. Tell her that, Mr. Wolfe. Convince her."

"I'll tell you what I think; I think you need to look at the Crissmans. Probably Lucy, as Linfield was her husband. Or maybe Layla. The 'black widow sisters.' Brianne Kilgore wouldn't hurt a fly."

* * *

Carrying their leftover pizza wrapped in aluminum foil in one hand, her cell phone in the other, Lucy followed Evie back inside the house. She'd texted Layla but hadn't heard back from her sister. Evie was holding the door from the garage open for her; it was on a spring lock that automatically closed, and it never failed but to bang into her when she was entering.

"Thanks," she told Evie, who skipped on ahead of her.

Lucy was just putting the pizza into the refrigerator when her cell rang. Her pulse jumped, and she glanced at the screen, expecting Layla, half-hoping for some reason it was Dallas, which was ridiculous, but seeing it was her brother.

She almost didn't answer. She'd ignored earlier calls. But there was no point in putting off the inevitable, so she clicked on. "Hey, Lyle," she said without much enthusiasm.

"Dad's had a heart attack," Lyle said soberly. "He's in an ambulance heading to Laurelton General. Kate and I are on our way. . . ."

Layla chewed on an open-faced slice of grilled cheese toast, the first thing she'd eaten all day. Off and on, she'd checked her phone for anything about Neil's death, but apart from Courtney's libelous comments, there wasn't more information. That knowledge had encouraged her until she'd tried to go down to the Starbucks and found a news team waiting outside her building. They'd descended on her like jackals and she'd done an about-face and raced back up the stairs and into her apartment, slamming the door behind her.

She hadn't texted Lucy back yet. She'd just felt too harassed and lethargic and sad. Neil was gone. Dead. Likely killed by someone . . .

She picked up her phone and saw the screen register a

call from Lucy. Layla hadn't turned her ringer back on, but now it seemed like she should. She flicked the sound back on at the same time she answered the call.

"Hi," she said. "Sorry I've been so hard to—"

"Layla, Dad's had a heart attack," Lucy clipped out. "I'm on my way to Laurelton General now. Kate and Lyle are probably already there."

"What . . . what?" She felt numb, sick, disbelieving.

"Are you doing okay?"

"I, uh, yes. I just turned my phone back on. I'll catch an Uber. They're probably gone by now."

"Who?" Lucy asked, confused.

"Reporters. Hanging outside my door."

"Oh . . . ugh . . . no, Layla, stay put. Let me see what the deal is. I'm closer to the hospital and I got Bella to sit for Evie, so I'll be there soon."

"I can battle my way through," Layla assured her, feeling better now that she had a plan of action. "But Dad . . . ? What happened?"

"I don't know. Stay put," she advised. "Give me half an hour to figure things out. I'll call you . . ." And she was gone.

Lucy entered the hospital ER and, as she crossed to a desk the first person she saw was the orderly who'd come to the car when she'd brought John in, hoping to get him to see a doctor. The man did a double take on her as well, then came her way.

"Are you looking for me?" he demanded.

"No. My father's here. He had a heart attack, and my brother called me."

"Oh." He seemed nonplussed.

"Lucy!"

She looked up and saw it was Lyle, Kate beside him in the waiting room, both talking to a man in a white coat. A doctor? Lucy swept past the orderly toward her family. "How is he?" she asked.

Lyle said, "Okay . . . it's not too bad. A light one, that's what they said." Nervously, he smoothed his hair from his forehead.

"Abbott's going to be fine," said Kate but glanced away.

Lucy stared at them both, wondering what it was they weren't saying. "Okay, well, then, I'm going to text Layla and tell her not to come. The press were camped outside her place today."

"Jesus," Lyle said. He walked over to a chair and sank into it. A pretty, somewhat dazed-looking woman scooted closer to him, taking the adjoining seat.

Who? Lucy wondered, and Kate answered the unspoken question, "Ainsley."

"Ah," Lucy said. "It happened at dinner? What happened, exactly?" She was already texting Layla that things looked okay with their father and she would call her soon.

She looked up from the text when Kate didn't answer her. Her sister-in-law's gaze was on Lyle. "You maybe should ask your brother," Kate finally said.

"Okay . . ."

"You know any good lawyers?"

Lucy's pulse leaped and she shot Kate a look. "Maybe," she said cautiously, before realizing it was a rhetorical question.

"You're all going to owe me for what I did," she said with a bitter smile.

Then she walked toward the glass doors that led to the reception area of the main floor of the hospital, away from Emergency and all of them.

Chapter Thirty

A second will.

A new will. The real one. The one Junior had expected would be used and *Lyle had waylaid it*!

Lucy could scarcely believe it. After Kate's dramatic departure from the hospital waiting room, Lucy had wrested Lyle away from a rather clingy Ainsley, walked him into the empty hall where Kate had disappeared, and demanded to know what the hell Kate had been talking about.

And the whole story came out . . . about their grandfather's will, which Abbott had wanted destroyed . . . about the witnesses to the will, one of whom had blackmailed Lyle . . . about Lyle taking the sixty thousand to pay off the blackmailer . . . about Abbott believing the will had been destroyed . . . about the reveal tonight that Abbott was apparently engaged and then Kate dropping the bomb on him that Junior's last will was safely tucked in a safe-deposit box . . . about Abbott's arrhythmia, the warning of a heart attack . . . and about the fact that Abbott had been systematically separating investments from the company, secreting money for himself.

While Lyle talked, stopping and starting, Lucy's emotions ran the gamut of shock, anger, and a little bit of hope at this recitation. It looked as if her father and brother's plans to sell Stonehenge were scuttled, at least until the will was settled. She'd been silent with disbelief and was furious with her brother, her anger mounting with each new revelation. When it seemed he'd said all he could, or all he wanted to divulge, she exploded.

"You should never have hidden the will," she hissed at him. "Then none of this would have happened!"

He had no good answer for her wrath, other than that he'd always been under their father's thumb. Abbott's favorite child. "You have no idea what it's like, the pressure I've been under," he said vehemently, as if he'd shouldered all the burden of being a Crissman.

She was utterly frustrated with him and had to draw a breath to pull herself under control.

As they stood in the hallway, she bit back a dozen harsh retorts and instead studied her brother. She and Layla had teased him mercilessly when they were young, calling him "Little Monster," among other things. His mother had complained about them to Abbott, and a division had occurred, a schism in the family. Then his mother had left, swanning off like their own mother, spending even less time with Lyle in the ensuing years than Layla and Lucy's mother had with them.

Still, he needed to man up. He should have a long time ago.

"You always liked Brianne Kilgore," she said aloud, bringing his head around in surprise.

"What's that got to do with anything?" He glared at her, stepping out of the way as an orderly pushed an elderly man in a wheelchair to a bank of elevators.

"You had a relationship with her, but you lied to her father," she charged, lowering her voice. "You told him Brianne was responsible for her little brother's death."

"What the hell are you talking about? Our dad just had

a heart attack and that's what's on your mind?" he asked, incredulous.

"I don't get you, Lyle. I don't get any part of you. You toyed with Brianne and you hid that will."

"I didn't toy with Brianne," he shot back.

"You had sex with her and she's not . . . she doesn't process well enough to have it be consensual!"

"Brianne broke it off with me," Lyle snapped. "Dad told me Brianne was responsible for her brother's death. I mentioned it to her father and it got back to her. I didn't want to stop seeing her, but that's what happened. And it's all old news."

Lucy had let it go after that. Other people were walking through the hall and stepping in front of the elevators. She'd wanted to argue with Lyle about something and so she had, but it hadn't made her feel any better.

They returned to the ER waiting area. Shortly thereafter, the doctor came out and told them Abbott was being moved to a private room and that he was resting comfortably and would likely be able to go home the next day. At that point, Lucy just left. She was glad her father was going to be okay, but she didn't want to see him. She needed to process. Leaving Lyle, she texted Layla as she walked outside to her car, letting her know their father was going to be fine.

Monday morning, Lucy was standing in the kitchen, drinking black coffee, planning the day. Lyle had said he and Kate were collecting the will from a safe-deposit box and taking it to a lawyer. Lucy had suggested Dallas, understanding Kate's cryptic comment now. Dallas might not be an estate attorney, but he could point them in the right direction.

With that in mind, she called him. She'd gotten his cell number, and though it was barely seven o'clock, she didn't care. She wanted to talk to him. There was so much to say. So many issues.

He answered on the third ring. "Hi, Lucy."

She opened her mouth and thought, *Oh, no, oh, God no* . . . as her throat closed with emotion.

"Lucy?" he asked.

"I'm sorry. I've got to talk to you . . ."

"What is it? About Layla? Or . . . your husband . . . ?" He sounded wide awake and alert. "Should we meet at my office?"

"Sure." She could barely get it out.

"Or . . . I could come there . . . ?"

"Yes. Please. Soon as you can." And she hung up before she broke down completely.

Her insides quaking, she went upstairs to collect herself and apply some makeup. She felt vulnerable and angry at all the men in her family, Lyle, Abbott, and yes, even John. She stopped by Evie's room on the way, checked in, and saw she was still sleeping. Then she went to the master bedroom and switched on the television as she walked toward the bathroom.

". . . authorities are looking into the nearly one hundred thousand dollars that passed from Neil Grassley's bank account to Layla Crissman's over the course of the last week. Sources say there was animosity between them, and their relationship had become contentious with a lawsuit pending. . . ."

Lucy stopped cold, staring at the screen in shock. Still listening, she found her phone and called Layla.

Layla couldn't take her eyes off the TV. The news was terrible. Terrible! She was being crucified and it was all lies! She was cold inside from head to toe and gripped the back

of one of her chairs for support. If the police believed she'd
stolen Neil's money . . . ?

She had answered the phone in a daze, and it took all her
powers of concentration to understand what Lucy was
saying. ". . . Dallas will figure it out. Don't worry. We know
the truth . . ." And then she went on to tell her about their
father, who apparently was recovering fine from a heart
attack and engaged to a woman almost half his age, and that
Lyle had secreted their grandfather's most recent will, which
cut out their father entirely—that fact being the catalyst for
Abbott's heart event—and that Kate had been the one to
force the truth to come out.

"Wow," was all Layla had been able to get out.

Talking fast, Lucy finished with, "Dad tried to cut us out
of our inheritance, Dad and *Lyle*. Our brother's been right
there all the time, knowing the truth and not doing anything
about it. He and Kate are turning the will over to Dallas
today, and he's coming over in a few minutes and I'm going
to . . . tell him everything."

"Everything?" That penetrated. She glanced away from
the TV for a second. "You mean . . ."

"I think so. Don't watch the news. It's just . . . I don't
know. Somebody's got their facts wrong."

"Okay."

But it was impossible not to look back. A reporter was
claiming the police had evidence—*evidence*!—that Layla
had been receiving payments from Neil! Impossible. She'd
taken the twenty thousand dollars from Neil and squirreled
it into an account, but that was it. They had no evidence.
They couldn't!

But . . .

Still holding her phone, she pressed the icon for her
bank's app and signed in. She wasn't all that computer savvy,
but she knew enough to handle the basic banking on her
phone. Her heart nearly stopped as she found two deposits

of fifty thousand dollars each, transferred into her account *last week*. Neil had done it. Somehow.

Layla groaned in disbelief, the cell slipping from her fingers. She felt persecuted by unseen forces. She groaned again when she realized she was due at Easy Street at eleven today. If the news reporters had been outside her door yesterday, they were bound to be there in full force again today.

As she picked up her cell, the phone jingled in her hand. Dallas Denton's name flashed onto the small screen. She answered, and he identified himself, mentioned he was meeting Lucy at her house this morning, and then got down to business. "They're doing the autopsy on Grassley today."

"Have you seen the news? Did you see what they're saying?" She was breathing hard, damn near hyperventilating.

"Yes. Don't watch it. I'm just pulling up to your sister's. We're working on it. Don't talk to them, the press."

"Dallas . . . I checked my bank account. That money's in there, but I didn't put it there! Neil must've." She was pacing, her thoughts swirling, panic growing.

"There'll be a record," he said calmly. "We'll follow the trail."

Suddenly, she wanted to be there with Dallas and Lucy. She felt like a traitor that she knew Lucy's secret and he didn't yet, when he was working so hard for her, for them both. "I have to go to work. They've been camped outside my door." Walking to the living-room window, she looked outside and saw a news van parked on the other side of the street. "Oh God. They're here again."

"Ignore them. Do you need a ride? I can send Luke to take you."

"No, thanks. I'll take care of it."

They ended their call and she slipped on her jacket and went down to the parking garage. She let herself out a back door, then zigzagged through the city blocks and traffic to a deli four blocks from the apartment building. On the way, she hired an Uber driver and found his black Honda with the Uber sticker in the rear window waiting at the corner. He dropped her off at Easy Street and she barely had time to wrap an apron around her waist when a young man with sharp eyes strolled in, looking around, his gaze falling on Layla. He'd been waiting for her, she realized.

Layla walked directly into the kitchen and said to her boss, "I'm going to have to leave."

The owners, both of them, didn't even bother to try to stop her. It was clear they thought there might be some teensy bit of truth in the fact that she was involved in Neil's death.

She walked out the back of the restaurant, sneaked around a few more blocks, ducked into another restaurant, and called Uber once more. To hell with it; she would go to Lucy's.

"For God's sake, Auggie, where's this information coming from?" September snapped into her cell as she paced back and forth from the kitchen to the back patio where the barbecue stood, cleaned and ready for use, though Jake had ended up leaving the steaks in the refrigerator and going to a nearby burger joint instead. The coffeepot gurgled away, and she could smell its scent each time she passed through the kitchen. "All this bank information on Layla Crissman. It's all over the papers. Is it verified?"

She'd already called her brother twice this morning, texted him, too, and he'd finally gotten back to her. "It came from Grassley's account last week," he said.

"How do you know this so fast?"

"From the bank. There was a flag on Grassley's account."

"Layla didn't do it, Auggie."

"It was done from his home computer, and she had

access. She had a key. She knew her way around. The money's in her accounts, and he was most likely dead or dying when she did it."

"It's a setup! Somehow." She grabbed a mug from the cupboard and waited for the last of the coffee to drip into the glass pot.

"I'm just telling you what it looks like. We've apparently got a leak around the department. That's how the word got out so fast. We weren't planning on making it public."

"Sounds like there was no attempt to cover up the transfer at all. She's smart. She would have tried harder," September argued, filling her cup. "And Grassley told her that he wanted to marry her. No prenup. She could have had it all."

"I'm giving you what I know, Nine," Auggie said, calling her by her nickname: September was the ninth month of the year.

"Layla's the least money motivated of the Crissmans. She didn't do it."

"Okay. Then who did?"

"Somebody else who had access. Courtney Mayfield, maybe." September remembered the computer at her parents' house as she took her first sip, nearly burning her tongue. "She's a data processor of some kind. It would be easy for her. Layla only uses the electronics she has to. She's an artist. A painter."

"I'll pass that along." He hesitated, then added, "There's something else that hasn't been put out there yet but probably will be soon. Grassley took a blow to the head, probably what killed him. Autopsy is tomorrow and we'll know for sure. But the tox screen came back. He was poisoned with the same stuff as John Linfield. Amanita . . ."

"Ocreata," September finished when he trailed off, her brain buzzing. "You think the mushrooms were the real cause of death?"

"Like I said, we'll know more after the autopsy."

"Okay." September felt slightly ill, thinking of Brianne Kilgore. Was she involved with Grassley's death? The angel of death mushroom sure suggested that. Had she taken September's advice and talked to Deputy Morant yet?

As soon as September was off the phone with Auggie, she put in a call to her ex-partner. Whatever Brianne Kilgore decided to do, Gretchen had likely taken over the Linfield case, and she needed to be informed. When Gretchen didn't answer, September tried Wes and failed to connect there, too. She was thinking of phoning George when she got an incoming call. Laurelton Police Department flashed on her screen.

Good timing, she thought, wondering which one of them was calling her. "September Raf-Westerly," she answered.

"Ms. Westerly, it's Dana Calvetti. Do you think it's possible you could come into the station for a follow-up interview this week?"

That brought September to attention. "I can be there . . . today?"

"That'll work. How about two o'clock?"

"Great. Thanks. I'll see you then. . . ."

Her heart was pounding fiercely as she hung up. Was she about to get her old job back?

Lucy answered the door before Dallas could even knock. She looked . . . great, actually, in slacks and a pink blouse open over a white camisole, face flushed, eyes bright. He put the blush down to fury over what was happening with Layla. He'd noticed, over the years, that some women's beauty seemed to heighten with anger and outrage, though he couldn't say the same for their improvement in judgment; but then, that was true for the entire human race, male or female.

Before he could say anything, an eight- or nine-year-old girl bounced down the stairs and said, "Hi!"

"Hi," he said, taking her in.

Lucy said, "Oh, um . . . Evie, this is Mr. Denton. He's a lawyer. Here to talk about Grandpa and Layla . . . and stuff."

"My grandpa's in the hospital," said Evie solemnly.

"I heard," said Dallas.

"But he's going to be fine." Lucy was brisk. "Hey, uh, give us some private time to talk, okay? Maybe head upstairs with your iPad."

"You're telling me to go to my room with my iPad?" she asked, as if she hadn't heard correctly.

"Yes. Knock yourself out."

"O . . . kay . . ." Evie raced back up the stairs, clearly afraid Lucy was going to come to her senses and change the plan.

As he followed Lucy into the family room, she kicked aside a metal figure of a snail used as a doorstop to close the door behind them. Clearly, this was something that didn't happen often; the door was usually left open.

"What?"

Turning to face him, her eyes were wide. She said in a rush, "I have a couple of things to say, and I want to just say them. First, my brother has been hiding my grandfather's true will. It cuts my father out entirely and we—my sister, brother, and I—need to do whatever needs to be done to put it in place and supersede the old one before my father sells Stonehenge to Jerome Wolfe."

"Okay," Dallas said in surprise. "Did this have anything to do with your father's heart—"

"Yes. Yes, it did." She clasped her hands together, holding on to them tightly, her knuckles blanching, her gaze sliding away. "But there's something else. It's not related to that . . . much . . . it's, um . . ." She unclasped her hands and placed them on either side of her face, pressing them against her cheeks, not looking at him. "Oh my God. I can't believe I'm going to do this. And no one knows, except Layla guessed, but otherwise *no one*. And I'm afraid if I don't get this out now I'll never do it, and you're going to hate me anyway . . . or something . . . I don't know how you'll feel. . . ."

Dallas knew a serious confession when he saw it coming. Oftentimes his clients initially worried more about what he would think of whatever transgression they were about to admit than their friends and family, a kind of tryout, a testing of the waters with their attorney first. "Tell me what happened," he said calmly.

Now Lucy looked up at him, her hazel eyes glittering with moisture.

She said, very quickly, "Evie's not John's daughter. I was pregnant with her about . . . about . . ." She exhaled heavily, emptying her lungs. "Ten years ago."

Dallas waited, but she stopped cold, just staring at him.

Realizing she was expecting something from him, he asked, "Does this have something to do with Evie's real father?"

And then he saw her tense face, did the addition, heard his own words still hanging in the air . . . "No," he said sharply, disbelieving. The girl—Evie?—was *his* daughter?

She nodded jerkily.

"No!" It was a blow to the solar plexus. His head was spinning. No way. But his mind brought back images of that night. Blurry, indistinct images.

Her nodding intensified. She placed her hands protectively over her chest. "Evie doesn't know," she said in a whisper. "No one does but Layla, and now . . . you. . . ."

"What are you doing? This is, this is . . ." *Not true!*

But he could tell it was. She wasn't making it up. And she'd never told him, never once reached out. . . .

"You knew this?" he demanded incredulously. "All this time, you knew this?"

"I didn't immediately know I was pregnant, and by the time I did . . . it was long after, and I thought, I just . . ."

He couldn't process. He couldn't believe what he was hearing. No, it had to be a lie. Had to be. But it wasn't. *He could tell it wasn't!*

Ding-dong.

Lucy's doorbell rang, but she didn't move. She was frozen in place. So was he.

"I'll get it," sang out Evie, and he could hear her bounding down the stairs again.

"Evie . . ." Dallas said, his gut wrenching.

Lucy swiped at the tears that had formed in her eyes as Evie greeted the newcomer warmly. He heard Layla's voice ask, "Where's your mom?" and Evie must have pointed because there was a moment of silence.

Lucy had alerted Layla to what was going on. She'd said as much.

"If Layla hadn't pushed it, would you ever have come to me?" he asked softly.

Lucy shook her head. "I don't know . . . I think so . . ."

"Luce?" Layla called tentatively.

Dallas turned and opened the door. He nodded to Layla and said something to her that he couldn't remember later as he brushed by. He said something to Evie, too, a good-bye, nice-meeting-you kind of thing, but all he was focused on was leaving . . . going somewhere to clear his head.

He believed her. He didn't want to, but he believed her. Even recognized some Denton traits in the girl. The dimple . . . the curly hair . . .

It wasn't anger that had caused Lucy's high color. It was fear.

But it was anger that drove him now.

He wanted to get as far away from her as possible.

Chapter Thirty-One

"Was he mad, Mom?" Evie asked, looking in the direction Dallas had departed, obviously bewildered by his abruptness.

Lucy sank onto the couch, her leg muscles quivering with reaction. "He just had somewhere to go." She surfaced enough to ask Layla, "How're you doing?"

"Oh, I'm okay." She gazed at Lucy with lots of questions in her eyes. Lucy gazed meaningfully at Evie, who said, somewhat dryly, "Should I go back upstairs?"

"Sure," Lucy said, as if Evie had been asking for permission.

This time, Evie took her time heading back up, drifting her hand along the banister, gazing down on Lucy and Layla, who remained silent until she was out of earshot, evidenced by the slamming of her door.

"You told him," Layla said quietly.

"I did."

"How did it go?"

"Just about like you'd expect, I think." Her voice was bitter. She heard it and pushed it aside. She couldn't deal with this yet. Not when there were other, more pressing matters. At least she'd told him. That secret was out, and the ball was in his court. "We need to talk about you. And Neil. And what's happening."

"I was going to talk to Dallas, and oh . . . I need to call back Neil's attorney. She phoned me last week and was trying to set up an appointment for Neil and me to meet with her about Neil changing his will. That was before we found him. I don't know if I should talk to Dallas first . . . Lucy?"

"I heard you," Lucy said, snapping back to the present. Despite telling herself to focus on the here and now, on Layla's urgent problems, she'd let her mind return to Dallas . . . and Evie . . . and what she was going to do. "Could you repeat the last part, though? About talking to Dallas about something?"

Layla came over to her, sank down on the couch beside her, put her arm around her, and pulled her close.

First Financial of Laurelton, where Lyle had secreted Junior's will, wasn't an institution Kate and Lyle normally banked with, and as they pulled into the lot, Kate wondered if Lyle had accounts there as well, ones without her name on them.

Like father, like son?

She'd been silent and stewing since they'd left the hospital the night before, and a tad embarrassed about blurting out the whole scheme at dinner. But witnessing Ainsley cozying up to Abbott had made her see red. She'd wanted to grab the little gold-digger by the hair and drag her out of there.

They went into the bank together and Lyle signed the signature card for entry into his safe-deposit box. The young woman helping them had dyed red hair and a chatty manner Kate found irritating. Something about her reminded Kate of someone on TV; one of those actresses, maybe?

She noticed Lyle's eye lingering a little too long on the

bank teller. He seemed sort of in a trance, and as the girl led
them into the vault, Kate nudged him in the ribs.

He didn't even register it, just moved forward and handed
the girl his key. Seeing that key winking under the fluorescent lights of the vault, and thinking about how Lyle had
kept this account from her, made Kate realize she was going
to have to be extra vigilant in the future. She just couldn't
trust him.

He quickly retrieved a manila envelope and returned the
box to its slot in the vault area with the redhead's help. He
handed the envelope to Kate and she tucked it under her
arm. As they were leaving the bank, Lyle said, "She looked
familiar."

"The girl in the bank?" Kate shook her head, so annoyed
she could scarcely see straight. "She looked like someone
on TV."

"That's not it . . ." He was thinking hard, trying to put it
together.

They both got into his car, Kate just managing not to
slam her door with extra force. If Lyle would try as hard at
their marriage as he was thinking about this *girl*, they might
have a chance.

She stared out the passenger window as he drove her back
home. Daphne was at a half-day art camp for Easter break,
so Kate was going to have to pick her up soon, right after she
and Lyle dropped off the will with Layla and Lucy's lawyer.

"They're keeping Dad at the hospital another day, just to
make sure," Lyle told her as they got in his car, "so we don't
have to pick him up till tomorrow."

We? "Are Lucy and Layla involved in this?" she asked
tautly.

"I guess they could be."

There it was. His wishy-washiness. He was a dishrag of
mass proportions. Kate looked out the window and thought
about her future, not liking the vista of grinding through

each day. Even with Lyle receiving one-third of the estate outright, once the lawyers were through with it, not having to grovel to Abbott, it didn't feel like enough.

At Lucy's house, Layla's cell phone rang from inside her purse. She glanced over to the spot she'd dropped the bag, on Lucy's counter, and crossed the room to retrieve it. Lucy had gone upstairs to corral Evie, and the three of them were going to head somewhere for lunch. Not that she and Lucy felt like doing anything, but it was better than sitting around listening to the news.

On the third ring, she pulled out the cell with trepidation, saw it was Mary Jo, so she answered. "Hi."

"Hi, yourself. Good God, Layla. You're a celebrity now!" She said it teasingly, but Layla knew Mary Jo well enough to realize she was probably put off by Layla's new infamy. Mary Jo rushed on. "Great news, though. We're in escrow on the property, but my buyer really wants your painting. You never got back to me on what you want to do with it."

"I've been kind of busy, Mary Jo," Layla said dryly.

She laughed uneasily. "I don't believe any of that craziness on the news. C'mon."

"It doesn't matter. I'm not selling the painting."

"Just think about a possible price," she encouraged.

"I actually sold it once for eight thousand. I have it back now, but—"

"Eight thousand!" She was aghast.

"—it's no longer on the market."

"Woo-wee . . ." Mary Jo said on a swift intake of breath. "Okay, I'll tell them . . . but if my buyer still wants it . . . ?"

"I'm not selling!" Layla said emphatically. Her eyes drifted to the television. It was turned off, but part of her wanted to know what they were saying about her. Of course, she could look on her phone. . . .

"Well, okay." Mary Jo was miffed, but she let it go. As if remembering she should stay positive, she told Layla to "hang in there" and clicked off.

"Yeah, right." Layla refused to let herself check the latest news on her phone, even though she wanted to. Instead, she placed a second call to the number Neil's attorney, Penelope Gaines, had given her. She wanted to call Dallas and have him be part of the conversation, but that wasn't going to work today.

This time the attorney was in and took Layla's call. After introductions, she said to Layla, "In light of Mr. Grassley's sudden death, we'll have to put off the meeting for now."

Read that to mean: we think you might have killed our client, so don't think you benefit in his will. . . .

Layla answered crisply, "Fine. In the future, you can contact me through my lawyer, Dallas Denton."

Lucy came downstairs as Layla was ending the call. "What was that about?" she asked.

"Neil's lawyer. I could be a killer, so . . . I guess the meeting to discuss his will is off."

Lucy's answer was a snort, but at least she seemed brighter, more like herself.

"It really pisses me off they're calling us the 'black widows.'" She paused, then asked, "Are you going to call Dallas?"

"I was thinking of waiting a little while, at least till after lunch."

"Good idea," she said with relief, then, "C'mon, Evie. Get your shoes on and your coat."

When Evie popped down, carrying a stuffed rabbit adorned with jewelry, Lucy clapped her hand to her forehead and closed her eyes, looking like she was praying for patience.

But she didn't say a word, and the three of them headed to the garage and Lucy's car.

Dallas drove directly to his office, parked in the underground garage, then sat with his hands on the wheel, staring blindly at the concrete wall in front of him. He was in a state of shock. Couldn't get his head wrapped around Lucy's bombshell.

Her daughter . . . his daughter . . . *their* daughter . . . Evie Linfield . . . or maybe Crissman?

Evie Denton.

He went up to his office and managed a brief hello to Billie before locking himself inside. There were several files on his desk, ones he'd asked Billie to pull, but he didn't open them. Instead, he looked out the window at the view and saw nothing but Lucy Linfield in her pink blouse, telling him he had a daughter.

He exhaled hard, as if someone had clapped him on his back. Hadn't realized he'd been holding his breath. He couldn't get his mind past what she'd said. Just couldn't do it.

But he had to. He'd always prided himself on his ability to separate fact from emotion. Today would be a test of that, but he had to force himself. For now. Then, though . . .

Hours later, he was at his desk, thinking over the information he'd learned about Layla's case. September had informed him that Grassley's tox screen showed Amanita ocreata poisoning and Luke, through his source from the IVF clinic, had nailed down that Courtney Mayfield definitely had been implanted with one or more of Grassley and Layla's embryos. It was a lot of information to go over, but he was still having trouble keeping focused.

Around one p.m., Billie buzzed him. "Penelope Gaines is on the line."

That sharpened his attention.

He drew in a long breath and said, "Put her through."

* * *

September parked at Lucille's and, once inside, took a booth by the door. She'd finally gotten through to Gretchen right before her two o'clock appointment with Captain Calvetti. Now, her ex-partner was meeting her at the diner.

She'd barely sat down when, through the window, she saw Gretchen wheel into the lot in one of the department's Jeeps. Gretchen caught sight of September as well, and she hurried across the lot, pushing through Lucille's front door to the ding-dong of the bell.

She slipped in opposite September and grumbled, "They gotta get rid of that god-awful noise. It's not like you can't see everybody who walks in."

"It seems to be part of the ambience."

"Bullshit." She slanted a knowing look at her. "You're seeing Calvetti."

"Like in half an hour."

"Be careful. Could be about your job. I want it to be. But she's tricky. Just letting you know."

"Thanks. I'll watch out. Are you the lead on the Linfield case?"

"Officially, that's Wes still, although he's a short-timer. Why?"

One of the waitresses came by with two cups and a pot of coffee. Both September and Gretchen let her pour them each a cup, but they waved off the menus. As soon as the waitress had moved to a nearby table, September drew a breath, then told Gretchen about Brianne Kilgore and the angel of death mushrooms growing beneath the "big oak," close to Wolfe Lodge, everything she could think of to bring her up-to-date on what she'd learned. She finished with, "I'm pretty sure Brianne was the one who called the sheriff's department and told them to look for Amanita ocreata poisoning in the Linfield autopsy."

Gretchen's brows lifted. "You think she's the poisoner?"

"I think she knows something. She's different—maybe on the autism spectrum, I don't know exactly—but she showed me the mushrooms at the base of that tree." She took a sip from her cooling coffee. "I don't know how she's involved, I just know she is. I'm afraid she's protecting someone. Her family is friends with Deputy Martin Morant at the sheriff's department. Last night, I told her to go to him, tell him what she knew."

"What'd she say?"

September made a face. "Nothing. There was a bit of a glitch. Jerome Wolfe was there. She's in love with him and he's using that to get what he wants, namely the Kilgore property. Her mother's terminally ill and the place will be Brianne's when she dies. Wolfe's making sure Brianne sells to him."

"Is the property that valuable?"

"Don't know. But there seems to be a revenge factor in there." September relayed what she'd learned about the Crissman/Wolfe history, the fact that there was no love lost between the two families.

"So, how does that come back to Linfield?"

"Brianne alluded to the fact that he wasn't the one who was supposed to be poisoned. Now, I don't know if that means anything," September added hastily, as Gretchen was looking at her as if she'd been sitting on critical information. "You'd have to meet Brianne to understand. She just says what's on her mind, and maybe it isn't always the real truth."

"You gonna tell Calvetti all this?" Gretchen asked as the door opened again and the bell rang.

"I want to keep on the case, so yeah, probably. There's something more . . ." September told Gretchen what Auggie had revealed about the tox screen as the alert waitress came by to refill their nearly empty coffee cups.

"The *same poison*?" Gretchen expelled when they were alone again. "Jesus. That reporter's already calling the

Crissman sisters 'black widows' and he doesn't even have that info yet."

"It's not the Crissmans."

Gretchen snorted. "Well, I've got something for you. The Wharton County Sheriff's Department phoned us this morning and Calvetti took the call. Bound to have something to do with this, so I'd lay my cards on the table early if I were you."

September's heart clutched. "I hope it doesn't have to do with Brianne."

Ten minutes later, Gretchen headed back to her Jeep. September sat for a while more, passing the time till her appointment, thinking over what she knew. She had an urgency to protect Brianne. She could call her house, she supposed. Try to talk to her. Or she could take another trip her way, although Brianne hadn't listened last night, so why would she now?

September paid the bill and headed to her Outback. She drove from Lucille's to Laurelton, and within five minutes of walking through the station's door, she was ushered into Captain Dana Calvetti's glass office, where the drapes were drawn against the rest of the squad. Maybe that was how the captain liked it. D'Annibal usually had kept them open. He liked to see what was going on.

"I'd like to give you a job," Calvetti broke right in, raising September's hopes as she sat down in one of the chairs opposite the captain's desk. "But I've run into a problem."

Those hopes took a nosedive. "What problem?"

"A deputy from Wharton County said you've been impersonating a police officer, and that's a crime."

September's heart started thudding. "That's not completely accurate."

"How so?"

"I alluded to knowing Detective Pelligree and Detective Sanders, and he just assumed I was on the force."

The captain's eyes were cold. "And you just let him?"

"Yes."

"What were you after?" She leaned back in her chair. It protested with a groan and a squeak, much as George's did, at least before he'd lost weight.

Figuring her goose was cooked either way, September went for total transparency and told the captain everything she'd just related to Gretchen, along with more about the steps of her investigation: interviews with the StopGo convenience store owners and Courtney Mayfield's parents, everything that applied to Wharton County.

When she was finished, Captain Calvetti tapped a pen on her desk and asked, "And who were you working for?"

"Um . . . myself, mainly. I wasn't paid, if that's what you mean."

"Other than yourself, who was involved?"

Gretchen was right. This was dangerous territory. "I worked with Dallas Denton, a defense attorney, and his brother, Luke Denton, who's a private investigator."

"I know who they are."

Calvetti's cool attitude didn't bode well. September waited nervously for the ax to fall, but then the captain said, "Luke Denton was a good cop. Loyal to a fault, maybe, but a talented investigator. Too bad he went to the other side."

September nodded, not quite sure what was expected.

"All right, Ms. Westerly. Your paperwork's being processed." Calvetti leaned forward and stuck out her hand.

September jumped up, reached across the desk, and shook the captain's outstretched fingers. "So . . . ?" she asked.

Calvetti said, "Pick up your badge tomorrow."

"Thank you." She wanted to dance for joy. "Thanks a lot."

"One more thing. We need a face to show the press. I saw some coverage on you. I'm making you our liaison with the press, so I'm counting on you to make us look good."

The idea of dealing with news people dampened her enjoyment a little, but September wasn't going to make waves. Fine. Whatever. All she cared about was that she was going to be on the force again.

In her Subaru again, September texted Jake before pulling out of the parking lot: Mr. Westerly, you are married to one of Laurelton PD's finest again.

He came back with: Congratulations! That's great! Can't celebrate tonight. Client dinner. Unless later on . . . ? Handcuffs optional.

Chuckling, she wrote: Funny man. See you later.

She wore a smile the rest of the way home, only sobering as she pulled into the garage . . . her mind turned back to Brianne Kilgore. As soon as she was inside, she looked up the number for the Wharton County Sheriff's Department, punched in the number, and when she was connected, asked to speak with Deputy Morant. Foot tapping with repressed anger, she waited for him to come on the line, and when he did, she said, "This is September Westerly. You called up Captain Calvetti and told her that I had impersonated an officer."

"That wasn't why I called!" he sputtered. "I was just looking for you. I got the captain and it kind of came out."

"I never said I was with the police," September reminded him.

"Yes, you . . . *implied* it."

She let that one go. "Why were you looking for me?"

"I wanted to talk to you about Brianne Kilgore."

"Were you going to tell me that you recognized her voice on the phone when she called and told you to check for angel of death mushroom poisoning?"

"What?" he blustered, but she could tell she'd jolted him.

"She's got a very distinctive way of speaking, and I'll bet you she didn't try to change her voice. She called because she was worried someone had used the mushrooms growing by her house on John Linfield."

"I don't know what you're talking about," he mumbled.

"You know the family. You knew it was Brianne and you didn't give her up. That's something you could lose your job over."

"You're saying Brianne made that call?" His voice had turned to a squeak and he had to clear his throat.

"I'm not interested in playing games with you, Morant." September let that sink in as she stared out her window to the deck, where a hummingbird was flitting around the clematis that wound around the covered areas. "What were you going to say about Brianne?"

"Um . . . she said you told her to talk to me." He cleared his throat, all seriousness now.

"Did she tell you anything?"

"No, but I think she kind of wanted to. . . . If you could . . ." He stopped himself.

"If I could what?"

"Check on her again," he blurted out. "She's listening to you, whether you know it or not. She's a good person. I don't trust Jerome Wolfe. He's playing her. I just want her to be okay, but she won't open up to me."

Finally. The truth. "I will," September told him. "I'll do it today."

"Thanks," he said, and there was a wealth of meaning in his words. She had the power to take his job away, and he'd almost derailed hers. But they both had Brianne Kilgore's best interests at heart.

Layla was just climbing out of an Uber car that had dropped her off three blocks from home when Mary Jo called again. A warm sunshine had sprung up, but Layla had on a jacket with a hood that she'd flipped over her head. She'd had the driver pass by her building and was encouraged that there weren't quite as many press people lurking about, although she saw the reporter who'd followed her to her work. She'd escaped him once, but she sensed he wouldn't be so easily shaken a second time.

By the time she was unlocking the door to her apartment, her cell phone was ringing. "Hold on," she said, quickly shutting and locking the door behind her. She swept back the hood and her eye fell on a small clock, fashioned to look old school, that Neil had bought her because he'd complained she was always late. She'd been a bit irked by the move, but she had to admit because of having the clock in her home, she'd been more prompt.

The cell was still ringing, and she pulled it from her purse and looked at the screen. Mary Jo again. She clicked it off without answering, which, of course, prompted Mary Jo to text: Buyer wants the painting. Will pay eight thousand directly to you.

What the hell?

Layla didn't immediately respond. She was still thinking it over when Mary Jo called again. She answered on a sigh. "I saw your text."

"This sale is moving fast," Mary Jo said in a rush. "It's all cash. The house is empty. The builder's eager to sell, and we've got a closing date next week, if you can believe that! And my buyer wants your painting!" Mary Jo cried in an orgasmic shriek.

Layla opened her mouth to tell her once and for all that she didn't want to sell, but she stopped herself. Why did she care? She was lucky, damn lucky, that a painting she'd offered up to charity had come back to her and now she had a chance to reap the profits. And she had no intention of splitting with Jerome Wolfe. He could come after her for his half, and good luck with that.

"Let me think about it," Layla said, compromising. It was

sounding like a better and better plan, if indeed this buyer was for real. Sometimes, she'd learned, they just talked.

"Okay, great. Think fast. She wants to meet you at the house. She'll write you a check for the painting right then!"

"She can just mail it to me," Layla declared.

"Layla, for God's sake, she wants to *meet* you. This all happened because you're in the news. She's like a . . . star fucker. If you were a man, she'd sleep with you."

"Now I'm really not selling it."

"Oh, just meet her. I'm joking. She's very personable."

"This isn't funny, Mary Jo."

"Nobody believes you did anything wrong, not really," she hurriedly assured her. "Really, Layla. It's just all the hype on TV." A brief hesitation, then, "How about tomorrow? Sometime in the afternoon?"

Talk about a dog with a bone. "Fine," Layla buckled, and Mary Jo quickly got off the phone to call her very personable buyer.

The conversation left her feeling worse, however. What if the truth didn't come out? What if the police arrested her for Neil's death? What about Eddie? Could she lose him? What would happen to him?

She called Naomi in a fit of panic. She hadn't given the transfer of money to her account enough serious thought, she realized. It was a mistake, and she expected it to be handled. And she'd treated the reporters outside her door more like a nuisance than a true threat. But now she felt physically ill.

Naomi picked up on the third ring, and before she could say anything, Layla suddenly burst into racking sobs, blubbering that she was innocent, that she was sorry Neil was gone, that it wasn't her fault, that all she wanted was Eddie and she would be a good mother, the best mother, and no one could take that away from her.

Naomi, bless her soul, was as calm as ever. "The police

will figure out what happened to Neil. It's so awful and scary, but you need to stay positive. This little guy's coming. He's going to need his mama."

That sent her into another spate of tears. She thanked Naomi, asked her how she was feeling, could barely hear her answer she was so distraught, but understood enough to know that everything was going fine.

"A few more weeks," Naomi said. "It'll be okay."

Layla thanked her again, and after a few more minutes, they both hung up, Naomi promising to call her if anything changed. Layla felt overwhelming gratitude that the surrogate Neil had picked was so incredibly sane. How, after choosing so well with Naomi, had Neil ever gotten involved with Courtney? A woman who was practically reveling in the attention Neil's death had afforded her?

When Layla thought about Courtney possibly carrying *her* baby, it made her batshit crazy. The situation was out of control.

A creeping thought, one that had nagged her but she'd tried to keep at bay, wormed into her consciousness: Had Courtney had something to do with Neil's death? Layla wouldn't put it past her.

Layla next called the bank about the unexplained funds in her account but was put on hold. When she finally got through and laid out the problem, she was informed a manager would have to call her back. Was there a coolness to the banker's tone, or was it her imagination? She hung up more worried than ever. So many things had happened, none of them good.

Who had deposited that money into her account? Neil . . . ? She wished she could trust that he hadn't had a secret agenda that would suddenly blow up in her face, but it just didn't make any sense.

And what about John's death . . . was that just coincidence? Lucy had said it looked like Brianne Kilgore was possibly involved with the poison, maybe peripherally or maybe not. Whatever the case, it sounded like that mystery might be solved soon. Layla fervently wished the one surrounding Neil's death would as well.

Her cell rang. She gazed at it with trepidation. Dallas Denton.

"Hello," she answered cautiously.

"Layla, I've talked to the detective in charge of Neil Grassley's homicide and he'd like you to come into the station for an interview. I'll go with you. Does tomorrow morning at ten work for you?"

No! She swallowed. "Yes."

"Okay, I'll pick you up at nine-thirty. . . ."

Brianne Kilgore looked up at the darkening sky, smelling the scents of hay and manure, mixed with a bit of pine from the trees that rimmed the back paddock at the Happy Times Animal Shelter. She was working outside while Myra and Jennifer, who owned the place, got ready to go home. On Mondays, Wednesdays, and some Saturdays, Brianne was the one who kept the animals safe until eleven o'clock, and then Tommy O'Toole took over. He stayed in the bunkhouse, but he wasn't as good as Brianne was. He liked the beer too much.

The two dogs, Scruffy, a terrier mix, and Delray the hound, followed Brianne as she went into the stables. They had two horses right now. They were too skinny when they came; Brianne had been able to count their ribs. It had taken a long, long time to see them not too skinny. They were in the stalls for the night. They stuck out their heads when they saw Brianne, and Corduroy whinnied. Brianne rubbed their noses and checked their hay. They were good.

One of the stable cats looked down from the top of a

feedbox and hissed at Delray the hound. Delray didn't care, but Scruffy started jumping and barking.

"You're making a racket," Brianne said. Scruffy stopped jumping, but he didn't take his eyes off the cat, and his barks turned into a long, grumpy growl. The cats had no names. They wanted to be petted, but they didn't want the dogs around. Brianne let the cats be and headed back outside.

Myra came to the back door of the office, stuck her head out, and said, "Jen and I are off, Brianne. Will you be okay?"

Myra always asked that.

"I will," Brianne always answered back.

As the women left, she watched them both get in their cars. The cars were hybrids, saved on gas. Brianne drove an old truck that wasn't a hybrid. She was a good driver, but she stayed only on the roads she knew. She could go to StopGo, but the road through the town of Glenn River was really crowded with cars and lots of people and Brianne knew better than to go there.

Brianne tugged on her ear. She didn't feel right. That September person had told her to go see Martin Morant, but she didn't want to. She had called him on the burner phone and told him what to do. She had then thrown that phone into the creek down behind the house.

Now, she went into the office, and Scruffy and Delray the hound joined her. They each had a crate and Myra and Jen were very strict about them going in their crates if they stayed inside the office. Brianne would let them stay outside if they wanted, but they liked their crates, so it was okay.

Brianne had a sandwich, and Scruffy and Delray the hound went into their crates, hoping she would give them some food. She gave them each a bite, then went to the refrigerator and got a bottle for the baby deer in the pen outside because those hunters had killed her mama. Brianne shut the doors to the crates and banged out the back door with the bottle. The dogs scared the baby deer.

She went into the small barn where the deer was and smiled as the animal tugged on the nipple. Sad little guy. No mama . . .

She thought of her own mama, who was dying. Mama didn't like Jerome Wolfe, but Brianne loved him and he loved her. Mama said he didn't. She said he only wanted the house. Brianne would give him the house. Mama said Brianne "wasn't thinking with her head" and that she should "plan for the future before he takes everything and leaves you." Brianne had pointed out that Mama was leaving, too, and Mama had gotten sad and said, "I wish I could stay and take care of you."

That September person had worried about Jerome, too. They didn't know him.

The rooster suddenly fluttered into the barn, flapping and hopping and crowing so loudly that Brianne said, "You're making a racket!"

Distantly, from the office, Delray the hound started baying, Scruffy yipping furiously.

The baby deer released the nipple and backed into the corner of the stall.

Brianne looked up, heard, "Good-bye," and something hard slammed into her chest. All around was animal noise. Roaring in her ears. All kinds.

She fell backward on the ground.

She felt pain. Big pain.

She saw the face. Saw the gun. Saw her own blood.

Saw dust specks.

She should have listened to that September person.

Chapter Thirty-Two

September pulled up to the Kilgore home. Neither Brianne's truck nor Jerome Wolfe's Mercedes was parked in front. She'd called the Kilgore home on the way, but there had been no answer, which had concerned her more. Maybe she was overreacting. Wolfe wasn't going to *do* anything to Brianne. He needed her to sign the papers. But Brianne knew something about somebody and the angel of death mushroom, and Deputy Morant was worried, too.

She climbed out of the Outback and stretched. Whether Brianne would actually listen to September was debatable, but it was worth a shot.

At the door, she knocked and heard the slow thumping coming her way. When Mona answered the door, Duke nosed past her to give September another doggy sniff. He then let out a keening wail that raised the hair on her arms.

"He's been doing that for about a half hour," Mona said, worried. "Can you go check on Brianne? She's at the shelter."

"Where is it?" September demanded shortly.

"Not far. Head toward Glenn River, but you turn off

before that. . . ." She quickly gave September the particulars
while Duke kept wailing and moaning.

In the car again, September slammed the Outback into
reverse, whipped around and headed back the way she'd
come. Now she berated herself for not listening to her inter-
nal radar sooner. Maybe nothing was wrong, but she didn't
think so. Duke knew something about his mistress.

She found the shelter fifteen minutes later. A light on a
tall pole illuminated the main yard, revealing several outbuildings. A dog was baying, a deep sound, and another was
barking furiously. They sounded muffled, as if they were
inside the first building, an office, it appeared. HAPPY
TIMES SHELTER was painted on an arcing sign above the
door. September threw the Outback into Park, made sure her
phone was in her pocket, and ran toward the office. She
pushed through the door, which was unlocked, and was
deafened by a couple of madly barking dogs barricaded in
crates. They increased their furor, if that was possible, and
September, without a weapon, thought about it for half a
heartbeat, then opened their cages.

The two animals tore toward the back of the office,
scratching, practically flinging themselves at the rear door.
She unlatched the lock and they barreled through, across the
grounds to a small barnlike structure. Everywhere there was
noise, a cacophony of animal sounds, grunts, squawks, and
yips building in the night.

She ran after the dogs, only slowing as she neared the
open door of the shadowed building. "Brianne?" she called,
looking around the darkening yard.

The dogs barking had changed to whining. September
moved forward, ducking her head around the edge of the
jamb, her heart racing.

No! Her worst fears were confirmed. Brianne was lying

on her back at the other side of the room, the dogs milling, whining, and nosing her.

September ran forward, saw the spreading darkness on her chest. Blood on her clothes. Gunshot wound, she would bet. "*Shit!*"

She yanked out her phone and punched in 9-1-1. Before the woman at the other end could finish her intro, September yelled, "Need an ambulance to the Happy Times Animal Shelter. Gunshot to the chest. Victim's name is Brianne Kilgore . . ."

Dallas was shrugging into his jacket when he heard Luke's voice in the outer office. Billie was standing by her desk, her purse over her arm, when Dallas opened his door, and Luke was heading straight to Dallas's door.

"Hey, brother," Luke said, but he appeared grim.

"Go ahead, Billie," Dallas said, stepping aside so Luke could precede him into the office.

"I can wait," Billie said, glancing from one brother to the other.

Dallas waved her away. "No need. I'll see you tomorrow."

She threw a look at Luke's disappearing back. There was a certain amount of disapproval in her gaze, but she gave Dallas a deep nod and headed out.

Dallas followed Luke, closing his door again.

Luke didn't waste time. "Someone's feeding that reporter, Jeb Duarte, information about Grassley's finances. The detective on the case is Charley Simms. I don't know him well, but he's tough and fair. The leak's not coming from him."

Dallas grunted an assent. He, Layla, and Lucy had met Simms at Grassley's apartment the night Layla had discovered his body. "Simms wants Layla to come in tomorrow morning for an interview."

"You talked to him today?"

"Yep."

"Good. The forensic accountants are taking apart Grassley's finances. Don't think they're coming up with quite the same results as what Duarte's been reporting."

"Who'd you talk to?"

"Opal Amberson."

Luke had worked for the Portland PD and still had a lot of friends there. "Opal hear anything more about the transferred funds into Layla's account?"

"Either Grassley did it himself or someone else used his computer. Knew his passwords. But it's a little more sophisticated than that. They hacked into Layla's accounts, got enough info to send the money."

"Never heard of hackers putting money in. Usually works the other way," Dallas pointed out.

"Whoever did it is probably the killer. It's right in the window of time of Grassley's death."

Luke was probably right on that, although they wouldn't hear the definitive word on time of death until the medical examiner gave his report, most likely when the results of the autopsy were released.

"Simms is looking at the videotape from the security cameras at Grassley's apartment, but the one on the eighth floor was messed with," Luke went on. "We were lucky to get some footage from the front gate."

Layla Crissman was on that camera; she'd gone to Neil's apartment a couple of times.

"What about Courtney Mayfield?" Dallas asked him.

"Still trying to pin her down. Everybody wants her, but she's gone silent after those interviews smearing Layla. Won't pick up her phone or answer her door. That can't last forever. And, per your request, I checked on Jerome Wolfe. It's known that he didn't like Grassley, but then, he doesn't like anyone he deems to have as much, or more, money as he does. And he really doesn't like the Crissmans. There's a long-standing feud between the two families. Wolfe thinks the Crissmans got the better part of the deal, and it's taken years for his family to catch up and surpass the Crissmans financially. As far as Grassley goes, haven't heard yet if he's on the security cameras. There's a way to avoid the front camera, if you come through the garage, side door, but you have to have a key. That camera was disabled, too."

Dallas absorbed all that and said, "If Layla were the killer, she wouldn't keep going through the front gate."

"If the doer wants to blame Layla, they're doing a piss-poor job. It's amateur hour," Luke agreed.

"The killing might have been more spur of the moment."

They talked it over for a while longer, and Dallas, whose attention was still sliding off point whenever he thought of Lucy and Evie, was brought back to the moment when Luke suddenly asked, "Something you're not telling me?"

He debated with himself for a moment but wasn't ready to go into his personal life. He said instead, "Grassley's lawyer, Penelope Gaines, called me. She and Grassley had been trying to set up a meeting with Layla to go over his will, but Grassley died before it happened. Grassley was apparently dead set on marrying Layla. He already rewrote the will, and Layla and his sons are his beneficiaries."

Luke whistled. "A lot of money coming her way."

"Strong motivation," Dallas agreed grimly.

"You said *sons*, plural," Luke said, his brows pulling together. "Meaning the child Mayfield's carrying, if she still is?"

"That's right. Gaines said she wants to meet with Layla and go over the will. She didn't immediately feel that way, with what's come out about the murder, so Layla referred her to me. But she's changed her mind. Maybe Layla's a beneficiary and Gaines is just being careful about how much to reveal."

"Something Gaines knows, but the police don't yet."

"Or maybe it's the other way around. There's a lot of money at stake. That deposit to Layla's account is only a fraction of the whole. . . . I don't know . . . maybe it's a smoke screen, meant to throw blame on Layla when the bulk of the estate goes elsewhere. But if Layla's a beneficiary, she has the right to know what her part of the estate is."

"Who's in charge of those kids, and Grassley's money, if Layla dies?"

"Don't know yet." Dallas nodded grimly. "In the meantime, I'm looking forward to seeing that will. In fact, as Layla's attorney, I'm demanding it. They can only stall so long."

Luke got to his feet. "Okay. I'll keep at it."

"Good. One more thing: Find out where Grassley was going on that business trip and why he canceled, if he did, or if something happened that kept him here."

Dallas's cell phone buzzed, a text.

Luke hesitated in the doorway to the outer office.

Dallas sucked in a breath. "It's from September. Brianne Kilgore has been shot in the chest and is in emergency surgery right now. . . ."

September stood in the waiting room outside the OR at St. Anne's Hospital in northwest Portland, where Brianne had been life flighted. She'd texted Dallas and called Gretchen, who was on her way. The Wharton County Sheriff's Department was in charge of the attempted murder case, and to that end, Deputy Morant had gone to be with Mona Kilgore. He would come to the hospital later.

September was sick with guilt. She'd known this was

going to happen. Had sensed it. Felt like it was all her fault, even though she knew she was being unfair to herself.

Gretchen strode into the OR waiting room, saw September, and crossed the carpeted expanse where she was standing. "You okay?" she asked, reading September's face.

"I should have been on this. I knew it was dangerous. She knew about the poisoning."

"You warned her. You talked to the sheriff's department."

September shook her head.

"You know this kind of thing happens," Gretchen reminded her. "You gotta get past this and think about what you need to do next. Who did this?"

September had been asking herself the same question over and over again. "I don't know. Jerome Wolfe, maybe. Or someone working for him. But it doesn't make sense if he wants the Kilgore property. He needs Brianne's signature."

"One of the Crissmans," Gretchen posed. "John Linfield knew something about them or their company that could have exposed them somehow."

"Brianne hinted Linfield wasn't the target," September reminded her.

"Then who was?"

"One of the Crissmans?" September asked. She and Gretchen discussed each of Abbott's children and Abbott himself but determined they didn't have enough information to point a finger at any one person. Yet. They were still discussing the possibilities, seated at two chairs in the semiprivate corner of the room, when Deputy Morant showed up about an hour later. He plopped onto a short vinyl couch and shook his head. "Jesus." He was beside himself over the shooting. "Nine-millimeter bullet was in the wall behind her."

September nodded. Brianne was lucky to be alive. "You spoke to Mona?" she asked Morant.

"Yes, and I waited for her friend to get to the house. The friend will drive Mona over ASAP."

"Good," said September.

A doctor appeared through a swinging door to the operating room and searched the waiting area. September caught his eye and moved toward him. "Brianne Kilgore?" September asked.

"Are you family?"

"I'm with Laurelton PD. I found her."

Gretchen flashed her badge.

The doctor nodded. "She's in recovery. She's stable . . ." He went on to explain that the bullet had missed her heart but had done damage to her lungs and blood vessels and there was nothing to do now but wait.

"Okay," September said. She took a seat near the OR desk.

Morant growled, "We gotta get this asshole. I've known Brianne since she was a kid."

"Find out who in her circle has a nine-millimeter gun," September said.

"On it already," Morant answered grimly, his eyes hard with determination as he headed out.

Gretchen checked her phone, then said, "You're staying?"

"For now."

"Okay. I'll let Calvetti know. And by the way, glad you're back with us. . . ."

Lucy was curled up on her couch, channel surfing through a number of television shows, finally snapping off the TV and tossing the remote aside. She was drinking a cup of decaf tea, unable to concentrate on anything. Evie was sitting by her, on her iPad, and she looked up when the television went off.

"Can we make some popcorn?" Evie asked hopefully.

Sure. Whatever. Why not?

Lucy went through the motions like an automaton, popping the corn in the microwave, then portioning out a bowl of buttered and salted popcorn for each of them. As Evie dug into her bowl, Lucy was still standing in the kitchen, eating her popcorn without tasting it, thinking hard. About Dallas. Of course. Her cell rang, bringing her back to the here and now. She looked around the room, listening to the muffled sound. The phone was in her purse, which was sitting on one of the barstools, just where she'd left it. As she reached for her handbag, she hooked the strap and knocked it to the ground. Shit. The phone bounced out, still ringing.

She saw the screen: Lyle.

She picked up the phone, which seemed no worse for wear, thank God, and answered. "Hello, Lyle."

"Hey, um, are you going to the hospital tomorrow? They said Dad would probably be released then."

"Are you going?" she asked. She took her half-eaten bowl and set it beside the sink. She'd been picking at the popcorn anyway. Lyle's call had squelched what little remained of her appetite.

"Yes, I think so. Somebody needs to be there," he pointed out, as if she might have forgotten that fact.

"What about Ainsley?" Lucy asked, a bit meanly. Her father's new fiancée had clung to Lyle and been more of a hindrance than a help.

"So, you're not going," he bit out.

"No, I'll go. He's my father, too." She didn't need this now. She hung up and stuffed her phone back into her purse.

Evie had been listening to the whole conversation. "You're talking about Grandpa."

"Yes, he's fine," she said flatly, not wanting Evie to get the wrong idea.

"What's wrong, then?"

"What do you mean?" she asked automatically.

"You've been in a bad mood since Aunt Layla was here."

Lucy blinked. Her mood had been mercurial ever since she'd told Dallas the truth about Evie. It hadn't had anything to do with Layla. But she couldn't say that to her daughter. "I'll try to be happier," she said, pulling her mouth into a wide, rictus grin and crossing her eyes.

Her daughter smiled and snorted. "Be careful or they might stay that way," throwing one of Lucy's own warnings back at her.

Lucy went to Evie and gave her a big, big hug. "I love you, y'know," she said.

"Yeah, I know."

After planting a kiss on her daughter's head, she swept up her purse and headed down the hall.

"Love you, too!" Evie called, which created a huge lump in Lucy's throat.

She swallowed hard. She'd done the right thing by telling Dallas, but now that he knew, he had the power to hurt her daughter.

Chapter Thirty-Three

Tuesday morning, Layla got up, took a shower, washed her hair, toweled off, and dressed carefully in black pants and a white blouse. Knocking the color out of her wardrobe just seemed like a good idea when she imagined herself being interviewed in a room at the police station.

When she turned off the blow dryer, she heard her cell phone ringing. She'd left the cell on her bedroom dresser and she approached it with a feeling of doom. When she saw the caller was Lucy, she expelled a relieved breath. "Hey, there," she answered.

Lucy said, "Hi. How're you doing?"

"Okay, I guess."

"Good. I've checked the news. Not as bad today. I haven't heard or seen Courtney once."

"That's an improvement."

"Yep, so Lyle and I are going to the hospital to pick up Dad."

"I feel like I should be there, but Dallas is picking me up and we're heading to the police station." She cleared her throat. "They want to interview me."

"Oh." Lucy was surprised. "Maybe I should go with you instead."

"You don't have to." But truthfully, she wanted her sister to be with her. She needed the emotional support.

"I could meet you there," Lucy offered. "Let me talk to Lyle. What time?"

"Ten o'clock."

"Okay. I'll make it happen and see you there."

Lucy immediately called her brother and was irked when he didn't pick up. She texted him and said she was going with Layla to the police station, so she couldn't go to the hospital at this moment. She waited for him to get back to her, but it was Kate who called.

"You're not going to the hospital?" she demanded.

"I'm going with Layla at ten to the police station. I think it's important. What time is Dad being released?"

"I don't know. You should talk to Lyle."

"Well, I've tried, but he's not picking up. Maybe you could have him call me?" Lucy suggested shortly.

"Lyle's taking time off for work for this."

"Okay, what do you want? You want me to pick up Dad, because I'm the one with time on my hands and Lyle's job is so important?"

"Lucy!"

"Kate, sorry. I don't have a lot of patience. As I said, I'm going with Layla, and then I'll go to the hospital. I've never known any hospital to release a patient early, so I'll probably be there in time anyway. If not, tell Lyle he's on his own."

She clicked off. She was sorry her father was ailing, but she sure as hell was still mad at both him and her brother.

At the downtown Portland police station, Dallas and Layla were led down the hall by a Hispanic officer to a drab, taupe-walled room where fiftysomething Detective Charley

Simms was talking to another officer and holding a paper cup full of coffee. The other officer left as Dallas and Layla were led into the room. Simms, tall, white, with a shaved bald head and a close-cropped beard, motioned them both to chairs.

Dallas had been through any number of these interviews. Mostly the detectives knew exactly what had transpired during the crime and were just learning what possible persons of interest might add to the mix.

Layla knew next to nothing about Neil's personal life except what he'd told her, and Dallas advised her to just tell them that. "Just answer them directly. Make your answers simple. Just be transparent."

The questions started, and he could practically see how tense she was, but as the interview went on, and she was able to answer clearly and calmly about her relationship with Neil and her whereabouts the last week, he thought she was relaxing a bit. The issue of hiring a surrogate required a lot of explanation, which she handled like a pro, and only when it came to her breakup with Neil, and his taking up with Courtney Mayfield, did Layla seem to falter. "I'd never met her before the Denim and Diamonds benefit auction," she said. "Neil and I hadn't been getting along for a while. I was surprised to see him there, too."

"Did you think he was surprised to see Courtney Mayfield?" the detective asked.

"Uh, Neil? No, I . . . thought they came together."

That caught Dallas's attention and he made a note of it.

The detective then asked her about her finances, coming back to the twenty thousand dollars Neil had paid her for her eggs. He asked whether she had any ownership in the embryos created from those eggs, to which she looked at Dallas. "Legally, no," Dallas said.

Layla said, "I was working to get them back."

In the end, Detective Simms thanked her and then

showed them both out. Dallas turned to Layla and said, "That went fine."

"You think so? I was scared, so scared."

"You didn't show it, you—" He broke off abruptly when he suddenly saw Lucy in the reception area of the station. It felt like a kick in the gut.

Layla turned her eyes from his and focused on her sister. She hurried to her and the two women embraced. Dallas pulled himself together, both annoyed and surprised at himself, then went to meet her as well. "Hi, Lucy," he said. Did his voice sound strained? He thought it did.

"Hi . . . Dallas . . ." she returned. The smile she was forcing was definitely strained. She focused on Layla. "How did it go? You look so businesslike. I'm sorry I didn't get here sooner."

"You wouldn't have been able to come into the interview room," said Dallas.

"I know. I didn't expect to. I just wanted to be here," Lucy answered, her gaze locked with Layla's as if she were afraid to look at him.

"Thought I'd try to look more . . . in control," Layla said of her clothes, her words ending on a slight hiccup, belying the effort. "The interview was okay, I guess. . . ." She turned to Dallas for corroboration.

"You did fine," he assured her as a couple of uniformed cops walked past.

There was an awkward pause, then Lucy asked Dallas diffidently, "How's the investigation going?"

Dallas thought about September's text the night before, and her follow-up phone call this morning. Brianne Kilgore was fighting for her life, and it likely had to do with John Linfield's death. He needed to tell her about it. "Do you have some time to talk?" he asked Lucy. "I have some things to go over."

Her brows lifted, but she said, "Um . . . yes. Evie's . . . with our babysitter."

"Bella?" Layla asked. She was looking from Dallas to Lucy and back again. Lucy had clearly informed her that she'd revealed Evie's parentage to him.

Lucy turned to Layla as if she were a lifeline. "You know what Bella told me? She's dating a guy on the school golf team. The golf team! I don't think you can be a Goth, or whatever she is, and date someone on the golf team."

Layla managed a smile. "You never know. Look, I'll take Uber back and let you two . . . talk. I've got an appointment at that house I'm staging in a few hours, and I think I'll just decompress first."

"The one in the West Hills?" Lucy asked.

"Yeah, on Cherry. The buyer wants my painting of the Columbia River, the one Jerome Wolfe gave me back."

"Well, good . . . right?" Lucy asked hopefully.

"We'll see," said Layla.

She gave Lucy a last hug and then took off. Alone with Lucy, Dallas wasn't sure quite where to pick up. Without Layla as a buffer, she appeared as uncomfortable as he was; then they both tried to talk at once.

"Is Layla really okay?" she asked.

"Do you want to go to my office?" he questioned, and he realized he was jangling his keys in his pocket. Nerves. He stopped.

"Sure," she answered.

"The worst of those reports came from Courtney May-field," Dallas said. "The police are going through the bank records. If they really were looking at Layla, we'd have gotten some sense of that today. I'd say their focus is else-where, but I don't know for sure."

"Okay."

"I'll meet you at my office, then," he said as they walked through the door to the parking area dappled with late-morning sunshine.

"Okay," she said again, and he could tell she was struggling to get something out.

"What?" he asked.

She blurted, "I didn't mean to drop it on you like that. I just . . . you needed to know. But Evie's my whole life. Whatever you decide, fine. You do it. But I'm not ever going to let you hurt her."

"Hurt her?" He was flabbergasted.

"Yes, hurt her," she declared, squinting up at him. "You're her father and you have the power to really do some damage. She's always wanted to know who her dad is, so just consider this fair warning. That's all I'm saying. If you don't want to be a part of her life, that's cool. You just needed to know."

"I just found out about her!" he reminded in a tense whisper.

"I know. I know. I'm sorry," Lucy whispered tensely right back. "I didn't know if I would ever tell you, but I did, and here we are. I'm just asking you to be careful with my daughter. Because as soon as she knows, she's going to want to meet you. Don't hurt her. That's all I'm saying."

"Let's talk about this at my office," he said, glancing at the pedestrians bustling along the busy sidewalk.

"Sure. Fine." She cleared her throat. "I'll see you in a few."

September finally gave up her vigil when Brianne was settled into ICU. She was stable. That was all the hospital staff would say.

Once at home, September fell into bed, caught about three hours of sleep, then dragged herself out to get ready for her first day of work. She was feeling a little bleary-eyed when she showed up at the station, but it felt good to be there, to have purpose. Calvetti called her into her office and asked to hear the blow-by-blow of what had transpired the night before. September, fortified on break-room coffee—always marginal at best, though today she drank in the faintly burned scent—reported everything she knew, to which Calvetti bestowed the Linfield case on September.

"Solve it," she said.

September was surprised but happy to comply. "The Linfield case may tie in to the Grassley homicide," she told the captain. "Grassley's tox screen found traces of Amanita ocreata poisoning, the angel of death mushroom, but that information hasn't gotten out yet. He also suffered a blow to the head. We're waiting on cause of death until the full autopsy report comes through. But the press is already calling the Crissman sisters 'black widows.' If and when the mushroom poisoning gets out, the Crissmans will be run over by the press."

"And you don't think they're guilty."

"That's what I want to prove," September admitted.

"No preconceived ideas. Do it," was all Calvetti said, and September took her leave.

Gretchen was at her desk, apparently waiting for September to be through with Calvetti, because as soon as September was outside the captain's office, Gretchen came over and dropped the Linfield file that Wes had started on her desk.

"Are you okay with me taking this?" September asked, riffling the pages of the file.

"It's been passed around, but you're the one who knows the most. I'll send you the digital file, too."

"Okay." She'd noticed that neither Wes nor George were at their desks. When September asked, Gretchen explained that Wes was basically gone and "Skinny" was taking a sick day. "He's been sick a lot since the breakup," Gretchen said.

"Maybe that's what the weight loss is all about," said September.

Gretchen snorted. "Yeah. Right."

As soon as Gretchen went back to her own work, September called St. Anne's for an update on Brianne's condition— she was stable—then sat back and really turned over in her mind what she knew about the Linfield case. Brianne Kilgore had given the mushrooms, or shown them to, someone associated with her. If she'd shown them to someone, then that person might be known to Mona Kilgore as well. Possibly.

Jerome Wolfe? She couldn't quite see where he fit in, other than what she knew about him: that he wanted the Crissman and Kilgore properties for some future endeavor and that he had a real problem with the Crissmans. The Crissmans, however, didn't seem to have the same animus toward him, and Abbott Crissman had signed, or was signing, the deal that would turn Stonehenge over to Wolfe.

Who else? She needed a list of Brianne's friends and co-workers. That was something else she could ask Mona Kilgore about.

And then there was the possible connection to Neil Grassley. The only link she had was Courtney Mayfield. Courtney was deeply involved with Grassley, but the Mayfield woman's only tie to Brianne Kilgore was the fact that she'd grown up in the same general area. Did they know each other? Maybe gone to school together . . . ? September wasn't sure Brianne had even attended public school, but maybe. She made a note.

"I think I'm going to head to Wharton County one more time," September told Gretchen a few minutes later.

"I'd come with you, but . . ." She spread her hands, indicating the file that was open on her computer screen.

"I've got this. I'm practically a commuter to Wharton County these days." September would have liked to partner with Gretchen again, but because today it was just the two of them in the station, the partnership would have to wait.

She took a call from Deputy Morant as she was heading out. They'd formed a bond over Brianne Kilgore. "Jerome Wolfe owns a nine-millimeter Glock," he said tautly. "The sheriff's not fooling around on this. He's picking up Wolfe and bringing him in for questioning."

"I'm heading your way," September said, her pulse beginning to race. Maybe there was more to the Wolfe story than she knew. She could see him thinking Brianne was expendable. He was already using her as a pawn in his real estate transaction.

"If he killed Brianne, I'm going to make sure he pays," said Morant.

Though she felt the same sentiment, September heard the barely leashed fury behind the deputy's words and said, "Keep that thought, but we gotta stay legal."

"Oh, I'm not going to do anything to jeopardize the case. I want to see the prick behind bars for the better part of his life."

Lucy sat down in one of the client chairs in front of Dallas's desk, while Dallas stood by the window, apparently lost in thought. He'd closed the door to his office, telling his receptionist to hold his calls.

She waited for him to say something, anything, and was kind of embarrassed about just blurting out what she felt. Not that she didn't feel that way.

Dallas finally looked up, and Lucy braced herself, but what he said took her by complete surprise. "Someone shot Brianne Kilgore last night. She's in intensive care."

"*Shot*? Shot? Oh my God . . . ! How? Why?"

"We think she knows who poisoned your husband. . . ." And then he went on to explain how September had discovered Brianne shortly after she'd been shot and had arranged for her to be taken to St. Anne's Hospital. Dallas then reiterated the steps of September's investigation, resulting in her finding the mushrooms on the Kilgore property that were believed to be the source of the poison, and September's fear that Brianne was covering for someone else, a lot of which Lucy had already heard, but now it hit home harder.

"Does Layla know?"

"I wasn't going to tell her if she hadn't seen it on the news because I wanted her to stay focused this morning. She should be informed now, though," he agreed, stepping toward his desk phone.

"I'll call her . . . and Lyle . . ." Lucy said, though she didn't feel quite the same urgency about informing her brother.

"Go ahead," Dallas said, and she got the feeling he was somewhat relieved to have a shift of focus.

As it turned out, Layla didn't pick up and Lyle told her rather abruptly that he'd seen on the news that Brianne had been attacked. Lucy was annoyed that he seemed so unaffected, but then she realized he was shaken up and just didn't want to talk. That was Lyle's way of dealing with any emotional trauma.

"I'm on the way to get Dad," he said, just before hanging up.

"I'm in a meeting," she answered, to which he gave a small bark of laughter, which basically meant "I knew it."

When she was off the phone, Dallas picked up where he'd left off. "Brianne hinted that your husband might not have been the target."

Lucy had heard that before. "Well, then, who?" she asked. "There were tons of people at the benefit. The food, and the drinks, were being passed out to everyone . . . although we were the only ones there earlier, and the caterers and some of the waitstaff . . . ?"

Dallas thought about that a moment, then said, "I know we went over this before, but can you remember what food was around earlier in the day, for lunch?"

"I didn't eat anything. I told you that, I know. Maybe Lyle went to Glenn River for sandwiches around lunchtime? There was talk about it. Lyle probably knows."

"I'll check with him. Can you remember if John had anything earlier in the day?"

"Not that I saw, but I wasn't really paying attention."

He nodded. "There's a window of time where the poisoning could have happened at the benefit. You've already said you and John ate the same food the night before and the morning of, so it looks like it happened at the benefit. But it would have been earlier, not long after you arrived."

"About lunchtime," she agreed. "I wish I'd paid more attention."

"Was John the kind of guy who would skip lunch?"

"No." She was definite on that.

"So, he likely had something between breakfast and dinner."

"Well, yes . . ."

Lucy had been so sure he was going to talk about Evie that she was having a bit of a delayed reaction when it came to his questions about John. And she was also struggling to process the fact that Brianne had been shot, *shot*, and that the shooting might be connected to John's death; at least that appeared to be the theory Dallas was working on.

"John would have eaten something, if something was around, and he would have complained if there wasn't something. I didn't hear him complain," she realized.

Lucy cast her mind back. She and John had arrived at the benefit and he'd gone his way and she'd gone hers. Though her father had requested, *demanded*, they all come early, there really hadn't been that much for them to do.

"Mostly, I remember John at the benefit," she said. "He could hardly let a tray of hors d'oeuvres go by without sampling something. We were grabbing what we could from the trays, except maybe Layla. I was having a hard time getting anything. The waiters were kind of sweeping through, then sweeping back out. But that was later. Earlier . . . ? I don't know, but it seems like I saw him eat something . . . maybe . . . ?"

"I know I've gone over this before. I don't want to put ideas in your head," Dallas said. "I'm just looking for something."

Lucy searched her memory, screwing up her forehead with the effort. The whole event had been kind of a blur, mixed in with all the eating and drinking during the evening hours, but she would swear she'd seen John earlier, maybe in the main foyer, holding something . . . ?

"A sandwich," she said suddenly. "He was eating a sandwich! I saw him for lunch. I'm pretty sure."

"You are?"

"Yeah . . . yeah . . . because it was a full-fledged sandwich, not a slider or an hors d'oeuvre of any kind."

"Do you recall where it came from? Your brother?" Dallas asked carefully. She could tell he didn't want to interrupt her memory.

"Maybe Lyle brought it from Glenn River. John was coming from the back of the main room when I saw him, from under the gallery by Layla's painting." She struggled hard to remember. "I think there was a tray of sandwiches back there . . . ?"

"Left out for anyone to take?"

"I don't know. Maybe." She inclined her head and said, "You're thinking, why didn't anyone else get sick, then, if the sandwiches were tampered with and available. I know. I'm sorry. I want to help, but I don't want to make up something either. I could be wrong about this."

He nodded. "I'll ask Lyle."

"You know, I think Layla was standing there, not far from the tray, close to her painting," Lucy mused. She could see her sister in her denim jumpsuit with that big sunset of color from her painting behind her.

"Layla?"

Lucy heard herself and instantly wanted to take the words back. "Well, she wasn't involved, of course. It's just an impression . . . I could be wrong. Layla wouldn't hurt a fly. She's just not made that way," Lucy hurried to say.

"Okay."

"Just, okay?"

"I'm on her side, Lucy. I don't think she's a killer. I just want to know who was targeted at that benefit and why, and also why Brianne is now in ICU, fighting for her life. And if it has anything to do with Neil Grassley's death."

"I want to know that, too," she said in a smaller voice.

Dallas nodded and finally took the chair behind his desk. He rested his elbows on the desktop and looked at her. "And I want to talk about Evie. I would never hurt her. She seems . . . like a wonderful girl. You've clearly done a great job raising her. I'm still getting used to the idea that I'm a father, but I'm not sorry about it. I want to know her, and I want to thank you for taking such good care of her."

Lucy's eyes bloomed with tears.

For all the mistakes she'd made, she'd inadvertently picked the right man to father her child.

Chapter Thirty-Four

Kate stood beside Lyle as they both watched Abbott being helped into a wheelchair. She and Lyle had stopped by his house to pick him up some clean clothes, but even so he looked disheveled and angry.

Ainsley was nowhere in sight, so Kate asked about her. His answer was a glare and a muttered, "She had things to do."

Yeah, like look for some other potential sugar daddy.

Lyle was particularly quiet on the drive back to his father's, while Abbott bitched and moaned and said he wasn't going to take the goddamn medication they were foisting on him.

They settled him into his house, but he was bound and determined not to go into his bedroom and relax. Kate found some cans of Campbell's Soup and offered to make him something to eat, but he flapped a hand at her as he was trying to call or text someone on his phone. Probably Ainsley.

As she and Lyle were getting ready to leave, Lyle suddenly jerked, as if someone had pinched him. "I know!" he said, as if he were having a eureka moment.

"What?"

But almost as soon as he uttered those words, he retreated into himself. "Nothing."

"*What*?" Kate repeated as they headed outside to his car.

"The girl at the bank . . ."

"Oh God," Kate said wearily.

"She looks like . . ." He shook his head. "I need to talk to Lucy."

"Oh, great. Go ahead. Talk to your sister." She flung her arms in the air and stomped to the car. "Don't talk to your wife. Don't ever, ever, ever talk to the wife who's been by your side through everything. Who's championed you. Who's done everything she can to make sure you get what's rightfully yours! Don't do that, God forbid!"

"You're mad at me? For trying to place why that red-headed girl looked so familiar?"

"I'm mad at you for a lot of things," she snapped back. "How about that making love to me is such a *chore*!"

"Kate, it's not you. . . ."

"Don't you dare say 'it's me.' If you do, I'll scream until your eardrums split."

He rolled his eyes and anger flared in their depths. "How about if I don't say anything?" he ground out.

"Why, that would be just fine."

The rest of the ride back to their house was made in cold, stony silence.

Layla got to the house on Cherry Street in the West Hills fifteen minutes early. She'd left on her "business attire" as a form of armor against all the rumors flying around about her. She didn't plan for this to take long, although she was still uncertain which way she was going to jump on selling the painting. Yes, she should. Yes, she could use the money.

Yes, there was no reason to hang on to a piece that seemed to be gathering bad mojo day by day.

But . . . she just wasn't sure. When she met Mary Jo's buyer, that was when she would make her choice.

There was a builder's lockbox on the outside of the house. Mary Jo had given her the code when she'd delivered the painting and other decorative pieces, so she punched in the four digits without waiting for the Realtor and the very personable buyer. Mary Jo had never mentioned anyone besides the woman, so maybe she was a single purchaser.

Layla extracted the key from inside the lockbox and threaded it into the front door lock. She twisted it and realized she'd ended up locking herself out. Mary Jo had already opened the house for them, or someone had forgotten to lock it back up.

She put the key back and snapped the box shut, then walked inside the house. Sunlight was filtering through the rim of firs and maples, and the huge laurel that turned the backyard into very private grounds, but also cut off any kind of view the lot would have toward the Willamette River and the east side of Portland. Mary Jo had told her the builder had seesawed about whether to take down the hedge when he razed the original house, sometimes thinking he should, other times backing off. Now, the thinking was: let the buyer decide. If they wanted the laurel removed and the backyard opened up, the builder would do it for them, no cost.

She set her purse down on a side table next to the couch. Her painting definitely drew the eye. It's large size, and the pop of color it added to the tone-on-tone room, changed the feel of it. Layla could see why someone might think it needed to be with the house. Of course, that and the red pillows and other items she'd added: the heavy silver candlesticks with their orange candles on the mantel, the glass balls surrounded by hemp that had been arranged in a canoe-shaped piece on the coffee table, the brass mallard that sat atop a fanned-out stack of copies of *Sunset Magazine*.

Who wouldn't want to live here now? Layla congratulated herself, feeling a tiny bit better.

Her cell phone rang, and she dug it out of her purse and looked at the screen: Mary Jo. "Hi, I'm already here," she answered without waiting for Mary Jo to identify herself.

"Oh, Layla, I'm sorry. My buyer, Amy Neilson, just called and she can't make it today. Are you available tomorrow?"

Wouldn't you know? "I'm not even sure I want to sell. Maybe we should just forget it."

"No, no. Just meet with her, please. Tomorrow. I'll set it up. Oh, but . . . well, never mind."

"Oh, but what?" Layla asked.

"I'm leaving town in the afternoon until next Monday, after Easter? We might have to make it the morning, but I'm kind of squeezed."

"Mary Jo, it's fine. We'll figure it out when you get back."

"I really need to get this done before I leave."

"Well, I can't help you there."

"You can meet her by yourself. You can go to the house anytime. I haven't fully listed it yet, so no one else will bother you. I just think this sale is going through, and I don't want to jinx it, so I'm waiting till after you and Amy meet. Can I give her your number?"

"Sure," Layla said. She could always tell this Amy herself that she didn't want to meet. It was probably easier than dealing with Mary Jo.

Delighted, Mary Jo quickly got off the phone to tell her client.

Layla walked through to the back flagstone patio. If the house didn't sell, maybe she would suggest some outdoor furniture as the weather got better. Yeah, if it were up to her, she would get rid of the laurel hedge.

She wanted to call Naomi again and make sure they were still okay, that Naomi still believed in her, but she'd just talked to her. She just needed reassurance.

She walked back inside and gasped; there was a woman

with bright red hair coming down the last step from upstairs. "Oh my God," Layla said, startled.

"Hi," the woman said, turning fully toward her.

Layla blinked, her lips parting in shock.

It was Courtney with red hair.

And she was holding a shiny, bluish gun, aimed right at Layla's chest.

September wheeled into the sheriff's department's parking lot and racewalked to the front door. The woman at the desk recognized her and told her Sheriff Kingston was already interviewing Mr. Wolfe, but she could join Deputy Morant and watch through the two-way mirror.

"Thank you," September said when she was shown to the right door. Morant was standing with his arms crossed, looking grave, staring into the room where Jerome Wolfe was seated across a table from a florid-faced man in uniform, about sixty with a gleaming pate and about fifty pounds too much body weight. Morant, being a friend of the Kilgores, had been relegated to bystander.

"How's it going?" September asked.

"He swears he had nothing to do with it. Says his gun was stolen out of his vehicle about a week ago."

"A week ago?"

"Says he remembers it before then. Keeps it in his glove box. Says he has a concealed weapon permit."

Morant clearly wasn't going to believe anything Wolfe said. September didn't blame him, but . . . "Does he have any idea where this gun could have been taken from his car?"

"Yeah. Says it had to have happened when he was at the Kilgores."

"Well, who would take it there? Mona doesn't seem like a likely candidate."

Morant slid his eyes toward September. "He says he

thinks you did it." September made a choking sound of disbelief, but Morant said, "Don't worry, sheriff's not buying it. Whatever Wolfe's hiding, he'll get it out of him."

But maybe not for a long while. Jerome Wolfe was some-what rattled, but he was too smart to incriminate himself at a first interview.

"I've got some questions for Mona, so I'm heading out," September said. "Keep me posted."

"Will do."

Dallas's cell rang, and Lucy was glad for the distraction. At this rate, she would be a puddle. She'd never let herself even hope that Dallas could be part of their family, that he would welcome Evie with open arms.

Her own cell jingled at the same time. She looked at the screen. Lyle. Well, they both had questions for him, so she took the call, aware Dallas was talking to Luke about something that had grabbed his attention.

"Speak of the devil," she said to Lyle. "I was just talking to Dallas Denton about you."

"Oh?" He sounded unsure about that. "Well, I'm just calling to tell you something."

"Okay." She prepared herself. When Lyle wanted to talk to her, it was generally something she didn't want to hear.

"At the Denim and Diamonds dinner, I saw someone who looked familiar, but I couldn't place her. She was there with Neil Grassley, but I couldn't put my finger on it."

"Courtney Mayfield?"

"Yeah. I finally remembered. I saw her maybe ten years earlier, only she had red hair then. Really red hair. Brianne's hair was sort of red, but Courtney—I didn't remember that was her name—her hair was bright red. Probably fake, I guess. Brianne was more auburn, like that detective who helped you get John in the car that night, although I heard

Brianne's really gone gray. I didn't see her at Stonehenge, but I guess she was there that night, too."

"Wait a minute. Why are you comparing Courtney to Brianne?"

"Because they're cousins. I just saw her that one time. We were all out in the woods together. Brianne told her I was her boyfriend. It wasn't long after that that . . . Brianne and I got together. . . ."

Courtney was Brianne's cousin.

She mumbled a good-bye to Lyle, even though he was still talking. She should have asked him about the sandwiches, but she was trying to process.

Dallas sensed her eyes on him and he realized something had happened. "I'll call you back," he said tersely, then asked, "What?"

"Lyle just told me that Courtney Mayfield is Brianne's cousin."

Dallas inhaled a sharp breath. "Luke just told me that besides being a data processor, Mayfield is an accomplished hacker. The police think she did a soft hack into Grassley's computer, meaning she used passwords and information to breach his accounts rather than hack straight into the bank, but she's capable of a lot more."

"Like sending money into Layla's account?" asked Lucy in alarm.

"Like breaching Layla's accounts through a hard hack, getting the information, then sending the money through Neil's computer, making it look like he sent the funds."

"Why? What's she doing?" Lucy was on her feet.

"Call Layla," he ordered.

Her phone was still in her hand. Immediately, she scrolled to her favorites and pressed Layla's name.

* * *

Layla's cell jingled merrily in her purse.

Courtney had motioned Layla to move over to the couch and ordered her to sit down. Layla had complied, but she hadn't taken her eyes off Courtney and the gun. She'd asked, "What . . . what are you doing?" and Courtney had said simply, "Finishing what I started."

Now, Courtney, who was dressed in jeans, sneakers, a black shirt, and a black leather jacket, glanced at Layla's purse. "I'm going to have to get rid of that thing," she said.

"Why are you here? What . . . what's happening?" Layla felt like she'd walked through the looking glass. She couldn't take her eyes off Courtney's hair.

"You like it? It was my natural color before I went gray. My mom still dyes hers, but I thought it was too noticeable. When you're tiptoeing through people's personal files, it seems more prudent to be a mouse, not a toucan. But you like color, don't you?" She waved the gun toward the painting, before immediately training it back on Layla. "Although today you look like your sister picked out your wardrobe."

"I don't understand," Layla murmured.

"Of course you don't." She smirked.

Layla tried to process. This Courtney was completely different from the woman Neil had introduced her to at the benefit. That Courtney had blurted out that she was pregnant and then looked stricken. That Courtney, she realized, was a fake. This was the real Courtney.

"Let me enlighten you. My cousin Brianne—you remember her—had a 'thing' with your brother. She had him wrapped around her finger. I could never figure out why. And he wasn't the only one. Now, it's Jerome Wolfe sniffing around, though he's got other aspirations. But, maybe, like your brother, he just got off on Brianne's strangeness. Whatever it was, it's over now. Brianne has left the building!"

"What?" Layla whispered.

"This gun was Jerome Wolfe's, but I appropriated it. And it shot Brianne. *Bang*!"

Layla shrieked, and Courtney laughed. She'd lifted the gun at Layla but had only been playacting. "Nah, I'm not going to shoot you . . . I brought something else along."

Her eyes and gun trained on Layla, she reached her free hand into her jacket pocket and brought out a vial of chopped-up mushrooms.

Layla's blood ran cold. She didn't have to be told that she was carrying around the angel of death.

"She's not answering," Lucy said. "Lots of times she doesn't answer. It's probably okay."

"Luke was keeping tabs on Courtney, hoping to catch her on the street, ask some questions, but she sneaked by him. She apparently knew he was watching."

"Where is she now?" Lucy asked in alarm.

"Luke is looking for her."

"I can't just sit here!" Lucy cried. "I need to go to her apartment!"

"Didn't she say she had an appointment?"

"Yes! The cold house . . . in the West Hills . . . on Cherry!"

"Do you have an address?"

"No, but that's not a long street. She probably took Uber, so there's no car. . . ."

"What about the real estate agent?"

"Mary Jo . . . yes . . . I can get that!"

She looked up Mary Jo's real estate agency and placed a call to them. The receptionist answered, but when Lucy asked for Mary Jo, she learned that she was with a client and currently not taking calls.

Beside herself, Lucy cried, "I need the address of her Portland listing on Cherry, in the West Hills!"

Lucy counted the seconds as the receptionist said, "Ummm, okay, ummm, I'm going to have to put you on hold."

"No!" Lucy fairly shrieked.

"Let's get in my car and head that way," Dallas said tersely.

She nodded, the phone to her ear, following Dallas, who was moving fast.

Finally, the receptionist came back on the line. "Mary Jo doesn't have an active listing on Cherry. Are you sure you have the right area?"

"Yes . . . yes . . . did she have a listing? Has it already sold?"

"No . . ."

Lucy was in the elevator, silently counting to ten. "Is there a listing coming up soon?" she asked the receptionist with all the patience she could muster.

"Possibly. Let me transfer you to our broker."

Click.

Another long wait.

She and Dallas were in his SUV and heading out of Portland city center toward the West Hills when the receptionist finally came back on the line. "Alice DeKamp, our broker, is on another call. If you give me your number, I'll have her phone you back when she's free."

"You do that," Lucy snapped, then rattled off her number before shutting off her phone and throwing it back in her purse.

September pulled up to the Kilgores' home and hurried to the front porch. She banged hard on the door. Duke started howling mournfully again, but September couldn't hear the thumping of Mona's walker. She peered through the window at the side of the door and saw Duke was the only one who'd made his way toward her.

"Oh no . . ."

The back door she'd seen Brianne enter through.

She quickly circled the house and found the door. It was locked, but the gap between the door and the sash was wide, and it only took one kick to break it in. She'd left her gun in her Outback. Wasn't used to carrying it again.

But it didn't matter anyway. Mona was on the floor in the family room and she raced to her side. Her eyelids fluttered and her pulse was thready.

"Mona . . . Mona . . . I'm calling nine-one-one."

"I fell. I just fell. . . . I wanted to call you and tell you, but I just fell . . ."

"Nine-one-one, what is the nature of your emergency?" the dispatcher said in September's ear.

September snapped out the address.

". . . It's Brianne's cousin . . . always been jealous . . . I know she did it . . . I know she did. . . ."

Brianne's cousin?

As soon as September hung up, a call came in. She looked at the screen. Luke Denton.

"It's Courtney Mayfield," he said. "She's a hacker, hacked into Layla's bank accounts. Dallas knows. He and Lucy are looking for Layla right now. . . ."

"Courtney . . ." Mona said. "I know she did it. . . . She shot my baby."

Layla's pulse was running fast. She'd believed she was going to die. She'd believed Courtney was going to shoot her straight out, but apparently, Courtney had other plans and was in no hurry to see them through. Time . . . time was what Layla needed . . . and a way to relay her predicament.

She purposely kept her eyes away from her purse and cell phone. If there was any chance, any moment . . .

"Come on," Courtney said, waving the blue nose of the gun at her. "Into the kitchen."

Layla reluctantly complied, watching her purse recede

from reach as she went past the two-sided fireplace into the large kitchen gleaming with stainless-steel appliances. A weapon . . . she needed a weapon . . . but where? How? This kitchen was empty.

Courtney began to twist open the top of the vial with one hand. The lid was barely closed.

"I'm not going to eat that," Layla said.

"Neil did. I served it right up to him. Buried the little pieces in a lasagna with spicy Italian sausage. Yum. You were supposed to eat the sandwiches I brought to the Denim and Diamonds event, but your brother-in-law was kind of a pig that day. Kept eating everything. He didn't even notice."

"You set the tray down beside me . . . that was you."

"A wig for every occasion," she said with a smile and a shrug. "You didn't even look at me, did you?"

"You meant it for me," Layla realized with a distinct shock. "You meant for me to eat the poison."

"Let me tell you something, Ms. Crissman, with all your money and all your prestige . . ."

"I don't have any mon—"

"Shut the fuck up, dearie, and listen. I wanted to be you. All of you. You don't know what it's like to grow up poor. It sucks. I had to trade on my looks, which was okay, but there were a lot of men out there who only wanted to use me. You know what I mean?"

"Yes . . ."

"But they wanted you, y'see. You're the forever girl. I'm just the throwaway girl. And you were with Neil Grassley and Jerome Wolfe was with Brianne, and there was all this money, just waiting to be grabbed. I slept with Wolfe first. What a bastard. As soon as that was over, he was done with me. The thrill was gone. Brianne kept him coming around because he thought she was 'interesting' and he wanted her property. But I took care of that in one fell swoop. Brianne's gone for good, so that's done, and Mona won't sell to him, so he loses.

"But you . . . you got Neil to fork up some sperm, didn't you? Got him to make a baby with your eggs!"

"Neil came to me—"

"You did it," she cut Layla off, growing angry. "*You.* I heard all about it when I struck up a friendship with him. He was really kind of a lonely guy. You weren't giving him anything. Not after you got what you wanted anyway. So, he turned to me. Some good conversation. Old Courtney just bent her ear and Neil poured his heart into it. I said, 'maybe you need another baby,' and he was like a kid in a candy store. You were such a bitch to him, so he turned to me."

"You used Neil and my embryos."

Her lips tightened and her eyes darkened. She'd set the open vial on the counter, but she still held the gun. Layla wasn't going to let her force that deadly poison down her throat. There was no way she could make her.

"You know Neil couldn't get it up, so we had to. Use your embryos."

Layla's brows lifted. Neil hadn't had that problem with her. She was beginning to see that Courtney's version of the truth was just that, a version. "I would never have agreed to that," Layla said.

"But you gave them away . . . sold your little babies, and then you wanted them back. Boo-hoo-hoo. Poor Layla. Can't hold a man. Can't even have a baby." She placed a hand on her abdomen. "But I can. I can have your baby."

"You lost it," Layla said, dry mouthed.

"Well, that's what Neil thought."

"If you . . . kill me, you'll get caught. It's going to come back on you."

"It's going to fall on you, dearie. You took the money. You killed Neil after he left you for me."

"He wanted to marry me. He told his lawyer. We were meeting this week."

"You're a bad liar." She laughed.

Layla had been passive, quivering, unfocused, and scared. She couldn't be that way any longer. She had to channel Lucy, think of what Lucy would say, Lucy would do.

"I'm not lying," Layla challenged. "Neil didn't love you. He wouldn't even have sex with you, and he could perform really well . . . *really well*. He just didn't want you. Like my brother . . . and Jerome Wolfe."

"I've got skills you don't know about," she said, but Layla could tell she'd gotten under her skin. "I can steal all your personal data and sell it to the highest bidder. I can ruin you . . . I am ruining you . . . even before you die."

"But you can't keep a man," Layla said slowly. "Neil wanted me. Not you."

Courtney's eyes bugged from her head with suppressed rage. "I'm going to shoot you right now! Like I did Brianne."

Heart thudding, knowing she was taking a huge risk, Layla grabbed up the vial and dumped it onto the floor.

Courtney shrieked and lunged for the vial as Layla dropped it to the floor, where it shattered into pieces. She pushed Courtney as hard as she could. The other woman staggered, but she still had the gun.

Blam! A round slammed into the fireplace, chips of stone flying through the room, the sound deafening Layla, who raced back around the fireplace to the living room. She stopped short, looked everywhere for a weapon, eyes stretched wide with fear.

Courtney was screaming and then laughing and then screaming again as she barreled around the fireplace, full tilt.

Layla met her with a swing of one of the brass candlesticks, connecting with a sickening thud in the center of Courtney's face. Blood gushed from her nose, and Courtney squeezed off another shot. Blam! The bullet went wild, tore through Layla's painting.

Now Courtney was shrieking like a banshee. "I can't see! I can't see!"

Layla lifted the candlestick again, ready to blast her to the moon.

"I'm pregnant! *Pregnant*! You can't hurt me. You'll hurt your baby! I've got your baby!"

She hesitated. She'd been about to slam the weapon into Courtney's stomach. She saw that one of the chips of stone had lodged in Courtney's eye.

And Courtney lifted the gun, aimed at Layla, and fired.

"Gunshots!" Dallas yelled as Lucy cried, "Stop, stop, stop! Right here!"

Dallas whipped into the drive of a newly constructed home on Cherry. Had to be the one. Had to be.

Lucy scrabbled for the door handle. Struggled to get out.

"Wait!" Dallas ordered as she leapt from the car.

But she was running, running, running to save her sister.

Dallas caught her at the door, pushed her hard against the side of the house. "Wait. Wait! *I'm not losing you.* Call nine-one-one."

"B-b-but Layla . . ."

"Get back in the car. I'm checking the door." The knob turned in his hand.

Lucy stumbled away a few paces, scared, but then she turned back. She wasn't losing him either.

Crash. Dallas kicked the door against the wall. He ducked in a quick peek, then straightened. Muffled sobbing came from the house. "Layla," he said, rushing inside.

Lucy staggered after him.

Layla was standing over a prone, red-haired woman who was bleeding profusely over the lovely tile floor and the fuzzy white area carpet, holding a candlestick like she was about to bludgeon her.

"She missed," she said in wonder, then kicked a handgun away from the woman's convulsively grasping fingers, where it skidded across the tile and landed near the base of what was left of Layla's painting.

Epilogue

Four days later, Lucy pulled her Outback up in front of Stonehenge's gray stone walls. It looked nicer than the last time she'd been there, she thought, though maybe that was more a trick of warm sunshine and the sense that spring had finally arrived than any real change in the building.

Evie bounced out of the car and ran for the door. Lucy heard squeals of delight and knew that Daphne, Kate, and Lyle must have beaten her here. They'd all agreed to congregate for Easter, Layla, too, bowing to Evie and Daphne's pressure, though Abbott and Ainsley—whose ardor for Abbott had really taken a nosedive—had chosen not to come. That put Kate and Lyle in the master suite, while Lucy and Evie were tagged for the smaller bedroom in the north wing, and Layla would be across the hall from them. Given the state of all the bedrooms, musty and mildewed as they were, it hardly mattered. Maybe in the future they would be able to renovate, but for now it was enough to know they had ownership.

Lucy hauled her bag inside and up the stairs to her room and then knocked on Layla's door, surprised when her sister answered. "I didn't think you'd beat me here."

"I caught a ride with Lyle and Kate. I almost drove, but . . . I changed my mind."

"This isn't the week for any more big changes," said Lucy, eyeing her sister. Though Layla looked no worse for wear after her harrowing experience, the aftermath had created a hellish past few days. And there were decisions yet to be made. Courtney was taken to the ER to remove the splinter of stone from her eye, and during the checkup, after her insistence that she was pregnant, she was tested, and they all found out she was telling the truth. With confirmation from the IVF clinic, Layla learned the baby Courtney was carrying was hers, and Dallas was making a legal case for Layla to have custody. Meanwhile, Brianne continued to improve, much to everyone's relief, and her mother, Mona Kilgore, having taken a fall in her distress over her daughter's shooting, was in a knee brace but otherwise doing fine.

"I guess you're right," Layla said. "I'm already going to be a mother, twice over. I'll start driving more later."

Lucy went into her room and began pulling out her toiletries, arranging them on the pine dresser. In a joint meeting she and Layla and Lyle had with September, Dallas, and Luke, she'd learned that Courtney had stolen Jerome Wolfe's gun and tried to kill Brianne, who figured out she'd been the one who'd taken the mushrooms and was close to giving her up. They theorized that when John Linfield died, Brianne worried that Courtney was responsible, but she couldn't figure out why she would kill Linfield, so she thought she was wrong. She called the Wharton County Sheriff's Department to send the authorities looking for the right cause, and only later came to believe that Courtney had killed the wrong person.

September was a detective with the Laurelton Police Department again, and she was someone Lucy thought could be a good friend.

And then there was Dallas . . . Lucy and he had hardly

been out of each other's sight since they found Layla and Courtney at the house on Cherry. Evie seemed to accept Dallas as part of their new normal, although that might be because she was so focused on this trip to Stonehenge.

There was a knock on her door and she opened it to see Layla.

"Hey, again," Lucy said, smiling.

Layla's eyes were shining. "Naomi called. She's dilated to three and they think it could be anytime. Maybe even this weekend. I might have to leave before it's over!"

"Oh my God!" Lucy whispered, excited.

"I know. I'm totally boggled. Can't get my head around it. And I've gotta look for a new place tout de suite."

"Maybe Mary Jo will help you find something," Lucy teased.

"Mary Jo is never going to use me again after what happened to that rug. And the fireplace. And even the tile."

"She'll get over it. Oh, I'm so happy for you!"

"So am I." Her smile slowly faded. "And for more blessings to come."

Lucy nodded. She knew Layla was thinking about the other baby due in about six months. "It's going to work out," she said, and Layla nodded.

Lucy hadn't been invited back to work at Crissman, and she didn't expect to be. A long legal wrangle lay in all of their futures, but Dallas was confident it would all work in their favor in the end.

"When's Dallas coming?"

"Soon. I would have come with him, but Evie was just crazy. These girls . . . I hope they're not disappointed. I mean, we love Stonehenge, but there's not that much to do."

"Have you and Dallas been . . . together yet?"

"Haven't really found the way for that to happen. Evie's still on school break and with everything else . . ."

"Well, Evie and Daphne are angling for that room at the end of the hall, so, if they go down early . . ."

Lucy snorted. "That room's in the worst shape of all. The leak two years ago stained the wall and no one's fixed it yet."

"But it was the grand master at one time, long ago, and it's chock full of old furniture and junk. A playhouse."

"And haunted, if you believe the lore. I don't see Evie throwing a sleeping bag down in there anytime soon. As soon as it gets dark, she'll be barreling back to my room."

"So, where is Mr. Denton going to sleep?"

"I believe there's a motel in Glenn River."

"If he gets drunk enough, he might have to stay," Layla said pragmatically.

"Why, I do believe you think I should sleep with him."

"I do believe you're right."

She headed back to her room and Lucy walked to her window, which looked out upon the grand entrance of the lodge. Her eyes strayed to the southeast and the Kilgore property. She could almost pinpoint where the Kilgore house was, and where the big oak would be, but the thick forest of Douglas firs obscured everything.

Sudden footsteps pounded down the hall from the north end, punctuated by high-pitched squeals and shrieking laughter. Daphne and Evie.

They burst into Lucy's room in a flurry, Evie clutching Lisa around the neck and Daphne her American Girl doll, Maddy. Both the beloved friends were bedecked in jewels of every kind, though there were rings falling off Lisa's toes that Evie scooped up and tried to smash back on twice while Lucy was watching.

"You gotta go for the necklaces," Daphne declared, holding out her doll for Lucy to inspect. Maddy looked as if she were being weighted down and drowned by the jewels around its neck.

"Where'd those come from?" Lucy asked, but her mind

was on what Layla had said about Dallas. Should she invite him to stay? The rooms were fine, just more rustic than he might prefer, but maybe that wouldn't matter. . . .

"Lisa and Maddy are going to a ball," Evie declared grandly.

"Yes," Daphne said, chin in the air. "A ball with a prince and a carriage!"

Kate appeared in Lucy's doorway, frowning at the giggling girls. "What are you two screaming about? They can hear you all the way to Portland!"

"They're fine," Lucy said. The girls had been in high spirits even before they demanded the key to the room at the end of the hall and raced each other to the door of the room used for storage. "They're just playing with their doll and stuffed animal. . . ." Her eye drifted over the girls' toys.

"Oh, sweet Jesus . . . !" Kate suddenly snatched Lisa out of Evie's hands.

"Hey!" Evie cried, affronted.

"Give it back, Mom." Daphne reached for Evie's dog, but Kate held up a hand.

Lucy, Daphne, and Evie all looked at her. She was staring at the plush dog. One of the rings slid off its leg again and dropped into Kate's hand. It was a large, ornate gold band with a magnificent ruby stone.

Evie yanked Lisa back, and Lucy stared at the gem in the ring, blood pounding in her head.

"They fell out of the wall and that's when we found them," Daphne said anxiously, picking up on the vibe.

"*I* found them," Evie said. "I told you about them. That's why we wanted to come back!"

"Yeah, and they're really, really valuable," Daphne added, unknowingly parroting her mother's know-it-all tone.

"I think . . . I think they really are valuable," Lucy said in wonder.

"Are they Edwina's?" Kate asked, her voice shaking.

Lucy turned to her daughter. "Where did you find them exactly?" Lucy asked her.

Reacting to her tone, Evie suddenly grew cagey. "In the wall . . ."

"In the west bedroom where you've been playing?" Lucy's pulse was beating even harder.

Evie was watching her mother, worried, trying to figure out what the correct answer would be. She nodded after a long moment.

Lucy pushed out of the room and practically ran down the hall, with Kate at her heels. Layla's door opened and she called after them, "What is it?"

Lucy didn't answer, just entered the room that was piled to the ceiling with desks, chairs, chests of drawers, rolled carpets, bedsteads, antique end tables, and more. "Show me," she ordered, and Evie squeezed around her and led the way along a narrow path through the furniture to the rain-dampened wall.

"This room is locked when people stay here," Layla said from the hallway.

"Right here," Evie said, her voice warbling a little. She knew something momentous had happened but wasn't sure how it was going to affect her.

There was a hole in the wall, a wrench of wood and lathe that looked as if it had been torn open for further viewing, probably by the girls. Inside was a pouch of what might have been faded purple velvet, though it had torn apart and apparently spilled out the rings and necklaces the girls had wound around their toys.

Lucy plucked another ring from the dust and debris. A diamond, dulled and dirty.

"Who sealed them into the wall?" Kate asked. Lucy glanced behind her. Kate was now clutching her daughter's American Girl doll, fingering a pendant necklace with a huge amethyst.

Lucy looked back at the wall, reaching farther past the torn pouch. "There's something more," she said, her hand touching something hard and pebbly. She grasped it, pulled it out, and stared at it. It was gray-white, grimy, and an odd shape.

"What is it? A pearl?" Kate asked.

"No. . . . Come on, let's all get out of here and clean up. It's filthy." Lucy stood up abruptly and shooed Evie away. The rest of them followed her into the hall. "Who's got the key to this room?" Lucy asked.

"Lyle," Kate said.

"Let's lock it back up."

"What is it?" Layla asked after the girls had gone on ahead. She and Kate were looking at Lucy as the three of them walked much more slowly back toward their rooms.

"It's a bone," Lucy revealed. "Human. I'd guess a toe." She drew a breath and exhaled slowly. "I don't think our great-grandmother ran off after all. . . ."

Dallas arrived about an hour later and Lucy pulled him aside toward the main dining room, which was cold and dark right now. She'd called him and told him there was something she wanted to show him when he got there, so now he asked, "Okay, another big secret? I don't think this'll top the last one."

"Well, maybe not, but this one'll give it a run for its money."

Lucy led the way back upstairs, holding on to Dallas's hand. Kate, Layla, and Lyle followed. They'd set the girls up with a jigsaw puzzle spread across the smaller kitchen table, and Lyle had found a claw hammer from a storeroom off the kitchen. When they got to the room, Lyle handed the hammer to Lucy, who dug it into the wet plaster at about chest height. The plaster fell away easily, and Lucy worked the hole until it was about the circumference of a baseball.

Inside was a crumple of human ribs, the bones having fallen into rubble without the benefit of connective tissue keeping them together. There were scraps of clothing wound through the bones, blue threads, and in the middle of them, a puddle of dull green gems. The bottom of a jaw could be seen.

"Edwina's emerald necklace," Lyle said; then, "He wouldn't let her leave."

They all turned to look at him.

Lyle stared at the bones and gems as if in a daze. "Junior told me. He never knew what happened, but he heard his father, Criss, say it enough times to his mother: 'I won't let you leave. I won't let you leave.' It always made him wonder that maybe she didn't run off."

Dallas said, "Better take some pictures. Chronicle it," and Lyle pulled out his cell phone and clicked off a number of shots.

They all headed back downstairs and paused to look at the girls and Maddy and Lisa.

"Do you think Jerome Wolfe knew about this?" Kate wondered. "Or suspected?"

Lucy looked at her sister-in-law. "Maybe," she said. "Maybe his great-grandfather knew something more than anyone else and Jerome was just waiting for a chance to gain control."

"Glad that didn't happen," Kate said fervently, and they all chorused their agreement, even Lyle, who looked a little sheepish about his part in pushing for the sale of Stonehenge.

Layla's phone dinged out a text. She sucked in a breath. "Here we go!" she declared.

"Naomi?" Lucy asked.

"She's on the way to the hospital."

"Do you need a ride?" Dallas asked.

"I do," she fretted.

"Can I go, too?" Lucy begged.

Evie dropped what she was doing and stood up. "Aunt Layla's having her baby?"

"Yes, in a manner of speaking," Lucy said.

"I want you to come," said Layla.

Kate stepped in. "Lyle and I will take care of the girls, the jewels, and Edwina. Go on. Bring that Crissman baby home. . . ."

Connect with Us

Visit us online at
KensingtonBooks.com
to read more from your favorite authors, see books
by series, view reading group guides, and more.

Join us on social media

for sneak peeks, chances to win books and prize packs,
and to share your thoughts with other readers.

facebook.com/kensingtonpublishing
twitter.com/kensingtonbooks

Tell us what you think!

To share your thoughts, submit a review,
or sign up for our eNewsletters, please visit:
KensingtonBooks.com/TellUs.

Romantic Suspense from
Lisa Jackson

Absolute Fear	0-8217-7936-2	$7.99US/$9.99CAN
Afraid to Die	1-4201-1850-1	$7.99US/$9.99CAN
Almost Dead	0-8217-7579-0	$7.99US/$10.99CAN
Born to Die	1-4201-0278-8	$7.99US/$9.99CAN
Chosen to Die	1-4201-0277-X	$7.99US/$10.99CAN
Cold Blooded	1-4201-2581-8	$7.99US/$8.99CAN
Deep Freeze	0-8217-7296-1	$7.99US/$10.99CAN
Devious	1-4201-0275-3	$7.99US/$9.99CAN
Fatal Burn	0-8217-7577-4	$7.99US/$10.99CAN
Final Scream	0-8217-7712-2	$7.99US/$10.99CAN
Hot Blooded	1-4201-0678-3	$7.99US/$9.49CAN
If She Only Knew	1-4201-3241-5	$7.99US/$9.99CAN
Left to Die	1-4201-0276-1	$7.99US/$10.99CAN
Lost Souls	0-8217-7938-9	$7.99US/$10.99CAN
Malice	0-8217-7940-0	$7.99US/$10.99CAN
The Morning After	1-4201-3370-5	$7.99US/$9.99CAN
The Night Before	1-4201-3371-3	$7.99US/$9.99CAN
Ready to Die	1-4201-1851-X	$7.99US/$9.99CAN
Running Scared	1-4201-0182-X	$7.99US/$10.99CAN
See How She Dies	1-4201-2584-2	$7.99US/$8.99CAN
Shiver	0-8217-7578-2	$7.99US/$10.99CAN
Tell Me	1-4201-1854-4	$7.99US/$9.99CAN
Twice Kissed	0-8217-7944-3	$7.99US/$9.99CAN
Unspoken	1-4201-0093-9	$7.99US/$9.99CAN
Whispers	1-4201-5158-4	$7.99US/$9.99CAN
Wicked Game	1-4201-0338-5	$7.99US/$9.99CAN
Wicked Lies	1-4201-0339-3	$7.99US/$9.99CAN
Without Mercy	1-4201-0274-5	$7.99US/$10.99CAN
You Don't Want to Know	1-4201-1853-6	$7.99US/$9.99CAN

Available Wherever Books Are Sold!
Visit our website at **www.kensingtonbooks.com**

Books by Bestselling Author
Fern Michaels

___	**The Jury**	0-8217-7878-1	$6.99US/$9.99CAN
___	**Sweet Revenge**	0-8217-7879-X	$6.99US/$9.99CAN
___	**Lethal Justice**	0-8217-7880-3	$6.99US/$9.99CAN
___	**Free Fall**	0-8217-7881-1	$6.99US/$9.99CAN
___	**Fool Me Once**	0-8217-8071-9	$7.99US/$10.99CAN
___	**Vegas Rich**	0-8217-8112-X	$7.99US/$10.99CAN
___	**Hide and Seek**	1-4201-0184-6	$6.99US/$9.99CAN
___	**Hokus Pokus**	1-4201-0185-4	$6.99US/$9.99CAN
___	**Fast Track**	1-4201-0186-2	$6.99US/$9.99CAN
___	**Collateral Damage**	1-4201-0187-0	$6.99US/$9.99CAN
___	**Final Justice**	1-4201-0188-9	$6.99US/$9.99CAN
___	**Up Close and Personal**	0-8217-7956-7	$7.99US/$9.99CAN
___	**Under the Radar**	1-4201-0683-X	$6.99US/$9.99CAN
___	**Razor Sharp**	1-4201-0684-8	$7.99US/$10.99CAN
___	**Yesterday**	1-4201-1494-8	$5.99US/$6.99CAN
___	**Vanishing Act**	1-4201-0685-6	$7.99US/$10.99CAN
___	**Sara's Song**	1-4201-1493-X	$5.99US/$6.99CAN
___	**Deadly Deals**	1-4201-0686-4	$7.99US/$10.99CAN
___	**Game Over**	1-4201-0687-2	$7.99US/$10.99CAN
___	**Sins of Omission**	1-4201-1153-1	$7.99US/$10.99CAN
___	**Sins of the Flesh**	1-4201-1154-X	$7.99US/$10.99CAN
___	**Cross Roads**	1-4201-1192-2	$7.99US/$10.99CAN

Available Wherever Books Are Sold!
Check out our website at www.kensingtonbooks.com

More by Bestselling Author
Hannah Howell